THE BOND STREET CAROLERS
Mary Balogh

A London street choir brings together a
nobleman who dislikes Christmas with a pretty
widow who can melt his icy heart.

MELODY
Anne Barbour

An American finds himself in an English village,
where a singer with the voice of an angel helps
him find not only his tie with the past—
but a future filled with love.

YULETIDE BELLES
Elisabeth Fairchild

The celebration of the Yuletide season helps a
grieving governess to discover that Christmas
can bring new hopes, new dreams, and
perhaps even a new love.

MAKE A JOYFUL NOISE
Carla Kelly

In this joyful tale, a widower discovers an
enchanting surprise in the Christmas choir: a
mysterious Welsh lady.

THE EARL'S NIGHTINGALE
Edith Layton

A lovely heroine pawns a music box, and begins
an odyssey that takes her to a handsome earl's
parlor . . . and into his heart.

A Regency Christmas Carol

FIVE STORIES BY

Mary Balogh

❄

Anne Barbour

❄

Elisabeth Fairchild

❄

Carla Kelly

❄

Edith Layton

A SIGNET BOOK

SIGNET
Published by the Penguin Group
Penguin Putnam Inc., 375 Hudson Street,
New York, New York 10014, U.S.A.
Penguin Books Ltd, 27 Wrights Lane,
London W8 5TZ, England
Penguin Books Australia Ltd, Ringwood,
Victoria, Australia
Penguin Books Canada Ltd, 10 Alcorn Avenue,
Toronto, Ontario, Canada M4V 3B2
Penguin Books (N.Z.) Ltd, 182–190 Wairau Road,
Auckland 10, New Zealand

Penguin Books Ltd, Registered Offices:
Harmondsworth, Middlesex, England

First published by Signet, an imprint of Dutton Signet,
a member of Penguin Putnam Inc.

First Printing, November, 1997
10 9 8 7 6 5 4 3 2 1

CONTENTS

The Bond Street Carolers

❄

Mary Balogh

The season of Christmas was irrevocably upon them, it seemed. Bond Street in London was crammed with fashionable shoppers, most of whom carried assorted packages and bandboxes and dodged impatiently about those similarly encumbered. Several of them had servants walking a pace or two behind, loaded to the eyebrows with larger, heavier, more unwieldy parcels, and suffering considerable verbal abuse from those whose path they obstructed. Carriages paused to pick up their passengers and were cursed at by impatient coachmen for blocking the thoroughfare. The general mood seemed to be one of irritability.

The rain had stopped for the moment, but the wind that howled along the street as if it were a funnel was damp and chill and cut through fashionable greatcoats and cloaks, setting their wearers to shivering and hurrying—and bumping all the more surely into one another. Both the road and the pavement were wet. Hems of cloaks and dresses were dark and heavy with moisture and boots were muddy. Heedless carriage drivers sprayed passersby with a mixture of dirty water and mud and were roundly berated for their impudence.

There was little evidence of the peace and goodwill for which the season was supposedly renowned.

Yet the group of carolers standing on one corner, red-nosed and bedraggled, exhorted everyone within hearing, the gentlemen in particular, to allow God to rest them merry and let nothing them dismay. The shoppers gave the group a wide berth lest they be importuned to contribute to whatever charity had set the singers to indulging in such blatant self-torture. Most of them appeared not to remember, though instructed to do so by the choir, that Christ our Savior was born on Christmas Day. Or if they did remember, there were more important things to occupy their minds for the coming four days—like completing their Christmas shopping so that they might return home and get themselves warm and dry again and rest their sore feet.

It was Christmas—that time of love and laughter and peace and merriment and religious observance. That most blissful of all times of the year. That persistent myth. Roderick Ames, Baron Heath, who was proceeding along Bond Street only because it offered the shortest route from where he had come to where he was going, was as fashionably dressed as anyone else on the street. More so, in fact. His greatcoat boasted twelve capes and his boots and gloves and beaver hat were all new and of the latest design and the most costly materials. But he carried only a silver-topped cane and did not even glance at the shops to either side of him. Their window displays did not entice him. Although he had brothers and sisters and their assorted spouses and offspring for whom to buy, not to mention a resident mistress, he also had a secretary who was perfectly capable of taking the unpleasant task of choosing and purchasing upon himself. He was paid handsomely enough, after all.

Lord Heath disliked Christmas. Traditionally it was always spent at Bloomfield Hall, his seat in Hampshire. His beloved home, except at Christmas, when it was invaded by every last person, he sometimes thought, who could claim some connection with the Ames family, however remote. And every last person's spouse as well, and all their children—and even occasionally their pets. His family had been remarkably prolific over the past century or so.

It was all a merry romp—or so family mythology described Bloomfield Christmases. By his own observation they were fraught with inebriated, overfed, sleepy, short-tempered gentlemen; demanding, complaining, vaporous, short-tempered ladies; frazzled, despairing, short-tempered nurses and governesses; and shrieking, unruly, petulant, short-tempered children. And himself—counting the days until he might expect to have his home to himself again and decidedly short-tempered in the meanwhile.

But not this year. This year the festivities would proceed without him. He did not believe he would be sorely missed. This year he would remain in town and would recognize no obligation to the season except to send off all the presents to Bloomfield and to host the concert that he usually gave during January. That was to be two days before Christmas. Christmas Day itself he intended to spend blissfully alone in his library with perhaps the indulgence of an afternoon or evening visit to Lucy. It would be a pleasant novelty to be able to make use of the services of a mistress on Christmas Day.

The carolers, he noticed with an inward grimace as he drew closer to them, were singing with surprising enthusiasm considering the inclement weather and the lack of appreciation with which their efforts were being greeted. They were also singing with a lamentable lack of musicality. One mature female voice, predominating over all the others, trilled and wobbled in the higher registers. Someone, Lord Heath guessed, had once told her she had a fine voice. He singled her out with his eyes. A buxom woman of late middle years, she sang with closed eyes as if in an ecstasy. The thin and elderly man behind her sang in a lusty bass voice. It took no connoisseur of music to recognize that the owner of the voice was tone-deaf.

"God Rest Ye, Merry Gentlemen" came to a close just as Lord Heath stepped out into the roadway in order to pass the group. They did have a small audience, he noticed. A lady, holding the hand of a small child, stood and listened to them. Though perhaps, he thought, she was one of them. She was young and doubtless personable, and the child was no more than an infant. Who better to take up the collection between renderings? Who could resist a pretty woman—unless perhaps another less pretty female? And who could resist a tiny child? He lifted one cynical eyebrow and walked on.

But the carolers had begun a new song. Not the whole group. A soloist began singing. "Lully, lulla, thou little tiny child," the voice sang—a soprano voice of such sweet purity that Lord Heath stopped in his tracks and unconsciously held his breath. It was like an angel's voice, he thought foolishly, and waited for the discordant sounds of the choir to join the voice after the opening lines. But it sang on alone.

A young boy he had not noticed before stood in the front ranks of the group, an open book across his two hands, his eyes directed downward at it. He was muffled up against the cold so that only his downcast eyes, two rosy cheeks, and an equally rosy nose were visible—and his mouth, which opened wide to release the heavenly sounds that held Lord Heath spellbound. He rested the tip of his cane on the wet and muddy curb and forgot everything but the music itself.

And the magic—if such was an appropriate word—of the Christmas story.

Fanny Berlinton was embarrassed—and cold. In equal measures. She was wearing a wool dress with long sleeves beneath her heavy cloak, and she had swallowed her pride by wearing her rather ugly half boots and an unfashionable bonnet with a brim large enough to shield her face from some of the wind's force, and from the intermittent rain. But Bond Street felt like an icy tunnel and she was unable even to hurry along it in order to build up some heat or duck inside one of the shops. She could not walk at all, in fact. She was forced to stand still.

She was forced to stand close to the carol singers and be associated with them by proximity. They were a group from the church she had attended since coming to live permanently in London at the end of the summer, and they prided themselves on having gone carol singing and raising money for church repairs every year for the past twenty-seven. With two or three exceptions, the members of the group were the same people who had begun the tradition. Fanny seriously doubted that they had ever been a tuneful choir, but she would give them the benefit of the doubt. Miss Kemp, their leader and star attraction, had perhaps had a passably good voice before it began to wobble with advancing age. Mr. Fothergill had perhaps been able to carry a tune before he lost most of his hearing.

If only Matthew had not opened his mouth one Sunday morning at the sound of a familiar hymn and sung like a nightingale, as the vicar had commented immediately afterward before launching into his ser-

mon. Matthew had been surrounded by kindly
parishioners after the service was over, and Miss
Kemp herself had announced that the dear boy really
must join the carolers and attend weekly practices, it
being October already.

He ought to be singing with the choir at Westminster Abbey or one of the other larger, more fashionable churches, the vicar had added, though he had
gone on to say that he hoped Mrs. Berlinton would
not deprive them of her son's heavenly voice.

Matthew, no ordinary child, had not cringed from
the idea of being part of an adult choir, as Fanny had
rather hoped he would. He had been charmed by the
prospect. Singing came more naturally to him than
talking, his mother often thought, and he would
never willingly pass by the opportunity to share his
talent with an audience.

Not that he was conceited. Far from it. Praise appeared to warm him but not to puff him up with any
sense of his own importance.

And so here she was, cold and embarrassed. The
carolers seemed to be more than usually off-key.
Though as usual she felt her heart swell with pride—
and apprehension—when Matthew began his solo.
How could anyone on busy Bond Street not stop to
take notice? she thought. But what if no one did?
Would Matthew notice and be crushed by the crowd's
indifference?

She glanced down at Katie, her daughter. She
hoped the child was warm. She was certainly bundled
up well enough. Katie was a strange mixture of quiet
dreaminess and occasional daring boldness. For the
moment she was still, content to hold hands and
watch her brother's performance. She set her head
against Fanny's side even as her mother looked down
at her.

Christmas would be quiet this year. Fanny had made the decision to let her brother-in-law and his family, with whom she lived because Boris had not left her sufficient funds for an independence on his death, go into the country without her. There would be a large house party there as usual and she had hesitated about depriving the children of the company of others of their own age. But she hated those Christmas parties, during which the adults and children were strictly segregated and the adult festivities consisted of too much eating, far too much drinking, and very much too much kissing and pinching beneath the mistletoe—kissing everyone, that is, except one's own spouse. For the past two Christmases, ever since coming out of mourning for Boris, Fanny had been kissed enough times to send her scurrying to her room on more than one occasion, feeling somewhat nauseated.

This year they would spend Christmas alone. Just the three of them. She hoped she was not being dreadfully selfish. She could imagine nothing lovelier than being in John's house without John and Mercy and their three children—just alone with her own two. Watching them open their gifts. Playing with them and reading to them. Spending the whole day with just them. It seemed like an unbelievable luxury. She still did not quite believe in it.

Matthew was not totally without an audience. One gentleman had stopped to listen. She turned her head to look at him. She recognized him though there was no chance that he would know her. Although she had had a come-out season when she was eighteen and had attended *ton* balls and parties, she had never moved in quite such exalted circles as Baron Heath— for which fact she had been thankful. Tall, handsome, fashionable, arrogant, and fabulously wealthy, he had also had a reputation as something of a rake, as a man on whom matchmaking mamas need not waste their time.

He still looked elegant and expensive. And supercilious, leaning on his came as if he very well might own Bond Street. But he was listening—and watching Matthew.

Fanny felt a sudden and wholly unexpected wave of loneliness. Boris had been dead for longer than three years and had not been much of a companion when he was alive. Amiable and good-looking and second son of a viscount, he had been a good match for her. But his amiability had concealed laziness, she had discovered after their marriage, and a lack of either strong feeling or principle. He had been frequently from home, spending his time with male companions as amiable and as shiftless as he, gaming, drinking, womanizing. He had not been a vicious man, merely one without character. She had not mourned him as deeply as conscience had suggested she ought.

Since his death there had been other suitors, though it seemed that the only ones she found remotely interesting wanted her as a mistress rather than as a wife. Widows, she had learned, were almost expected to take lovers rather than new husbands. A few of her suitors had seemed genuinely surprised to be rejected.

And sometimes she thought that perhaps she was foolish to have rejected them. Sometimes she longed for closeness with another adult. She had women friends, but they did not totally satisfy. Companionship with a man was important to her—she had discovered that when she had not found it with Boris. But she was not so dishonest with herself that she would not admit she wanted more than companionship. Sometimes she craved physical closeness—touching, kissing, caressing. And, oh yes, she would not deny it, the joining of bodies. She could remember that at the start of her marriage at least she had come to enjoy that. She had come to need it.

But she shook off the loneliness in order to gaze with pride at her son, whose voice had drawn the attention of a few other people on the street. He really did sing like a nightingale. Or like an angel. She listened to the words of the Christmas story he told in song. Perhaps this year Christmas as it was meant to be would come alive again and be more than an orgy of eating and drinking and flirting.

She longed for love and joy and peace and all the other feelings that were associated with Christmas yet were so rarely a real part of it.

Katie Berlinton was a little bit cold. She imagined that the wind was a bad-tempered old man with puffed cheeks and angry eyes. He was a rude man, too. He blew right through a person without having the courtesy to go around. She pressed closer to her mother and set the side of her face against Mama's cloak. She felt instantly warmer. She had realized before that feeling safe was a warm feeling.

She liked listening to the carolers. She did not know the tunes well enough to sing them herself and she did not know all the words. But she did know that she had heard the same carols every year at Christmastime. There was a special feel about carols and about Christmas. A warm feeling. A dreamy feeling. She was glad Matthew had a chance to sing alone. He loved to sing. She had tried to sing like him, but she could not do it. Nurse had told her once that she sounded like a rusty saw, but Nurse had laughed and hugged her as she said it, so the words had not really hurt a great deal. Though the truth of them had made her a little sad. Sad, but not jealous. She loved Matt. He was her hero.

She and Matt were to spend Christmas alone with Mama this year. Uncle John and Aunt Mercy and the cousins had gone into the country, where there would be all the children to play with there had been last year—she could remember the fun they had had. But she did not mind remaining behind as long as Matt and Mama were with her. She especially would not mind if she got what she wanted for Christmas. Numerous people had asked her what she wanted— Mama, Aunt Mercy, Miss Kemp among others—and she always gave the same answer because she knew it was the answer they all expected. She always dutifully said that she would like a doll.

But that was not what she really wanted. She wanted a new papa. Papas were fun. They came to the nursery every day and praised their children even when there was nothing particular to praise them for and pretended to fight with their sons until the boys shrieked with laughter. And they tossed their daughters at the ceiling and caught them and laughed at them for screaming with fright—and enjoyment. And they gave their children gifts even when it was not Christmas or a birthday and took them to the Tower of London and Astley's Amphitheater. They bought ices for them at Gunter's.

Uncles were nice too, of course. Sometimes they noticed that one felt left out and smiled and talked to one. Once they even took one along to Gunter's, though they scolded if one dropped ice cream on one's dress. Their own daughters never did any such bad thing.

Uncles were nice, but they did not belong to one. Uncles had to force themselves to be nice. Papas were always patient and loving. Papas belonged to one's very own self.

Sometimes Mama went driving with a gentleman. Once she went to the theater with one. Katie had seen some of the gentlemen, either by peering downstairs through the banister when she was supposed to be in the nursery or by looking out through the window. But none of those gentlemen had looked like papas.

Katie could not remember her own papa. She had had one. Mama had said so. But he had gone to heaven because God had wanted him. She thought it rather selfish of God, but Nurse had shrieked and looked quite frightened when she had once said so aloud. She had kept the thought to herself since then.

There was a gentleman watching Matt. He was leaning on his cane, and Katie could tell that he was really listening. He was not just being polite. She thought she could probably walk up to him and pinch his leg and he would not notice. But she would not do so. He was an extremely large gentleman—larger than Uncle John. And he looked like the kind of gentleman who would not take kindly to having his leg pinched—even though she did not believe he would notice.

Katie gazed at him. She thought she might be a little afraid if he looked at her as intently as he was looking at Matt. But she also thought that if he were her friend—not that he ever *would* be because she had never seen him before and obviously he and Mama had never seen each other before or they would be bowing and curtsying and he would be touching the brim of his hat. One never *ever* spoke to strangers, Mama always said. And so did Nurse. But if he *were* her friend, she thought, he would be utterly trustworthy. She imagined herself being lifted from the ground by him and held in the folds of all those capes. She would be wonderfully warm. And she would feel marvelously safe. She wondered if he was a papa. How she envied his children if he were. She wished she was one of them.

Secretly and silently she had added a rider to her evening prayers for ages and ages past, even though she knew she was praying to the same God who had wanted her papa and had taken him from her. She had prayed for a new papa, preferably for Christmas. Gifts were always more special at Christmas. And it struck her that it was an eminently unselfish gift for which to pray since if she had a new papa then Matt would have one too—as well as the gift for which he hoped. And Mama would perhaps like one too, though he would not be her papa, of course. Aunt Mercy seemed to like Uncle John and they often went to concerts and balls and things like that together while Mama as often as not stayed at home. Mama would like having someone to take her to concerts—*perhaps* she would like it. Not that Katie would love her one little bit the less just because there would be a papa to play with her as well.

She wished *that* gentleman could be her papa. Perhaps she would add that detail to her prayers tonight. The gentleman with the silver-headed cane and the many capes and the big nose and the piercing eyes, she would tell God. The gentleman who had loved Matt's singing so much that he looked as if he had forgotten where he was.

But Matt finished singing even as she was composing the prayer she would recite to herself that evening after she had finished the official version in her mother's hearing. And the gentleman jumped almost immediately into action.

"You!" he said, pointing his cane to Miss Kemp as there was a smattering of applause from some of the bystanders and one of the other ladies stepped forward with an upside down hat to collect money. "You, ma'am. Who is this boy?"

Miss Kemp, looking flustered, bobbed a curtsy. "He sings like an angel, does he not, sir?" she said. "We are proud this year—"

"Who is he?" Nurse would have said he was rude to interrupt, but Katie doubted Nurse would have said so to his face. She doubted that *anyone* would say so to his face.

"He is Master Matthew Berlinton, sir," Miss Kemp said. "He is—"

"Matthew Berlinton," the gentleman said, turning to Matt, "you have an extraordinary talent. It should be displayed before a larger and more appreciative audience."

"If it had not rained this morning, sir—" Miss Kemp began.

The gentleman was praising Matt just like a papa. Uncle John had once told Matt, though kindly enough, that he must stop singing all the time because he was giving Aunt Mercy headaches. Katie left the almost warm cocoon of her mother's side, completely forgetting what she had been taught about strangers, and crossed the distance to the gentleman. She stood on the curb before him and tugged at his greatcoat.

He looked down, astonishment on his face. He seemed even larger from close to and he did not smile. For a moment Katie felt frightened, but she remembered that he had told Matt that he had an extraordinary talent. Katie did not know quite what that meant, but she could guess from his tone that it was something good.

"I am Katie Berlinton," she said. And then she remembered to add, "Sir."

"Indeed?" he said, and Katie noticed that he did not

sound like a papa now—and that from among the
folds of his capes he had somehow produced a
quizzing glass, through which he looked down at her.
His enlarged eye looked somewhat colder than Uncle
John's had when she had dripped ice cream down
herself.

"Yes," she said.

Lord Heath had never particularly liked children.
Perhaps it was that he had never had a great deal to
do with them and that his numerous nieces and
nephews appeared mortally afraid of him. In fact, of
course, he had deliberately cultivated the fear by
never smiling in their presence and by making free
use of his quizzing glass. Only so could he preserve
even a modicum of privacy at Christmas while his
brothers and brothers-in-law and male cousins were
constantly being climbed upon and pestered to come
and play. Children, Lord Heath had concluded, shortened male tempers in a hurry. He avoided having his
own shortened by the simple expedient of avoiding
children.

And now a little cherub of an infant had had the ef-
frontery to pull at his greatcoat in the middle of the
street and to present herself to him. After his hand, almost by its own volition, had found his quizzing glass
and raised it to his eye, she still clung to his coat and
still gazed steadily upward, her head tipped sharply
back.

The child's mother, he decided, deserved a severe
tongue-lashing for allowing such impertinence—and
for keeping a less than careful eye on her offspring.
What would she do if he tucked the child beneath his
arm and made off with her? There would be nothing
she could do except have a first-class fit of the vapors.

She would never see the child again. And it would serve her right too.

But the mother—the woman who had been standing watching the carolers when he arrived—was there before him, only a stride or two behind her daughter, and she was pulling the child away and scolding her and looking remarkably flustered—as well she might.

"I *do* apologize," she said, presumably to him even though she did not raise her eyes to his. She sounded suitably mortified.

But he was distracted. His hearing had just caught up to his thoughts. Katie *Berlinton*, the child had said. The young soprano was Matthew Berlinton.

"Mrs. Berlinton?" he said.

She looked more mortified than before as she curtsied slightly. But of course, she was a *lady*. His manners had certainly gone begging. It was not at all the thing to accost a genteel stranger in the middle of the street without anyone to perform a formal introduction. But that boy was too precious to be lost on account of a few social niceties.

"I must commend you, ma'am, on your son's voice," he said. "It is quite exquisite."

"Thank you, my lord," she murmured, curtsying again and gathering the infant's hand firmly in her own before turning with the obvious intention of gathering her son beneath her other wing.

Ah. So she knew him. He did not know her. She was clearly a lady and was well dressed. But she was not clad in the first stare of fashion. There was no sign of hovering servants or of a carriage waiting to convey her home. The other carolers were gathered about, gawking and beaming.

"Pardon me, ma'am," he said, desperation causing him to fling aside the vestiges of good manners, "may I be allowed to present myself?" He did not wait for an answer. "Roderick Ames, Baron Heath, at your service. You may have heard of me as something of a connoisseur of musical talent."

The leader of the carolers, the woman of the wobbly voice, curtsied just as if she were being presented at the queen's drawing room. The other women of the group hastily followed suit, while two or three of the men bobbed their heads.

"Eh?" the tone-deaf chorister said, cupping one hand about his left ear.

"His lordship is Baron Heath, Mr. Fothergill," the lady leader said in a voice that announced his identity to at least half of Bond Street.

The tone-deaf man was also deaf, his lordship concluded.

Mrs. Berlinton did not curtsy again, but she did raise her eyes to his for the first time. He had realized from the start that she was young and probably pleasing to look at. He was surprised to find that actually she was quite exquisitely beautiful, with large hazel eyes, a straight little nose, and a soft mouth that was neither too small nor too large—a mouth made for kissing, in fact. Mr. Berlinton was a fortunate man. Even reddened cheeks and nose could not quite disguise the delicacy of her complexion.

"No, my lord," she said, "I had not heard that. Please excuse us." And she turned back to her children.

"Your son has a talent that is wasted on such an audience," he said, gesturing with his cane at the street around them.

She turned back to him then, and he could see anger in her eyes. "My son is a *child*, my lord," she said. "He does not need an audience."

Lord Heath was not a man to act from impulse. He was not sure quite what impelled him now, except that the boy's voice was exceptionally beautiful and that it was such an ephemeral gift—it would disappear with puberty. It was not a voice to be wasted on Bond Street shoppers and to be drowned out by an unmusical adult group of carolers.

"I will provide him with an audience, ma'am," he said, "the most discriminating audience in London." He always prepared the guest list for his concerts with care, choosing not necessarily the most fashionable guests, but those with a sincere appreciation for music. Consequently, he knew, his invitations were much sought after and were scarcely ever refused. "He will sing at a concert in my home the evening after tomorrow. I beg leave to call upon Mr. Berlinton to discuss the details."

He could not understand her anger—or perhaps he would in a more rational moment when he would surely recall with some discomfort discussing such matters with a stranger in the middle of Bond Street during a busy afternoon. But angry she was—her eyes flashed and her nostrils flared and she would surely have flushed if her cheeks had not already been fiery red.

"This is distasteful, my lord," she said with all the disdain of a dowager duchess. "My son is not for hire and not for display before the *ton*. He seeks no remuneration. I assume you *were* offering to pay him?"

He had not considered the matter. He always did pay the performers at his concerts, those who would accept payment, anyway. Some would not. He opened his mouth to reply. But she had turned from him once more.

"Come, Matthew," she said. "Make your bow to Miss Kemp and the other ladies and gentlemen. I regret, Miss Kemp, that we cannot stay for the rest of the carols. Katie is cold and tired."

Lord Heath shut his mouth with a clack of teeth
and turned on his heel. He had been roundly snubbed
and deservedly so. But he was not accustomed to
being snubbed. He would not wait to see Mrs. Berlinton take her leave with her offspring. He could not
imagine what had possessed him. He was not given
to encouraging child performers—or to engaging performers at the last minute and on the spur of the moment. He had already selected with care, with
consideration to both the talent of his chosen performers and the variety of their talents. He already had a
soprano on his program, a much acclaimed opera
singer, whose services he had felt honored and delighted to attain. She was a woman soprano, of
course.

He would doubtless have been laughed at if he had
presented a mere boy, of whom no one had ever
heard and whose voice, though undoubtedly lovely,
was also untrained.

No, he would not have been laughed at. His audience would have been spellbound, as he had been just
minutes ago.

He felt an unaccountable wave of sadness—yes,
sadness, not chagrin, he thought, testing the word in
his mind—at the knowledge that he would never hear
that voice again. How the shepherds of Bethlehem, he
thought with an unaccustomed flight of fancy, must
have found their lives blighted by their inability to
hear again the heavenly host of angels after the night
when they had proclaimed the birth of a baby in a sta-
ble.

His mind ached with the memory of that youthful,
pure voice.

Fanny was still feeling cross and out of sorts the following morning. And a little guilty, though she had

no reason to feel that at least, she assured herself. How dared he address her in the middle of Bond Street, even if Katie *had* pulled at his greatcoat and introduced herself. How dared he assume that she would jump at the chance of putting Matthew on display for his rakish friends.

Oh no, that was not quite true, of course. After Lord Heath had stalked away in high dudgeon at having his will crossed, Mr. Parkinson, one of the quieter and more genteel of the carol singers, had informed her that his lordship did indeed have a reputation as a connoisseur of good music. He gave an annual concert in his London home at which he gathered some of the most prestigious performers in all of Europe. Invitations to his concerts were much coveted.

Matthew might have sung at such a concert.

But Matthew was an eight-year-old child. She had no wish to put him on display as if he were some sort of circus performer, even if the audience was to be a knowledgeable and appreciative one.

Matthew himself had seen the matter differently, of course. He had been severely disappointed and had made her know it by pouting and being unusually quiet for the rest of the day. The most irritating fact was that he had said nothing, and so she had not had the opportunity to work out her irritation on him. And how dreadful to think that she might have done so.

She had scolded Katie and given her the usual lecture about talking to strangers and about ladylike conduct. And the child had been punished when they arrived home by being made to sit on a hard chair in the nursery for a whole hour without talking and without occupation.

But Katie had borne the scold with quiet, wide-eyed patience, and when Fanny had stood in the doorway of the nursery after half an hour, trying not to give in to weakness and release her daughter early, it had been to find Katie sitting with her eyes tightly shut, her hands pressed together, and her lips silently moving, for all the world as if she were in prayer. She had been deeply involved in some game and had clearly not been suffering unduly from the punishment.

Now today Fanny felt depressed. She had deprived her children of company over Christmas; she had taken Matthew away early from yesterday's carol singing although he had been wildly excited in anticipation of it; she had been forced to punish Katie; and she was more aware of her own loneliness even than she had been every other Christmas since Boris's death.

The truth was, she thought with sheepish annoyance, that she had had a foolish tendre for Lord Heath during her girlhood. All the young ladies of her acquaintance had, of course. Everything about him—his looks, his wealth, his arrogance, his elegance, his reputation—had given him an irresistible appeal. She had been very sensible. She had dutifully looked about her for a suitable husband and had equally dutifully fallen in love with Boris when it had become obvious that he was the one. But it was about Lord Heath that she had woven dreams right up until the time of her wedding. She could recall feeling mortally envious of Miss Dryden, one of her friends, with whom he had danced on one occasion.

And yesterday, she thought with brutal honesty, she had noticed how everything about him had only improved with the passage of nine years—including the harsh perfection of his features and the arrogance of his expression. And she had felt breathless and weak at the knees.

How despicable! The very thought made her feel embarrassed, just as if someone had caught her at it.

She sighed and made her way to the nursery. She had half promised to meet a few of her lady friends at the library, but she felt the need to spend the time with her children and to try to mend bridges. She was intercepted before she arrived there, however, first by the sound of the door knocker below, then by the sound of male voices—more than one—and then, as she stood still waiting, by the appearance of John's butler, who had come upstairs to announce to her the arrival of the vicar of her church. She looked down at herself, decided she was presentable enough, ran her hands over her hair to make sure that no curl had broken free of her careful chignon, and went down to the visitors' salon.

The Reverend Josiah Barker was not alone. As he bowed and greeted her with his usual hearty smile and voice, she became aware of another gentleman standing some distance away, before the window. A large man with a many-caped greatcoat. *Him.* She scarcely needed to turn her head to ascertain the fact.

"Mrs. Berlinton, ma'am," the vicar said, rubbing his hands together as if washing them, "may I have the great honor of presenting to you his lordship, Baron Heath?"

Lord Heath bowed. Fanny curtsied and felt astonishment—and anger. And that weakness in the knees again. He seemed to half fill the salon. He seemed to have sucked half the air out of it.

"A quite astonishing stroke of good fortune, Mrs. Berlinton," the vicar said. "His lordship heard our dear carolers on Bond Street yesterday and was so impressed by their singing that he has engaged them to sing during a concert at his town house tomorrow evening. He has agreed to make a most generous donation to our repairs fund."

His lordship was looking at her quite intently, his lips pursed.

"And his lordship has specifically requested that your dear son sing his solo piece," the vicar said. "I can only applaud his taste, ma'am. It is a great honor for our carolers and for your young Matthew in particular."

How dared he! He had tricked her, made it almost impossible for her to say no.

"It is an evening concert?" she asked the vicar, ignoring her other, silent visitor. "I regret that it will be too late for Matthew, Mr. Barker. But the carolers have functioned very well without him for twenty-seven years. I am sure they will acquit themselves very well indeed without him tomorrow evening."

Lord Heath spoke for the first time. "But I have made my invitation to the carolers conditional upon their bringing your son with them, ma'am," he said.

Ah. So he had her. Miss Kemp and everyone else would be ecstatic. The Reverend Barker was fair to bursting with pride—and with excitement over the projected boost to his repairs fund. And really she had no good reason for preventing her son from sharing his talent with true music lovers.

But she seethed with resentment at the trickery.

"I see," she said as icily as she could, her eyes directly on Lord Heath's so that he would know that indeed she did see. Obviously he had discovered that she was a widow, that her brother-in-law, Matthew's male guardian, was from home. Doubtless he had thought—quite correctly—that she would be easily vanquished.

"I should like to speak with your son," he said. "There is little time for rehearsal, but I would like to discuss with him what he will sing. I would like you to bring him today or tomorrow—or perhaps both days—so that he may practice in the music room and accustom himself to its acoustics."

Her chin shot up. "And has this invitation been extended to the whole group of carolers, my lord?" she asked. "I shall send to Miss Kemp and find out when they are planning to call at your house for rehearsal."

He pursed his lips again. "A group of carolers may simply be themselves, ma'am," he said. "A child soloist—"

"—will also simply be himself," she said sharply.

He raised his eyebrows and looked at least twice as arrogant as usual. Doubtless he was unaccustomed to being interrupted.

"Miss Kemp has kindly offered to accompany you and dear Matthew for rehearsal, Mrs. Berlinton," the vicar said. "She will call upon you early this afternoon to see if today is convenient to you. The child does indeed have an angelic voice, my lord, as you so perceptively remarked. And a disposition to match."

"*May* I speak with him, ma'am?" Lord Heath asked, a trace of well-bred impatience in his voice.

Fanny compressed her lips. Perhaps, she thought, she would feel the honor if this offer were being made by anyone except him. She could not reconcile her image of him as elegant rake with that of connoisseur of musical talent. And she did not appreciate the idea that she was being treated as some sort of servant, providing her son to offer entertainment to his *tonnish* friends. She wondered if she would be kept waiting in the kitchen while he sang.

She was being foolish, she decided. It *was* an honor. Matthew would be thrilled. And it would happen only once. It would not be wrong for a child to participate in a Christmas concert. Christmas was about a child.

"I shall fetch him down myself," she said, addressing herself to the vicar. "Though I do not know what there is to discuss. He will sing what his lordship overheard yesterday. That is all."

"Yes, do fetch the boy," Lord Heath said, sounding faintly bored as she turned to the door.

Katie had not been at all sure her prayers would be listened to, let alone answered, since she had been sitting in the punishment chair when she had said them. Sometimes she wished Mama would simply spank her when she was bad as Aunt Mercy did with the cousins, but Mama never did spank.

But perhaps God had thought the tedious time in the chair punishment enough, because He had answered her prayer. At least she thought He had answered. That gentleman had come this morning—Matt had returned to the nursery after being taken down by Mama and had said that it was the very same man who pointed his cane at Miss Kemp and looked at her, Katie, with his huge, magnified eye.

And now this afternoon they had come, the three of them, with Miss Kemp, to the gentleman's own house and had been shown into a huge room with a pianoforte set right in the middle of it and a big thing beside it that Mama said was a harp. Matt was going to sing, and he was so horribly excited that he had been unable to eat his midday meal even though Nurse had tried to coax and even force him.

Katie did not know how coming to this house so that Matt could sing was going to make the gentleman into her papa, but she trusted God. At least she thought she did. She still remembered uneasily that

He had wanted her first papa and had taken him away without a by-your-leave.

Even after the gentleman had come into the room and bowed and she and Mama and Miss Kemp had curtsied and Matt had bowed, she did not know how he was going to be her papa. He looked far smarter in his clothes than Uncle John did, but he did not smile and Mama did not smile and for some reason there was a terrible stiffness in the room despite the fact that Miss Kemp was telling the gentleman what a splendid room it was. But she did not have to tell him that. He must have known it for himself.

His eyes warmed when he looked at Matt, though, and he spoke to him as if he were a real person.

"Well, Matthew," he said, "do you find the room daunting?"

"No, sir," Matthew said, but Katie could tell from his voice that he did really, though she could only guess at the meaning of that unfamiliar word.

Katie did not listen closely to what followed. They talked about what Matt would sing. He would sing only one song, Mama said, sounding firm as she did when Matthew tried to wheedle her into letting them stay up a little later at night. But the gentleman said there would have to be something else called an encore. Miss Kemp said something about the harp, causing the gentleman to frown. And then he had Mama and Miss Kemp sit down on two chairs close to the pianoforte and had Matt stand beside it. And Matt started to sing the song about the little tiny child. His voice wobbled almost as Miss Kemp's always did and the gentleman told him to stop, to draw a few breaths, to take his time, and to try again. After that Matt sang more properly. The gentleman went to stand a long distance away, near the door.

Katie wondered if she had been mistaken, if perhaps he could not be her new papa after all. He had not once looked at her. She could not quite imagine him wrestling with Matt or tossing her at the ceiling. Though she wished he would try it. He looked very big and strong. If Uncle John could catch the cousins, she was sure this gentleman would catch her. She would not even shriek in terror. She would *know* that he would not drop her.

She wandered away from her place after a minute or two. Mama did not notice, or anyone else either. They were all listening to Matt, whose voice sounded very loud in this great room. She walked toward the gentleman. She wanted to test her own feelings. She rather thought she would be frightened when she got close, but she was not sure. His pantaloons were very tight, she thought. In fact, if they had been pink, she would not have been quite sure they were not simply skin. The thought amused her and she reached out a hand to feel them, to assure herself that they really were just pantaloons and not biscuit-colored skin.

He looked down at her, startled, and she almost jumped back in alarm. But she did something else instead, something really very silly because Nurse had told her long ago that it was a babyish thing to do. She stretched both arms above her head.

The gentleman continued to look down at her, just as if he did not quite know what it was she wanted— or as if he did not want to know. God was playing tricks with her, Katie decided, and was about to let her arms fall. She thought she very well might cry, but that was a really babyish thing to do and she would not do two such things in a row. She was four years old and no baby.

And then he stooped down and picked her up. She was amazed at his strength. Up she went with seemingly no effort at all, just as if she weighed a feather.

She came to rest seated securely and comfortably on one of his arms, with her face only inches from his own. He turned away when she gazed into his eyes, and looked back at Matt. They were blue eyes. She liked the idea of a papa with blue eyes.

Matt faltered and Miss Kemp had to remind him of the words. He started again.

There was something strange about the gentleman's face. It looked different from Mama's or Nurse's. Katie stared at it until curiosity got the better of good manners. She touched his jaw with one finger and ran it lightly downward. Smooth. She ran the finger upward. Not quite so smooth. She pressed harder and pushed her finger upward again. There was a funny tickling feeling.

And then she looked up to find the gentleman's eyes on her. "Well, little one," he said very softly, "did I not shave closely enough for you this morning?" And for the merest moment—she almost missed it—his eyes smiled at her.

It was at that moment that Katie fell irrevocably in love with him and decided that she must, she simply *must* have him as a papa. Uncle John had never *almost* smiled at her in quite that way. And she had been quite right in her guess yesterday. She felt wonderfully safe up where she was.

"No, sir," she whispered, not knowing quite what his words had meant but giving the reply she thought he wanted. His lips twitched. He wanted to smile outright, she thought, but would not do so for some reason.

A few minutes later Katie was sure that she was bound for the punishment chair again as soon as she arrived home. Mama spun about, her eyes grew as large as saucers, her hand flew to her mouth, and she jumped to her feet. Miss Kemp was saying something to Matt about expression. But the gentleman spoke up.

"I beg you not to agitate yourself, ma'am," he said out loud. "She is safe here with me. You will find, Matthew, that in a room that has been designed for music, as this one has, you do not need to sing with full volume in order to be heard. I would like you to sing again, forgetting the presence of your mother and of Miss Kemp, forgetting my presence. Let yourself feel the room and what it requires of you. Listen to your own voice and work with the room. Relax and let your own musical instinct guide you."

Miss Kemp sat down without another word. So did Mama. Katie gazed at the gentleman, who had understood that Matt felt small and bewildered and frightened. He had not softened his voice as adults usually did when they wanted children to think them kind, but Katie had understood his kindness anyway. So had Matt. He visibly relaxed.

"Well, little one," the gentleman asked quietly before Matt started singing again, "and what do you want for Christmas?"

A doll, she almost said in answer to the familiar question. But she stopped herself. "It is a secret," she told him. "But I will whisper it to you if you wish."

He raised his eyebrows. They arched very nicely. She must look in the mirror to see if she could do that.

"I want a new papa," she whispered to him.

"Indeed?" His eyebrows lifted even higher. "And do you have anyone in mind, pray?"

She nodded firmly and felt a shiver of excitement all along her spine. But soon it was a shiver of something else. His look of near amusement disappeared and his eyes flattened if eyes could do that. They looked as if they had flattened.

"Indeed?" he said again.

Matt started to sing again then and Katie could tell immediately that he had forgotten his excitement and indeed everybody and everything except the carol he sang. The gentleman watched him intently, and she could tell that he had forgotten all about her. She was glad of it. He did not want to be her papa, she thought. She had been very bold and had almost told him that that was what she wanted, but he had turned chilly and flat-eyed and had said, "Indeed?" in that voice she would try to imitate when she was alone with her dolls. How she would make her dolls tremble!

She felt again a little like crying but stayed still until Matt came near to the end of his song. Then she wriggled.

"Down, please," she demanded, trying to use the same expression and tone of voice as he had used when he had said, "Indeed?"

He set her down without a word and she scurried back to her mother, wishing that she had asked God only for a doll for Christmas. She was more sure of getting a doll than a papa. There would be less chance of disappointment. But it was too late now. She had made her wish and set her heart on having it granted. She was going to be awfully disappointed.

Perhaps the gentleman had merely meant that he wished her to say no more so that the Christmas gift would be a surprise. Perhaps that was what he had meant and why he had sounded so chilly when he had said, "Indeed?" Perhaps after all he was going to be her papa.

Her mother took her firmly by the hand.

Lord Heath halfheartedly supervised the decoration of his hall and his music room the next day. Really, he conceded, his servants were quite efficient and needed no direction from him at all. But the idea of decorating for Christmas had struck him just yesterday morning as a good one. Although his concert was an annual event, it had never before come within two days of Christmas. He might as well make it a suitably festive occasion.

The thought had quite buoyed him up. He had forgotten for a moment that his very reason for remaining in town this year was so that he might avoid Christmas altogether. After all, he had thought, there would be children present at his concert this year. Children would appreciate some of the atmosphere of Christmas. He had forgotten too that he had remained in London so that he might avoid children.

This morning he was feeling irritable. And sorry that he had decided to make the connection between the concert and Christmas. And sorry about a number of other things. That he had not gone to visit Lucy last night, for example. He had intended to go. He had sent word to her. He had got ready to go. He had even left the house. But at the last moment he had rapped on the front panel of his carriage and instructed his coachman to take him to White's instead. It had been almost deserted so close to the holiday and he had spent a tedious evening and come home early to lie awake half the night staring at the canopy above his bed. Perhaps he would have felt better this morning if he had spent the night in Lucy's bed, even if it had been an equally sleepless night. At least his sleeplessness would have been more productive and infinitely more pleasurable.

She had more than a lovely face—he was not thinking of Lucy. She had thick and shining chestnut hair, whose glory she disguised but could not quite hide in a careful chignon. She was not slender. Neither was she fat or even buxom. She had a mature woman's full and shapely figure, and she carried herself proudly and gracefully. He had noticed her beauty and appreciated it during the morning visit to her home with the vicar of her church—he was a connoisseur of female beauty as well as of music. He had noticed it again during the afternoon. He had even felt a stirring of the loins for her—he was a perfectly normal male after all. She would undoubtedly be satisfying to bed.

What he had not noticed was any personal emotion toward her. Not, that was, until that strange and impudent child had said what she had—and how foolish he felt to remember that he had been somewhat touched by her lack of fear of him, almost honored by her raising her arms to be picked up, and charmed by her innocent curiosity about his whiskers.

She wanted a new papa for Christmas. And she had someone in mind. The Widow Berlinton was being courted, then, by a gentleman wise enough to court her children also. And he must be very close to success if the child hoped to net him as a papa by Christmas. The widow was about to remarry. Fortunate man!

But that had not been Lord Heath's first thought. His first thought had been of another man's hands releasing and burying themselves in that glorious hair and of another man's body lying atop hers, pleasuring both her and himself. It was a thought so unexpected and so startling—and so mortifying—that he had indulged it for several seconds before ruthlessly suppressing it.

But not quite in time. He had made himself irritable and restless and he had done a somewhat foolish thing considering the fact that she was about to remarry. He had assured her that the boy would need another rehearsal this afternoon. He had mastered

both the acoustics of the room and his own nervousness and had sung even more beautifully than Lord
Heath had expected, but the day of the concert would
bring fresh nerves to so young a child. He must come
back, then, to accustom himself to the atmosphere, to
settle his excitement. And since there would be little
point in Mrs. Berlinton's returning home with her
children afterward merely to come back again in the
evening, she must agree to join his other guests and
dine with him. His housekeeper would be quite delighted to look after the children. He would make a
guest room available for them and for her, so that she
might change into evening clothes.

Miss Kemp had not been included in the invitation.
However, he had assured Mrs. Berlinton that the
house would be filled with milling servants and
guests all day so that there would be no impropriety
in her coming alone with her children. He had emphasized the benefits for her son, of course, and she
had accepted, though with obvious reluctance.

And so he was pursuing an interest in a widow
who was about to remarry. A widow with two young
children. He never pursued other men's women. He
rarely consorted with widows. Too many of them
were eager to return to the married state. He always
avoided women with children. He liked to be assured
of the undivided attention of the women he bedded.

Besides, Mrs. Berlinton was dignified and aloof and
even hostile. He knew from an instinct developed
through long experience that she would not easily
enter upon a sexual liaison for the mere sake of pleasure.

He had known that before he invited her.

"No," he said now to his housekeeper, who had interrupted his thoughts to ask if he wanted any mistletoe pinned up. No mistletoe. The very thought made

him shudder. If he was to kiss her, it would not be through such trickery.

If he was to kiss her?

All his irritability returned. This was the day for which he had planned meticulously for months past, the day he had looked forward to more than any other since his last concert. He wished to be able to focus all his thoughts, all his energies, all his emotions on the music with which his guests were to have their spirits lifted into another dimension this evening. He wished to anticipate in some excitement the sensation the boy soprano was certain to create.

He did not want to be thinking, like a randy schoolboy, about stealing kisses from lovely widows.

And he did not want to be remembering, he thought with a grimace, that his concert was to end with a rendition from a group of carolers whose enthusiasm and good intentions could not in any way make up for the fact that they murdered every piece of music they chose to attack. But such had been the price of his boy soprano—and of his lovely widow.

Matthew had vomited once during the morning and had been so restless with nervous energy that his nurse had sent for Fanny and suggested that perhaps they should send for a physician. Fanny had taken her son on her knee, something he would rarely allow these days since he was eight years old, cuddled him, and asked if he would like her to send word to Lord Heath that he would not sing at this evening's concert.

"You must really not feel that you are being pushed into it, sweetheart," she had assured him. "No one is going to force you to sing against your will."

Katie had stood beside them, silent and wide-eyed,

and had also regressed a couple of years. She had put her thumb in her mouth and sucked on it.

But then Matthew had almost panicked in the conviction that she would forbid him to sing.

"I want to, Mama," he had wailed, "more than anything else in this whole wide world. I want to please *him*. He knows about music and he understands about me."

Fanny had hated to admit that he was right. Lord Heath had shown unexpected sensitivity the afternoon before and had calmed Matthew and helped him with a few well-chosen words. He had not calmed *her*, especially when she had seen him with Katie on his arm, but that was quite beside the point.

And so now they were at Lord Heath's house again and Matthew's rehearsal was quickly finished—he was relaxed and confident now that they were here, his excitement under control. Lord Heath's housekeeper had borne the children away to give them their tea and to see to it that they lay down and had a rest while Fanny was to take tea in the drawing room with the guests who were to stay at the house tonight. But Lord Heath was in no hurry to take her to the drawing room. The milling servants and guests he had promised just yesterday certainly were nowhere to be seen in the music room. He seated himself in the chair beside hers.

Fanny looked around surreptitiously for mistletoe, but she could not see any among the holly wreaths and the pine boughs and the ribbons and bows with which the room was lavishly decorated. It looked like Christmas here, she thought, and felt a moment's unreasonable pang when she remembered that in just two days' time she and the children would be spending Christmas alone in John's house.

"Your son has enormous talent, ma'am," Lord

Heath said. "But I am sure I need not tell you that. Not only does he have a pure and uniquely lovely voice, but he also has a rare feel for music. His voice, alas, will change within a few years, but the musicality will remain and perhaps his man's voice will be as lovely. Does he show aptitude on any instrument?"

John's two daughters had pianoforte lessons, but Mercy was prone to migraine headaches and John had decreed that the privilege should be extended to no one else, his own son included.

"I do not know," she said.

He stared at her for a long time. His very blue eyes and his proximity made her uncomfortable, together with the subtle fragrance of some expensive cologne that clung about him. She tried to breathe evenly. How humiliating it would be if she became breathless and he were to suspect that she found him attractive—knee-weakeningly attractive.

"Does he have voice lessons?" he asked.

"My brother-in-law believes in bringing up boys to be masculine, my lord," she said. "He is my son's guardian." She tried to keep the bitterness from her voice. Matthew's love of music must be squashed, John always said, or he would be laughed at when he went to school. Besides, Mercy's migraines . . .

"I see," he said. "Are you not his guardian too, ma'am? Could you not at least see to it that he have an audition with a reputable church choir? At Westminster Abbey, for example? There he would be among boys like himself and would not appear strange or less masculine than they."

She was angry. How dare he take it upon himself to advise her or suggest that she had less than total control over the upbringing of her children. That he was right did not lessen her anger.

"He is a child," she said. "I will not have him exploited."

"He loves music, ma'am," he said. "My guess is that he would love nothing more than encouragement to pursue his talent—and his dream."

"My lord," she said, no longer trying to hide her anger, "do you presume to know my son better than I know him?" But he was quite right. Oh, he was *right*. Perhaps Boris would have understood. Perhaps . . .

She gazed down, startled at the ringed, well-manicured, very masculine hand that reached across and covered her two hands in her lap. And looked up into his blue eyes.

"Will you permit me," he asked quietly, "to have a word with your brother-in-law? He is the elder son of the ailing Viscount Milford, I believe? My word on musical matters carries some weight, I do assure you, and no one has ever questioned my masculinity. Not to my face, at least."

Two *men* deciding the fate of *her* son? Fanny's nostrils flared. But anger was all mixed up with desire. He had not removed his hand

"I am Matthew's *mother*, my lord," she said. "I will speak myself to my brother-in-law when I feel it necessary to do so."

"Some men," he said, "feel it a weakness to grant the wishes of a woman." His fingers, she noticed with a twinge of discomfort and intensified desire in the pit of her stomach, had curled about her two hands so that he held them fast. His hand was warmer than hers. "Perhaps you could persuade your betrothed to speak with him."

"My—betrothed?" She frowned at him. "To whom do you refer, my lord?"

"I understood," he said, "that you were about to remarry. Did I misunderstand?"

Who could have given him such an idea? The vicar? But she did not even have a regular suitor.

"I am not betrothed," she said, "or about to remarry, my lord." She spoke with unwise lack of consideration. "There is enough male interference in my life and in those of my children without my giving up all my freedom again to another."

He looked steadily into her eyes for several moments before glancing down once at her lips. She felt the terrified certainty that he was going to kiss her—and that she was not going to stop him. But then she felt merely foolish. He squeezed her hands once, released them, and got to his feet.

"Come, ma'am," he said. "My guests will be in the drawing room by now and you must be ready for your tea. You must not be afraid for your son tonight. I have experience with talented performers. All the excitement and nervousness and sometimes even illness that precede a performance invariably disappear when the time comes and merely ensure that the performance itself is flawless. Tonight your son will leave even you breathless with wonder."

There was a rush of tears to her eyes and she blinked them back, feeling foolish. "Are you ever wrong?" she asked.

He took her hand and drew her arm through his. "Rarely," he said. "On this particular matter, never. But you will not believe me, of course, until the performance is over."

He had a very firm and steady arm. She felt comforted even though her terror for Matthew was still like a ball of ice deep inside her.

How had he known she was terrified?

What *was* that cologne? she wondered. She had never smelled it on any other man.

*   *   *

Katie was all dressed up in her red Christmas dress
with white stockings and shoes and a white bow in
her hair. All the ladies in the music room had smiled
at her and told her—or Mama—that she looked like a
princess or a doll or an angel. But Katie had sat down
beside Matthew in the front row of chairs that went
all about the room and had taken hold of his hand. He
had not shaken her off as he sometimes did, but had
clung, his own hand cold and damp. Katie had not
cared for anyone but Matt at that moment. Matt was
dreadfully afraid and terribly excited, but he was
going to be wonderful. Katie just knew he was. She
sat quietly telling him so with her hand while a lady
with a limp played the pianoforte and then a great fat
man sang with a deep voice and then another lady
played that harp—Katie was going to play it too
when she was grown up. It sounded lovelier than the
pianoforte and the lady was able to play it with great
sweeps of her arms that made her look very pretty.

And then it was Matt's turn. When he got up and
dropped Katie's hand, she got up too and sat on
Mama's lap, and the gentleman came and sat down
beside them. Katie gazed at him. He was all in black
and white tonight and looked marvelously splendid.
She wished she could tell everyone that he was to be
her papa, but she was not quite sure it was true. This
morning for a few minutes she had even been afraid
that they were never going to see him again. She had
found herself doing something dreadfully babyish.
She had sucked her thumb.

He did not look at her or at Mama. He looked at
Matt—and Matt looked at him with great frightened
eyes. And then the gentleman's eyes did what they
had almost done for her yesterday. Except that it was
definite this time and lasted a long time. His eyes

smiled at Matt and he beamed at him without moving any part of his face. That was another expression Katie was going to practice. She had had no success with her eyebrows this morning. She wondered if she could smile without moving her face.

And then Matthew started to sing and Katie, who had been contemplating getting down and climbing onto the gentleman's lap, sat very still because Mama was holding her very tightly indeed. Matt was wonderful, as Katie had known he would be. He was more than wonderful, but she did not know another word. She was going to tell everyone when the concert was over that Matt was her brother.

A funny thing happened when he had finished singing about the little tiny child. Everyone clapped, as they were supposed to do, but some people started roaring—at least, it *sounded* like roaring—and some even jumped to their feet and started calling out that word the gentleman had used yesterday—"Encore!" Mama was holding her so tightly that Katie felt short of breath, and Mama was crying. And the gentleman—well, he was blinking fast. He was crying too, Katie thought, but he would not want anyone to know. Matt always said that men never cried.

She wriggled free of her mother, got down, and climbed up onto one of the gentleman's legs. "I knew he would be wonderful," she whispered to him as the noise about them began to subside. "I could have told you so. Matthew is my brother."

And then *he* hugged her even harder than Mama had done. "You can be justly proud of him, little one," he said. "And he of you."

She gazed up into his face as Matt began to sing again. The gentleman closed his eyes and frowned. He looked as if he were in pain, but Katie understood that it was only the music and the sound of Matt's voice that were almost too much for him to bear. She heard him swallow during one pause in the music.

He hugged her again when Matt was finished and everyone was roaring again, and kissed her on top of the head, right where her bow was. Then he got to his feet and set her back on Mama's lap before walking over to set a hand on Matt's shoulder and to tell everyone what a privilege they had all been permitted to experience tonight. Almost, he said with a smile, as if they were the shepherds outside Bethlehem listening to angel voices—except that it was one day early.

Katie knew the story of the shepherds outside Bethlehem. They had been looking after their sheep, but no one had been able to tell her what happened to the sheep when the shepherds went to Bethlehem to see the baby.

And no, the gentleman said, there would be no other encore. Matthew must be allowed to rest his voice.

And then Matt was sitting beside them again and cuddling against Mama, his face hidden against her side. Katie, touching his hand, found that it was cold and trembling now that it was all over.

The gentleman had understood that he could sing no more. And he had said Matt was someone to be proud of. And that she was too. He *was* like a real papa. He was proud of them even though she had done nothing of which anyone could be really proud. And he had smiled at them and been kind to them and had had that lady give them the creamiest cakes for tea that she had ever tasted. She had eaten two. And before he had crossed the room to Matt, after setting her down on Mama's lap, he had looked into Mama's eyes and touched her hand. He liked Mama, and surely Mama liked him. How could she not?

Christmas was soon. Not tomorrow. Two more sleeps, Mama had said when Katie had asked earlier. After two more sleeps she would really have a papa. She just knew it. She was not even going to worry about it anymore. She yawned and set her head against her mother's bosom. Someone was playing a violin.

Well before the end of the concert Lord Heath had suggested to Mrs. Berlinton that his housekeeper take the children to the guest room set aside for their use and put them to bed until it was time to take them home. The little one was fast asleep against her mother's bosom, her cheeks flushed, her mouth open. Matthew was clearly exhausted, both physically and emotionally. He picked the boy up while she got carefully to her feet so as not to wake the child.

And so the concert continued and came to its grand finale with the carol singers. They were not nearly the disastrous anticlimax he had feared. They were all dressed up in their finest outdoor garments and all carried sheet music except for the two appointed to hold high lit lanterns. Lord Heath had the presence of mind to signal for all the candles in the room to be extinguished so that the atmosphere would be right and distract attention from the inferiority of the music.

But the warbling voice of Miss Kemp sounded almost musical, and Mr. Fothergill sounded—merely earnest. Everyone else did a passable job of singing for that jolliest and holiest of all seasons. And the audience, pleased and mellowed by an evening of exceptional music, sang along with the group after the first carol and declared afterward that the idea of hiring carol singers had been an inspired one on his lordship's part. Now they were all fully in the mood to celebrate Christmas Day just the day after tomorrow.

Drinks and dainties were served in the dining room immediately after the concert, and the guests divided themselves between the music room, the drawing room, and the dining room. It was a merry, festive occasion, far more so than was usual with his concerts. It was not so much the hiring of the carol singers that had been inspired, he thought, but the placement of the concert so close to Christmas. He must do the same every year.

"My lord?" Mrs. Berlinton was standing before him—it had irked him that the demands of being host had kept him away from her since the end of the concert. Crofton, that damned *rake*, had been engaging her in conversation for all of fifteen minutes. "If you would be so good as to order around your carriage, we will be taking our leave. I am anxious to get the children into their own beds."

He turned with her to leave the room and picked up a branch of candles from the hall table. He walked beside her up the stairs, having sent a message to the coach house with a servant. There was nothing left to say. He could not keep heaping praises on her son, and he would not renew his offer to speak with her brother-in-law. Though it was imperative that *someone* do something for the boy.

He would not see her again, he thought. There would be no reason to. And did it matter to him that he would not? There was no fiancé or favored suitor waiting in the wings, it appeared, but that made no difference to anything. She was a virtuous woman. He was a—well, yes, he supposed the word applied to a certain degree. He was a rake. Certainly he had no honorable intentions where women were concerned.

Tomorrow, he decided, he would spend the whole afternoon with Lucy, and probably the whole night as well. He would immerse himself in an orgy of sensual delights. He would stay for the whole of Christmas Day. To hell with the notion of spending part of the day quietly in his library. A boudoir was a better place for forgetfulness. He would forget about virtuous widows and about their immensely talented sons—and their curiously adorable daughters.

They walked in silence—up the stairs and along the dark, deserted corridor to the chamber where the children slept. There was a small table a short distance from their door. Lord Heath stopped when he came to it and set down the candlestick. She stopped walking too.

She looked at him quietly, with noncommittal eyes. In the flickering of the candlelight her skin looked like porcelain and her eyes large and mysterious. Red lights tangled with the darkness of her hair. Her pale gown was modestly cut but it did not disguise her magnificent bosom or the beginnings of cleavage.

She must know what was coming, he thought, yet she was making no attempt to turn the moment. He set his hands on either side of her waist and drew her toward him.

Her lips were cool, soft, trembling against his own. She smelled of roses. Her breasts were firm against his waistcoat. Her hands were on his shoulders. He parted his lips and traced the seam of her lips lightly with the tip of his tongue. When her lips parted and her mouth opened, he slid his tongue deeply inside, feeling the warmth and moisture of her, delving into the very essence of her.

Her breasts were generous and youthfully firm. He caressed them with his hands, drew down the light fabric of her gown until he could set the pads of his thumbs against her bare nipples, and rubbed lightly. He slid his hands down her back, spread them over her firm buttocks and drew her snugly against him, pressing her against the pain of his erection. Her arms were about his neck. She was making soft guttural sounds in her throat.

Someone might come upstairs at any moment.

"Stay with me," he said softly against her mouth. "The children will sleep." To hell with his guests downstairs.

"Come to bed with you?" she asked, opening her eyes. "Is that what you mean?"

"It will be good," he promised her. "Believe me, it will be good."

"I believe you," she said. Her eyes were becoming more aware. "The answer is no, my lord. Take me to my children, please."

He held her against him for a few moments longer while he closed his eyes and tipped back his head. He swallowed twice. He released her and picked up the candlestick.

"Why not?" he asked her. A stupid question. He knew very well why not.

"There has to be more," she said. "More than just the physical."

"Like love?" he said. "And marriage, I suppose."

"Yes," she said. "Like love and marriage."

"I am not the marrying kind," he told her. "Or the loving kind."

"No," she said. "I know. And *I* feel no love for *you*. Nor any desire to marry you. Only to lie with you. It is not nearly enough."

Well, he had asked for it. Now he would not even be able to console himself with the sneering conviction that she had been trying to trap him into marriage.

"On the contrary, my dear," he said, "it is everything. But I will not waste any more of your time. I

can see that you are not to be either convinced or seduced. I thank you for allowing your son to share his
talent with me and my guests. I will never forget this
evening."

"Neither will I," she said quietly.

Neither will I. Neither will I. The words echoed in his
head for the rest of the long evening, after she had left
with her children, and for the rest of a longer night.
They echoed in his head for all of the following morning, even after he had sent to Lucy to instruct her to
be ready for him during the afternoon.

He did not go to Lucy's during the afternoon. He
went shopping instead. In person. On Bond Street.

Fanny was feeling mortally depressed by the time
Christmas Eve drew to an end. It did not help to remind herself that she would be feeling no better if she
had gone into the country with John and Mercy. The
point was that she expected to be depressed in the
country. She had dreamed of a real Christmas, with
her home and her children and her church and nothing to distract them from remembering the meaning
of it all and experiencing the peace and goodwill that
were supposed to be a part of the season.

The dream had come true, and it was hollow.

The weather had been dreary with heavy gray
clouds and a biting wind. It had done nothing to lift
the spirits.

Matthew had been suffering from reaction after his
success of the evening before. He had been listless
and inclined to whine and had asked if Lord Heath
would be calling upon them again. She had told him
that he would not.

Katie had been more than usually quiet and had
been scolded gently twice—once by her nurse and
once by Fanny herself—for sucking her thumb. She

had said nothing when reminded that there was only one more sleep left before Christmas, but had merely grown wider-eyed, though whether with excitement or with disappointment that she was not surrounded by other children as she had been last year her mother did not know.

Fanny had been unable to settle to anything. She had spent far longer than necessary decorating the house, yet even after she had finished she was not satisfied that the atmosphere of Christmas had been captured. She had wandered down to the kitchen more than once on the unnecessary errand of seeing that all the Christmas baking was well in hand. Yet even the smell of Christmas pudding and mince pies had been unable to stir that old magic that had always been Christmas.

She had remembered with a horrible feeling of embarrassment. She had allowed him to put his tongue in her mouth. Had anyone else ever allowed such a thing to happen? She had allowed him to bare her breasts and set his hands on them. She had allowed his hands to move below her waist, to draw her right against him. There had been no mistaking his own involvement in what had been happening.

They had been in an open corridor. Any of the guests or servants could have come along at any moment. One of the children might have come out of the bedchamber.

He was a man she deeply despised.

He was a man very highly respected in the world of music. He had recognized Matthew's talent and had treated it with respect and something bordering on awe. He had not allowed his guests to cajole her son into singing yet another encore. He had allowed Katie to climb into his lap and sit gazing up at him.

He was a man she had wanted more than she had

known it possible to want a man. She had throbbed with desire. She had been almost desperate with the need to open for him, to receive him deep inside, to take his seed into her womb.

It would have been good, he had told her. Of course it would have been good. It would have been the most ecstatic experience of her life. All night and all day too there was a part of her that had cursed herself for not having had the courage to stay with him as he had suggested. Where would have been the harm?

The harm would have been in becoming the mistress of a rake. The harm would have been in beginning an addiction that he would feed only until he grew bored with her. The harm would have been in fornicating under the same roof as her sleeping children. The harm would have been in setting physical pleasure before morality and plain common sense.

Oh, she could go on forever. The harm would have been catastrophic. She was simply not a woman made for casual affairs.

She hated him. And hated her own childishness in feeling such an irrational emotion.

The Christmas Eve church service that evening was lovely. It was not one of London's most fashionable churches—Fanny had chosen it for that reason—and was not very full, several of the parishioners being from home for the holiday. But there was the feeling of being among friends who cared, and the vicar's kindliness went a long way to making up for the tedium of his sermon. And there was the memory as the congregation, most notably the carolers, sang the Christmas hymns with unmusical enthusiasm, of the night before and the way in which they had offered a strangely moving finale to a very professional concert.

Matthew was made much of after the service was

over, and Katie, on the verge of sleep, her head against Fanny's shoulder, was fussed over.

"And what have you requested for Christmas?" the vicar asked her in the jovial voice he reserved for children and the very elderly.

But Katie was not telling. "It is a secret," she said just before her thumb found its way to her mouth. Fanny did not scold, and the vicar and other parishioners who were in earshot laughed heartily.

Fanny stood at the window of her bedchamber late that night, absently brushing her hair and gazing outward on a night that was almost as light as day. She must make an effort at greater cheerfulness tomorrow, she decided. For the children's sake she must be festive. She had been very selfish keeping them at home. She must make them happy.

And then the brush stilled in her hand and she half smiled. What a strange irony it was that it had begun to snow. On Christmas morning, or very close to it—it was not quite midnight. It *never* snowed at Christmas. Everyone always hoped that it would and sometimes persuaded themselves that it would. But it usually snowed before Christmas, just when people were trying to travel to house parties, or just after Christmas, when everyone was trying to return home. Or not at all. Winter moisture usually came down as chill rain. But it never snowed at Christmas.

Except now, this year, when she and the children were stuck in town. They might have been in the countryside, where there would have been a whole park to frolic in tomorrow. But they were in town, thanks to her.

Perhaps it would come to nothing, she thought, closing the curtains firmly and extinguishing the candle before climbing into bed. An empty, cold, lonely bed. She closed her eyes and felt his mouth against her own and his thumbs stroking and tautening her aching nipples. She felt him hard and large against her abdomen as his hands fitted her against him. She ached with unfulfilled desire. And regret. And self-hatred.

Tomorrow was Christmas. She was going to have to be happy tomorrow.

Sleeping, or at least hovering blissfully on the very brink of sleep, had been easy at church when there were voices droning around her and there had been Mama's comfortable lap and Mama's comfortable bosom to lull her. It had been easy on the way home when Mama had carried her. But it had fled entirely after she had been laid down in her own bed and the candles had been blown out and all was peace and quiet and warmth.

There was only one sleep left to Christmas. If only she could start having that one sleep, Katie thought, yawning loudly, it would come. Yet she was half afraid to have it. Tomorrow was Christmas and the Christmas gifts. If she had a doll, how would she contain her disappointment? How would she smile and look pleased so that Mama would not know that she did not want a doll at all. Or rather she did, but she wanted a papa more and if she had a doll, then that would mean that she was not going to have her new papa.

Mama had told Matt that the gentleman was not going to come again. And he had not come all day. She had waited for him anyway, but he had not come. She had thought maybe he would come to church, but he had not been there.

If she just stayed awake and did not have that one sleep to Christmas, she would never know for sure that she was not to have her new papa. But what if she was? If he was going to come, she wanted to sleep immediately so that he would come quickly.

But what if she had a doll instead?

The choice of sleeping or staying awake was ultimately not hers to make. She slept—and woke with a start, knowing that there were no sleeps left, that it was Christmas, even though it was still dark outside. She felt suddenly almost sick with excitement. There would be presents and that very special feeling there was at Christmas—she could remember it from last year.

She also felt almost sick with apprehension. She knew she had to act quickly, without giving herself time to think. Perhaps his horse or his carriage would be below her window and she would know that her Christmas wish had been granted. She jumped out of bed without even feeling the cold, raced over to the window, and pulled back the curtain with one hand. Her mouth dropped open and her eyes widened.

Snow! Heaps and heaps of white snow just waiting to be played in. Excitement welled in her for a moment and she was on the verge of turning and rushing, shrieking, into Matthew's room next door. But then she noticed that there was no horse and no carriage and no footsteps in the snow. And snow was hard to travel in. It was deep and slippery. She could remember that from some other time. He would not be able to come. She would not be able to have a new papa for Christmas.

She let the curtain fall back into place. And noticed that she was cold. And wanted her mama. She opened her door quietly so as not to wake Nurse in the room opposite and went to her mother's room. She let herself in quietly and closed the door behind her. Mama was asleep and did not stir when Katie stood beside her bed.

A doll would be nice, Katie thought. Surely she would have a doll. She would be happy. She would be able to play with it all day. The doll was probably here already and would not have to come through the snow. Perhaps she would have a papa next year.

She climbed up onto the bed and burrowed beneath the bedclothes, helped by her mother, who stirred, smiled sleepily at her, and drew her close before kissing her on top of the head—just where the gentleman had kissed her that night she had been wearing her white bow. Mama was all warm. Katie put her cold feet against her and wriggled even closer. She sighed and went back to sleep.

Snow! A great heavy blanket of it. Lord Heath stood at the window of his bedchamber, scowling out at it. He would not be able to go to Lucy's today. She lived a considerable distance away, and he knew he would not risk the safety of any of his horses by taking them out until it had melted. Snow this thick would not melt for a day or two at least and then the slush would be even more treacherous.

He had received a letter from Lucy last evening, badly spelled and reeking of her particular brand of perfume. If he could not keep his appointments when he had sent her specific instructions and she had denied herself an outing on both occasions in order to comply with them, she had written, then she knew another gent—another half-dozen gents, in fact—who would be only too willing to engage her services.

The note had irritated him to the point of fury. *He* was to be dismissed by a mere kept woman? And one whom he paid and housed and clothed very generously indeed. He would go on Christmas Day, he had decided, and leave her in no doubt about what was what. He would spend as many hours with her as he chose—and then dismiss her. The childish peevishness of his plan only added to his irritation. Even whores, he supposed, had a right to fair dealing. And he had not been quite fair to Lucy in the past few days.

Besides, he had not wanted to spend part of the day with her. He did not want to do so now. But there was only one other thing that he *did* want to do and that was impossible—despite his shopping expedition yesterday.

She was within walking distance.

She would probably have the door slammed in his face.

He could not spoil Christmas for her.

He did not know if she intended to spend it alone with her children. Probably not. Possibly she had plans to join some party. But this morning they were probably alone. If he went now, or perhaps in an hour's time, after breakfast . . .

She would covet the morning alone with the children. She would be giving them their gifts. They would perhaps dine early, before they went out. He would be the last person she would wish to see—her would-be seducer of two nights ago. Though she had been just as pantingly eager as he. It was not that she had not wanted it.

Drat the snow. He had planned to go to Lucy's to take his mind off where he really wanted to go. He had planned to satisfy his appetites on her and imagine that she was . . .

No, no no. That would be grossly distasteful. And quite impossible anyway.

He could call for half an hour—to take the boy a gift as a sort of thank-you for singing at his concert. And one for the infant just because she *was* an infant and it was Christmas. It was the proper thing to do. The public thanks he had given the boy during the concert needed to be followed up with a more personal thank-you a day or two later. It was mere coincidence that it was Christmas Day.

She would see through his ruse in a twinkling.

So what? He would stay for half an hour and then return home to enjoy the quiet day he had planned for himself.

But he was so damned lonely. The thought was out before he could guard against it. And now it was too late to deny it. He had never before felt consciously lonely. But a few streets away there was a woman he wanted to bed. No, it was not quite that, though un-doubtedly he did want to bed her. Very badly. But what he wanted more was for her to smile at him. She had never smiled at him. He had never felt the warmth of her regard. A smile from her would go a long way toward alleviating loneliness—strange thought!

And a few streets away there was a boy who looked at him with trust and liking—and a little infant girl who held up her arms to him and climbed on his knee and felt his whiskers with one tiny finger—and gazed into his eyes without blinking.

A few streets away there was a family of which he was no part. They were celebrating Christmas. With-out him. He was alone, looking out at a blanket of snow.

He smiled ruefully and even chuckled when he caught the self-pitying bent of his thoughts. But he did not feel particularly comforted. Just half an hour? He would not disturb her peace for longer than that.

He wanted to see those children again.

And he *had* to see her again. Just once. Just for half an hour.

He left a note on his secretary's desk before leaving the house, for immediate attention when the man returned to work. Lucy was to be settled with—quite amicably and quite generously. He would not see her again. He felt enormously relieved at the thought.

He wondered as he lifted the knocker of Mrs. Berlinton's house later and let it fall back against the door if he had come unpardonably early for a morning visit. There was no sign of life anywhere on the street. His bootprints were the only ones to mar the smooth surface of the snow. But it was Christmas Day, of course, and there were no tradesmen about. It was really not as early as it appeared. The door opened.

She came down alone to the salon into which he had been shown. He bowed to her; she curtsied.

"Good morning, ma'am," he said. "Happy Christmas."

"And to you, my lord," she said. And blushed hotly, and caught her lower lip in her teeth.

"I have brought gifts for the children," he said, indicating the parcels he had set down on a table.

"That is extremely kind of you," she said, "though there was no need. Thank you. I shall take them up." She hesitated. "Thank you."

Ah, so he was not to have even his half hour. Or to see the children. And she had not smiled—only blushed.

But the door behind her opened again and both children stepped inside the room. Matthew was bursting with excitement.

"I got a stagecoach and horses," he yelled, "and passengers and parcels that can be taken in and out and doors that really open. And the horses go up and down when you push the carriage along. The coachman has a horn and—"

"Matthew," his mother said, sounding appalled, "remember your manners and make your bow to Lord Heath."

Matthew bobbed his head in an approximation of a bow and Lord Heath smiled at him—and at the little child, who stood just inside the door with excitement and wonder in her wide eyes, which were fixed unblinkingly on his face.

"And you, little one," he asked, "what have you had for Christmas?"

"A doll," she whispered. She did not move from where she was or take her eyes from his face. Or blink.

He smiled at her and felt a strange pain about the heart. He remembered what she had said to him a few days before. She had told him her secret wish for Christmas. She had wanted a new papa. And she had had someone in mind—the nonexistent fiancé he had asked her mother about.

It was as if a lit candle had suddenly been set in the middle of his head. He suddenly saw the light. She wanted a new papa—*and she had someone picked out*.

Oh no, little one, he told her with his eyes. *Oh no.*

But she gazed unblinkingly back.

"You were not told that you could come downstairs," Mrs. Berlinton was saying. "We are taking too much of Lord Heath's time when he merely came to drop off some gifts for you. What very fortunate children you are. Do say thank you."

The little one's eyes widened further if that were possible. But she did not look at the parcels, as the boy did, with a whoop of delight. She continued to gaze at him. He felt that he had betrayed her in some way. He wondered if her mother knew about her secret wish and guessed not.

"I would like to see you open the gifts," he told the children. "I am in no hurry to go anywhere else." Now he was being unfair to their mother, who had hoped to get him back out through the door almost before he had come through it.

Matthew tore the wrappings off his and gazed in awe at the miniature man's watch inside. "Oh," he said, "just like Uncle John's. Better than Uncle John's. Oh, thank you, sir. It is the best present in all the world. Look, Mama."

The little one opened her fur muff and small parasol more carefully. She slipped her hands inside the muff and ran her cheek over the fur. "Thank you," she whispered. But her eyes looked wounded.

"I want to show his lordship my stagecoach," Matthew yelled, remembering his primary gift. "May I, Mama? The coachman's horn actually makes a noise, sir, though it is more like a whistle than a horn."

"I think his lordship must be eager to be on his way, Matthew," his mother said firmly. "We must not keep him."

"But I would be delighted to see the stagecoach," he said. "And the doll. If I may, ma'am?" He would not exceed the half hour, he promised himself. She need not look so stricken.

"You must not allow them to delay you," she said, as Matthew raced from the room toward the stairs. She looked down at her daughter. "Katie, *why* have you started to suck your thumb again? Run along and bring your doll to the drawing room to show Lord Heath."

The child went on ahead, her hands back inside her muff. Lord Heath looked at Mrs. Berlinton and extended an arm for hers.

"I shall ring for hot punch and mince pies," she said. "You must be cold from the outdoors. It was most kind of you to come through all this snow and to bring gifts. But you must not feel obliged to stay long or to allow the children to bore you."

"I am expected nowhere else," he said. "And I am not expecting to be bored."

She blushed. "You are kind," she murmured.
She smelled of roses.

She wished him a thousand miles away. When a
servant had come to the nursery to inform her that
Lord Heath was waiting below in the salon, she had
wanted to send back the message that they were from
home—but it would have been churlish to do so. As
soon as she saw him, she wished she had been churlish. And when she knew he was coming up to the
drawing room to view the children's gifts and to partake of punch and mince pies, she wished she had
taken the children into the country. She wished she
had never met him.

And yet as he gave his full attention first to Katie's
doll and then to Matthew's stagecoach and even went
down on one knee to watch the horses prancing as the
carriage was pushed along, she knew beyond a doubt
that *this* was her Christmas gift. Just this. A secret gift
she would cherish for days to come. Perhaps weeks.
Probably years.

She had seen him smile at her children—his smile
transformed him from aristocratic austerity to breath-
taking attractiveness. She had heard him say that he
was expected nowhere else, rejecting the easy escape
route she had offered him. She had held his arm and
felt his body heat and smelled his expensive cologne.
She had heard him comment on the white silk and the
lace frills and satin bows of the doll's dress and declare that the doll was *almost* as pretty as Katie. And
she had seen him try to blow the stagecoach driver's
horn and laugh as he produced only a sad little
squeak.

After half an hour she had enough memories on
which to feed for a long time to come. She was, of
course—she did not even try to deny the truth to her-

self—in love with him. It would have been strange if she had not been. A lonely widow and a handsome, virile gentleman reputed to be a rake. Of course she was in love with him.

She held her breath when he got to his feet and turned to her. Half an hour had passed. It was time for him to take his leave. She wished he had not come at all. She wished he could stay forever.

"I cannot help thinking," he said, "how your children are shut up indoors here, ma'am, while there is a whole world of new white snow out there going to waste. And Hyde Park a mere five-minute walk away."

"I plan to take them outside after dinner, my lord," she said, flushing. Did he think that she denied her children all pleasure? And Hyde Park was all of a ten-minute walk away.

"But I will wager," he said, "that you will not take them sliding along the paths or engage them in a ferocious battle with snowballs or build a snowman with them tall enough to bump his head against the clouds." He glanced down at Katie, who was as usual gazing steadily into his face. "Or teach them how to make snow angels."

"Ye-e-es!" Matthew started to jump on the spot. "A snowball fight."

"Will he hurt his head?" Katie whispered.

"We will give him a hat," Lord Heath said.

We?

"And it seems to me altogether possible," he said, glancing at the window, "that the snow might begin to melt by this afternoon."

We? What did he mean by *we*?

"We had better go out this morning," he said, looking directly into Fanny's eyes. "Would you not agree, ma'am?"

"Yes." She did not know why both she and Katie were whispering. She cleared her throat. "Yes, my lord, if you can spare the time and if it is no trouble to you." She rushed onward before she could talk herself out of it. "Perhaps you would care to join us for Christmas dinner afterward."

He inclined his head to her. "I would indeed," he said. "Now, who wants to go out into the snow? Within the next ten minutes?"

Matthew cheered and Katie whispered, "I do."

She was being very foolish, Fanny thought as she hurried upstairs to get ready, Katie's hand in hers. His motive for showing such an interest in her children was crystal clear. Doing so was the surest route to her affections. Not that he cared about her affections, of course. But clearly he had not given up on his desire to get her into bed. He thought to win her this way. And he might well be right. She was not at all sure quite how strong she was.

There was something overwhelmingly attractive about a man who was kind to one's children. She could not quite imagine the elegant and immaculately tailored Lord Heath romping in the snow.

Katie had made a million snow angels. At least that was how many the gentleman said she had made. She had counted up to eleven herself, but she knew she was not a good counter. Mama had made two. After the first one she had said the snow going down inside her collar felt horrid and she would make no more, but the gentleman had called her a coward and so she had made one more.

They had thrown snowballs at one another until Matthew had hurled himself backward into the snow, laughing, and she, Katie, had been so helpless with giggles that she had been unable to throw even one

more. The gentleman called them *all* cowards and
Mama threw a snowball that hit him right in the middle of the face. And then he threw one that hit *her* in
the face—and it dripped down inside her collar. And
so the battle had ended in a draw, the gentleman said,
but since his and Katie's side had thrown the last
snowball, he would declare Mama and Matthew vanquished. And so Mama hit him on the shoulder with
another snowball, and that was the end of that.

They built a tall, thin snowman. It was so tall that
the gentleman had to lift her up to set her handfuls of
snow on its head. They had brought coal from the
kitchen for eyes and nose and buttons and a carrot for
a pipe.

Katie did not think it was quite tall enough to bump
its head against the clouds, but perhaps the clouds
would come lower later on.

"Where is his hat?" she asked the gentleman, and he
took off his own and set it on the snowman's head at a
funny angle so that Katie started to giggle again. But
she would not let the gentleman leave the hat there.
He might get a cold head, she told him, and he bowed
to her and told her she was kindness itself.

Mama would absolutely not—those were her very
words, *absolutely not*—slide along the slippery path the
gentleman and Matthew made. Katie was afraid to try.
She clung to her mother's hand and watched. But then
the gentleman was bending over her and offering to
pick her up and slide with her.

"I will not let you fall, little one," he assured her.

She knew he would not let her fall even though
Matthew had come to grief several times. She lifted
her arms. And of course he did not let her fall. She felt
as safe as safe could be while they slid along faster
than the wind. After a few times, when she kept asking for more, he did fall, but he did not drop her. He

merely held her more tightly so that she came to a bumpy but quite safe rest against his chest while he laughed, sprawled out on his back.

"My boots moved faster than we did that time, little one," he told her.

And then Mama was exclaiming over him and slapping at the snow caked all down his back and telling him he was as foolish as any child and if they did not hurry, their dinner would spoil and she would instruct the cook to blame him.

And so they set out for home again and Katie thought with some longing of the warm fires in the nursery and drawing room. She burrowed her hands deeper inside her new muff.

No one had told her yet that the gentleman was her new papa, and she did not like to ask. But surely he must be. He had praised them and played with them and given them presents. And he liked Mama and she liked him. But no one had said anything yet and so she could not quite let go of her anxiety. Perhaps they would tell her—and Matt—at dinner. Or perhaps at tea. Or perhaps at bedtime.

He was a wonderful papa. Far more wonderful than Uncle John, though she would never say so aloud to the cousins. She yawned loudly and the gentleman stooped down and picked her up and carried her the rest of the way home even though Mama told him she was no longer a baby.

But that was what papas did. They treated one like a baby when one was cold and tired and wished one really were still a baby. Papas did not force one to remember all the time that one was a big girl. She yawned again.

He had been very selfish and very unfair to her. By the evening it was very obvious that she had had no plans for Christmas Day. No plans that involved any company or party, anyway. Like him, she had probably planned a quiet Christmas at home, just herself and her two children. And he had spoiled that plan by intruding—he, a stranger.

He stayed for Christmas dinner and then he prolonged his visit in order to take coffee in the drawing room. The boy wanted to sing for him and the infant wanted to show him the story book she had received from her uncle and aunt. And that reminded Matthew that the same uncle and aunt had given him a spillikins game and he wondered if Lord Heath would care to play it with him. And so they played game after game. He let Matthew win all but once or twice.

He found himself late in the afternoon stretched out on one side of the floor, his head propped on one hand while the boy sat cross-legged beside him. The little girl had some time before climbed onto her mother's lap and had watched with increasingly drooping eyes until she had fallen asleep.

The Yule log crackled in the fireplace. The air was perfumed with the scent of pine boughs.

It was an achingly domestic scene. A family Christmas. Except that they were not a family and he had stayed in town this year in order to avoid that shudderingly awful thing, a family Christmas.

Mrs. Berlinton went herself, when it was already getting dark outside, to fetch the tea tray since she was determined to give the servants as much time off as possible. He should have taken his leave then, or at least immediately afterward. She must be wishing him to the devil. The children were not. Matthew chattered to him all through tea, the little one climbed onto his lap and startled him by methodically opening all the buttons down the front of his waistcoat and then doing them up again.

But he was keeping her children away from her on Christmas Day. He looked at her and smiled rather ruefully, but she lowered her eyes to her plate and reached for the piece of cake she had already eaten.

He did not leave immediately after tea. He carried one of the trays back to the kitchen and then returned to the drawing room to join them all in singing carols and other songs and to hear Mrs. Berlinton—what the *devil* was her name?—continue a story of adventure and intrigue that she had obviously been inventing over many evenings for her children's entertainment. And then he told a story, using an imagination he had not suspected he had, about a fierce dragon and a princess in a white silk gown with lace frills and satin bows and a prince disguised as a stagecoachman and blowing loudly on his coachman's horn as his horses came prancing to the rescue.

"The princess had a dress like my doll," the little one said.

Matthew giggled. "Did the horn whistle, sir?" he asked.

"Indeed not." Lord Heath raised haughty eyebrows. "It blew so loudly that the dragon's head vibrated for a whole week after and made him horribly dizzy and sick. He did not breathe flames for a whole month afterward. The prince was able to rescue his princess and take her away in the stagecoach without even having to use his magic sword."

"Magic?" the little one said, her eyes widening.

"There is a story attached to that sword," he said. "But it will have to wait for another night."

"Ah," she said while her brother groaned.

The groans were renewed when their mother announced quite firmly that it was bedtime—an hour past bedtime, in fact.

And even *then* he did not take his leave. He remained alone in the drawing room after shaking hands with Matthew and taking Katie's tiny hand into his own and raising it to his lips. Her eyes clung to his and looked wounded again before she was led away to bed, but he could say nothing to reassure her.

"Good night, little one," he said. "Sleep well."

He waited alone in the drawing room, one arm propped against the high mantel, gazing into the flames. He waited for her to come back downstairs. He tried not to think about how he might have ruined her Christmas.

He was still there. She had half expected to come downstairs to find him gone. She had half hoped he would be gone. She had almost panicked at the thought that she might find the drawing room empty. But he was still there, gazing into the fire. He did not turn when she came back into the room. She sat down quietly on a chair some distance from the fire.

What was she going to do?

She hoped that at least she would have the strength to insist that it happen on another day, in a place where her children were not. She did not know if she had even that much strength. She had been beguiled all day by his kindness and his gaiety and his smiles— and his hopeless attractiveness. And by that certain something that was Christmas.

He turned his head and looked at her. If empty air could crackle between two people who were some distance apart, she thought, then the air between them did just that.

"Please," she heard herself say, "would you grant me one wish?"

"What is it?" he asked her.

"Will you promise not to touch me?" she asked. "If you do not touch me, I believe I might be strong enough to resist what you have come here to do. I am being honest with you, you see. You know that I desire you. You know too that I do not wish to give in to that desire. And so I ask you not to touch me. I appeal to your honor."

"What is your name?" he asked her.

She looked at him with raised eyebrows.

"I cannot continue calling you Mrs. Berlinton," he said. "Berlinton was your husband's name. What is *your* name?"

"Fanny." She was whispering again.

"Fanny," he said. "Did you love him? You had two sweet children with him. Do you still mourn him? How long has he been dead?"

"For over three years," she said. She would not answer the other questions. She was bewildered at the turn in the conversation. Though she had admitted that it had been longer than three years. That was what he wished to know. "Yes, my lord. It has been that long."

"Is that your only reason for desiring me, then?" he asked her. "Would you desire any reasonably personable man who happened to be standing here at this moment?"

She closed her eyes tightly and lowered her head, feeling the hot flush in her cheeks. "You are impertinent, my lord," she said.

"I want you to desire only me," he said. "I am jealous even of your husband."

She kept her eyes tightly closed. "I cannot play your games," she said. "I have no skill or experience. I would desire only you. So much so that I would make a horrid scene when you had done with me and would hate myself for the rest of my life. I beg you to leave. Please leave." She was going to be strong enough after all. She had been wise enough to look into the future and know without any doubt what it would be like, what it would feel like. She got to her feet and raised her head to look at him. "Please leave. And please do not come back."

He did not move. Or say anything for a while. "Smile for me, Fanny," he said. "Let me once see you smile."

He was not an honorable man after all. He was not going to play fair. Why had she expected that he would?

"It is more than desire, is it not?" he said. "Tell me it is more than desire." But he raised a staying hand even as her vision blurred with the welling tears and she swallowed awkwardly. "No, that is unfair. It is just that I have no skill or experience either. Not at this. I want to bring up your children with you, Fanny. I want to spend my life with you. Ah, that is bland. I love you. I love you so much that my whole world has been turned upside down. I love you so much that I am terrified of leaving here and stepping out into the void. If you send me away, you see, I will make a horrid scene and hate myself for the rest of my life." He smiled crookedly—and looked quite impossibly adorable. "Tell me it is more than desire you feel for me."

She swallowed again and tried not to grasp too tenaciously at her Christmas gift. "It is more than desire," she whispered. *Why* was she always whispering?

"How much more?" He looked at her so wistfully that no one seeing him now for the first time would guess that he had a reputation as a rake.

"I love you." She forced herself to speak out loud.

"Will you do two things for me?" he asked.

"Yes." But she hoped she did not know what one of them was. Not tonight. Not under the same roof as the children.

"Will you smile for me?" he asked.

She smiled—and he smiled back.

"And will you rescind your request?" he asked. "Will you let me touch you? Only to hold you and kiss you, my love. I will not bed you until our wedding night. Not even if you beg me. Will you marry me?"

"Yes," she said.

He smiled again. "Yes, I may touch you?" he asked. "Or yes, you will marry me?"

"Both," she said.

She was in his arms then and all the breath was whooshing out of her. Before she could gasp in another lungful his mouth was on hers—open and yearning and dizzyingly wonderful.

"Fanny, my love, my love," he was saying against her mouth.

"Yes," she told him. "Yes. Oh, my love."

The children, she thought fuzzily. She must ask the children. She should have asked them before she said yes. She would ask them tomorrow. Surely they would say yes too. Surely they would. Oh, surely they would.

She wrapped her arms about his neck and abandoned herself to the embrace. She trusted him to end it before they had gone too far. She trusted him. She loved him. He was going to be her husband.

Oh, he was going to be her husband. Lord Heath. Roderick.

Katie could not sleep no matter how much she tried. No one had said anything. Not once had anyone called him Papa even though Matt had said to her when they were alone that wished the gentleman could be their father. But that had been only a wish. No one had said anything. Perhaps, Katie thought, she

would **wake** up in the morning and he would be gone
and would never come back again.

Perhaps he was not her papa after all.

She had had a doll. She would not have had the doll
if she had had a new papa. That was proof enough.
But he had *acted* like a papa.

There was nothing else for it, she thought at last, but
to go back down and ask straight out. Mama would be
dreadfully cross and perhaps Papa—if he *was* Papa—
would be too. Perhaps she would have to sit in the
punishment chair tomorrow. But she had to go. Otherwise she would never sleep.

When she opened the drawing room door, everything was so quiet that for one awful moment she
thought that he must have gone home and Mama had
gone to bed. But they were there, both of them, and
Katie's heart leapt for joy. The gentleman was hugging
Mama very tightly and kissing her. And Mama was
doing it right back to him. She had *known* they liked
each other. And she would bet anything that that was
what mamas and papas did when their children had
gone to bed. She closed the door quietly behind her
and gazed. Mama called the gentleman "My love,"
though she did not stop kissing him while she did so.

And then the gentleman opened his eyes and
stopped kissing Mama and hugged her less tightly and
spoke to her. He spoke very softly, but Katie heard.

"We have company," he said, and Mama's head
shot around and Katie could almost see the punishment chair looming.

The gentleman stretched out a hand toward her.
"Come here, little one," he said and he smiled at her.
He did not look cross at all.

He stooped down when she came close so that his
face was much closer to hers, and he took her two
hands in his. She had not noticed that she was cold.

"You cannot sleep?" he asked. "I might as well ask you tonight then instead of waiting until tomorrow. May I be your papa, Katie? Your Mama has said yes but I will need you and Matthew to say yes too. May I?"

Oh. She would sit in the punishment chair all morning if she had to and all afternoon too and not once squirm or ask to get down. Oh.

She nodded.

"It was your Christmas wish," he said. "You wished for a new papa. You told me you had someone in mind. Was it me?"

"Katie!" Mama said, sounding half scolding and half laughing.

But Katie looked only at the gentleman and nodded.

"I am your Christmas gift, then," he said. "And you are mine. You and your mama and Matthew—if he will have me. I have a whole family for my Christmas gift."

"Matthew said he wished *ever so much* that you could be our papa," Katie said.

"Oh, Katie." She could tell from the tone of her mother's voice that there would be no punishment chair in the morning after all. There was definitely laughter in it.

Katie took a step forward and put her arms about her new papa's neck. She shivered.

"You are like a block of ice, little one," he said, clucking his tongue, and he wrapped his warm coat about her and held her against his warm shirt and waistcoat as he stood up with her and drew Mama closer with his free arm so that there was warmth against Katie's back too.

"She is already half asleep," he said. "Now that the suspense is over, her body is reminding her how tired she is."

"Oh, Roderick," Mama said, "did you *know*? Did

she *tell* you? How embarrassing!" But she was half laughing.

"And how very touching," he said. "I fell in love with your daughter, ma'am, long before I fell in love with you."

"But it has been only five *days*," Mama said. She was laughing outright.

"I fall in love fast," Papa said. "Lead the way to her bed. I will carry her up. Katie, are you still a little bit awake? I will not be here when you wake in the morning. But I will come soon after breakfast to talk with Matthew and to wish you a good morning and to give your mama a kiss. That is a promise. I am your papa, little one, and always will be. Soon I am going to take my new family to live with me in my own home, but your mama and I have to have a wedding first. Are you warm enough to go back under the bedcovers?"

She was. Though her bed did not smell nearly as nice as he did. Not that she really noticed the difference or even felt herself being put down. She was sinking into a warm, safe world where there was a papa as well as a mama and always would be.

She had a mama and a papa.

Next year she was going to ask Papa if he would give her a new brother or sister for Christmas. She did not mind which. He could choose. Perhaps Mama would help him.

Christmas was over. But it had been wonderful as it always was. And always would be.

She was going to get Papa to tell them the story of the magic sword tomorrow. Papas always told one stories.

And when she went to live at Papa's house, she was going to get him to show her how to play that harp.

The Earl's Nightingale

❄

Edith Layton

She entered the shop quietly, as evening was falling.
The proprietor didn't bother to look up immediately. This sort of customer could wait. Anyone wanting to buy would come to his shop in broad daylight.
Those who wished to sell came late, and quietly. A
customer with money in pocket came stepping
smartly, often laughing and always accompanied, especially if female. He'd barely heard a footstep, which
meant slippers, not boots. A soft perfume wafted in as
the door swung shut. A woman then. Alone, with
something to sell, and likely a sad story to go with it.

The proprietor sighed, put down his pen, and prepared to deal with her. Business was business. If a
man had no stomach for it, he might as well be a
farmer—and not owner of a fine jewelry shop in the
heart of London town, catering to the nobs, and
priced to make sure of it.

He tugged down his waistcoat, rubbed his hands
together, stepped forward, and looked at his customer. And was instantly sorry for it. She was lovely.
Young, with a petal smooth complexion, fine features,
and a plump shapely mouth that trembled and turned
down at the corners, as though she was trying not to
cry. That wasn't a good thing to look at if a man
wished to keep his head, and a businessman had to
forget he had a heart.

Glancing into her eyes was worse. Large and expressive, they shone gold in the lamplight, awash with unshed tears. The hood on her cape concealed her hair, and he realized she'd probably also used it to conceal that lovely face as she'd gone down the twilight streets. A respectable young female then, or trying to be.

He quickly glanced down at the paper-wrapped parcel she held in her arms. That was no better. She held it tenderly as a newborn. This was definitely trouble.

"May I help you?" he asked, hoping he couldn't. He had a business to run. She was obviously on the road to ruin. He did not run a charity.

"Yes, if you please," she said in a soft cultured voice. "I have an item I believe you might be interested in?"

"I'm afraid not. This is a jewelry shop. That is certainly no necklace or brooch," he said jovially, eyeing her parcel, much relieved.

She smiled. He was devastated. She spoke, he felt hunted.

"No, of course not," she said gently, "but I was told you also sell lovely oddments, objects of virtue? At least, Mr. Hale, down the street, said so."

"Indeed, I do, but very few, very few, my dear. And they must be exceptional, even so. My clientele, you see, consists of persons of refinement who are interested in jewelry. While it is true that I carry the occasional jeweled comb or silver dresser set, ormolu vase or mantel clock"—he waved a hand at the row of fine articles on the shelf behind him—"they must be rare, in perfect condition, and rather magnificent, as you can see. I do wish I could help you but . . . oh, I say! Please don't. If you unwrap that parcel it will take forever to do up again and I am closing soon, so . . . Ah . . . oh . . . Oh!"

She placed the item on his counter so he could have a better look. He put his looking glass to his eye. It was worth staring at.

A birdcage, or at least, a fanciful representation of one, ornate as Prinny's own palace. It was all done in gilt wire, light as sunlight, with turrets and turns to it that no living bird could navigate. But the jeweled bird that sat on a perch in the middle seemed content. A lavish little thing, all over finely wrought golden scales, with a ridge of shining opal on its bright head for a crest and a spray of gold wire for a tail. The lamplight made its topaz eyes shine bright as the young woman's living ones.

"Charming," the proprietor muttered, examining it from every angle, "charming." Then he fell silent, aghast at forgetting himself so much as to say so, since he knew he had just increased its price.

"But that's not the whole of it," the young woman said eagerly. She took a little golden key from her purse. Her hands were trembling, but she managed to hold the cage steady so she could insert the key in a slot in its base. She turned the key three times and stood back, holding her gloved hands together at her waist, like a little nun, waiting.

The bird turned on its perch. It lowered its head to one side, and then to the other, for all the world like any living bird on a May morning, listening for a worm. The proprietor was captivated as a child might be. When the bird turned again and opened its beak, it was all he could do not to clap his hands together. And when it sang, his own mouth fell open.

Because the bird whistled two true notes, two pure notes. Then the music box in the base of the cage began to play, and the bird whistled, in accompaniment, keeping the beat, clear as a bell. In a little still sane corner of his mind, the proprietor realized the birdsong was more a hooting whistle really, than a warble. And though the music box was appealing, he'd heard more elaborate ones. But together, the effect was enchanting, and he listened raptly to the duet, as the little golden bird hopped and fluttered and sparkled like sunlight on his perch, trilling a rippling song to the merry tune.

When the last note died away, the proprietor frowned. It was deafeningly silent. Quieter than in the morning when he came in to open the shop. Not just silent, but bereft now, because of the absence of recent delight. And darker, somehow.

"It's by Mozart," the young woman said nervously, when the proprietor didn't speak at once. "A piece of light, I—I mean a light piece," she stammered, "from his *Magic Flute*—the bird-seller's song? Papageno's. Apt, isn't it? The bird sings the *'Papa-papa-papa-geno'* part as the music plays."

"Mmm," the proprietor answered absently, scarcely hearing her because he was still staring at the bird in the cage as though he expected it to sing again. One little topaz eye seemed to wink at him. He blinked. "How much?" he suddenly said, turning to the young woman, all business.

"It's not for sale," she said.

"What?" he said angrily. "My dear young woman, let us have the truth with no bark on it. You came into this shop at this hour with that bird, you obviously wish to sell it. I tell you, such foolishness will not increase the price!"

She took a deep breath and held her hands together hard. "That wasn't my intention," she said. "But you see, I don't wish to *sell* it, I wish to leave it for pawn. I—I have some pressing bills to pay," she said, lifting her chin as though it were some great honor she was discussing and not the fact that she was a debtor. "I find myself temporarily in need of funds. I thought, if I could get a sum for it, leaving it here as earnest, I could pay you back in a month's time—with interest, of course.

"But by leaving something so obviously worth-while"—she went on eagerly—"why then, if I had to forfeit—which I will not, I assure you—you'd have something you could easily sell, given your clientele."

The proprietor stood still while his mind turned over the facts. He wasn't a pawnbroker. But there was a possibility he wouldn't have to act as one, even if he took the bird in pawn. He gazed at the young woman closely now, overlooking the lovely face and trying hard to overlook the enchanting figure her partly opened cape revealed. The cape was not new. The glimpse of her gown beneath showed it was fashion-able—a year past. Her gloves were mended. A young woman fallen on hard times. Another thought in-truded.

"You have proof the item is yours to pawn?" he asked.

Her head went back as though he'd slapped her. "How dare"— she checked—". . . but of course," she murmured. "Forgive me, you've every right. Yes, I do. It was left to me by my grandmother. And if I must, I can produce a copy of her legal will. It is mine."

Not for long, the proprietor thought, eyeing the bird again. He'd give her a sum for the pawn of it. But that was all he'd have to pay. It would be sheer profit. He'd wager every cent in his till, and half that in his wall safe—that she could never come back to reclaim the bird. Noble persons sold their birthrights to him on a regular basis. Reckless young men, gamesters, wastrels, men and woman of good birth and bad sense, those of bad luck or mischance: he saw them all. It was why he stayed open so late.

His merchandise came and went in waves, like the

tides. Goods came in at night, went out by day. Persons of fortune came in sunlight, to spend. Those of misfortune crept in by dark to sell. And they never came back. In his experience, once a man began to sell off his estate, he never regained it. Or if he did, he never bothered to buy back what he'd sold, as though it was unlucky to do so, as though admitting it would bring back bad fortune. But it could also be because they seldom did regain their wealth. And a female was far less likely to come about.

"Done, then!" he said, and named a sum that made her swallow hard. It was too much, but he wanted the bird, he wanted it now, he wanted no glimpse of her eyes, or further discussion or twinge of conscience to disturb him.

"At how much interest?" she asked bravely.

The sum mentioned made her swallow again, but she lifted her head and said, "Fine. And a month's time for me to pay."

"No," he said. Looking away from her dismay, he told her one truth, at least. "You must understand that I am not in the normal way of things a pawnbroker. I doubt a pawnbroker could give you the price I offer, because they'd have no market for such an item. I do. But Christmas is coming. I have the best chance to sell it now. In a month's time, it will be a new year, then it will have to sit on my shelves for another twelve-month. Surely you see that? Where's the profit in that? So. A week's time. Or I must ask you to take it elsewhere."

He held his breath, not daring to glance at her, or the bird. If he didn't sell it, he'd be glad to keep it. It had enchanted him, no doubt of it.

"And if you cannot raise the wind in a week, my dear," he added, because he could not bear to see her leave with the bird, to leave in it some unworthy place, out of his sight, out of his grasp, "how shall you ever do so? Time is not the issue for you. Face it: if you can't reclaim it in a week, it's doubtful you can do so in a month. Time is a pawnbroker's illusion. We all know Fortune either smiles or she does not, and time is of really little moment in the matter."

He paused, smiling at his jest to show he wasn't such a bad sort. But he was anxious to conclude the business, pay her and let her out, so he could listen to the bird again. "I offer a fair price. The rest is up to you. I doubt you'll do better in all London town. And so? It grows late . . ." He glanced at the clocks lined on the shelf.

She bit her lip. Then she lifted her head again, her fine eyes sparking bright as any bits of topaz. "Done," she said.

He counted out the coins quickly, before either of them could think better of it, scribbled a receipt, and showed her out, saying it was time for him to close shop. It wasn't strictly true, but he couldn't wait to be alone with the bird.

"I'll be back within the week," she said, casting a longing glance back at it.

"Indeed, indeed," he said, hardly knowing what he said, so eager was he to be rid of her.

When she'd gone and a peek out his window showed no trace of her shadow on his street, the proprietor closed his curtains, locked the shutters and the door, and went to the cage. There was a moment of terror, before he realized she'd left the key on the counter, after all. He rubbed his hands together, and then carefully wound the cage and stood back, prepared for delight.

The bird tilted its golden head and went *"Fweee,"* rather sadly, and then hooted a *"Whooo"* that had nothing of music in it. The box groaned into play. But it sounded tinny this time, and the bird's accompaniment, feeble. The proprietor frowned, and snatching up the key, wound the cage again, this time vigorously. Now the bird jiggled a bit, croaked a windy whoop or two, and then stood stone still on its perch, with not even a "Fweee" to say for itself. The music box tinkled a note or three, and stuttered out.

The proprietor stared at the bird. It looked more like gilt than gold now, the jeweled eyes like glass, the opal crest, muddy marble. There was nothing rare or vivacious about it at all now.

"Gammoned, gulled, and taken over the coals like a raw boy!!"

He stood alone in his dim shop, cursing, regretting assays not taken, mechanisms unchecked. A pretty face and a melting smile, and she'd unloaded an expensive piece of junk on him. *Him*—who should be the one gulling, not the plucked pigeon!!

He grabbed the cage, climbed a stepladder, and slammed the bird onto a shelf near the window. But carefully. He didn't want to break it. He might yet be able to sell it during the fervor of the coming Christmas shopping season. He consoled himself. He'd paid so little he wouldn't lose any money, it was decorative and he, an excellent salesman, after all.

But he was still grumbling as he left his shop. He felt a fool, and it didn't help at all that when he looked back as he slammed the door closed, he saw the bird still rocking on its perch, and could swear he saw the damned thing's eyes twinkling.

"Diamonds," the rich tenor voice said. The proprietor's head snapped up. The door swung open, flooding the shop with sunlight as two men entered. "No," the voice continued, "no, not diamonds. Too much of a statement I don't wish to make yet.

"As for emeralds?" the gentleman went on saying to the friend who'd come into the shop with him, "No. Too passionate. The same for rubies. Sapphires . . . sapphires are for fidelity, again a thing I don't want to even hint at right now. Pearls?" he mused, staring down into one of the cases. "Charming, but a father's gift. No, not jewels, Simon. I can't give any kind of jewels. They're too personal for a gentleman to give to a lady—unless he's willing to give her far more."

The proprietor bustled to the fore, bobbing and bowing. One glance showed him the quality of these customers. The man who had spoken was a paragon of gentlemanly splendor. In the prime of his thirtieth year, perhaps; in the prime of his life, certainly. Tall, fit, muscular, yet elegant with it. His fitted jacket was flawlessly tailored, his tightly-knit nether garments, perfection. His highly polished boots were as expensive as most men's jewelry, and as for that, he wore none but one signet ring—obviously handed down through the centuries to him, as his name must have been. His linen was fine and clean, his carriage erect, his barber and valet had done him proud.

The proprietor was not in the habit of admiring men's faces; it was their financial condition he always saw first. But even he had to admit the gentleman was attractive, with his lean clever face all planes and cheekbones, his eyes dark and knowing, the whole elegant effect capped by thick dark auburn hair brushed back from that noble forehead.

Women would catch their breath at seeing him. The proprietor considered the years of expensive breeding that had produced him, and caught his. The other man was not so impressive, but also obviously a gentleman born. The proprietor waited for a chance to speak, and sell.

"Flowers are too insubstantial and everything else I

can think of too personal, or inappropriate. And so," the tall gentleman said, addressing the proprietor at last, "what am I to do? I seek a gift for a young lady. Something . . . delightful. But not so delightful as to be mistaken for a gesture of commitment."

"Of course, sir," the proprietor said, "and the occasion?"

"Ah, well. The occasion is nominally Christmas. But as the lady in question will be out of town by then, and I want her to remember me, it is to be Christmas . . . with a hint of things to come . . . perhaps. You see the difficulty?" he asked with a white-toothed smile that made the proprietor's heart swell, for it was almost as if this magnificent fellow was talking to him man to man, which he knew of course, was impossible.

"Indeed, indeed," the proprietor said, thinking furiously.

"Nice brooch here, Elliot," the other gentleman said, peering down into a showcase. "Looks like a spray of flowers. Awfully pretty, actually, ain't it?"

"Diamonds," the man he'd called Elliot said, gazing at the brooch, "but you're right. It is handsome. I think I'll take it."

"So then, the problem is solved," the proprietor said happily, rushing to pick up the diamond spray, because it was very expensive, and had just gotten more so.

"No, no," the tall gentleman said with a laugh, "a different problem solved. You've an eye, Simon. I think they'll be much appreciated."

"Dash it, Elliot! I thought you said jewels were too personal, and diamonds too much of a commitment!" his friend complained.

"They are. And certainly would be for the *lady* in question," Elliot said with a rueful grin. "But I think La Starr will see them far differently, don't you?"

"Oh, aye," Simon said. "You're personal enough with her, after all. As who wouldn't be—if he could afford it . . . So, you ain't giving her up yet, neither."

"No need, since I'm not shopping for anything . . . *definite* for the lady, after all," his friend commented. "So. A trifle purchased—for a trifling purpose. But with another, more carefully considered trifle still to be suggested. So, my good fellow," he told the proprietor, "what have you got for a young lady? A lady of discernment, who might be expecting more," he added with a merry look to his friend. "But something so charming that when she sees it, she'll not be too disappointed, even so."

"Ha!" his friend said without a touch of laughter. "Not in this life. She's expecting you to come up to scratch, so if it ain't a ring, it ain't going to be received in good part. Don't give me that lifted eyebrow, neither. Everybody's wondering. You danced with her at the last three assemblies, you've driven out with her in your phaeton, took her and her mama to the theater. You even had dinner at her house last week."

"Oh?" the tall gentleman asked haughtily. "Dining with a lady is tantamount to a proposal these days? Or is it attending the theater with her that tied the knot? Now, I thought it was in the nature of an investigation, myself. I was unaware it meant I was pledging myself for life. Changed the rules since I last looked, have they?"

"You know they haven't, but you know what she's thinking too. Don't know why you're playing this game, she'll slip through your fingers if you ain't careful."

"I know," the tall gentleman said, suddenly serious, "the damnable thing of it is that I don't know if that will really bother me that much. *That's* the problem."

"A looking glass!" the proprietor exclaimed, rushing

back behind his showcases. "I have the very thing! A lovely thing it is, mother-of-pearl, with tiny seed pearls set around it, on a golden chain it would be very fine . . . see?"

"Very fine, very fine," the gentleman mused, gazing at it, "but for an older lady, surely?"

"A . . . snuff box?" the proprietor said quickly. "Some ladies consider it quite the thing. Some use antique patch boxes for it. See, here I have a delightful one from the realm of Charles II?"

"Yes. Delightful for a hoydenish sort of female, which the lady is decidedly not," the gentleman said, clearly growing bored, his quick eyes roving the shop, summing it up, preparing to pay for his brooch and leave for greener pastures.

"A vanity set in rococo gold? The back of the hairbrush is all repoussé roses . . . A watch? If gold is too elaborate, then certainly a young lady could use . . . a lovely silver watch?" The proprietor began to despair, ". . . then what about a little posy holder to pin to her gown? Chased silver, with room for an initial on it? Perhaps a—"

"What's that?" the gentleman asked, his gaze arrested.

They all looked up at the shelf he was staring at. A trick of sunlight; a random beam had slipped in the window, touching a golden spark in the golden bird in its gilt cage, lighting it spectacularly. The topaz eyes shone out like beacons, the cage glowed richly gold, it was as if it were spotlighted there, high on its shelf near the window. It shouted its presence in the dimly lit shop.

"Oh yes!" the proprietor said, almost stumbling up the stepladder in his haste to reach the bird. "It's lovely, to be sure. It has a mechanism. It's supposed to sing, but sadly, it's in need of repair . . ."

"Is that the key?" the gentleman asked, holding out one long slender hand. But his question was like a command.

The proprietor placed the key in his palm.

The gentleman found the slot at once, and wound it once.

They all stood, waiting; the proprietor with sinking heart. Because the bird was beautiful but no man would give a young lady a broken toy, however beautiful. And because he was belatedly remembering the bird was not actually his to sell yet.

The bird turned its pretty golden head to the left, and then to the right, cocking it as though eyeing the tall gentleman. Then it opened its beak. And sang, charmingly. The music began to play, beautifully. The three men stood silent, and listened, raptly. Only when the bird fell still and the last notes died, did they speak again.

"Perfect!!" the gentleman said in astonished pleasure. "Who could not love that? It's charming. Not intimate, nor insignificant, the perfect compromise, but more than that—memorable and unique. Why, if I didn't have a lady to give it to, I'd take it for myself. Whatever . . . Wrap it, I'll take it, or rather—give you the direction of Lady Georgina Lattimore, where I wish it to be sent, immediately."

"Er, but," the proprietor said, sweating lightly, "the thing of it is, I am not at liberty to sell the piece until the end of the week—"

"I'll not need it by the end of the week," the gentleman said firmly, "I need it now. Look here. If you oblige me now, you have an excellent chance of doing so in future. You'll note I don't ask the price. Not because I don't care. I'll pay a fair price for it, and now. *Immediately.* Yes, an oddity, to be sure. But unlike most of my cronies," the gentleman said with a sparkling look at his companion, "I pay my way as I go. It may be eccentric, but I'll not be left in the suds like some others I could name. The Earl of Elliot does not have any creditors, you may ask anyone."

It wasn't the promise of future business, although that certainly set the proprietor's heart pounding. It was the title. And, a look at the coins being placed on his counter. They were gold as the eyes of the young woman who had left him the bird. But he was rapidly forgetting those beautiful tearful eyes, because this gold was here and now, and a good deal more beautiful to him.

"Certainly, my lord," the proprietor said, bowing, casting all inhibitions to the winds, exactly as so many women had done for his customer, the Earl of Elliot, "at once."

The footman gave the parcel to the butler, who delivered it to my lady's maid, who took it to her lady's bedchamber. The lady's maid waited in the dressing room until noon, when her lady opened her eyes to a new day. The maid showed the lady the parcel after she'd served her morning chocolate. And when she did, the lady screeched and leapt from bed and danced around like a mad thing, shouting, "Mama, Mama!"

Her mother came puffing down the hall, her hair still in curl papers, trailing lady's maids, chambermaids, and footmen in her wake, all rushing to see what had caused the commotion.

"Come see! At last!" her daughter cried. "At last! A gift! From that jeweler's down on Bond Street. You know, the one that costs the earth. It's from Elliot! Yes! At last!"

Her mother saw, and then shooed all extraneous servants from the room, leaving only a pair of lady's maids, and a chambermaid to clean up the mess of spilled morning chocolate.

"Yes, a gift," the elderly lady sniffed, "and far too large a parcel to be a ring, my dear."

"Oh fiddle," her daughter said as she attacked the paper covering the parcel, "it's a joke. Elliot's a famous jokester. He's probably taken the ring and wrapped it in yards and yards of paper, to tease me. I hope it's diamonds and rubies, I do so love rubies and you always said they're too old for me, but if I'm to be a married lady I can drape myself in yards of rubies," she said as she tore the last of the paper off the box, and struggled with opening the string on it.

The young lady was fair, and only her youth saved her from being pallid to the point of insipidness, so perhaps her mama had the right of it. Because when she ripped open the box and lifted out what it contained, her face grew red as a ruby. And it didn't suit her at all.

She held up the gift.

It was a golden cage, containing a golden bird on a perch. The young lady shook it hard, and turned it upside down and shook it harder. But no ring fell out, though the thing gave out a few chiming clanks. It clanked harder when she flung it across the room. It crashed against the wall in a cacophony of harsh notes.

"Oh, damn him, damn him, damn him!" the young lady sobbed. "No ring, no pin, no—wait! No, only a key to the filthy thing," she said, flinging the key after the cage. "The note! Perhaps it *is* a jest and there's a clue to where the ring is in the note!"

She tore the accompanying note wide and read it aloud:

'*When this you see, remember me. When this you hear, Happy Christmas my dear, warmest regards, Elliot*' . . . Oh blast!" she raged, crumpling the note. "He didn't even sign if 'Frauncis'! Well, he's not the only gentleman in the *ton*," she said, sniffing. "He'll learn, I'll have a dozen other offers by Christmas. I might just accept one, and then where will he be?"

"Wherever he wishes. He hasn't asked," her mother said with brutal frankness.

"I'm sure he intends to. He's just being difficult. Let him," the young woman snarled. "I'll be married by spring, and don't be surprised if it is to him, even so."

"My lady?" the little chambermaid said, pausing in her cleaning to gaze at the bird in its cage. "What shall I do with it, if you please?"

"Throw it in the rubbish, for all I care."

"It ain't ruint," the chambermaid persisted, lifting the cage to look. "There's a dent in its side now, to be sure," she said, staring in at the bird. It still sat on its perch, and it seemed that the topaz eyes winked at her, "but it's still a lovely thing, it is."

"I said, throw it out!" the young lady roared.

"I know," the chambermaid said, still on her knees, looking frightened, for it was not her place to speak and well she knew it, "But, if you don't mind . . ." she persisted nervously, because now the lady's maids—leagues above her in power—were frowning at her. "If you please, my lady," she said in a rush, "would you mind if I gave it to my poor little brother for Christmas, instead? He's that crippled, you see, he don't get out much, and this would amuse him something wonderful, for I believe it's got a music box in it too—"

"Take it, take it, I don't care what you do with it, just get it out of here!"

The girl raised the cage like a Grail and sighed. "Thank you, with all my heart. My brother thanks you too."

"Get on with the cleaning," one of the maids said.

There was a smile on the girl's face as she did.

She wasn't smiling the next morning. She scowled at the filthy little old man behind the counter where she'd placed the birdcage. She'd hurried to the dark, cramped shop as the sun rose and was fidgeting because she had to leave before it got much higher. A tear and tale had gotten her a half-day off, and she had to make good use of it.

"Wot? Think I'll take that for it? Ho! Think again, you old skint!"

He laughed. "Aye, I think you'll take it and be glad, luv, for where will you take it else? Besides, I'm fair, and you knows it. Now, one more time. Did you come by it legal?"

She frowned, but the money he had put on the counter disappeared into her apron pocket quickly. She gazed around his shop. "Three parts junk and one part priceless," she muttered, eyeing the dusty stacks of books, the mounds of paintings, the random piles of objects.

"Aye, but none knows which is which—'cept for myself," the old man cackled, "which makes it a waste of time for anyone to steal from me. And since I'm the only fair dealer in town, a complete waste to murder me. I do good business out of bad business. Again: is it yours to sell? I'll buy it anyway, but I got to know."

"Yes," she said curtly. "My lady had a fit when her beau sent it 'stead of a ring. There's a dent in the side, where it hit the wall. It's fine elsewise . . . 'cept maybe it used to play music, 'cause it has a key. But it don't work no more, I tried. The wall didn't do it any good. Ah, don't look at me like that. I know she don't give away ice in wintertime, but she was in a taking. I told her it was for my crippled brother, that's why she gave it to me."

He roared with laughter. "Why then, lass, your crippled brother thanks you kindly." He pantomimed a mocking bow before he turned his attention back to the birdcage.

She saw him fiddling with it. "Well, at least you got something to play with, good day to you," she sneered as she left his shop.

He didn't answer. In fact, he hardly noticed her leave—while she was there to notice. Once she'd gone, and he was sure of it, he put the key in the slot in the side of the cage, and turned it.

The bird turned its head, and seemed to look at him. He held his breath. Its jeweled eyes caught the little light there was, and glistened. It opened its beak—and sang, while the music box played.

The song was like true birdsong, the music box played soft accompaniment. The sound took the old man far from his dusty shop, back to the green fields of his youth, back to a sweet voice singing him a lullaby—the last sweet words any woman had ever addressed to him—while in the background, a murmurous wind rustled in the tree outside his window . . .

"Silly slut," the old man said when the last notes died away, and he could breathe again. "Didn't know what you could do, did she, my beautiful lad?" he cooed to the bird. "Well, but I do. Aye, and I know just where you belong."

"Eliza! Enough. Pacing won't move the clock any faster," the fair-haired woman complained as her daughter kept marching to and fro in the parlor.

"I know," the young woman with the golden eyes said, "it would already be tomorrow if it did. But how I wish it were time! I have the speech rehearsed. I know I must do it. I know how to do it. I'm *ready* to do it. But even so, I'm . . . frightened of doing it. But I will, I will."

"It's not fair," the older woman said sadly. "You've worked for the money, it should be in your pocket. I don't make much with my sewing, but I'm paid the moment I deliver it. And what you do is so much better, so much more important—"

". . . So much blather, Mother," Eliza said, interrupting. She looked at her mother fondly.

With fifty years in her cup, Maria Dumont was still attractive. Still slender, with a lovely complexion marred by few lines of age—or trouble, which she'd had in plenty. Widowed, and thrust from her family long before that unhappy time, just because she'd wed unwisely. Eliza admired the soft fair hair that scarcely showed the encroaching gray. She had her mother's features, but had inherited her father's heavy mahogany hair. It was the only thing she had inherited from him, since when he'd died he'd only left the earth richer by three children.

"It's just that your skills: being a good mother and a brilliant conversationalist, aren't much in demand—for pay, that is. Though of course, you're beyond price." They grinned at each other. "I wish I could cook as well as you," Eliza went on, "and I'd be happy to cope on so little money half so well. You can sew and embroider too. I can't. And how you can sing! If I could sing like that I'd make our fortune on the stage."

"Over my entirely dead body, of course," her mother commented.

"Well, but the argument is academic—as am I now." Eliza giggled, "I can't sing; it's all I can do to carry a tune on the harp. But that I can do, so I can at least teach to help keep our mediocre roof over our heads."

They exchanged sympathetic looks. They hated their rented rooms on the outer fringe of fashionable London, so perilously close to terrifying London.

"So I teach," Eliza sighed. "And since you sew like

an angel—though I'm sure angels have better things to amuse themselves with—you do that. The only difference is that the tailor you work for is lower class, and so pays his debts. While most of my students' mamas aspire to the upper class, and so feel they need not. But needs must when the devil drives. We need the money now. I'll ask for it. And I'll get it!"

This was said with far more confidence than either of the women felt and they both knew it. Mrs. Dumont looked out the window, and Eliza down at her toes.

She'd pawned the bird in the golden cage, and they were both suffering because of it. But if she hadn't, they wouldn't have been able to pay the rent. Because they'd needed money for her brothers too. A sum for Everett, to pay his fare home from school for the holidays. Somewhat more so they could send something fine to Charles: a man in the service of his country far from home deserved a memorable Christmas gift. The watch and fob the bird had helped finance was that.

But though the money had met their needs, they needed the bird. It was their last link to a better life.

"Grandmother said the bird would bring me happiness," Eliza said, bravely. She neglected to mention that as she'd never actually met the lady—and had only gotten the musical bird and nothing else when her estranged grandmother had died last year—the gift of happiness hadn't been very apparent. *So far*, Eliza thought, and said, more bravely than she felt, "Well, there's the carriage pulling up, and there's Mrs. Pomfret with her daughter." She shuddered.

"And here I go," she muttered, taking a deep breath. "I do think I deserve *some* reward for not forcing little Melissa right through the strings of the harp just for the pleasure of watching her being sliced into dozens of neat little slivers," she said fervently.

"Eliza!" her mother said, half in shock, half in jest.

"Well, it would be the only neat thing about her," Eliza said bitterly. "I even have to wash down the harp strings when she leaves. The child is sticky as the inside of a wasp's nest, she's always eating, and it's always something gummy. And she can't play anything but spillikins, and I'll bet she cheats at that!" she whispered harshly as she squared her shoulders and went to answer the door.

"Mrs. Pomfret, Melissa, do come in," Eliza said as the broad woman in furs and her little daughter swept past her. Melissa headed straight for the harp in the front parlor Mrs. Dumont had just hastily vacated. Mrs. Pomfret marched after her daughter, until she was halted in her tracks. Because Eliza stepped in front of her.

"I should like a word with you, ma'am," Eliza said, "if you please."

Mrs. Pomfret looked affronted. She did that very well. Her frown said eloquently that in her experience, music teachers should speak *after* a lesson, and then only to praise. It was a terrifying frown that had quelled countless tradespeople asking for payment. It terrified Eliza too. But she had to be brave today.

"There's a matter of back services for rendered payment to be settled," Eliza said, and then scolded herself, realizing that in her nervousness she'd said it the wrong way around. But since she had managed to dumbfound Mrs. Pomfret, she pressed her advantage and went on quickly. "If you wish Melissa to have further harp lessons, I must be paid—and now, ma'am."

"WELL!" Mrs. Pomfret said, swelling with outrage, for whatever the girl had said before, the last was clear enough. "I never! Nor shall I ever again. Come along, Melissa, we shall find a more accommodating teacher. The woods are full of music masters, young woman. We need not stay and be insulted!"

"No, you need not," Eliza said, almost entertained by visions of a forest filled with hungry, prowling out-of-work musicians—except she knew too well it was almost true, "then, I suppose, Melissa will not be present at the spring recital my students are giving?"

"I should think not!" Mrs. Pomfret boomed. ". . . spring recital?"

"Yes, the one the Saunders, the Cummings, Baron FitzWilliams, and the Frobishers' children are performing in. So, that is too bad. But c'est la vie. Very well, good day, Mrs. Pomfret."

"The Baron FitzWilliams, you say?"

Eliza had buried the baron in the middle, but as she'd suspected, Mrs. Pomfret heard it loudly and clearly. Eliza nodded. "Yes. One of my students, a charming child."

"Ah," Mrs. Pomfret said, "perhaps, I have been hasty."

When the last strains of the tortured harp had died away, and Mrs. Dumont felt it was safe to come out of the kitchen, it was to see her daughter alone, dancing like a gypsy around a little stack of coins.

"I did it!" Eliza caroled. "And after Mrs. Pomfret, the others can only be easier!"

"So you did," Mrs. Dumont said slowly. "But Baron FitzWilliams? Whoever is he?"

"I haven't the foggiest notion." Eliza laughed breathlessly. "But the very idea of him opened the Pomfret purse, and with that open, the others will surely follow."

"But a baron—"

"I said the recital will be in the spring. By spring, Mama, anything may happen. I may even meet a baron somewhere! But one thing's sure. By the week's end, we shall have our bird back, and by Christmas, enough to celebrate by having a roast bird for dinner as well. Grandmother was right. I'm sorry I never met her, but so glad she left the birdcage to me. It *has* brought me happiness! For when I get it back, I'll never be intimidated by any of my pupils' horrid mamas again."

Mrs. Dumont frowned. Surely, that couldn't have been what her mother had meant. That poor lady had obviously finally been permitted to forgive her daughter for marrying her music master so many years ago. Or at least, to forgive her granddaughter for being born to such a union. For although she'd never dared get in touch with her, she'd been allowed to leave her unknown granddaughter something.

It had only been a musical bird, but the note had been warm, and specific. Her mother had been a weak woman, Mrs. Dumont thought now, dominated by her husband and his family. She'd also been a woman of fancies and fantasies, since, unlike the daughter who had run away, it was the only way she could escape their domineering. But she'd never been a fool. Surely, she'd meant a truer, lasting sort of happiness?

Mrs. Dumont shook herself from her reveries. She was getting as bad as her poor lost mama. For what sort of nonsense was this? As if a mechanical songbird could bring happiness!

Frauncis, Earl of Elliot, sat in his drawing room, trying to decide what to do with the rest of his afternoon, and far less urgently, with the rest of his life. He'd planned to take a lady for a drive in the park today, but that lady had definitely snubbed him last night. It still astonished him. He'd seen the Lady Lattimore at the assembly, began to cross the room to her, and she'd turned up her nose and then turned away from him, as though she hadn't seen him at all. He might have thought she was shortsighted, but her mama had turned crimson and given him an agonized apologetic glance, which was high coin from such a high-nosed hatchet-faced lady.

He'd paused, reviewing his sins. None of them were new, or extraordinary for a man of his ilk. The only other thing it could have been was his gift. It was exquisite, in exquisite taste, and unexceptional. So she couldn't have been insulted. But it was also exquisitely noncommittal. So it was that then. *Fare thee well, my lady*, he had thought, and left the assembly, amused, annoyed, and vengeful.

The other gift was very well received. He gave it himself rather than sending it, because he wanted to reap the immediate rewards. He did. But that ended up leaving him amused, annoyed, and sorrowful—precisely because the lovely La Starr, an opera dancer, newly in his keeping, was very grateful. So was his body, actually. But his mind was not.

Because it had occurred to him, at the worst possible moment, that her intimate attentions were exactly that: a reward he was getting. And moreover, a paltry one, since he'd had to pay for it. Well, a man of his class had little choice; after all, it wasn't as if he could bed a woman of birth and character without wedding her. Or cuckolding her husband. But it was a lonely, damnable thing, and he was sorry for it, *during*—instead of immediately afterward, as usual.

Two gifts, two mistakes, he was in a vile mood today, wondering whether to snub the lady to show her what it felt like, ignore it and get on with either courting her, or leave off the pursuit of her altogether. He'd already decided the opera dancer would do better with someone who appreciated her more, and a charming farewell note with regrets, a face-saving lie and sum as severance, was already on its way to her.

So he was glad to be distracted by his butler.

"A young woman insists on seeing you, my lord," the butler said. "She is most agitated," he added. Which meant that in his opinion the young woman ought to be seen. He usually only gave a "young lady" such an honor. Not a discarded mistress then, unless the actresses he had known in the biblical sense were better actresses than he remembered, the earl thought with a hidden grin.

"Show her in, then," he said, diverted.

She came in breathlessly. Yes, *very* agitated, the earl thought with interest, and that was fine, because it suited her very well. It brought color to her pale face and sparkle to those remarkable eyes. She was a lovely creature, with exquisite features and great speaking topaz eyes. The form revealed by her half-closed cape spoke volumes to him too. He couldn't wait to hear what she had to say. She hardly waited a second to say it.

"My lord," she said firmly, holding a piece of paper in front of her, as though for support, "I believe you belong to something that I have . . . I mean, I believe you have my belonging. My lord," she said a little desperately as the formidably elegant handsome nobleman behind the desk looked at her in bemusement, "I want my bird back."

"Your bird . . . ?" he asked, buying time, reviewing all the birds he'd had, and suddenly realizing what she was trying to say, but refusing to help her precisely because her distress was so fetching. And besides, he didn't have the bird anymore.

"I p-pawned it," she said, spitting the shameful, hated word out. But once it was out, like a bad tooth, the pain stopped, and she could go on rationally. "Here, this is the chit I received for it," she said thrusting the receipt at him, careful to not actually give it to him. It was her only proof, and she hung on to it like grim death. He was a man of wealth and power. But the paper made them equals in this—she hoped.

"It states I can retrieve the bird from pawn until the twelfth of the month—which is tomorrow," she said triumphantly. "But when I went to the shop with the sum in my hand this morning, I was told you'd bought it! But as you can see, it's mine. And I want it back."

"Oh, the *musical* bird," he said. "But I purchased it legally and honestly."

"You couldn't have—it wasn't for sale. The proprietor said he'd made a mistake. He said he'd reimburse you, and that you would understand. I must have it back. It was my grandmother's. It means a great deal to me—oh, why am I begging? It's mine!"

"Not anymore, I'm afraid," he said, "Miss . . . ?"

"Dumont," she said helpfully, watching his mouth, so eager was she to hear what he was going to say. It was a very fine mouth to watch, even more so because she was so fearful of gazing too long into those dark, knowing, fathomless indigo eyes of his.

"Miss Dumont," he said with satisfaction, as though she'd given him more than her name. "I think we must discuss this. May I offer you tea? And a seat, so we can try to thrash this out between us?"

"I'd rather have the bird," she said worriedly.

"We'll get to that," he said, enchanted.

"I'll go there this afternoon," the earl promised Eliza at last. Because he really couldn't keep her any longer. He would, of course, he'd decided, keep her—and for far longer. But that was in the future. For now, he'd agreed to get the musical birdcage back for her. His offer of protection would come later.

He gazed down into her face as he helped her on with her cloak. The faint scent of perfume released from its opened folds as she snuggled into it sent a shaft of longing straight to his heart. And other personal body parts. Of course he'd help her. Then, he'd help himself to her. She was just what he needed.

She was beautiful, charming, and well-spoken. And very available. It was astonishingly, amazingly lucky for him. Because she looked every inch a lady. But she couldn't be one. He'd discovered that within five minutes. He'd placed careful telling questions. She was so eager to recover the birdcage she'd answered immediately and artlessly. All the facts added up.

First: she'd pawned something. A lady did *not* go to pawnshops. A lady's husband or maid did that for her.

Second: she had no social standing. She'd visited a gentleman without an escort to act as chaperone. Which also meant she had no reputation to speak of. Well, it wasn't her reputation he was interested in, or rather, only the lack of it was. A wife required a reputation. A mistress required one of a different sort. Someday, he'd know what had led her into such difficulties. It was enough that those difficulties had led her to him.

Third: she taught music to the petite bourgeois of London. She worked! Whether it was at teaching or dancing at the opera, no lady *worked* at anything.

Fourth and fifth and so on and on, her situation came clear. She lived in rented rooms in a district on the margins of respectable London. She had no servants. Servants? She obviously had scarcely enough money for herself: her clothing was serviceable and well worn. She said she lived with her mother. Well, but a wise woman would say that, to keep herself safe until she found better protection. She had.

She'd live with him, he thought with satisfaction. He'd keep her safe enough, in comfort and pleasure. Why not? She seemed to like him very well. And how she amused him. They'd laughed together after she'd got over her anxiety. He couldn't remember ever laughing so comfortably with any mistress, or lady.

"I'll go directly after luncheon—which you, cruel creature—won't take with me," he finally told her, "and retrieve the bird. It was a present for a friend's . . . birthday. I'll have to lie to get it back. That pains me, but I bear it for your sake. And since I want to be sure you get it—I'll bring it round to your rooms. I'll be hungry and exhausted by then," he said with a winning grim. "After all my efforts on your behalf—you *will* have dinner with me? It would be surpassing cruel of you not to."

"Of course," she said, smiling, "but look at the time! I must go! My first lesson is at two! Thank you so much, my lord. I was so distressed to think I'd lost my inheritance."

"*Frauncis*," he said gently, "if you please."

Her eyes grew very wide. "I—I don't think so," she said, "at least, not yet. We scarcely know each other."

"We will," he said.

The earl couldn't wait to see Lady Lattimore again. She could have saved him and herself a great time of time if she'd known it wasn't her blue eyes or blond hair he was fantasizing about as he cooled his heels in her salon, as she tried on gown after gown, seeking the one that would absolutely blind him with desire. It was her mechanical bird he craved.

"My dear," he said with such heartfelt relief and gladness when she entered the room she couldn't help looking in triumph at her mama.

"Frauncis," she said, dimpling as he took her hand, "to what do we owe this honor?"

"Does a man need a reason to seek your company— other than the delight he takes in it?" he asked, wondering when he could ask the question he'd come to ask.

So did she. They both endured her mama's chatter, a service of tea and biscuits, a retelling of old gossip and an attempt to start some new. But when the correct visiting time was almost up, her mama rose, leaving them alone, having supposedly found something fascinating to look at by the window.

The earl was thinking of fascinating things too. He couldn't wait to get back to Eliza Dumont to discover more about them. She'd beguiled him entirely. Yet unless she was the most accomplished actress he'd ever known, it was clear she hadn't been trying to. That boggled him. He was a man of wide experience with females, but for all that, he didn't know them very well.

An only child of elderly parents, he'd been sent to school at an early age. There, he'd learned about women. He'd been taught they were distinctly different, mind and body, from males. They'd been portrayed as rare and mythical creatures, either sensual sirens or sacred mothers and wives. He'd been on fire to find out which was true. He had. It seemed both things were so. And in the years since, he'd found no other purpose for them. Nor they, for him.

Because since he'd reached his majority, women only wanted to make use of him too. Those of his own class were either trying to marry him, or get him to marry their daughters, sisters, or nieces. Sometimes, it was true, they tried to cuckold their husbands with him. But they never simply *spoke* with him, with no ulterior purpose, as a man might do.

The women he did sport with were no more interesting to talk with. They were willing to trade the incredible pleasures their bodies provided for a fee, but were usually ignorant and avaricious. When he was lucky enough to find a clever female to share his bed, that intelligence was never really shared with him. The women he bought were totally self-serving, and seldom honest with him. Nor could be blame them for it. Business was business.

But Eliza had been different, or so it seemed to him. They'd chatted about many things and she'd never once flirted or been coy, or sought anything of him but her own property. When they'd done speaking of that, she seemed to enjoy talking to him simply because he said interesting things. So had she. They'd begun discussing music, naturally, and then naturally enough, London and weather: all sorts of common things that made up everyday life. He couldn't remember a one of them. It had been delicious. She treated him like a man, but an equal, and a friend. He found he wanted that. He discovered he needed that.

In an all too brief hour, Eliza Dumont had spoken to him as a man—on all levels. Or so it seemed. He was eager to find out if it was true, and if so, if it would last.

He was being asked something now. ". . . Hmm?" he asked, having lost the thread of whatever the lady he'd only yesterday been contemplating as a possible wife was prattling on about.

". . . and so I'm sorry to leave London," she said. "But as I said, Mama was wondering just this morning if you'd like to be a guest at Lattimore Hall for the holidays? It would be so jolly! We hunt, we ride, we have such a lot of company."

"*Ah!*" he said, as though he'd sat on a pin, realizing his wandering thoughts had almost gotten him caught in a net he hadn't seen. "How generous! But I'm afraid I can't. Family obligations, you know."

He hoped she did, because for the life of him, he couldn't invent any. Both parents were long gone; he had many more friends than relatives. He'd read the name of his heir somewhere, and always intended to meet him. That saddened him now, suddenly. He realized it must be the coming season, although Christmas was as alien to him as women had been at school. He'd learned about them both the same way, after all: from acquaintances and strangers, and had always enjoyed them both far from his own home.

"Oh, too bad," she said. Then eyeing him brightly as a robin watches something wriggling in dewy grass, she said sweetly, "But then when shall we meet again? I'll be away until the New Year."

"Oh, too bad," he echoed. "But 'fast away the old year passes' and all that. It won't be long until we have you back in London, will it? Umm, but—that reminds me . . . before then, I must ask . . . This is embarrassing, but—I did send you a little token for Christmas . . ."

"Yes," she snapped. "How remiss of me. I meant to thank you."

"No, no, not at all, better you didn't, actually," he said. "You see, I've just discovered that by some accident you received the wrong parcel. One meant for . . . my little cousin, Eliza. A charming child, always one of my favorites, very musical, she is," he said quickly. "But you see, she received *your* present, and her mama was confused by it, as you might imagine . . ."

She imagined too well. Her eyes lit up, her smile widened, she became absolutely incandescent. He'd never seen her looking so lovely, her usual pale blondness was all a-sparkle. If he weren't already planning rapturous hours with a chestnut-haired, topaz-eyed delight, he might have even regretted his decision not to spend the holidays with this suddenly radiant lady.

"So, if you could give me the musical bird?" he

asked. "Then, I'd be able to have dear Eliza send you the . . . gift meant for you. I wish she weren't so badly spoiled, then I'd be able to hand you your rightful gift right now. But she's a terror, and won't give it up until she gets her own."

He reminded himself to ask his secretary to get the lady a vanity set or silver-backed hairbrush or something, and waited for her to send for a maid to retrieve the birdcage. Instead, she blinked. Her sparkle faded.

"Oh," she said weakly, "the *bird* . . ." She darted a frantic glance at her mama. "Umm," she said, dimpling to distract him as she cudgeled her brain, "as to the birdcage . . . You see, my dear sir . . ."

"We took it to be mended, my lord," her mother said, cleaving to the truth, in part.

"Mended?" the earl asked in surprise.

The lady felt her mouth go dry. Shooting a threatening glance at her mama to silence her, she thought furiously. She couldn't say she'd shied it across the room. But *mended* . . . "Yes. I, ah—wound it once too often," she said with sudden inspiration, thinking of the clanks it had made and remembering at the last second that the blasted thing had been a musical box, "and it refused to . . . Ah . . . go."

She paused. If it hadn't been a music box, she'd look a fool. But so what? Men loved silly females. Well, he'd loved her as one or he wouldn't be here now, would he? And if he'd given her a broken music box to start with, he'd feel like a fool himself, and that would be all right too. But he was frowning.

"I expect we can have it back for you by . . . tomorrow, don't you, Mama?" she said quickly.

"Oh, indeed," her mother said nervously.

They bade him farewell at the door, all dimples and promises.

"Until the morning then," the lady said, "when I'll

have the bird—and you will have my rightful gift, I do hope?"

She said it archly. He replied with a bow. She closed the door with a sigh of pure pleasure, wondering if it would be a diamond or a pearl.

He was thinking of a goose. He'd bring a roast goose, he thought, as he strode to his carriage. Yes. And a bottle of wine. To make himself a warm welcome and warm Eliza up too. By the time he changed and drove to her unfashionable quarter of town, it would be too late to go to a restaurant. Besides, he didn't want to share her company. She hadn't the clothes for the sort of place he wanted to take her to, either—yet. Two bottles of wine then, and a nice cake, besides. He'd have Cook see to it, he thought with pleasure—before he saw to her.

Night was complete, and the earl, complete to a shade, as he stepped from his carriage in front of the modest house Eliza said she lived in. He wore his cape open over a black jacket, his linen was dazzling even in the flickering gaslight. If he'd worn knee breeches he could have gained admittance to Almack's. As it was, he was attired magnificently—except for the huge wicker basket he'd hung from his arm.

"You might as well take the rig home, John," he told his coachman and consulting his watch by the light of the moon, added, ". . . you might come back in three hours, and stay a half hour. If I'm not out by then, go home—and return tomorrow, early."

There was every reason to expect he would not leave until morning, the earl thought happily, as the sound of the departing carriage faded away. He strolled to the door and lifted the knocker. It sounded loudly in the silent evening. It was a cold, still, starry night. The street was quiet, the row of houses simple, the pavement clean. It was respectable, but only just. A few streets away there was noise, litter, and too much activity for this hour.

He'd do better for her, he thought smugly. He'd broach the subject at the first decent opportunity; he didn't want her to think he was trifling with her— wanting only this one night with her. In fact, he'd amaze her with his forbearance. There'd be no physical overture until the thing was settled. Even though that would be difficult. Just thinking about that slender yet rounded, perfumed figure, those high breasts, those wide topaz eyes widening further with pleasure . . .

But no, he wanted to do it right. First the wine, he mused as he waited, then the ham . . . well, but the cook couldn't get his hands on a goose that fast. Then the cake, and then . . . Then, he'd see how persuasive he could be. He had three allies: charm, flattery, and money. Surely one—or two—he told himself more realistically—of them would do the trick.

It promised to be a delicious evening. He drew in an anticipatory breath as the door opened—and then frowned as light and heat, and the delicious scent—of dinner, filled the air as the door went wide.

The woman in the doorway looked entirely respectable, and vaguely familiar. Except she had fair hair, he mused, and was old enough to be Eliza's mother . . .

Her voice was sweetly melodic as she said, "My lord? Do come in. My daughter will be here directly. May I take your cape and . . . basket?"

He felt heat rising in his face and was glad he had to bend low to put the basket down. He felt even lower. It was if all his lavish sexual fantasies had just been printed out boldly—in church.

"May I take your hat? I'm Maria Dumont. Eliza told me you promised to retrieve the birdcage—"

"Oh, and I see you have!" Eliza exclaimed as she came into the parlor. She wore a cinnamon-colored gown of some luminous silken stuff, and even in the candlelight, he could see her golden eyes were shining too. She clapped her hands together, like a child. "Thank you, thank you, this is wonderful!"

He didn't think he could feel much worse, clumsier, or more degenerate, but he'd been wrong. If he'd just had the damned goose he could have tried to pass it off as a jest—a tasty bird as a token for the mechanical bird that was to come. Instead, he cleared his throat. "No, I'm afraid I don't have it—yet," he said, and as Eliza's smile faded, added quickly, "tomorrow—it's been promised to me for tomorrow. This—this is . . . ah—dinner. You remember I asked you to dinner? But when I saw the hour, I decided to bring it to you instead of having you wait."

"No need," she said with a gurgle of laughter. "Great minds with but a single thought! For we noted the hour too . . . well, Mama's a famous cook, and we've soup, fowl and"—she noted his surprise and added, bravely—"we may have no servants, but I promise you, you've never tasted better."

Clear water over smooth stones, her motives were so pure, he realized, that so were her thoughts about his. He felt chastened, humbled—and yet was purely delighted—in the most literal sense.

"Ladies," he said, removing his hat as he bowed, "I'd be pleased, and honored." And he meant it.

The soup was excellent, the fowl delicious. So was the conversation. The ladies loved his jests: Eliza had a way of making him laugh without warning, and Mrs. Dumont had a sly way with words too. His hostesses made sure his interest never flagged, his plate was never empty, his wineglass was never allowed to go lower than his spirits. And if he sometimes stared at

Eliza when she spoke, and found himself still staring while they waited for his answer, they were too well-bred to chide him, as he silently did himself. As if he'd never seen a beautiful girl! But it was as if he never had.

Because he had never loved to listen to a female equally as much as he delighted in looking at her. He'd never desired any woman just as much as he desired her good opinion, either. He hadn't needed to bring a cooked goose tonight, he thought as he finally rose from the table. Because, for a certainty: he was one.

"We have no other gentleman to leave you with while you enjoy your port—well, but we haven't any port either!" Eliza said as she led him into the parlor and sat opposite him.

"I couldn't take a sip of anything else," he swore, and stopped himself before the easy words slipped out . . . *except for your sweet lips* . . . It was true, and what he would have said if things were different. But they weren't. And they were. Very much so. Now he had a wholly different course to pursue.

Eliza's mother had subtly let him know that she was from a good family, even though she'd been out of touch with them since her marriage to an impecunious music master. She'd made a point of letting him know. He suspected she'd noted his shock at seeing her and had a glimmering of an idea of what the basket of dinner had been really meant for. But she was indeed well-bred. Not a hint of it escaped her lips, even if the knowledge sometimes showed in her eyes as she watched him watching her daughter.

Eliza was eminently respectable then. And a respectable female of good—even if impoverished—circumstances, required a different form of address. A *courtship*, he realized. He waited for the familiar chill of dread—and felt suffused with warmth instead.

So, there it was, he thought—the thing he'd never really expected to find. Such a momentous moment, he had expected cataclysm. But love had stolen up on him—when he looked, it was simply there. Simply, undeniably, marvelously there. He sat astonished and elated. Until he saw Eliza's mama manfully trying to stifle a yawn.

But she'd cooked and served, and since they both obviously weren't ladies of leisure who went to bed when the sun rose, their day likely started with the new day.

He made a show of pulling out his watch and staring at it, amazed. "Circes, a pair of them," he marveled, as though to himself, as he rose, shaking his head, "invite a fellow for dinner and the years slip away! By the time I get back to my house I'll probably find *another* new century's dawned, and whatever will such a paltry fellow as me find to do in the twentieth century, I wonder?"

"Lecture about ours, of course." Eliza giggled.

He said his good-byes and left his thanks—and his basket, to her mama. Eliza walked him to the door.

"Tomorrow," he said as he took her hand. "I'll bring you the birdcage." His eyes said much more, and when his lips touched her hand, it was as though she heard them. Because she took a sudden sharp breath and her eyes went wide. "Tomorrow," he said again. But his voice was a little uneven.

The young upstairs maidservant's voice was uneven too—but because she was screaming so loud. The old man she was shouting at winced.

"You ain't got it no more?" she screeched in disbelief. "G'wan—who'd a bought it? It was banged up and broke besides. Ah. I see," she said on a sneer and a sigh. "Aye, I got it. All right, you old villain, I'll pay more'n you paid me for it. But don't go mad with power, they don't pay me much, you know. I'll pay, only 'cause it's my position on the line here."

"Really?" the old man said. "Odd that I didn't see you all day then. Not until just now—when I went to close up shop."

She looked a little embarrassed, then turned defiant. "Well, they gave me the whole day off so I could talk my little crippled brother into giving up the bird, didn't they? And such a day. Fair and bright . . . If you had to scrub and wash all the days of your life, locked up inside a big dark house, wouldn't you go to the park on such a day—if they give it to you out of the blue like that?"

His expression told her he never left the shop, except to sleep. "*Anyways*," she said, "they want the thing back, 'cause he sent it to her by mistake and she won't get the right present unless she coughs it up. Ha. Were it a ring, like they hope, why wouldn't he have give it to her right off, no matter where the bird is, I'd like to know. But who's listening to me? Not you, any road. How much?"

He shrugged. "Too late. Not for sale no more. Some fellow and his girl came in this very morning. She saw the birdcage, commenced cooing over it, and he said he was a handy lad and could fix it up for her. I sold it, and that's that!"

"No!" she said, her face going so ashen her freckles stood out in bold relief. "S'truth?"

"Ever known me to turn down money in hand?" he asked as answer.

"Lud!" she said, holding on to the counter for support. "It's gone? Then so am I! What am I to do?"

*   *   *

"*Gone?*" the lady shrieked. "What do you mean, you wicked, wicked girl?"

"All's I said was that my grandma, her that lives in Lancaster?" The little maid stammered. "She went and took pity on my poor crippled little brother, she did, and sent for him so he could have a proper Christmas in the country, is wot she said, my lady. So my poor old mam, she put him on the stage not yesterday morn, and waved him off with many a tear, and he went, clutching his precious birdcage to his thin little chest, my lady, it would have done your heart that much good to see him."

"Damn, damn, damn!" her lady raged. But after a moment, she calmed herself. "Lancaster, in Yorkshire, you say?"

The little maid was too nervous to speak; she only nodded.

"Mmm," my lady said, pacing, "and how many days will it take for him to get there?"

"Well . . ." the maid said, trembling visibly now.

"Three by mail, perhaps five by common coach," Lady Lattimore's mama snapped, "why bother to ask? The thing is gone."

"Not necessarily. Look you, girl," her daughter said to the trembling chambermaid, "I'll give you money for coach fare and pay you something for the birdcage—and your trouble—if you go get the thing and bring it back to me, quickly! We'll be in the country by then, but I'll give you the direction. Bring it there. Now mind: if you say you can't, I have no choice but to let you go—without a letter of reference. Well?"

"What's the point?" her mother moaned before the maid could answer.

"We can have it back by Christmas, Mother, that's the point. Moreover, he'll have to come to us at Lattimore Hall to get it, and once there, we may be able to bring him to the point even faster! *Now* do you see?"

"The fare alone will be costly," her mother complained, because like most wealthy persons in London, she hated to part with actual cash.

"It will be well worth it," her daughter said. And her mama, for once, didn't argue the point.

"He'll be here by two!" Eliza sang as she whirled around the parlor, looking for something else to re-arrange. "Then we're going for a drive! In an open carriage, he said, so there's no hint of impropriety but I don't know if I'll ever get over such elegance! Why so silent? I thought you liked him."

"Oh, I do, very much," her mama said, "how could I not? That's the point," she said sadly, "my dear, he's top of the trees. Titled, wealthy, in the prime of life, and most unfairly handsome to boot. Eliza, my love, you're the loveliest girl in London, so far as I'm concerned. And you know there's a dozen good lads here in the neighborhood who would agree."

Eliza stilled. So there might be, and they might have been good lads too, but not good enough, mind or body, for her to take seriously. There hadn't been any fellow she'd fancied that much in all her one and twenty years. Until Frauncis, Earl of Elliot—who in two brief visits had turned her head, and her heart had followed. He was clever, handsome, and charming . . . My goodness, she thought, what was there to dislike?

"But we're talking apples and oranges here," her mother persisted. "We've decent connections, but only that. No money at all, either, as you know far too well, poor child. Oh, Eliza, love, he *can't* be serious about you."

"You think he means to trifle with me?" Eliza asked, wide-eyed.

"I think he meant to, once upon a time. Now, I think, perhaps, to give him the benefit of the doubt—he means to amuse himself with you. Which is not the same, I know. But which will hurt you just as much in the end, I think, if you take his attentions seriously."

"Oh." Eliza carefully put the pillow she'd just fluffed back on the settee. "I see, well, yes," she said seriously, "you're right, Mama." She raised her head, her eyes sparkling, "But, if I *don't* take it seriously, all I can have is a wonderfully good time, you agree?"

"If you don't get carried away by his attentions," her mother said carefully. She raised a hand to still Eliza's protests. "Don't think it can't happen. Remember, you and your brothers would not be here if it were impossible. I loved your father dearly, but, oh, my dear, I never intended to wed him! He was just so different from my other admirers . . ."

She shook her head. "But that's an entirely different story. I only warn you it's likely the only time you *will* drive out with him, and I didn't want you hurt because of it. He's probably just paying you a courtesy after he delivers the birdcage. But remember that once it's back, he will be gone. You're too well born for him to take on any level but wife, and not well dowered enough to be that I'm afraid. I—I just didn't want you to take his attentions seriously, on any level."

Eliza raised her chin. "I won't," she said, and smiled bravely, because she'd never told her mama such a whopping lie.

" '*Not—repaired—yet*,' " Frauncis repeated. "I see. When is it supposed to be done?"

"Now that's the fortunate part," Lady Lattimore said gleefully, "not until the week before Christmas!

Imagine. So that means, my dear sir," she said gaily, tapping him with her fan, "you'll have to come to Lattimore Hall to fetch it home for your darling little Eliza. In fact, Mama and I were thinking—why don't you bring Eliza to the Hall for our Christmas fete, instead? There'll be dozens of other children there for her to play with."

"I think not," Frauncis said slowly, deciding to stay with the truth as far as he could, as he always did when he lied. "I can't imagine her mother allowing me to take her so far at Christmastime."

"Oh, too bad, then I suppose you'll just have to get the bird after Christmas . . . and to give me my present that late too," she added with a pout designed to melt his heart. It only melted his patience.

"Yes, it is too bad, isn't it?" he said, bowed, and left, leaving her to pace her salon in furious thought.

He got as far as the curb when he heard a hissing sound. He turned and paced around his horses. He frowned as he looked for the source, frightening the little chambermaid who had crept up to the carriage on the street side so she wouldn't be seen from the house.

"*Hist!* My lord," she whispered frantically, "over here. No, no, I'm not begging, put away your coins, do! I've a thing to tell you. You *are* the Earl of Elliot, right?" When he nodded tersely she went on. "Well, if it's the golden birdcage you're after, you won't be finding it here, nor at the Hall. Not never. But I can't talk here, they'll skin me if they see me with you."

"Round the corner then?" he asked, still frowning.

She nodded. "Round and down a street, if you please." She scurried off as the earl climbed into his phaeton and drove after her, his attention well and truly captured.

He heard the girl out when they met again, frowning more as he did. But it wasn't at her, and he paid her handsomely for her recital, so she went away happy enough. But he still looked troubled when he got to Eliza's house. A glance at his frown and another at his hands—empty except for a bouquet—made the two women try to hide their own troubled expressions.

"I haven't got the birdcage, no," he said, sweeping off his hat and presenting the flowers to Eliza's mama. "But I think I soon will. It's a roundabout tale. Suffice it to say I foolishly gave it to someone who obviously didn't deserve it. It was then sold. No—don't worry, I know where to find it. Would you like to come with me to fetch it now?" he asked Eliza. "Then we can take a triumphant turn around the park with it."

"Let me get my cape," she said.

"We'll be back before sun goes down," he told Mrs. Dumont. "I've good horseflesh, a well-sprung carriage, and am considered a decent driver," he said, as though oblivious to the fact that the many capes on his great-coat announced his membership in the prestigious Four in Hand driving club. "Don't worry, I'll take very good care of her," he added.

Since that was exactly what Mrs. Dumont was fretting about, all she could do was smile as she saw them off in his carriage. It was a high-perch phaeton, complete in every detail, even to the boy serving as the earl's tiger, standing on the back of it for balance, pride in his position clear to see in his young face.

"It's not in a good section of town," Frauncis told Eliza as he drove, "but not in the worst either. You'll be safe with me."

"Oh, I know that," she said so simply he was charmed, "but this is delicious! I thought I'd be terrified," she confided, "so high up, the ground so far away, moving so fast! But it's exhilarating. What fun! I never guessed. No wonder I see you gentlemen tooling around in your phaetons, when sometimes the traffic is so bad it seems much easier to walk around London."

The wind teased color into her cheeks, scattered some of her heavy hair into enticing ringlets around her face. Her eyes sparkled. She was so genuine in her appreciation and pleasure, Frauncis felt proud of thinking of taking her in his carriage. The curious, envious looks he was getting from passing men made him feel even more so.

"Ah, here we are. Hold the horses, Tom," he said as he helped Eliza down from her high seat, "shouldn't be a minute."

The shop's windows were opaque with dirt, the interior so dark in contrast to the bright day that Eliza and the earl were temporarily blinded when they walked in. A tiny bell on the door announced them. The place smelled like mushrooms. It was hard to see anything even when their eyes adjusted to the light, because there were stacks of things: mismatched chairs, piles of picture frames, mounds of objects haphazardly strewn everywhere.

"Hullo?" Frauncis called. "Anyone here?"

Something moved behind the counter and Eliza stepped back, afraid for a moment that it was a rat. But it was only a small old man, wrapped in layers of shawls. She hadn't seen him at once, because his face was almost as grimy as the interior of his filthy shop.

"I'm here," the old man cackled, "have been since before you were born, young sir. What can I do for you? Seeking a match to a set of glasses, dishes, a pitcher, an urn or a chair? I got most everything. Nothing stolen, never fear. Oh, no, honest trade's my middle name."

"No, nothing like that. I'm looking for a golden birdcage, with a musical bird in it," Frauncis said.

The old man blinked. "Nothing like that here, young sir!" he said, "Oh, no. Haven't seen nothing like that in many a long year. Look around, only the lost and discarded end up here."

"Interesting," Frauncis said smoothly, "since the girl who sold it to you told me she did so only yesterday."

"Did she?" the old man said scowling, "damn the wench for a—oh, pardon me and my terrible bad tongue, lady. I'm forgetting myself, I don't deal with the gentry much here. Well, *now* I recall . . . So she did, so she did. I suspected it were ill-got, but I've a heart, you see, and she were so needy."

"It wasn't stolen," Frauncis said, "but it wasn't precisely hers to sell either. It was a mistake all around. I know what you gave her for it; I'll double it. So. The birdcage, if you please."

"I would please!" the old man said. "Wouldn't I just! But you see, I sold the thing just yesterday, just like I told her. And for less, damn— Ah . . . blast it!"

"So that's true too," Frauncis said in chagrin. "I'd hoped . . . never mind. Can you tell me who purchased it?"

"That, yes," the old man said, and as Eliza began to smile added, "what they look like, I mean to say, for who asks a customer for a name and address when they pays cold cash?"

"So," Frauncis said as they drove to the park, "'*a pretty young miss all gingery hair in a red dress, and a dark-haired, likely looking lad with brown eyes.*' I'm so sorry, Eliza. Believe me, I am."

"Oh," she said in a mournful but brave little voice, "but it wasn't your fault, not really, you know."

He looked at her averted face, and felt his heart sinking at the sorrow he saw there. "Maybe . . . if I put an advertisement in the *Times*?" he suggested. "Contact Bow Street? Yes, and have someone draw up an illustration of it, with a description, pass out handbills. That might work. Someone will hear of it. Don't despair, I'll try my best to get it back for you.

". . . but," he added thoughtfully, his voice becoming brighter, "that does mean you and I will have to be together constantly, you know. That is to say, I intend to investigate every lead, every hint, every faintest suggestion as to its whereabouts. And of course, you'll have to be with me, won't you? To identify the thing, because I only got a glance at it when I bought it."

"Oh!" she said, turning to look at him.

"Yes," he said cheerfully, "absolutely imperative, that."

"Oh," she said, her eyes widening, "I imagine it would be, wouldn't it?"

"Absolutely," he said, smiling at her, paying so little attention to the horses that they almost ran down a young man in a sporty landau. "Absolutely," he repeated, deaf to the unfortunate young man's protests, blinded to all but Eliza's answering smile.

They forgot the birdcage that day. They drove around the serpentine paths of the park, so enrapt with each other they didn't see all the persons of Quality noting their fascination with each other any more than they saw all the people of little note, noting them with envy or pleasure, depending on their own state of love affairs.

Because obviously, as the baron DeWilde told Mr. Armstead that night at his club, "Elliot's got himself a charming new little armful."

"Well, but don't he always?" Mr. Armstead said enviously. "Still," he added brightening, "that must mean La Starr's looking for protection again."

"Yes," Mrs. Armstead told Lady Breen at her assembly the next evening. "At Astleys, no less. Looking into each other's eyes as if there was nothing on the stage, or so Henry said. Shocking, isn't it? I mean, a *gentleman* ought to keep such liaisons private. I'm surprised at him!"

"No, no," Lady Breen insisted the next day, over tea, "the shocking thing is that he must be serious about her! Because I saw them myself only yesterday, taking ices at Gunter's together, but with the most respectable female as chaperone!"

"No!" her friend said.

"Elliot? Drove right past, and passed me up without a 'howdyado,'" Lord Greyville complained to the dashing Harry Fabian at their favorite gaming hell the next night, "though with that little lovely at his side, who could blame him?"

"Charlie's right. Haven't seen hide nor hair of him here in days—rather nights, neither," Harry Fabian commented at a faro table the next week.

"Hooked, cooked and taken," Sir Stephen agreed, "m'sister's in despair, fancied him, y'know? But what female didn't? The chit ain't any lightskirt neither, my wife says the girl's well-born."

"No!" Mrs. McQueen whispered to the Countess of Chad, when they saw the pair, and the lady's very respectable mama, at the opera that night, "my maid says she's not connected to the Lewises of Cork, at all, but to the D'Arcys of Suffolk. Look! There's the mama. She may have been foolish in her youth, but she's a respectable widow now. The girl's the product of a misalliance, yes. And there's no money there. But with his money and her birth, the match would be acceptable, my dear. Pretty thing, isn't she?"

*   *   *

"*Ahhhhhhhhhhh!*" Lady Lattimore cried when her best friend arrived at the Hall for the holiday, ran from her coach, threw off her cape, and flushed with excitement, immediately told her the news. Lady Lattimore responded by slapping her friend silly, and then storming upstairs in hysterics. Her mama later said it was because she was suffering from a toothache.

And Eliza got dressed every morning, gave lessons every afternoon, and drove out with the earl every other minute she had. They saw silver birds in silver cages, bronze birds on pedestals, music boxes that played everything from foreign anthems to Christmas carols. But they never saw the golden cage.

"It's foolish to want it so much, I know," she told Frauncis one day after they'd followed up yet another false trail, "but Grandmother's note said it would bring me happiness. I don't really believe in such things, but she was a mystical sort of lady. Her note just said: *'The bird's song will bring you great happiness. Once you hear it and have it in your heart, set it free, as I have done.'* She meant me to have it last Christmas, but the bequest was held up so long I only just got it.

"Getting it before the holiday seemed like an extra gift," she said sadly, "because I thought I could pawn it to buy Christmas presents, and bring my brother Everett home for the holiday too. I meant to have it back at Christmas, as my gift from the grandmother I never met. I wanted to hand it to my own granddaughter someday."

"You'll have it again," he promised.

They did more than search for the birdcage. When they weren't pursuing it, they drove through the park, they went to the theater, they went out to dine. They strolled the frigid streets as though it were April or May, and gazed into each other's faces as often as they did into shop windows. The shops glittered with Christmas treats. They didn't seem to notice. If by chance they were hailed, the earl introduced Eliza to everyone he knew—when he could take his eyes off her long enough to realize they weren't alone.

But the thing of it was, he thought with a sigh as he dressed for dinner on Christmas Eve, that he never saw her alone. She had a mother, he thought in amusement, the way other girls had eyelashes.

He'd have to send her a letter to tell her his intentions, he thought as his butler handed him some gaily wrapped parcels. He'd have to mail her his kiss, he thought darkly as he went out his door. And as for what he most wanted to do, he'd have to write a book about it, have it bound, and delivered to her, he thought on a frustrated sigh as he drove to her house.

So he looked a little gloomy when he arrived at her door.

"Oh," she said nervously, when she saw him, "you're early. But . . . Everett just arrived from school . . ."

His spirits fell further. Another obstacle.

". . . and Mama took him down the street to visit with his best friend before dinner. So I'm alone here, and although there's no one to see, and so, to talk, I don't know if it's at all the thing for you to come in now . . ."

"It's absolutely the thing!" he said enthusiastically as he swept in, closing the door firmly behind him. "I've a gift for you and I . . . Oh, Eliza!" Because every other word failed him when he looked down into her face.

He placed his parcels on the hall table. Then he swept her up into his arms and kissed her with all the accumulated passion, fervor, and desire he had. Which was a great deal. Because it was a long time before they both realized he had his greatcoat on and it was greatly in their way. They separated, flushed, embarrassed, shy. He took off his greatcoat. And dropped it on the floor as he took her in his arms again.

The next time they parted they realized they needed someplace to sit or lie down. Only the thought of how inappropriate, desirable, and outrageous that was made them stop and stare at each other. They were mussed, disarranged, and pink-faced, and neither of them had ever seen anything more wonderful. There was some question as to whether Mrs. Dumont and young Everett thought the same thing, though.

"Oh!" Mrs. Dumont said as she came in and saw the disheveled pair standing, staring at each other in the little hall.

Everett, schoolboy to his toes, gaped. Then snickered, of course.

"Ah. Mrs. Dumont. I've brought your Christmas presents early," Frauncis said, as he tried to smooth his hair and arrange his cravat at the same time, "and as you can see, to offer for your daughter's hand."

"Oh, Frauncis, you don't have to do that," Eliza cried. "Mama will understand."

He turned to her in astonishment. "Why, of course I do, Eliza. Oh. You mean, I ought to have asked you first? But what do you think I was just doing? What sort of fellow do you think I am?"

"A wealthy titled man," Eliza said sadly, "with a conscience and a tender heart. I can't take advantage of that."

"I'm a wealthy, titled, lonely man," he said, "who never knew his conscience till he met you, and will certainly have no use for his heart if you don't say yes to his suit. I'll be a good husband, Eliza, let me take advantage of your tender heart. Say yes, please."

He couldn't hear exactly what she said as she came back into his arms and mumbled something suspiciously watery into his waistcoat. But Mrs. Dumont knew.

When she returned from the kitchen with a bottle and some glasses, they all adjourned to the parlor and toasted each other, introducing Everett to his future brother-in-law and wine at the same time. Then Frauncis remembered his parcels.

"I meant these to be opened tomorrow, but since tonight's so festive—let's have Christmas ahead of time. I was going to give you this one last, with an appropriate speech," he told Eliza softly, handing her a little box, "for it isn't really a Christmas present. Mind, if you take it, you'll have to accept a great deal more— for the rest of your life. Six feet of pure trouble, and a whole new name, my love."

When she got done kissing him, and then with weeping over her beautiful diamond-and-sapphire ring, holding her hand up to show it off, taking it down so she could wipe her eyes—she ran a finger under her nose and sniffed. "My gift will look so paltry by comparison," she sighed.

"Your gift is you, yourself, and so is priceless," he whispered over the sounds of Mrs. Dumont exclaiming happily over the paisley shawl he'd brought, and Everett rejoicing over his metal soldiers.

"And this," Frauncis said more loudly, "is for both of you." The shape of the parcel made Eliza's hands shake as she unwrapped it. "No, I couldn't find the original," he said regretfully, "so I had another made. I hope you like it."

It was an ornate cage made of golden wire, with a golden bird sitting on a perch within it. It was splendid, but very different from the one they'd had. Because although it was gold, it was somehow less gold, and while it was ornate, it was not as amazing in design.

"It's lovely," Eliza said firmly. "We'll start a new tradition. After all, the old cage did bring me great happiness, and I did set it free . . . perhaps that's what Grandmama meant. I can't wait to hear it."

She turned the golden key. The little bird hopped on its perch, and whistled merrily as the gay little tune played. They all sighed when the song ended.

"Oh, it's charming!" Eliza said, "Not 'Papageno's Song', but lovely, even so."

"But our bird didn't sing 'Papageno's Song', dear," Mrs. Dumont said. "It was a Bach cantata, one of my favorites."

Frauncis cocked his head to the side. "But no. I'm quite sure I heard it sing my favorite theme from Handel, I've always enjoyed it."

They looked at each other. They cleared their throats and fidgeted.

"Well," Eliza finally said, "it did bring me happiness whatever it sang. Maybe it will bring it to that lucky couple who bought it. I can't be greedy. I couldn't want more."

Frauncis, Earl of Elliot could. And did. But he could wait. They'd soon be wed. "Happy Christmas," he said, raising his toast, "may all of them forever after bring us happiness and be filled with the music of our laughter, and all our best loved songs."

All the church bells in London seemed to be singing this Christmas morn. It was cold and bright; some snow had fallen in the night, but only enough to give the city a festive air, disguising the smoke-darkened buildings, gilding the bare branches in the park.

The little chambermaid walked slowly. All her worldly possessions were in the carpetbag she dragged at her side. She sniffled from time to time, and more often than that, ran a ragged mitten over her eyes.

When she passed the little shop, she turned up her freckled nose and made a face, and struggled onward. But a tap on the window made her turn. Even through the smudged glass, she saw the figure inside gesturing at her. She sniffed, and moved on.

"Here, girl, you!" the old man shouted, coming out his door, drawing all his shawls around him against the bright chill of the morning. "I thought it was you. Listen, the bird—the one you sold me, in the golden cage? Well, that couple brung it back to me. So. You still got the money? It's yours. There was another buyer interested," he mumbled, "but he didn't leave no name."

But she knew the name. She looked up, and narrowed her eyes. "I got the boot 'cause I couldn't put my hands on the blasted thing when I needed it. So I can't pay you wot I said then. Tell you wot though, I'll give you half that. Half and that's it, mind," she said firmly, 'cause there's no guarantee I'll get my position back no more."

"Done," he said.

She took the cage, and hurried away before he could change his mind. He took the money and locked his shop before she could change hers. Half the money was better than nothing, he thought, and even nothing was better than trouble. The blasted bird had never sung for him again. He was beginning to think he'd never heard it. Moreover, now he discovered Bow Street was looking for the thing. *Bow Street!* The last thing *he* needed, what with all the stolen goods he had, the old man thought as he hid the money in his safe.

*   *   *

Her ex-mistress was out of town, the little maid
thought as she sat on a bench near the park. Not that
she'd give it to *her* anyway. But it was Christmas, so
she couldn't go to the Earl of Elliot today, either. She'd
have to hire a room for the night. But then she'd have a
great deal of money, and maybe she could even get
him to write her a reference so she could find work
again. Oh, it was a sad, cold world for a good girl with
no family or education, only a willing pair of hands
and a strong back.

She turned her attention to the golden cage. It
seemed to her that the little bird's eyes shone with interest and compassion. *Fool*, she told herself, so lonely
that a look from an artificial bird brought her near to
tears. Still, she found the key tied to the bars of the
cage. She took it and wound the thing, knowing it was
futile but half hoping for a song to cheer her cold
morning.

The bird cocked its head toward her. It opened its
beak—and sang. And the music box played on as
though joining in with all the bells of Christmas morning.

"A lovely tune, that," a masculine voice said, next to
her ear.

The maid's head popped up, and she gathered the
cage close. He was a well-built, rough-and-ready-look-
ing young fellow in seaman's clothing. He had a knapsack on his back, and a broad white smile on his ruddy
honest-looking face. But a girl alone had to have a care.

"Aye, a lovely tune," he said, putting down his
knapsack and sitting on the bench beside her.

She moved over, primly, though she liked the look
of him. "It's mine," she said.

"Oh, I don't doubt it. That's not what I was about to
ask next. No, I'm only after wondering why a fine-

looking lass like yerself be sitting by yerself of a Christmas morning?"

"That's my own business, thank you," she said pertly. "I might ask what a young fellow like yourself is doing alone this fine morning."

"Ah, ye might, and I might be glad to tell ye," he sighed, looking at her, "for I just put in to shore, and I'm trying to get meself as far from the sea as I can now, Christmas, or no. For it was a tavern by the sea where the press gang found me five years past, and sent me to sea to serve His Majesty, willy-nilly. I'll not have that again. No, it's off to the countryside for me, lass, back where I belong. Though my heart will be heavy when I get there. For my intended took another while I was away, and now I have an empty heart—as well as an empty cottage—waiting for me at home."

"Indeed," she said, "well, that's a sad story. But I'm a good girl—"

"I never thought else!" he vowed.

She nodded. "Well, but you might wonder, indeed you might and who would blame you? But I'm only alone today 'cause I lost my position as my lady's maid—through no fault of my own."

"I never thought else," he said again, "but it's cold here. Might ye care to come have a dram of something warming with me, lass? Ye can tell me yer story, I'll tell ye mine. I'm a good fellow, though rough about the edges. We'll go somewhere warm and decent, I promise ye. In fact, as it's yer town, ye can pick it!"

"Not much is open, it being Christmas Day, but I think I know of a place . . ." she said, gazing up into his honest blue eyes.

"Done, and done then," he said happily, shouldering his knapsack, picking up her heavy carpetbag with ease. "Here, I'll carry yer load, and ye can pick up that lovely cage. Wouldn't want to forget it, would ye? For

I've never hear a thing prettier. Imagine, wandering by myself in the heart of old London town, lonely as a motherless calf, and what do I hear but 'The Sailor's Hornpipe'? It was like an omen, it was."

"I should think," she said, smiling at his charming lie, for of course she'd ears, hadn't she? "Hornpipe" indeed! It was even the wrong rhythm! The bird sang a slow stately sweet old hymn. But she wasn't going to argue. No, and if things worked out, why she'd never sell off the thing, neither. Not if he liked it.

"An omen and a good one, I hope," she said, "on Christmas Day in the morning."

So it was. And so it wasn't odd, that after they had their dram or five, and talked for hours, and she agreed to go with him to find a preacher so she could travel on with him—legally and forever—that in all the happy confusion they forgot and left the bird on the seat in the tavern.

. . . Where the weary taproom girl found it hours later, when she was cleaning up after fourteen hours of hard work. And after winding it with work-reddened fingers, sat back to listen, enchanted, as it sang the merry rounds of her favorite Christmas carol to her. She thought it the finest Christmas present she'd ever gotten.

And, as it turned out—of course it was.

The Mistletoe Kiss

❊

Elisabeth Fairchild

TOLLING THE DEVIL'S KNELL

Every Christmas Eve in the parish church of Dewsbury Yorkshire, a team of bell ringers toll the tenor bell—once for every year since Christ was born. The final stroke is timed for midnight. Legend has it the practice began in the thirteenth century when a local baron, as penance for killing a servant boy, gave a bell to All Saint's and ordered it rung every Christmas to remind him of his crime. Some of the parishioners believe the ringing of the bell drives the devil away from Dewsbury for the next twelve months.

I

St. Thomas's Day, December 21
Dewsbury, West Yorkshire

Bells were ringing. Of all sounds, it was the toll of bells Constance Conyngham most associated with Christmas. From the tower of All Saint's they rang today, a merry carillon peeling across the fog-bound expanse of Calder Valley, nothing to do with sadness and yet she was saddened, echoes bouncing from the past, echoes bouncing from the foothills of the Pennines. Constance stood at one of the misted windows

of Leland Manor, the better to hear, the better to remind herself these happy bells rang in St. Thomas's
Day, December twenty-first. Nothing more. Five days
until Christmas, the fifth she had spent in Dewsbury.

She took a deep breath, as if in so doing she could
inhale the spirit of the season in the biting, fresh, out-
doorsy smell of the evergreen boughs decorating the
windowsill. The schoolroom smelled today, not of
chalk dust, glue, ink, and book mold, but of fresh cut
greenery, of pungent cloves and the zest of citrus. Lili
was making wardrobe pomanders as gifts for the servants, studding hothouse oranges, lemons, and limes
with whole cloves. The smell overpowered the fainter
perfume with which Cook had lately inundated the
entire house. Five days until Christmas, fewer than a
dozen days until the old year was rung out and a new
one rung in. Seven years since Constance had heard
the bells in Dover clanging, announcing not St.
Thomas's Day, but a ship gone down, no trace of the
crew to be found—her world changed forever. Bitter-
sweet, the bells.

"To the devil, did you say?"

Shocking words to hear fall from Florabelle Leland's
innocent, young mouth.

"Inappropriate language for a young lady, Flora,"
Constance said, standing back from the window,
drawing the drapes over her chilly view, recalled to
her duties as governess. Clarabelle, Florabelle, and
Lilibelle Leland—Mrs. Leland had insisted in the nam-
ing of them, that all of her girl's must-be belles—were
engrossed today in the making of gifts; Christmas gifts
for the servants, Twelfth Day gifts for their parents.
What had any of it to do with the devil?

"Lili said it first." Flo's usually cheerful countenance
was marred by a pout. "You do not mean to let her go.
Do you?"

"Go? Where is it you mean to go, Lili? I was not attending."

Lili looked like a little Christmas angel. The youngest at six, she was all golden hair, bright eyes, and soulful expressions. "I would go 'a gooding,' Mrs. Conyngham. To the Devil's Keep." She nodded decisively as she said it, curls bouncing, her expression serious. "It is my right as a female, is it not? Betsy told me the practice was only open to females. She and Mary mean to go about the entire neighborhood today."

"You spend far too much time fraternizing with the servants, Lilibelle." Clara, a stiff-necked mothering sort of nine-year-old, looked up from the penmanship she was practicing in sending Yuletide greetings to all her relatives. "It does not set the proper tone, does it, Mrs. Conyngham?"

"It is a 'gooding' onion she is after." Flora giggled over the embroidered L she was stitching into a handkerchief for her father. At thirteen, she giggled over most things, especially if it had anything to do with boys. "It is your future husband you wish to dream about tonight, is it not, Lili?"

"It is not!" Lili sat up very straight in her chair and set aside the orange she was studding. "Sleeping on an onion sounds silly and smelly! And I do not spend too much time with the servants. I overheard Betsy asking to have the day free. She says it is not just widows who go 'a gooding' these days, but all the women in the neighborhood."

"But why should you wish to go 'gooding,' my dear?" Constance was surprised. "You want for nothing. It is no more than a sprig of greenery or a piece of fruit you may hope to gather."

Lili was quite serious in her reply. "Father tells me that the women who are blessed with 'gooding' day goodies wish all that is good on the master of the house for the coming year. He will be blessed many times today."

"And what has that to do with the Devil's Keep, of all places you might wish to go?" Clara asked.

"I would hear none of you speak of our neighbor as the devil again, girls. It is vulgar. You will refer to the earl by his proper title."

"But Freddie calls him devil, and within Father's hearing," Flora chortled. "He says Lucian Deleval is just the devil misspelled twice. That the earl is no gentleman at all."

"Neither is Freddie a gentleman if he spreads such malicious gossip," Constance corrected her softly. "Nor is it the least ladylike to find Freddie's rudeness amusing. Now, Lili, please explain, if you will, what possessed you of this notion to go 'gooding' at Deleval Keep?"

Lili plucked at her lip uneasily. "Betsy said she and Mary meant to go everywhere—except the Keep, that no one will walk so far with expectation of little more than a door slammed in their faces. But it occurred to me, Mrs. Conyngham, that surely none needed a 'gooding' day blessing more than a man everyone calls the devil."

"True enough." Flora laughed. "I have heard he has a dreadful temper. That he never comes into the village, never receives visitors."

"They say he is rebuilding the old Keep," Clara said.

Flora nodded. "Has money enough to build an entirely new one from what I have heard, though he spends so little with the local tradesmen they cannot find much good to say of his improvements."

Clara stopped her pen. "I find it odd that an earl should choose to live in that dark, dreary old place when he might take up housekeeping anywhere."

Constance chose not to add her mite to the gossip all of Dewsbury had been abuzz with these many months. Lucian Deleval's temper had been soured by a jilting. Accounts of the scandal had littered the columns of several London newspapers. He had been left standing at the altar, in a church filled to bursting with family and friends, by a young woman of good family whom he had known all of his life. The Honorable Celia Sebastion had shocked all concerned by running away with a dashing young German, a violinist, of all things, a gentleman of limited means and few connections.

Constance considered Lord Deleval a tragic and much misused figure. It did not surprise her that he chose to remove himself from London to the bleakness of a long neglected property outside of Dewsbury. She had, in her own way, done the same thing, in removing herself from Dover.

"If anyone is in need of some goodness it is he. Do you not agree?"

Sweet Lili, to take the 'gooding' day custom so seriously. Constance could not but say yes.

Bells were jingling.

An annoyingly friendly sound, it played hide-and-seek, losing itself now and again in the fog-bound outcroppings that backed the fourteenth-century keep Lucian Deleval had of late begun to think of as home. High in one of the ancient linden trees that lined the avenue leading to the gatehouse, he assumed the noise came from a flock of the sheep he had recently introduced into his valley. The land was good for little other than grazing.

But in peering through the damp, denuded branches, he spotted not sheep, but another, far less welcome source. Swearing, he hacked free a great bunch of the mistletoe that threatened to choke the old tree, and with a cry of "Tallyho!" and a peltering of pearly berries, cast it into the waiting arms of Patrick, the lad who helped him at his task.

"Bloody parasites," Lucian growled, scrambling nimbly down from his perch. "Choke the life right out of a man."

"Tree, don't you mean, sir?" Patrick assumed he meant the mistletoe.

Lucian snorted contemptuously and pointed the curved blade of his knife at the approaching vehicle, a trap, full of females. "I was referring to women, lad." Lucian rubbed sticky hands and damp blade down the canvas apron he wore. "Cannot leave a man alone, you see, when it is separation from their company he wants above all else in the world."

Bells lined the pony's trappings. The lighthearted sound vexed him.

For nine months they had descended on the Keep, the good people of Dewsbury. The vicar, the local gentry, tradesmen, masons and roofers. For nine months all but a few had been turned away. Most assumed he would cordially bid them welcome, dared to think him interested in whatever excuse they might have concocted to come peer at him, at the slow rebuilding of the Keep. They could not fathom why he met their intrusions with impatience, why he had no desire to circulate among their boring company, why he neglected the needs of his soul in never visiting their unremarkable church. They could not understand the contentment he found in solitude.

"They'll be wanting onions, my lord," Patrick predicted.

"Onions?" Lucian repeated. "Why the devil would they be coming to *me* for onions?"

"They've come 'a gooding,' sir. It is the twenty-first." Patrick nodded briskly, as if this baffling pronouncement explained all.

Some foolish local custom, Lucian supposed. Some ancient pagan connection between onions and fertility.

The trap drew nigh, fog eddying about the pony's hocks, whirling through the wheel spokes. The cart bore not women as he had at first supposed, but children, three of them, and none above the age of fifteen. Too young for fertility rites, surely. The only adult held the reins, a young woman plainly dressed, pale complected, dark haired, and even featured. The sturdy serviceability of her attire bespoke the lower orders, and yet the creature fixed dark eyes on him with unflinching directness.

"Sir. We have come to call upon Lord Deleval. Can you tell us where we might find him?"

Ah. So she believed him her peer, clad as he was in rough clothing and canvas apron, his hair wet with mist, dangling in lank disarray about his ears and forehead. Lucian wanted to laugh, to ask if no shred of evidence remained to mark him a gentleman. Instead, he winked at Patrick and played the part expected of him.

"What business have you with the master?" He made no effort to mask his irritation. "He does not take kindly to uninvited visitors."

"Are all Lord Deleval's servants impertinent, sir?" Her voice, gentle as the morning mist, cloaked the sharpness of her set-down.

The youngest of the girls, dimples dancing, piped up. "We have come 'a gooding,' sir." Golden curls spilled from the bonnet she wore. Her eyes sparkled like sapphires. Her cheeks bloomed rosy in the morning chill. Destined to break hearts, this one.

"Come for an onion, have you?"

She laughed as she shook her head. "No, but—"

"And you?" he pointed a grimy finger at the girl beside her.

"Of course not, sir. I have no desire to sleep with an onion." This one had light brown hair, a proud arch to her eyebrows, and a faintly shrewish tone. She was not amused by his ludicrous supposition. A man-managing sort of female he would warrant, given a few more years.

"And you?"

The eldest child—of an age to be both silly girl and blushing coquette—giggled, colored prettily, and dipped her nose into the fur lining of her cloak. "I would not mind a 'gooding' onion, sir," she said, "if it brings me sweet dreams of a happy future."

So it was not fertility rights but divination they engaged in. "And you, marm? Are you desirous of a night with his lordship's onion?" He stepped closer to the trap, not above goading in a wholly inappropriate manner any female who instigated impertinent excursions for impressionable youngsters.

The woman glared at him, affronted, dark eyes flashing, the color of her cheeks heightened. Anger drew her mouth—and it was a pretty mouth—into a formidably straight line.

"Who are you, sir? What do they call you here?" Her breath plumed with the heat of her indignation.

He smiled. "Luce. Among other things."

"Well, Mr. Loose, who I am and what my business, is none of your concern. I shall inquire after your master at the house. It might interest him to hear of your churlish incivility."

With a vigorous slap of the reins she urged the pony onward, bells ringing with a merry sort of anger.

Patrick watched the cart depart with slack-jawed awe.

"Catching flies, boy," Lucian said.

Patrick clapped his teeth together only temporarily. "Told you off, didn't she, my lord? And rightly so, if you was to ask me."

"Whatever possessed you of the notion I should require your opinion, young man?" Lucian inquired dryly.

Patrick grinned. "Because I know who she is, sir, and if you was to know, you would be hying up to the house even now, begging her pardon."

"Who is she, then, scamp, that you think it would induce me to apologize to an unwelcome guest I have no intention of receiving?"

"Governess to Sir Leland's girls, sir. The widow Conyngham. If anyone is due 'gooding' gifts today, it is she."

Constance found Deleval Keep—even freshly reroofed and refurbished—an oppressive place, a looming medieval monstrosity designed to remind all who approached of the power and means of those who dwelt therein. The gatehouse seemed a face set in a squinty scowl so few were its dark, leaded windows. The crenelated roofline and moss-darkened stone seemed as unwelcoming as the rude young man they had met in the lane. She could not dismiss him from her mind, despite his rudeness, perhaps because of it. She was not at all accustomed to such arrogance from an inferior.

"Frightfully gloomy," Clara whispered.

"The perfect setting for a Gothic romance," Flora suggested.

A Friday-faced female answered the booming echo of Constance's assault on the knocker, and informed them curtly the master would have to be fetched. He was not on the premises. It might take some time.

Constance considered leaving, but one look at Lili's

beseeching countenance and she said quietly, "We do not mind waiting."

Through a bare, chilly, echoing passageway across a roughly cobbled courtyard they were led, to the keep's Great Hall. It proved an immense, darkly paneled room dedicated to the display of the family coat of arms and armor of an age long past. The place smelled of stone, leather, polished metal, and burning wood. The only chairs available to them ringed the walls in a less than sociable arrangement, and were of the armless, stiff-backed, uncushioned variety that had cutouts in the backs for the facility of removing jack boots.

Clara pronounced it, "Cold and unfriendly."

Flora nodded, all smiles driven from her usually merry countenance. "No sign of Christmas here. Not a single bough of greenery. It is very bleak."

"Perhaps they follow the old custom of decking the hall on Christmas Eve," Clara suggested doubtfully.

"The man in the drive was cutting mistletoe," Lili said. "They must mean to have a kissing bunch."

Constance held tongue on all opinion of the place or the man in the drive, intent instead on taking advantage of their surroundings. "History hangs before us, girls. Only look at that beautifully carved music screen." An immense paneled partition cut off one end of the room.

But carved oak was small competition for the brooding menace the wicked glitter lining the walls— crossed swords, poleaxes, pikes, halberds, and helmets.

"Imagine how many people have been killed with these things," Flora whispered.

"Unless you long for nightmares, I would prefer you did not," Constance suggested mildly.

"Do you suppose there is still blood on any of them?" Clara wondered.

"I am sure they have all been carefully cleaned. If they were ever used." Too eagerly, Constance thought, her charges studied the deadly collection. Odd, how females, even those well-bred and well-educated, were drawn to darkness, to danger. She had, herself, been drawn to the forbidding countenance of the troubling young man in the lane.

Pointing to a menacing club with a studded ball cosh, Lili asked curiously, "What's that?"

"A mace." Flora identified it without hesitation.

"And that?" An intriguing spiked metal ball chained to the end of another club drew her eye.

"A morning star."

"What does one do with it?"

"Flora." The warning note in Constance's voice diverted the eldest girl's attention, but Clara paid her no mind, explaining with relish, "It is for the bashing of heads."

"No!" Lili gasped.

"That is quite enough detail, Clara."

Lili frowned and turned to ask, "Head bashing? Really?"

Constance nodded gravely. "A pity, is it not, that man has come up with so many ingenious devices for killing his fellow man? As if life were not already fraught with enough peril, anger, and violence." Taking Lili by the hand she led her across the room. "Far more interesting than the weapons, my dear, is the room itself. Only look at that huge old fireplace. Imagine the size of the Yule logs it has cradled. Think of this room as it must have once been, a crowd of people all dressed in their most festive woolens and velvets. The walls covered in bright tapestries."

"The ladies had long pointy laps on their sleeves

then"—Clara attempted to restore herself to her governess' good graces—"and the gentlemen wore poofy breeches and—"

"Codpieces," Flora blurted.

"Flora, really!" Clara protested, the scolded ready to scold.

"What's a codpiece?" Lili asked.

"An article of clothing gentlemen no longer wear," Constance said and smoothly went on to mention "windows and doors hung with holly and ivy, the floor covered in sweet-smelling rushes, a table as long as the room groaning with a Christmas feast, and behind the richly carved music screen, musicians. Can you tell me what instruments might have been played?"

"Clavichord," Clara said.

"The lute, the lute," Lili crowed.

"A virginal." Flora giggled.

Constance wanted to laugh but refrained. "Yes. Imagine so many strange sounds filling the hall to the rafters with old Yuletide ballads."

"You make it seem merry, Mrs. Conyngham." Flo's eyes had gone dreamy.

"And so it once was." A deep voice from the far side of the screen made them all jump. Flora let fly a little squeak.

One of two doors that led into the choir swung wide. Through it stepped a gentleman vaguely familiar. The man from the lane, freshly shaven, his unkempt locks neatly combed and pomaded, his rough clothing replaced by the finest lawn, nankeen, and superfine. Only his eyes were the same—jade green, openly mocking and faintly irritated.

"Mr. Loose?" Constance asked uneasily, and then closed her eyes briefly as truth dawned. "Or it is Luce, short for Lucian and you are Lord Deleval after all?"

"At your service, ladies." He executed a bow. "I am afraid you have the better of me."

Collecting herself in the rote of formalities, Constance introduced the girls. Each curtsied prettily in her turn. A cool dip of the head and Constance enunciated her role as governess and uttered her own name. Mrs. Conyngham. Inappropriate, the title seemed. Married for less than three months, a widow seven years, she always thought of Daniel's mother when the name was uttered, even by her own mouth. Its awkwardness on her tongue seemed emphasized by her errand here today. "My lord," she concluded. "Forgive me."

"Whatever for, Mrs. Conyngham?"

"For addressing you as I did in the lane. It was very rude of me."

"As was I." His gaze, keenly penetrating, focused with implacable intensity on Constance as he drew from his pocket first an onion, and then a small drawstring bag. "I understand you have come 'a gooding'?"

As he held out the bag to her, it jingled.

The sound struck Constance like a slap in the face. He meant to give her money!

When Constance made no effort either to take his gift, or to fill a growing silence, Clara said primly, "We come, sir, at our sister's request."

He frowned, turned to regard Clara with cocked head, and assuming incorrectly that she meant Florabelle, fixed her with the strength of his gaze and held out the onion.

Flora blushed crimson under such scrutiny, awkwardly accepted the onion offering, and nervously bleated, "Not me, my lord. It is Lili insisted we come."

The line between his brows deepened. Pocketing the coin pouch, he bent, the better to peer at Lili, who ducked her head and nodded as he chucked her under the chin. "You, little one? But you refused all offer of onions in the lane. What is it you would have of me?"

"I have come to bless you and your household, sir." Lili uncertainly addressed her well-shod toes.

The earl frowned and turned to gaze at Constance, as if for explanation.

"Lili believed that you required a 'gooding,' sir, and the blessings of goodness that go with it," Constance said quietly.

She did not think highly of him, this dark-eyed governess, this well-deserving widow, Mrs. Conyngham. He could tell she did not. He had offended her with the very bag of silver with which he had thought to send her merrily on her way. A cold, tight-mouthed contempt had met him in her regard when he had drawn the money from his pocket. It was not an expression ingrained in her. The frost melted when she regarded any one of her charges. But then, he had the habit of bringing out the worst in women.

He eyed the fairy-bright little girl they called Lili. Here was a flower he would not bruise. "What goodie would you have from me, Miss Lilibelle Leland, in return for your blessing of goodness? A sugarplum, perhaps? Or a pear? Or is it after all a 'gooding' onion you desire, and dreams of future husbands?"

She considered the question with solemn dignity. "I should like some of your mistletoe, have you any to spare. We have yet to fashion our kissing bunch."

"Do you long, then, for kisses rather than husbands, young lady?"

"Does not everyone?" Lili seemed surprised he should ask.

Lucian laughed. For a moment his amused gaze locked with the widow Conyngham's. She was not amused, nor was she any longer coldly contemptuous in her regard. There was, instead, a hint of concern, could it be pity in her gaze? It left him irritable rather than amused that he should seem pitiable to a governess. "You may take it all, if you like. I've no need of it."

"You do not care for kisses, my lord?" Lili's amazement reached new heights.

"Lilibelle!" Both of the elder girls sang out in unison, turning on their younger sister with dismay.

"That is a very personal question, Lili," the widow reprimanded softly, very suitable in her role. "You must not expect an answer."

Lucian did not care for the question, but the innocent naïveté of the girl's disappointment touched him, as did her interest in a matter no one else dared question. "I did once enjoy kisses." He forced a lightness he in no way felt. "Too much, perhaps."

"No more?" Little Lili seemed much struck by the idea.

"Very rarely." In so saying he caught sight of the widow Conyngham's expression and lost all sense of what to say next. For a fleeting moment, she regarded him with warmth, a brief beautiful softening of features he had once judged hard and unyielding. It was an expression he could define as nothing less than affection, and something more akin to love.

Whatever the emotion, it had more to do with Lilibelle than him. And yet so long had it been since any female glanced at him with anything other than contempt, pity, or disregard that she dazzled him for an instant, and stole every word from his mouth.

Lili saved him, bringing him back to the moment. "You must not give all of your mistletoe away, my lord," she insisted. "There is no telling when you might change your mind about kisses."

He nodded, summoned his housekeeper, and when

the woman arrived, instructed her, "Have Patrick place such mistletoe as we shall not require, in the trap that waits at the door."

"Not require, my lord?" Like a breathless fish, she blinked and gawked before dipping into an obedient bob and hastening away to do his bidding.

In wishing his guests good day—the girls laughing, up to their knees in the surfeit of mistletoe with which the trap had been filled to overflowing—Lucian found himself once again disconcerted by evidence of approval in the widow Conyngham's gaze.

"You are generous, sir." She said it wryly as he helped her into the trap and handed over the pony's reins. "May our blessings, on you and your household, be equally generous."

Laughing, Flora held up the onion he had blessed her with, saying, "And may all your dreams be sweet."

Clara, the serious one, could not refrain from a hint of reproof as she maneuvered her way through the excess of greenery. "As you have overwhelmed us, sir, with mistletoe, may you be equally overwhelmed with blessings."

"And kisses." Lili leaned over the edge of the cart to kiss him, butterfly soft, on the cheek.

The unexpected contact alarmed him. As if burned, he drew back.

Clara yanked her sister's arm. "Lili!" she hissed. "Young ladies do not throw themselves at gentlemen. It is very common behavior."

Round-eyed with disappointment, Lili ignored her. "You really don't like kisses, do you?" Her voice was very small. "I thought you were only funning."

He laughed awkwardly and tried to explain to one too young to comprehend. "You startled me."

Mrs. Conyngham watched him, an unexpected level

of understanding in her gaze, a trace of melancholy dousing the shine of her eyes. "Do you mean to join everyone else in Dewsbury, sir, in listening to the handbell concert at All Saint's on Christmas Day?"

Convinced she asked for no more reason than to change the subject, that her charge might no longer plague him with the question of kisses—an appropriate ploy for a governess—he asked with equally detached interest, "You will be there?"

"We are obliged to attend," Clara said stiffly.

"We are ringers," Flora explained.

The widow nodded. "Yes, and nothing would please us more than to see you in the audience."

Her invitation sounded genuine, warmer than he might have expected. And yet, she spoke without hint of coyness or flirtation, as became her station.

"Do come," Flora coaxed.

Lilibelle popped up from her seat, mistletoe clutched gleefully in both hands, his slight of her freely offered kiss forgiven. "Oh yes," she said. "Do. The music will be splendid! We have practiced and practiced. Tonight we practice again."

"I do not much care for music," Lucian said gruffly, his mind on a certain violinist.

"Not care for music?" Lili dropped the mistletoe, leaned over the bench on which her governess perched, and taking his hand in hers, patted it in a soothing manner. "Poor Lord Deleval," she said. "No music. No kisses. No mistletoe. What do you do to make Christmas merry, sir?"

"Lili!" Again her sisters cried out their mortification in unison, yanking her back into place in the trap.

"We will trouble you no more, sir," the widow Conyngham said, appropriately polite. "Thank you very much for humoring Lili's notion to partake in 'gooding' blessings."

He heard her only peripherally. The child's simple question still rang in his mind. What *did* he do to make Christmas merry? What event had so captured his attention, so cheered him of late as the unexpected blessings from this cartload of females? Impulsively, Lucian leapt onto the step that led to the driver's bench in the trap, and leaning in a wholly inappropriate manner over Mrs. Conyngham's shoulder—so close he could hear the sharp intake of her breath, so close he could smell the rosewater cologne she favored, so close the bone of her shoulder pressed for a moment against his chest—he gave the worried six-year-old a smacking kiss on the cheek.

"Oh my!" Lilibelle gasped, flushing completely crimson.

He jumped down from the trap, his heart racing in a manner he had almost forgotten, his gaze flickering from Lilibelle's flushed face to her equally rosy governess. "Good day to you, ladies," he said gruffly, and strode away, an inexplicable emptiness troubling him at the sound of bells again, as the trap was set in motion.

II

December 23

The ringing of the handbells broke off in the middle of a halting rendition of "Greensleeves" when Aubrey Trent strode down the middle aisle of the chapel, his broad, freckled face a picture of concern.

Mrs. White muted her bells and gave Constance a nudge. "Will's had some trouble. I told Freddie it was not like him to miss a practice. Not this close to a performance."

Freddie was frowning. Whatever Aubrey had to say, it was not good news.

"Jesus, Joseph, and Mary! Only look." Mrs. White was nudging again, eyes agleam. "There, in the shadows at the back. The devil himself has come to chapel."

Constance did not need to be told. She was all too aware of the earl's presence. Every evening since first they had met him on St. Thomas's Day—since the night her pillow had enveloped the "gooding" onion, Flora had planted there on a lark—Lucian Deleval had haunted the darker corners and passageways of the chapel as much as he had haunted her dreams.

Unobtrusively he watched and listened as the bell ringers practiced. Each night, wraithlike, he slipped out before they were finished, galloping away on the big black horse he favored, without a word to anyone. And yet there had been an exchange of sorts, a communication unlike any Constance had shared before, for every evening Lucian Deleval positioned himself in such a way that he might stare at her from the shadows. The intensity of his regard as she practiced was such that Constance grew uneasy in his visitations, occasionally awkward with the bells, as uncomfortable as if he stretched across the space that separated them and touched her.

"Bad news." Freddie's voice was too loud, too coarse, for the peaceful beauty of the chapel. "Will's fallen from his horse and broken his arm."

"Good Lord!"

"Is he in a bad way?"

"Poor man."

Aubrey nodded his head with a suitably dour expression and assured them: "Stout lad. He'll soon mend. It is kicking himself he is, about letting you lot down."

"Good God," Freddie blurted. "We shall require a replacement. Any ideas? How about you, Aubrey? Care to step in?"

Eyes wide, Aubrey shook his head, clutched his hat uneasily, and backed his way up the aisle. "Not me, lad." He sounded panicked. "No sense of rhythm, don't you know."

"Not just one replacement, Freddie. Two." Mrs. White spoke up as Aubrey made a break for the door. "Will's a four-in-hand beller, my dear. We shall require two people, if they are unskilled, and while my Susan might be able to handle a simple bit, we shall need at least one person with greater ability than hers."

Two new recruits to fit into a performance that must be perfected in two days' time! A troubled silence fell.

Into which rang the voice of Lucian Deleval. Stepping from the shadows he asked, "May I render any assistance?"

"I do not think you can, my lord, unless you are acquainted with someone who plays the bells."

Freddie's response was so abrupt, stiff-backed, and ungracious that Deleval was left open-mouthed.

"Ah. Perhaps not then," Deleval agreed mildly. Inclining his head in the slightest of bows, he turned on his polished heel, black cloak whirling, and made for the door.

"You would turn away our first volunteer?" Constance was amazed, both by Freddie's dismissive attitude and by her own swift leap to defend a gentleman she barely knew.

"Shall I fetch him back again?" Lili, skirts flying, was already halfway up the aisle.

"Yes." Constance shooed her after him before fixing her attention on Fredrick Tomes's belligerent scowl.

The balding tailor muttered, "Volunteer or no, Constance, I cannot abide the fellow."

"Has he done you some injury, Freddie?" she asked.

His complexion blotchy with sudden color, Fredrick grabbed her by the elbow and dragged her out of hearing of the others. Lips thinned, his breath raspy with suppressed anger, he blurted, "Rude to me, he was, when I took samples of my work, and some fabrics I thought he might be interested in, all the way out to that bloody castle he is rebuilding." He spat the memory at her.

She backed away from his vitriol and smoothed the sleeve by which he had grabbed her. "Everyone is rude on occasion, Freddie."

"He is rude to everyone, all of the time," someone muttered, and in so doing released a spate of similar epitaphs from the others.

"Requires nothing of the local townspeople."

"Nothing at all."

"Prefers to spend his sovereigns elsewhere, he does."

Freddie nodded. "More reason than ever I would prefer not to rely on any assistance Mr. Nose-in-the-Air has to offer. Insulted me, he did. Not at all to his taste, he said, of my finest worsted. Rely on my London tailor, he said. Trusts no one else with the cut of his clothes."

"And you do not think him capable of changing his mind?" She turned to face each of the ringers, one by one. "Is it not worth your while to give him a second chance? Show a little Christmas charity until our Christmas bells have rung? Come now. We need him if he is truly willing and able."

Freddie crossed narrow arms across his narrow chest. "Oh, all right, Constance. But do not expect me to be anything more than polite to him. I can only hope he is tone-deaf. I shall send him away then, with clear conscience and no objection from anyone."

Lord Deleval did not return with Lili, despite a great deal of pleading, which Lili breathlessly recounted in detail before she bothered to inform Constance. "He waits without. Asked me to send you for a word with him, if you would be so kind."

Constance frowned, alarmed that she should be singled out.

"You know him then?" Freddie asked in amazement, as if she had in some way betrayed him, an emotion that seemed to be mirrored in the faces of every one of the bell ringers.

"We have spoken. Once," she said. The words emerged far too defensively. "I know him no better than any of you. Would it not be best if you went, Freddie? As leader of the bell ringers."

"Me? When he has asked for you specifically and you have set yourself up in the role of his defender?" Freddie puffed out his chest like an underfed gaming cock and shook his head. "No. I will not grovel to the man, no matter what his title and position. You must coax him, Constance, if he is to be coaxed."

She squared her shoulders with a sigh. "Give me a minute, then."

"Take two or three, my dear." Mrs. White chuckled. "I have never known a man, much less an earl, to change his mind in less."

"If he is a man at all," someone muttered wryly, drawing laughter from the others.

She did not mean to come, he decided. Chilled, sitting horseback in the dark, he recalled the last time he had waited for a woman, tense with anticipation, with hope, with expectations never realized. He hated waiting. Turning Styx with the mildest pressure of his knee he might have ridden away had she not called out.

"Wait."

Her voice, he recognized it instantly, echoed from the blackness of the stone archway behind him. She stepped from the darkness, cloak billowing, hair teased by the wind, her appearance pleasing him all out of proportion. So dark were her eyes in the meager light they seemed fathomless. "You wished to speak to me?"

"Yes." He leaned down to ask in a confidential tone, "Did you change his mind?"

"Freddie?" She laughed. "He changed his own mind."

"Not without some coaxing I'll be bound."

Her cheeks reddened, but whether it was embarrassment or the cold he could not be certain.

"Will you come back in? I am cold." She drew her cloak close and pulled the hood over her head.

"Come and stand by the horse. He is warm."

Her hair spilling like ink from beneath the hood, she obeyed him, leaning into the animal's withers, no more than inches between the curve of her breast and the bend of his knee, her cloak flapping briskly against his leg, as if to scold him for his rudeness in enticing her into the wind.

"Well, my lord, do you mean to help us or not?"

He had forgotten how completely uncowed she was in speaking to him, how direct despite gloved tones.

"I am a proud man, Mrs. Conyngham."

"I had noticed." She reached up to stroke the horse's neck. Styx shifted his weight, forcing her to move. She bumped Lucian's knee, stepped quickly back so that their bodies no longer made contact, and ducked her head in embarrassment, murmuring, "I beg your pardon, sir."

"No harm done," he said. Indeed he rather liked it that she stood so close. "I would not make a complete fool of myself," he admitted.

Her head came up quickly, her eyes shining like obsidian beneath the shadowed lip of the hood. She was beautiful in the mist and moonlight, this outspoken governess.

"A fool?" she repeated. "In what way?"

"Is this bell-ringing business difficult?"

She laughed, as if his question surprised her. "The bells? Not terribly difficult, no."

"Will you teach me?"

She stepped back to wave in the direction of the chapel. "That is what we mean to do."

"No. It is what *you* mean to do. I realize I shall find little support from the rest of them."

"Why do you think that is?" Hers was the most gentle and coaxing of voices he had ever heard. He felt he could safely answer any question it posed, had felt it from the first moment she had addressed him in the avenue leading to the Keep.

"I have given them no reason to offer me their support."

She said nothing.

He laughed. "You do not deny it."

"No. You do not ingratiate yourself with the locals, do you?"

"I have never seen reason to, until now."

"And what has changed?" A gust of wind threw the hood away from her head. Styx cavorted, unnerved by the sudden movement.

"I have," Lucian said evenly, calming the horse with a touch.

"I know," she whispered.

"What do you know?"

"You are reawakening, my lord, after a long sleep."

That she should understand so perfectly surprised him. His shock telegraphed itself to the horse, who

backed away from her uneasily, head tossing, long
black mane stinging his cheeks.

The wind whipped the words from his mouth, but
he had to ask her, "How long did you sleep after the
death of your husband?"

"Too long," she said, lifting the hood again, en-
veloping the darkness of her hair in more darkness. "I
still require, now and again, a soporific for the pain."

He longed to stroke a windblown strand from her
cheek, to straighten the peak of her hood, to offer himself as soporific. Instead he asked, "Will you teach me,
Constance?"

Her chin rose abruptly. He could see her lips in the
moonlight, just her lips, slightly parted, more than a
little vulnerable. "Teach you, my lord?" The lower lip
trembled. As if unnerved by his request, she stepped
away from the horse.

He gave Styx the slightest nudge. The horse followed as she backed away. "Tonight. After the others
have gone. Teach me. I ask no more than an hour of
you, perhaps two? I will pay you well for such a kindness. You have but to name the price."

She threw back her head to stare at him, her eyes
glittering with a passion he could not name. "Carte
blanche, is it? Have you no fear I should charge you
dear?"

"I trust you will take advantage of me no more than
I take advantage of you."

She shook her head, her expression wooden. "You
overestimate the limitations of my kindness, sir. I cannot oblige you. It would not be proper. I must take the
children home."

"And if I see to getting them safely home, and
arrange that your sense of propriety should not be
questioned?"

Her laugh sounded a brittle thing in the cold. "How is that to be arranged?"

He shrugged. "Shall we bring in the vicar?"

"The vicar?" She blinked at him, as if he suggested something quite outrageous.

"You do not think I can convince him to indulge me?"

"I should be amazed indeed, if you could."

"Surely he will understand that I've no great desire to hold up the practice sessions with foolish questions and stupid mistakes."

She wore a stunned look. A silence stretched uneasily between them before she blurted, "Is it the bells you mean?"

"But of course. What else?"

He thought she flushed. Certainly she ducked her head, so that all expression was hid from him beneath the dark shadow of her hood. His mind ranged over every word he had said to her, searching out reason for her reaction.

She was embarrassed. He could hear it as she choked in saying, "The vicar is a very good idea."

"You will do it, then?"

"I will," she agreed, and clutching her cloak ran for the chapel door, her hem flaring out behind her like the dark flame of anticipation she had, unknowing, lit within him.

The music must be the focus of all conversation, she decided. There was no danger in the music, nothing to trip her up, nothing to betray the foolish, fluttery state of her nerves, the uneasy quickening of her heartbeat as she waited in an expectant stillness that had so recently been full and friendly with noise and people. She picked up one of the bells. It betrayed her shaking hand, an echoing musical tremor that made her won-

der what moonlight madness had beset her. Why had
she agreed to spend an evening alone with the devil?
He was a devil, a handsome, unnerving devil with
knowing green eyes that peered into the deepest,
darkest, most vulnerable places in her soul and saw no
more than a governess whose talents he might hire for
the evening.

All was as Deleval had promised. A groom had
been waiting with the carriage to take the girls safely
home to Leland Manor. Deleval himself, the groom
said, had spoken with the master. Such a pity about
poor Will. Mrs. Leland would send over some calf's-
foot jelly in the morning. A light would be left burning
for her return this evening. What a blessing his lordship meant to step in. The girls were so looking forward to their musical performance.

She muted the bell against her shoulder. Her pulse,
heartbeat, and breathing were as uneven as her grip.
Foolish that she should feel drawn to a gentleman so
far above her touch as to be unreachable. Laughable
that she deigned to think he propositioned her for
lessons in something more scandalous than bell ringing. Silly she should feel threatened in the chapel. She
started like a frightened kitten when wind whistled
through the stained-glass windows of the nave, when
footsteps echoed on stone and she was confronted not
by a cloud of brimstone and Lucian Deleval with
horns and forked tail, but by the appearance of the
vicar, who peered at her over the rim of his spectacles.

"The earl has explained the whole to me. I am
pleased Constance, that you would extend such charity as would allow him to join in our Christmas service."

But was it kindness that goaded her to agree? Constance pondered her own motivation. She had plenty
of time in which to judge it. The earl kept her waiting

while the vicar lit candles and arranged his paperwork and became engrossed in his reading, while she arranged a grouping of bells, searched out a pair of practice gloves that might fit the earl, and selected music. It had just crossed Constance's mind that she had some sense of the anxious anticipation Deleval himself must have suffered in waiting for a bride who never arrived, when movement caught her eye, and his silhouette filled the archway at the back of the church.

She watched him as he came down the aisle, could not take her eyes off him. He was tall and lithe, his movements graceful, his face strangely leonine in the candlelight, imbued with the confidence most gentlemen blessed since birth with power and means possessed. He raked windblown locks from his eyes, swept his cape from his shoulders, tossed it nonchalantly into one of the pews as he approached, and excused his tardiness by alluding to the business of temporary stabling for his horse.

Everything about him moved and swirled and eddied. All but his eyes. They were hard and bright and steady. The glittering green of them pinned her from the minute he walked in. They strayed not at all until he stood before her, and then only to glance at the bells.

"Where shall we begin?" he asked, her odd pupil.

"Gloves," she said, surprised she could speak, surprised he removed the beautiful buff leather in which his fingers were already encased and donned the smudged white practice gloves without demur.

"Avoid touching the metal," she instructed. "It takes away the shine."

"Heaven forbid, I should take away the shine on the metal of anything with careless touching," he said with a wry smile and a look so penetrating, she knew he meant to tease her.

"You should be familiar with the anatomy of the bell." She rattled away like an empty kettle on the boil, her tongue seeking safety in the familiar. "This is the crown. This the handguard. Here the shoulder, waist, hip, lip, and clapper."

"Provocative these bells," he said softly, his eyes sparkling with mischief. "But you move too fast for me, Mrs. Conyngham."

"Too fast, sir?"

"Yes. Already we discuss intimate body parts and you have yet to name your price for this evening's anatomy lesson."

Flustered, Constance turned her back on him to hide a smile. She ought not to be amused by his suggestiveness, and yet she was. She did, in fact, feel terribly staid, almost prudish, not at all clever, in responding, "Two things, I would ask, in return for my services."

"Ask away."

"First, in exchange for each different thing you learn about the bells, I require an act of kindness."

"A what?"

The vicar, who sat reading, just out of earshot, looked up inquisitively.

She cleared her throat. "Acts of kindness, my lord. Surely they require no explanation."

"No. Of course not." He frowned. "Do you consider me an unkind man, Mrs. Conyngham?"

She felt rash in her demand—rash, impertinent, and completely out of the bounds of her position. She tried to oil the waters she had stirred. "To the contrary. You have exhibited great kindness and condescension to me and my charges."

"Condescending and unkind? You think very little of me indeed."

Flustered, tongue tripping, she did her best to recover. "I do not think you are inherently unkind at all, my lord. It has been my observation, however, that a gentleman in your position does on occasion cultivate a certain dismissive brusqueness that convinces others you dislike them."

"You are very direct for a governess, Mrs. Conyngham."

"Am I?"

She felt the fool and was sure she offended him though he responded with no more show of emotion than a mild sarcasm.

"Of these 'others' who are convinced I hold them in disfavor—is the tailor who leads your little band of bell ringers, one of them?"

"It is not my place—"

"No. Of course not." He waved a hand dismissively. "Let me put it another way. Would you have me suffer ill-cut patterns, binding seams, and the most provincial of fabrics in throwing him the bone of some business?"

"It would be a kindness."

"Is it a kindness to appear in public ill-clad?"

She lost patience with him. "Is there nothing he can sew to your satisfaction? No single, simple article of clothing? Neck cloths, perhaps, or nightcaps?"

He frowned. "Nightcaps? Do you envision me, then, Mrs. Conyngham, as the sort of fellow who wears nightcaps to bed?"

Embarrassed, she shook her head, cast a desperate look the vicar's way, but the vicar, blinking owlishly, and too distant to overhear the earl's suggestive remark, looked far more prepared for forty winks than any intervention on her behalf. "I do not envision, no . . . but, that is beside the point. You mean to unnerve me with such leading remarks, do you not, my lord?"

He laughed softly. Nodded. "And that is not a kindness, is it?"

"No."

"What else, then? Who else deserves these acts of kindness you insist upon?"

"Any number of people, in any number of ways. I rely on your own creative sense of observation to fulfill that part of our bargain."

"Do you mean to keep a running tally on these kindnesses?"

"No. I rely on your honor, as a gentleman, to satisfy our terms."

"Do you? I am pleasantly surprised. I had begun to think you found nothing honorable or gentlemanly in me. And the other half of your demand? I shudder to think what next you will ask of me."

"Four shillings and sixpence."

He blinked at her, his expression one of incredulity. "Money? Is that all?" Wind rattled the windows again.

She, who had never had the means to disdain money so cavalierly, nodded and said, "Not a penny less."

With a thoughtful expression he fished in the pocket of his waistcoat for the coins and handed them over to her. "You drive a hard bargain, Mrs. Conyngham, when it was a favor I meant to offer in the first place."

"We are in agreement, then, sir?"

"We are," he said.

And so, they spent the evening in some contentment together, while she instructed him in the downstroke and backstroke, taught him how to dampen the sound of the bells and the best way to ring them full voice and tiny tone, tremulando and trill. He practiced handling the bells, first one, then two, struggling with three, and sending her at last into a bout of laughter in failing miserably an attempt to master the four-in-hand presentation that seemed, he said, "child's play" when she held the bells.

Lucian enjoyed their private lesson, enjoyed every opportunity the passing moments offered of examining closely the young widow he had for several days eyed from afar—the widow who had mourned the loss of her beloved for seven years without faltering. Her loyalty drew him, the possibility of love, steadfast and true, that she embodied. More than the beauty of her eyes, or the glossy promise of her neatly coiled hair, more than the fullness of her lips, or the sweet swell of her hips, it was the character of this sober young woman that bewitched him.

Three hours had flown and the vicar long since begun to snore from his position in the pews, before she packed away the bells saying, "You must wake the vicar and see me home. The hour grows very late."

"Of course," he agreed. "Shall I ask for use of the vicar's gig? Or would you count it a kindness if I refrained from further disturbing his rest by offering you my horse?"

He almost laughed to watch the progression of emotion that possessed her features before she said uncertainly, "You must decide, sir."

He sent the vicar off to bed, choosing to seat her on Styx while he walked beside them. She was not missish about the absence of a sidesaddle, straddling the horse with as much grace as was possible draped in a dress. She arranged her cloak demurely about her legs. Both he and the animal approved, not only for the practical reason that she was far less likely to be thrown, but because he was afforded an attractive view of eyelet-edged petticoat floating above practical lace-up boots. His shoulder bumped the bend of the widow's knee now and again, but not so often that she complained.

She remarked on his rapid improvement in mastering the bells, commented on the beauty of his horse, on the velvet darkness of the sky and the crisp bite of the wind. He thanked her for her time, for the informative evening, for her forbearance in straddling Styx.

They ran out of polite conversation.

Alone in the quiet, dark, empty chill of the night, the road stretched before them. A blank void, it waited, like the silence, fraught with possibilities that Lucian Deleval had not allowed himself to consider since Celia Sebastion had left him standing in the uneasy silence of a chapel full of his peers.

He shivered, not with cold, but with the pain, anger, and humiliation the past could still provoke in him. He frowned into the darkness and asked Mrs. Conyngham why she had first become a bell ringer.

Her answer was slow in coming, but at last her voice floated softly in the wind. "I had to ring the bells or forever let them leave me weeping."

"Weeping?" he repeated stupidly.

"Four fours," she whispered, and immediately he understood. She referred to the tolling of the bells to announce her husband's demise.

She laughed softly, an uneasy sound. "I could not go about shuddering at the sound of all bells."

Styx whickered, as if moved by the woman's gentle courage.

"A kind man, was he?" Lucian dared ask.

"Daniel?" She pronounced the name fondly. "There was no kinder. He did not deserve to die."

The horse clopped along in silence for a time, the two of them lost in separate thoughts.

"Are you cold, my lord?" she asked at last.

He was, at that moment ice to the bone, frozen to the core of all emotion by the unexpected pain of realizing that Celia had not been kind. Not at all kind, and yet it was not a characteristic he had ever bothered to consider when he had chosen her as his wife. He took a deep breath, the cold knifing at his lungs, and admitted gravely, "I am chilled. Forgive me. It was thoughtless of me not to have asked for the gig. Are you freezing?"

"The wind cuts right through me." Her chattering teeth bore out the truth of it. "Will the horse hold the weight of two, sir?"

That she should suggest such a thing took his breath away. What manner of kindness was this? He had placed her on a pedestal, this widow of spotless reputation, "gooding"-day impulse and legal tender in kindnesses. Could it be that given a few hours attention she was no less eager than Celia had been to throw herself at a virtual stranger? Disappointment sat heavy in his gut. He had believed this woman a cure for what ailed him. He had dared to think her pure enough, loyal enough to the memory of her husband, to dissolve in him his disgust of the frailties of the weaker sex. Fool that he was.

"Indeed, he is prodigious strong." Cynically, an acid taste in his mouth, he clapped Styx on the neck.

"Ho, there." She drew in the reins, removed her boot from the stirrup, and slid forward on the saddle.

The governess had yet a thing or two to teach him, it would seem. Lucian took a bitter pleasure in swinging up behind her, his thighs enwrapping her hips as warmly as he swathed the two of them in the expansive circle of his cloak. Pressing his chest to the curve of her back, he snaked his arms about her waist. He could take pleasure, even in his disappointment.

She did not pull away, indeed seemed as happy as

he in their combined heat. He believed himself in a position to take further advantage of the situation, and would have done just that, had not her shoulders begun to shake.

At first he thought she laughed, nervous of their sudden physical contact. He leaned into the uneven sway of her back, pressed his cheek to hers, and was stopped from whispering something suggestive only by the unexpected sensation of warmth and wetness. Tears! He jerked away in alarm, all libidinous thoughts driven from his brain.

"You are crying," he accused her.

She nodded, sniffed. The sniff became a sob.

"Shall I get down? Have I offended you?" He distanced himself from her—started to put action to words—but she reached back to stay him, shook her head with some violence, and managed to utter a rather sodden, "No! Please."

"What is the matter? Are you all right?" He thrust his handkerchief at her.

The sniffing sounds decreased. She dabbed her cheeks, blew her nose, and straightened her back. "Forgive me." She sounded more than a little embarrassed. "I never expected . . . It is very foolish of me, but—"

"But what?"

"Silly." She exhaled heavily, dabbed at her eyes again, took a deep breath, and blurted, "I am so sorry. It has been seven years, you see."

"Seven years?"

"Yes. I . . . I had forgotten . . . how it felt."

"Felt?"

Her voice faded. "To be—to be held."

Such wistful words. They caught him off guard, pricked the balloon of his anger in an instant, left him deflated, humiliated, and foolishly in envy of a dead man.

III

December 24
Christmas Eve—10:00

The tenor bell at All Saint's began to toll promptly at ten. The steady ringing added to the festive spirit of celebration at Leland Manor, where the Yule log had just been dragged in and lit with great fanfare by the younger, more spritely members of the gathering of gentry who had stuffed themselves on a sumptuous banquet of roasted goose with chestnut stuffing, a rare joint of roast beef, hare pie, a half-dozen side dishes, and a thick plum pudding the size of a coach wheel that Mrs. Leland herself had poked little silver charms into. Glasses were raised, to toast Leland over the best Madeira his cellar had to offer, and Florabelle, who was to be allowed the special privilege of staying up late this evening, was asked by her proud mother to entertain them with her skill on the pianaforte.

"Time for bed," Constance chided Clara, who had the vacuous, heavy-lidded look of a child kept too long from slumber. Signaling to Lili with a gesture toward the ceiling, Constance encouraged Clara to wish her parents good night and moved through the crowded drawing room, toward the door that would most swiftly lead them upstairs.

Lili was busy talking to the one guest who had surprised all concerned by making an appearance. That Lord Deleval chose to honor the Lelands with his presence after snubbing every other invitation he had to date received from those who counted in Dewsbury's very limited society, pleased his host and hostess no end. That he took such an interest in their daughters could not but make them even happier. It was only Constance who was not pleased to see the earl, even less pleased that he should accompany Lili toward the door. His attentiveness did not fit in well with the plan she had in mind—to slip quietly up the stairs and away from this most prestigious of guests, away from the sharp-edged ache she experienced beneath her ribs every time she set eyes on the man.

It was an ache that had begun last night when Lucian Deleval had kindly, with gentlemanly restraint and a flattering level of respect and understanding, warmed her in the circle of his arms as if it were the most natural of positions for an earl and a governess, virtual strangers to one another, to assume. The ache had grown more painful with their every encounter, in practicing the handbells together this afternoon, in circulating among the guests before dinner.

He still stared at her too much. He stared at her now, as he approached, a shift in his gaze reminding Constance of the mistletoe she had so carefully avoided all evening. The stuff dangled everywhere. A great deal of lighthearted cheek smacking had been the result. But apart from kisses from each of her charges, Constance had skirted the kissing bunches with which the girls had gleefully strung every doorway, chandelier, and window bay as well as halls, walls, and stairwell.

Sidestepping the danger in the doorway, Constance met Lord Deleval with the cool confidence that came in knowing that her part of the evening was almost done and she had not succumbed to her own irrational desire to be kissed by this gentleman. His kisses, on any occasion, seemed an incomprehensible indulgence of "gooding" onion daydreams. Today, of all days, they would be indulged, even condoned, if issued within proximity of a permissive bit of greenery and wax-white berries.

He was the first to speak. As he should be.

"Lili has promised to go obediently up the stairs and straight to bed, if allowed but five minutes in the garden, listening to Black Tom chase away the devil for another year," he said.

"Can you not hear the bell clearly from your room, Lili?" Constance asked.

"Yes, but . . ." Lili beckoned her closer, insisted on whispering in her ear quite seriously, "I must be sure the bells do not make Lord Deleval disappear."

"Ah," Constance said. "No need to worry, my dear."

"Please, Mrs. Conyngham. Five minutes?" Lili begged, her expression tragic in its concern.

Constance could see no harm in indulging her. "All right, then, if you will be so good as to fetch Clara, and are both quick to don cloaks and gloves, you may have five minutes in the garden with Lord Deleval and Black Tom."

"You will not go away, will you?" Lili hung for a moment on Lucian's arm.

"Do you think the bells might ring me away, little one, in the time it takes you to put on gloves?" His tone, in asking, was indulgent.

"Mrs. Conyngham did tell me I must not be concerned."

The earl smiled. "And so you must not."

"Good!" Lili let go of him to summon Clara.

Constance bit her lip, darted a glance in the earl's direction, and would have hastened after Lili had he not said with gentle sarcasm: "You do not believe, then, in the legend of the devil's knell, Mrs. Conyngham?"

"If by legend, you mean I do not believe you the

devil, who will be driven from Dewsbury by the tolling of the bell, then no, sir, I do not."

"And yet, I have been possessed of the feeling all evening that you avoid me, Mrs. Conyngham, as if I was the very devil."

"Oh?"

"Yes. You do, most pointedly, shun my company, especially when there is mistletoe in the vicinity. It is not at all kind of you, who has taught me so much of kindnesses."

"I am surprised you should notice such a thing, my lord. I have it on excellent authority that you do not care for kisses."

The hint of a smile teased the corners of a mouth she had given far too much thought of late. "It is true, I did not care for kisses not so long ago. There are, in fact, a great many things I did not care for that I have begun, once again, to enjoy."

"Such as?"

"I have enjoyed these past few days, the music, and those who make it." His eyes sparkled when he mentioned the makers of music. His mouth drew her attention again. She sidled a little farther from the kissing bunch in the doorway.

"You made quite an impression, playing as well as you did at this afternoon's practice."

"Thanks to you, and thanks to the price of a few kindnesses, of which I can only hope you have taken note."

She smiled. "I have heard that every shopkeeper for miles scurries to provide you with items for celebrating the Yuletide season."

He shrugged. "I have ordered an item or two."

"Vicar tells me you are planning a number of New Year's festivities. That mummers have been hired? Sword dancers? An orchestra? I have heard that invitations are even now being printed on Mrs. White's very best vellum. That virtually everyone in Dewsbury and the surrounding countryside is to be invited to a New Year's fete at the Keep?"

Again he nodded, which surprised her. She had been sure some part of the rampant gossip must be a hum.

"I hear, as well, that you have commissioned every seamstress in the district for a bit of sewing." She could not resist smiling. "And from Freddie Tomes, a number of striped nightshirts."

He nodded. "With matching nightcaps, I'll have you know."

"Which you will never wear," she scolded.

"No," he agreed with a smile. "But there are two old gentlemen residing in a nearby almshouse who will sleep very warm this winter."

She could not disguise the fact that he charmed her.

"I have pleased you with this little kindness, Mrs. Conyngham?"

"You have. But you had better please yourself, my lord, rather than the tastes of a governess."

"On this one matter I would beg to differ, Mrs. Conyngham."

"Why so, sir? Surely it is better to satisfy our own sense of goodness rather than someone else's?"

He shook his head. "Ah, but I am, you see, bound to repay my debt to you." He held out his arm to her. "Will you accompany me and your charges into the garden?"

"I will," she agreed, "if you will do me yet another kindness, my lord."

His brows lifted.

She stepped into the doorway, pointing at the mistletoe hanging above her head. "You will not take advantage of the mistletoe?"

"You call that a kindness?" He frowned. "I would call it something else entirely."

She nodded. "I cannot think it a good example to set the girls in allowing their governess too much freedom with kissing, sir."

"I see," he said with a nod toward the girls, who were busy buttoning cloaks and gloves at the end of the long, dark, echoing hall that would take them into the garden. "You have no other objection to them, then?" Holding out his arm, he tucked her fingers into the crook of it.

She tried to stop her hand from trembling at his touch. "Objection, sir?"

"To mistletoe kisses, Mrs. Conyngham?"

She could not tell him her real reason for avoiding his lips, and so she shook her head, trying to sound carefree as she said, "They are one of the joys of Christmas."

"Come along you two. No dawdling." Lili called to them as if she had, for the moment, assumed the role of governess. But then she giggled and gleefully danced about on tiptoe, while Clara stood with her thumb on the door latch, tapping her foot in time with Flora's pianoforte performance from the other room.

"Off with you, then." Deleval gave them a wave. "We are right behind you."

There was no need to tell them twice. With a bang of the door, the girls were gone and just as suddenly Constance was whirled into the earl's arms as if he were inspired by Lili's little dance, and the music, and the darkness of the hall—as if he meant to waltz with her.

"Really, sir!"

"Really, Mrs. Conyngham," he murmured, guiding her progress with the heat of his hand at her waist. "You ask too much of me, you know, in requiring me to ignore my own kindness in providing so much of the Christmas joy, as you call it, that hangs everywhere. I have been blessed with the kindness of kisses from every female present, save the one I would most gladly suffer them from."

"Suffer them, sir?" she whispered in protest. "Sir! Really, sir! I do not think—"

"A little kindness, Mrs. Conyngham. I beg of you." He directed her attention to the stag's head above them. It was crowned with mistletoe.

As she lifted her face to regard it, he lowered his to kiss her lips not once, but several times. She, breathless, spellbound, and dizzy, let him.

She broke from his embrace. "This will not do! It is a wickedness." The door hinge squealed as she fled into the darkness of the garden without benefit of an outer wrap.

Warmed by the sweet fire of her briefly lit ardor, Lucian snatched up her cloak from the peg by the door before following her into the night, into the swollen sound of the tolling of the devil's knell.

There was a sadness to the bell, a chill to the garden. A jumble of black silhouettes against a background of black, here was layered darkness, layered sound. A fountain splashed against a backdrop of muted pianoforte and the steady, distant ringing of Black Tom. Rectangles of yellowed light fell from the windows of the manor. A haze of silver emanated from the slip of moon and stars above. The tolling bell seemed an endless thing, as endless as the stillness that surrounded him, for neither Constance nor the girls were to be seen.

Lucian stood in the doorway, searching, a woman's wrap clutched in his hand, the cold fingering him.

"Mrs. Conyngham?" he called hoarsely, the heat of

her name a fog before his face. "Constance!" he called again.

The tolling of the bell was his only answer, the steady pulse of it echoing his heartbeat.

When Lord Deleval burst through the door to the garden calling her name, Constance froze like a rabbit, hand to mouth, heart racing, paralyzed with fear, guilt and an almost overwhelming longing.

He looked right at her. She was sure she was discovered, and yet so completely had she become one with the shadows, he did not see her. She bit back the urge to respond when he called her by her given name. In kissing him beneath the mistletoe she had suffered a foolish, delirious capitulation to passion—a moment's indulgence of unrealistic dreams and unmet desires.

The bell rang Constance back to reality.

On and on, like a nagging tongue, it rang, a reminder of the devils that must be chased from man, of the devil that tempted her. How dear such folly could cost her. She, a governess of happy circumstances, could not indulge herself in the fairy-tale nonsense of a romance with an earl. She must, for her own and the children's sake, remember herself—and resist temptation.

As Leland thrust open a low window, a gush of sound from the drawing room followed by a wave of laughing guests, spilled over the sill into the lawn, saying, "Come! No dallying, you lot. Through here! The bell is to be heard quite clearly from the garden."

The sounds of laughter, of voices raised in jest, drifted ghostlike, reminding Lucian too much of another woman, another bell ringing—summoning friends and family to a wedding that never took place.

Was he the devil, after all, that women ran from him? Was his touch so hellish a torment?

The weight of the widow Conyngham's woolen cape slipped from his hand, and with it Lucian's confidence. Driven by old demons, by the constant reminder of the bell, he turned his back on lighthearted revelry, on honeyed lips and mistletoe kisses.

He went to the golden, lamp-lit warmth of the stables, the bell marking time for his footsteps. The groom did not move fast enough for him. He threw the saddle in place himself, impatiently tightening the girth. Incessant, the sound drove him, goaded him, taunted him.

The children had gone to their favorite spot, a wooden swing, from which one might look out over the valley. Constance joined them there, in the dark beneath the tree. A cold sliver of moon looked down at her. It judged her negligent, she thought, for too long abandoning her charges.

"Where is Lord Deleval?" were the first words from Lili's mouth.

"Is that not his horse?" Clara asked as a rider swept past them on the far side of the hedge.

"It is." Constance forced her voice to remain even. She had not expected him to flee.

"Oh dear!" Lili gasped. "He is the devil. He is!"

Fraught with a heart-racing sense of unfinished business, Constance stifled her own regret in soothing Lili's fears. "No, Lili, not the devil."

"But he left in such a hurry." She was not in a mood to be convinced.

"He had his reasons."

"It was the bell."

"No, not the bell."

"He promised to come to the garden!"

"Adults do on occasion break their promises." Her heart ached to think how often it was so. Daniel had promised to come back safely from the sea, had promised they should be happy together until they were both old and gray, had promised she would have children of her own to care for.

"We did not have the chance to say good-bye." Lili's anguish echoed her own.

"No. All too often that is the case," Constance said softly.

"But why?"

An age-old question. Constance had not the answer.

Spurring Styx to a bell-punctuated gallop along the dark lane, it occurred to Lucian that Black Tom had done its job. Here he was, chased from Leland Manor, just as Lili had feared, if not by the damn bell, then by the devils of his past. He had allowed a woman to leave him standing, unanswered and abandoned, a fool of feelings, a slave to emotion and animal urges. He had promised himself it would never happen again.

At the crossroads that would lead him home, he paused, anger rising, realization banging away at his head like the bell that would not stop.

An irrational need to strangle the noise, to cut off the heartbeat of sound, possessed him. He goaded Styx toward the town, not away from it. The muted ringing became one with the rhythm of the horse's hooves. Sliding from the saddle, the noise swelling like madness in his ears, he raced through the chapel and up the cold stone stairs of the bell tower, unable to hear his own footsteps, unable to think of anything but Constance Conyngham's lips on his.

Black Tom's voice washed over and through him, vibrating in his ears, his backbone, in his very shoes. A wave of sadness and melancholy closed in over his head. He drowned in the throbbing pulse, coming up for breath only when he burst into the bare openness of a high-ceilinged room, casement windows opened to a cold countryside pinpricked by the warm glow of those who had yet to snuff their lights.

The bell ringer, expression rapt, sweat drenched despite the chill, was oblivious at first to Lucian's presence. He seemed lost in reverie, a lunging rhythmic, physical sort of meditation.

Lucian grabbed the bell pull from his hands.

As persistent as the bell the question echoed in her mind, as an exhausted, despondent Constance climbed the back stairs to her room, the girls safely tucked into bed. Why? Of all men she should be drawn to, why Lord Deleval?

The stairs offered no answer. And yet, perhaps they did. Plain, narrow, and none too well lit, they measured the distance each step took her from the sheltering arms and heated kisses of an earl who never climbed to servant's quarters. In the slanted confines of her attic room she loosed the strings that fastened the back of her Sunday best, a three-year-old velvet gown that was hopelessly out of fashion, but too expensive to replace.

The gold watchpin she unfastened from its bodice was her only ornamentation. The highly polished boots she bent to unlace, the only pair she possessed. She had little else to her name, except her reputation and a happy placement as governess to Leland's belles. She had almost thrown that much away this evening. Unbuttoned, unbound, and unpinned, she allowed the tightness in her chest similar release.

Breathless sobs shook her. Hot tears rained on her cheeks, dripped into her lace. With reckless haste she tore the meager finery of the fichu from her throat. She must keep in mind her station, must remember her place. Her future was fixed, as unremarkable as the petticoat she stepped out of, as predictable as the steady ringing of the distant bell.

Caught off guard, the bell ringer let go the rope, turning to gape at the earl who would interfere with his task.

Lucian held fast the pull, determined to wrestle the big bell to silence.

A mistake. It was a live thing at the end of the tether, a massive, vibrating body of sound, hundreds of pounds of clanging brass, given life with no more than the tug of a rope. The bell ringer shouted at him, his words muffled in the blanket of sound. Lucian read his lips. Red-faced, the fellow waved his hands and mouthed, "Let go. Let go!"

Lucian was too focused on his purpose to see the sense of letting go. He would stop the bell. He would. He fought the pull of it. And yet, the bell laughed, undaunted, deep throated, and deafening. Lifting him from his feet as it laughed, he was dragged some six feet into the dark well of the belfry by the power of Black Tom's bulk. He was a marionette, the bell his puppeteer.

Lucian let go of the rope.

Another mistake. The floor rushed up to meet him with bruising force.

The baffled bellman helped him to his feet. The bell boomed heartily above their heads.

Struck by his own foolishness, by the thought that this man must be wondering just what it was he meant to accomplish in flinging himself at the rope pull, Lucian gave in. He laughed along with the bell.

The bellman smiled uneasily, as if at a madman. Motioning Lucian to back away for the next pull, he grabbed hold of the rope, gave it a good tug, and as it rose, grabbed hold that he might fly into the belfry with it. For an instant he dangled six feet off the floor, just as Lucian had. But the man wisely maintained his grasp, and light as goose down, the handgrip swung him to earth. He landed nimbly on his toes. Letting go of the pull, and grinning, he jabbed his thumb at Lucian as if to say, that's how it's done.

Lucian considered the rope, considered the booming voice of the bell that he had so recently been bent on stilling. Abandoning himself to the vibration, to the deafening noise, he waited for the grip to swing low again, gave it a tug, and as the velvet-covered hemp raced up into the dark well of the belfry, rushed into the air with it, lifted as a child is lifted and swung, light, carefree, and trusting.

Light he had felt in kissing Constance Conyngham—innocent, as he had not allowed himself to be in a very long time. Like the bell, she resounded in him, swept him off his feet. He laughed out loud. The bell laughed along with him, as if it understood perfectly his feelings.

The bell her only constant—sense and sensibilities in a turmoil—a hopeless anguish beset Constance. Breaking the ice on her pitcher, she poured a basin of water, splashed away the heat of her tears, sponged down the heat of her chest. As water trailed chill fingers along her breasts and arms she remembered in complete, evocative detail every shining, tempting moment she had lived, caught up in Deleval's arms, in his lips, in the sweet madness called mistletoe.

The bell, always the bell. It seemed an extension of the pounding in both her head and heart. Constance settled herself restlessly in the narrow bed that fit so well the dimensions of both her life and room. She lay listening, candle extinguished, eyes wide to velvet blackness, heart and soul thrown wide to the mistaken notion that with the ringing she drove all trace of the devil of desire from her mind, from her heart, from the throbbing, heated drum of her pulse.

He no longer wished to stop the ringing. He wanted to be a part of it, to share in the responsibility for filling the night with the passion of noise. He hoped Constance Conyngham heard this ringing—his ringing.

The bellman let him toll the bell until he was exhausted. Until, like the sweat that rained from his hair and nose, every bit of anger, pain, doubt, and loneliness had drained from his body. Humming with elation, filled to overflowing with the same sated contentment he had first noticed in the bell ringer, Lucian saluted the man and relinquished the velvet grip as if it were a prize. Donning his coat, he rode home, warmed to the night, warming to the notion he knew what he wanted as much as he knew what was needed to claim it. The knowing satisfied him. Like the echo of his intent, the sound of the bell, still ringing, followed him all the way to the keep.

IV

December 25, Christmas Day

Lucian Deleval awoke to a wet, cold, Christmas morning bursting with purpose and self-confidence, eager to participate in the ringing of the handbells, eager to see Constance, eager to reveal his feelings. The earl was at last prepared for intimacies with a female.

He was not prepared to find Constance Conyngham as resistant to the fire of his feelings as was the weather. She was chill in her politeness in responding to his good morning when the bell ringers gathered briefly before the service to don gloves, give the bells a final polish, and to review exactly where they must stand during the performance.

"You are here! You are here!" It was not Constance, but Lili who met his appearance with the exuberant excess of joy he would rather witness in her governess.

Of all he might regret from the previous night, it was his abandonment of Lili that troubled Lucian most. "I am sorry I did not find you in the garden, little one. Can you forgive me? It was most unkind."

"It was. It was most unkind."

"You did not think me the devil, after all, chased away by the bell, did you?"

Lili was unwilling to admit as much, but there was no denying that her lower lip thrust itself in a pout as she demanded, "Why did you leave, my lord? When you knew we waited?"

"Do you run away sometimes, Lili?" He knelt to ask her, well aware that Constance, though she tried to appear disinterested, overheard them.

"Yes. When I am afraid."

"I ran away last night. Fear chased me."

"You, sir? But what have you to fear?"

There was a stillness to Constance, though she would not look at him, that convinced Lucian she waited his response as pensively as her charge.

"I was afraid, my dear Lili, of abandonment."

"By whom, sir? We did not abandon you. You abandoned us."

"Not whom—what. It is self-control abandons me, and wisdom and good sense and propriety. I would let it all go, if I might hold onto one thing." His words, meant more for Mrs. Conyngham's ears than for her charge's, confused the child.

Lili frowned. "One thing, sir? What is that?"

"Love, Lili. Of all things you might abandon, do not let that slip through your fingers. Let your love ring out like a bell, clear and true and resounding."

Mrs. Conyngham turned at last to meet his gaze, but not with a smile as he had hoped. She wore a troubled look.

"I have brought you a Christmas keepsake," he said.

Constance blushed, bit her lip, and glanced uneasily about her when he held out a small tissue-wrapped box, not to Lili, but to her.

"A little kindness, nothing more." Realizing their exchange was observed from all sides, he handed a second, identical box to Lili, and then emptied his pockets of more boxes, saying to the room at large, "A token for each of the bell ringers."

The gifts proved to be diminutive silver bells, dainty, silver glove buttons. A great many pleased thanks were directed his way. Everyone, in fact, voiced their approval except Constance. She was the last to slip the shiny new buttons into the holes at the wrist of each glove, because she saw to each of the girls before attending to herself.

"May I offer any assistance?" he asked.

"I do thank you." Her head rose as abruptly as the defensiveness of her tone. "But I can manage quite well on my own."

She dropped a button.

He bent to retrieve it for her.

She accepted its return with a prickly, "Thank you." And when he might have offered his assistance once again, she turned to Flora and asked the child if she would be so good as to help her.

Throughout the service, throughout the actual ringing of the bells, stiff, silent, and unsmiling, she refused to look his way, to acknowledge his presence at all. Constance played her part without flaw, and yet she could not enjoy herself, could not relax in the company of a man whose gaze she knew to be fixed on her every move. She suffered a troubling sense of suppressed words, suppressed feelings, of anticipation and nervous expectation, that had nothing at all to do with the bells, and everything to do with the young man whom she had taught the use of them.

The muted precision, the methodical controlled rhythms of the bells usually soothed her nerves. Today they tested her patience to the snapping point. She was, in contrast to the smooth perfection of the sounds she created, feeling edgy, snappish, and completely out of sorts.

She felt as if she sinned, in some way hard to define, as if she, and she alone, were responsible for the undercurrent of gossip and speculation that ran rife before and after the service.

"Do you mean to partake of the festivities planned for New Year's Day?"

Everyone asked. That, and one other question.

"What has come over the earl?"

"A changed man, he is," Farmer Bayley said with a wink.

"Generous of him, to give us each a gift that way." The butcher's brows wagged suggestively.

"Quite the bell ringer he has become." Mrs. White gave her a playful nudge.

"Aye. And planning such a to-do as we have not witnessed in many a year." It was Freddie Tomes who had become the earl's greatest supporter.

Word had gotten around, as word always did in a community no bigger than Dewsbury, that Constance had been instrumental in giving the earl music lessons. There were those who went so far as to question the

extent of those lessons. What else, after all, so neatly
explained the earl's transformation but a woman's
touch?

"Do you mean to go to the Keep on New Year's
Day, Constance, lass?" The draper was the fifth of a
dozen who asked. His gaze fixed on her with speculative, canniness, an arch, I-know-what-you're-up-to expression that annoyed Constance.

"Plan to go to the Keep? Of course we do." She took
refuge in the plural afforded her position. "Is there
anyone in the valley who chooses not to?"

There were a handful of kinder, less cynical souls
who credited Leland's little belles with the earl's transformation. It was no secret Deleval had attended Leland's Annual Christmas Eve party, nor that he
lavished the girls with gifts, but that too, could be at-
tributed to the presence of their governess by those
who believed themselves wise to the ways of the
world.

Constance did her utmost to stifle her emotions
where the earl was concerned, to disguise the light-
headed, short-of-breath ebullience she suffered whenever she so much as caught a glimpse of him.

It would not do! She kept reminding herself. It
would not do at all for a governess to allow daydreams and infatuation to get the better of her common sense. Nothing but ruin lay down that pathway,
heartache and ruin.

Her gift, of glove buttons, exactly like any one of the
dozen others, yet managed to set her heart racing
when the earl himself insisted on tucking them into
the buttonholes for her. The very thought of his fingers haphazardly stroking the pulse at her wrist had
set it racing. But in so singling her out, in handing her
his gift first, in the very offer of his assistance, in the
manner he had studied so relentlessly her reaction to

its opening—the whispers intensified behind her back, and over and over like the tolling of a death knell to her reputation, her name was linked with that of Lucian Deleval.

V

January 1, New Year's Day

Constance Conyngham went to Deleval Keep unsure of herself, of her reception, of her very standing in Dewsbury, especially in the Leland household, now that she had become an object of gossip, speculation, and rumor. She was no good to the girls, no good at all as an example of how to behave, if gossip was to be believed.

Her arrival on that cold, crisp day roused scant attention. The Keep, its incredible transformation, and the entertainments that had been amassed for the day therein, transfixed all eyes and occupied all tongues.

"Amazing!" Florabelle rubbed mist from the window of her father's carriage with mittened fingers. "Have we come to the right place? The Keep is so changed!"

The Devil's Keep was indeed changed—a once grim face now wreathed in smiles. The exterior was certainly bedecked in holiday cheer. Decorative evergreen boughs and swags of red bunting and the cheerful flicker of additional lamplight warmed the old facade. The decorations intensified as one passed through the gatehouse and into the courtyard. Evergreens again: holly, ivy, and mistletoe, plus yards and yards of fabric, holly-berry red, had been made into swags and flags and canopies. Lamps and candles brightened every dark corner.

"How warm! How welcoming!" Clarabelle whispered as they were led to the Great Hall.

Warm indeed! An enormous Yule log blazed cheerfully on the hearth. The floor was ankle deep in fresh rushes and fragrant herbs. A table stretched the length of the room, perfuming the air with the smells of mince pie and plum pudding, roast turkey, haunch of venison, and the fruity spice of mulled wine and hot cider.

"What fun!" Lilibelle crowed in an undervoice. "It is just as you described, Mrs. Conyngham. Do you remember?"

It was true. The room was very much as Constance had described it on their last visit to the Keep. Walls once bristling with arms were now covered with richly colored tapestries. Greenery decked all the doorways and windows, the mantel and the music screen, from behind whose polished carvings wafted the pleasant stirrings of a chamber orchestra.

The place was packed. As a result, Constance had small duty in watching over her charges. The girls paired off with their friends, to mingle among giggling, fresh-faced clusters of their peers just as their parents sought out their equals among the local landowners. Constance found herself swept into a happy, gossip-raddled circle of governesses, nurses, nannies, and maids. Thankfully, none of the gossip centered on her. The earl figured very large, but it was in relation to the transformation both of the Keep and his attitude that occupied most of the wagging tongues, not his relationship to a local governess. Constance felt a little more at ease.

Everyone in the valley had come. Crisply starched, pressed, and polished, they filled the Hall and spilled out into the courtyard. A pieman, an orange girl, and several boys bearing jugs of ale catered to those who had not the courage to partake more than once of the bounty in the Great Hall. Flaming braziers chased away the chill.

Rather like the juggler and the troupe of acrobats who tossed one another about in the most amazing flips and flying leaps, Lord Deleval circulated among the guests, the best of hosts, making sure everyone was welcomed, warmed, and well-fed.

Constance was relieved to see him so fully occupied. She exchanged a polite good day with him. He acknowledged her with a direct look and a nod in greeting their party. They shared no further contact beyond a glance or two across the width of the room, his attention claimed by new arrivals. The day progressed far better than she had hoped until the main attraction arrived, in the form of sword dancers.

Everything stopped, including her feelings of security, when five men trouped into the courtyard clad in gaily beribboned vests, full-sleeved white shirts, and dark breeches with white stockings and silver buckle shoes. The dancers bore simple, hilted swords of about three feet in length which they wielded with a practiced ease as they marched in a tight circle.

All eyes were drawn to them.

All eyes save Constance's and Lord Deleval's.

As if by mutual agreement, their gazes met across the crowded courtyard. Heated looks, they came together with the same kind of impact to be heard in the sliding clash of metal upon metal as the sword dancers crossed blades.

Sun glinted dangerously on steel as the dancers, gleaming blade flats riding their shoulders, cavalierly grasped one another's sword points.

A jog of his head, and Lucian conveyed to Constance his direction, away from the crowd in the courtyard, away from the Great Hall.

The dancers jigged in a circle, breath pluming, weapons lowered to waist level, linked, glittering hilt to wicked point. With them jigged Constance's nerves. She courted danger in responding to the suggestive cant of the earl's head.

Breathless and wary, she skirted the flashing blades. She never thought to refuse him, to ignore the suggestive tilt of his head, to stand her ground. Keenly-felt desire pierced all resolve. She leapt into danger as blithely as the dancers leapt and lunged, passing their weapons in more and more complex maneuvers. Nerves on edge, she followed the earl through an archway and up a series of steps. They opened onto a gallery that overlooked the courtyard.

She could not stop herself from taking one nervous, peril-ridden step after another up the vast, cold stone steps. She would speak to him, one last time. She would allow him to kiss her, one last time. She would take a moment to bid this new and highly illogical love of hers farewell.

He took her in his arms at the top of the steps and kissed her soundly. His embrace, his very proximity, warmed her more than any Yule log. The mulled-wine taste of his mouth fueled her hunger for more.

She responded to his kiss with unstinted enthusiasm, but when she tried to speak, he pressed his finger to her freshly dewed lips, saying, "Come, my love. There is something you must see."

His love? She followed him without question, the words resounding in her memory. His love!

He led her to a spot where they might, from a bird's-eye view, observe the whirling, clashing finale of the sword dance. From above, the pattern of the dancers was, if possible, more spectacular than before. Constance could not stay the gasp of delight in watching the remarkable final maneuver, which ingeniously wove all of the swords together in a wreath of glittering hilts and blades so cleverly locked the entire thing might be passed from hand to hand.

"What a marvelous view!" she whispered.

"Box seats for the mummer's show," Lucian whispered softly, from so close beside her she started, almost missing the entrance to the courtyard of a trio of men in mummer's costumes, paper strips flying about them in gay abandon.

The tallest of the mummers, unusually tall because a leering, horned-topped, paper strip mask perched atop his actual head, wore paper strips in the earl's colors across his chest.

"Who do you suppose they mean to lampoon? It is generally a local they tease." She asked the question facetiously, brows raised, sure Lucian had planned this as carefully as all else.

He smiled. "I've no memory of having invited the devil here today."

A crier announced, "My Lord Beelzebub, Prince of Darkness, the Devil of Deleval Keep!" for those who stood so far to the back that they might not clearly see.

The crowd laughed when the mummer's bow threatened to topple the papier-mâché head.

"Never fear." Constance chuckled, in a mood to be amused. "The swordsmen mean to dispatch your unwelcome doppleganger."

As if she had directed it, with a shout the sword dancers, as one, lifted their woven "knot" of locked blades and dropped it over the fake head of the devil. With a second shout and a grating slide of blade against blade, the knot of swords was suddenly and simultaneously untangled, beheading the evil in their midst.

The papier-mâché head rolled across the courtyard accompanied by great laughter and a colorful spatter of tissue-paper blood. The corpse the devil's head had been attached to, in a melodramatic spasm of paper strips and red confetti, sank to the ground and lay still.

The devil's head was not allowed to rest in peace.

A second, hefty fellow, fitted out rather buxomly to portray "Milady Mummer" as he was introduced by the crier—in a passionate flutter of paper skirt and long paper tresses, swept up the decapitated devil's head. With provocatively swaying hips, hairy fore-arms, and beefy hands, the creature made a great show of tidying the paper locks, of plucking out the paper horns, which were thrown into the laughing crowd. With a final flourish, "Milady" turned upside down the paper frown the devil had been wearing.

Accompanied by the crier's explanation that "Mi-lady Mummer" was a healer who had come to Dews-bury from a great distance, the galumphing great "girl" returned to the side of the corpse, and effected a "cure" by jamming the rearranged papier-mâché head onto the real head of the fallen mummer. When the corpse remained prone, "Milady" kissed his paper mouth with loud smacking noises, to the uproarious amusement of the crowd.

When this, too, failed to resurrect the dead, "Mi-lady" hit upon another idea. Drawing forth a large, clapperless bell from her enormous bosom, with the broadest of gestures, she rang it over the body again and again, until the dead rose, smacked her lascivi-ously on the lips, and joined her in a triumphant jig.

The bell might as well have been a knife. It pierced Constance's pride, inflicting pain, shame, and contri-tion with its every silent clang.

"Dear God!" she murmured. "What cruel trick is this?"

Turning her back on folly, its dreadful enactment,

and the appreciative guffaws of the crowd beneath them, Constance dashed from the gallery.

"Constance! Don't go!"

He raced after her, his agitated cry stopping her on the landing, echoing in the stone stairwell. "Don't go. Don't go!" The words bounced from the walls, the steps, the ceiling, an Indian rubber ball of regret, careening down to the level of the courtyard, where the faint shadow of Lord Deleval's plea met the ears of a man lounging in the archway at the base of the stairwell.

To Fredrick Tomes, this plaintive cry, of a name quite familiar to him, was far more interesting than any antics the mummers might have imagined. Curious, ears on the prick, he turned and peered into the darkness from whence it came. There was nothing to be seen in the bottom half of the stairwell, nothing more to be heard save a distant masculine rumble.

At the top of the stairs, Lucian had lowered his voice. "You must believe me, I had no idea what tragedy the mummers meant to enact."

"Had you not?" Constance was skeptical, her jaw rigid.

"You cannot think I would condone such an insult?"

Her mouth worked a moment. Her chin trembled. "It would hurt me grievously to believe you had," she said at last.

"Do not leave," he coaxed. "Not now, on this dreadful note." He crossed the landing, held out his hand to her, might have touched her had she not backed away from him, to the edge of the stairs, where she felt she teetered, on the edge of darkness, on the brink of falling head over heels.

She put one hand to the damply cold wall, to steady herself before she shook her head. "I have the headache, sir. I think it would be best if I left." She pressed hand to breast, as if she might steady pulse as easily as dizziness.

He closed the distance between them. "Is it really your head that hurts, Constance?"

"What do you mean?"

He took up the fingers that clutched so anxiously the lace at her neckline and pressed the back of his hand to the spot from which he had lifted hers. "I thought perhaps it was something else that ached. I hoped, in fact, that might be the case, for while I have just the means for soothing such aches, I've nothing at all for your head."

She stood transfixed for a moment before flinging his hand away, before asking indignantly as she started down the stairs, "Do you mean to insult me, sir? Perhaps to seduce me?"

Her voice rang in the stairwell, rang all the way to the bottom of the steps and into the courtyard, where Frederick Tomes again heard every word, along with eight other souls who turned their heads, then stepped closer to listen.

Oblivious to the growing number of his audience, Lucian smiled mischievously and sent his reply echoing after hers. "If you care at all to be seduced, Mrs. Conyngham, I would be most happy to oblige."

"Sir!" Her response was quick, brisk, and indignant, like the click of her heels on the stone steps. "It is not a kindness, my lord, to lead me to believe you care for me more than the ordinary—to tease me."

"Tease you?" He stood at the top of the stairs, his voice rising with every step she distanced herself from him.

"Yes!" She stopped halfway above the middle landing, turning, that she might call out, "I am mindful, if you are not, that we are unequal in station, in family, in property, in means."

He flung up his hands, and with them the volume of his response. "What has any of that to do with how much I may care for you? Or you for me?"

"It is a torture, sir, not a kindness . . ."—her voice broke unevenly on the word *kindness*—"when nothing can come of it." The pain in her words bounced back from the walls.

"Nothing come of it?" His voice rose along with his ire. "You are mistaken. A great deal can come of it."

"Nothing honorable, sir, when I am a governess, a widow. I've little means. No connections. You are an earl. A titled peer of the realm, with obligations to name, rank, and fortune."

"I have a heart as well, or had you forgotten?" He bit out every word as if they tasted bad.

His challenge brought her very close to tears. "I am aware that you have some feelings of affection for me, that you have the means to offer me more than I may be able to refuse. I beg you will honor those affections by refraining from the tempting of me."

He smiled and took the first of the steps that led down to hers. "A tempter, am I?"

His approach dizzied her. She grabbed the wall, and turned her back on him to steady herself. Without risking a look at him, as he continued to approach, she threw words between them, the most formidable she could muster. "I will not be your mistress, my lord, no matter the depths of what I may feel for you. I beg you will let me go now, unhindered. I would consider it a great kindness."

"You may go," he agreed softly from the step above hers. "If you will promise me but one kindness in return, Constance."

She froze, unable to move. "What kindness, sir?"

He waited until at last she dared to look up at him before he joined her on the same step.

"Will you agree to let me call on you?"

"Call?" she whispered.

"To court you—openly, earnestly, with every honorable intention." He moved close with each question. "To make every attempt to win you, hand, body, and heart."

"But"—she was weeping—"I am a governess and you . . ."

He brushed away her tears with the flat of his thumb. "I am well aware of who I am, and what it is I would have of you."

"Oh dear," she moaned, her knees going weak, bending, that she might descend the steps, might move closer to the safety of the landing. She clutched the wall, that she might not fall.

"Have you no room in your heart for me, Constance?" He followed, close on her heels, so close she was sure they must both trip.

"Room?" Her heart was full to bursting. There was no room for anything or anyone but him at the moment.

"Does Daniel stand between us?" he asked earnestly, his hand on her shoulder, his breath in her ear. He turned her so that his green-eyed gaze might search hers intently.

"Daniel?" She shivered, tried to laugh, and failed. "No, not Daniel."

His eyes were hard and bright as polished agate. His mouth was pinched. "Seven years you have mourned him. The bells still bring tears. I have seen them."

She sighed. So close did they stand that her breath stirred the lock of hair at his temple. His lashes fluttered. He took a quick breath.

"Do not mistake me, my lord. I loved my husband dearly, but we were married no more than three months. It is the lost potential of our love I have so long regretted."

His gaze softened, as did the set of his mouth. He nodded. Silence hung between them, like the memories of the past.

"Do you think we might find that lost potential together, Constance?"

She hesitated a moment, and into the pregnant silence burst the anxious voice of a child. "Tell him yes, Mrs. Conyngham. Please, you must tell him yes."

"Lilibelle?" Constance gasped in alarm.

"Yes." The voice had a muffled sound, and was accompanied by a shushing noise and the hushed voice of Clara uttering "Oh, Lili!" and Flora giggling, "Be still!"

"Dear God!" Constance whispered, flushing with embarrassment. "We have been overheard." She might have fled down the stairs had not Lucian caught her and stilled her in his arms.

"Aye!" A voice that sounded very much like Freddie Tomes' carried up to them. "Heard every word, love. Clear as a bell."

Constance, distraught, caught her breath in a gasp.

Lord Deleval, with a devilish chuckle, stifled the gasp with a kiss. "Say yes," he admonished and kissing her again, "yes," he repeated. "Say yes, my love."

"Yes," she murmured faintly, giving in to a fresh onslaught of the sweetest of kisses.

From the base of the steps came the sound of Freddie's triumphant, "She said yes!"

A swelling of mingled laughter and applause met his announcement—a girlish giggle, a squeal or two, and Lili's voice again.

"I hear bells."

It was true. Even deep in the all absorbing warmth and comfort of the earl's arms, Constance heard them. Bells. In the distance, very faintly, all manner of bells, echoing in the hills—borne on the wind from every direction—ringing in the promise of the New Year.

Make a Joyful Noise

❄

by Carla Kelly

"Son, I own that being a Christian is onerous, at times."

Like many of his mother's pronouncements, this one was a bolt out of the blue. Peter Chard smiled behind his napkin as he blotted the remnants of dinner from his lips, and then did the same for his little daughter Emma. He winked at Will, who sat next to Mama on the other side of the table.

"How do you mean, Mama?" he asked. He draped his arm over the back of Emma's chair so he could fiddle with her curls. "Seems to me that Our Lord mentioned on at least one occasion that His yoke was easy, and His burden light."

"Peter, Jesus could say that because He never had to deal with our vicar!"

Chard laughed. "Mama, some would argue that He probably deals with the vicar more than we do! But please explain yourself."

It was all the encouragement she needed. "Pete, I find myself trussed as neatly a Christmas goose and it is only October."

"Grandmama, if you would not stop to talk to Mr. Woodhull, but only shake his hand and walk on, you would stay out of trouble at church," Will said as he reached for the last apple tart.

Peter laughed again and pushed the bowl a little

closer to his son. "Mama, it seems I cannot take you anywhere!" he teased. "And here I thought Sunday was harmless. Am I to assume that you have promised something that you are already regretting?" He pulled out his pocket watch. "We are only two hours out of church, and you are already repentant. It must be serious."

Louisa Chard, the Dowager Lady Wythe, sighed. "Oh, Pete, what a stupid thing I did! Son, I made the mistake of asking about the Christmas choir."

Will ceased chewing. Emma, as young as she was, tensed under Chard's hand. *Lord, are my insides churning? Dare I blame it on dinner?* he asked himself.

The choir. Too little could not be said about it, and here was Mama, tempting the devil. By some awesome, cosmic twist, St. Philemon's Christmas choir was a freak of nature. During the year, a choir occasionally accompanied services with no complaint. But Christmas? He shuddered. *Are we too proud? Do we not listen to each other? Are there poor among us that we ignore too much? Does the Lord use the annual parish choir competition at Christmas to flog us for sins real and imagined?*

It seemed so. What had begun when he was a boy as a friendly competition between three small parish churches had grown into a monster. "What, Mama, did the vicar ask you to assassinate one of this year's judges, and you have second thoughts?" he quizzed.

"I would not have second thoughts!" she exclaimed, then blew a kiss to her granddaughter, who regarded her with large eyes. "Emmie dear, I would never," she assured the child. "No, son. In a weak moment, I agreed to help in this year's recruitment. That is all."

Chard relaxed. "Mama, I know how much you love to gad about and drink tea. Now you are only adding

recruitment to your agenda as you career about the
parish boundaries."

Lady Wythe sighed again. "People will run from
me," she declared as she rose from the table and sig-
naled to the footman to do his duty.

"Papa, I am tired," Emma said as he picked her up.

"So am I, kitten. If I tell you a story, will you take a
nap?"

"If I don't take a nap, I *know* you will, Papa!" she
teased as he carried her upstairs.

Emma love, if I were to tell you how much I like
Sunday afternoon and napping with you, my friends
would hoot and make rude noises, he thought as he
stretched out on her little bed and let her cuddle close
to him. The rain began before he was too far into a
somewhat convoluted story about an Indian princess
and her golden ball. The soothing sound of rain thankfully sent Emma to sleep before he had to create an
ending where there was none.

Funny that I am forgetting my stories of India, he
thought as he undid the top button of his breeches and
eased his shoes off. It has not been so long since I adventured there. He seldom thought of Assaye anymore, a battle cruelly fought and hardly won. When
the morning paper brought him news now of Beau
Wellington in Portugal and advancing to retake Spain,
he could read the accounts over porridge with detach-
ment unthinkable six years ago in humid, bloody
India.

That is what hard work does to my body, he
thought, as he kissed Emma's head and let her burrow
in close to him in warm, heavy slumber. I can be kinder
to the Almighty than Mama, he thought as his eyes
closed. Thank thee, dear Lord, for my children, my
land, and our own good life. He frowned. But please,
Lord, not the Christmas choir.

When he woke, the bed was absent Emma, as he knew it would be. He turned onto his side and raised on one elbow to watch his children sitting on the carpet, playing with Will's wooden horses and cart. Will looks like me, he thought with some pleasure, and not for the first time. He will be tall and will likely stay blond, too. He has Lucy's eyes, he thought, but not her pouty mouth, thank God. Both children had his mild temperament, and he was more grateful for that than any physical blessings. There will be no tantrums in these darlings, he told himself. No railings, no bitterness, no accusations where none were warranted, no recriminations. When they go to their wife and husband someday, pray God they will go in peace and confidence.

It was his continual prayer, and he could see it answered almost daily. He and Mama were raising beautiful, kindly children. If that meant doing without wifely comforts, so be it. He had known few enough of those, anyway. He lay on his back and covered his eyes with his arm. To be honest, he thought, I know that someday I will have to face a heavenly tribunal and receive some chastisement for the relief I felt when I learned of Lucy's death. I will take my stripes and I will not complain. God is just, and quite possibly merciful.

How peaceful it was to lie there and listen to his children play, knowing that tomorrow he would be in the fields again—always in the fields!—seeing to the last of the harvest, and attending to the thousand duties that a man of considerable property rejoiced in. Tomorrow night he would likely fall asleep before Mama was through talking to him over her solitaire table, or before Will had finished explaining his latest lesson from Mr. Brett's school. He would quickly fall asleep again in his bed. There was no wife to reach for; he was too tired, anyway.

By breakfast next morning, Mama had still not relinquished her agonies over the Christmas choir. "I can count on you, can I not?" she asked.

"Of course! What is it that our choirmaster wants us to torture this year?"

"I heard him mention something about Haydn, and 'The Heavens Are Telling,' " she said.

He winced. "Perhaps our salvation lies in our simplicity?" he suggested.

Mama regarded her tea and toast somewhat moodily. "It lies in good voices, son, and you know it! Why is it that no good singers lurk within parish boundaries? I call it unfair."

"They are only hiding. You will find them, Mama," he assured her. "I have every confidence in you."

She glared at him again. "All I want is to win just once, Peter. Just once."

If you say so, Mama, he thought later as he swung his leg over his horse and settled into the saddle for another day. His route took him past St. Philemon's, and as usual he raised his hat to Deity within, then raised his eyes to the distant hill where he could see St. Anselm's, only slightly larger, but filled with singers, apparently. A half turn in the saddle and a glance over his left shoulder showed him St. Peter's, a parish blessed with golden throats. He smiled to himself, wondering, as he always did, what strange geographical quirk in property and parish boundaries had located three churches so close together. The living at St. Phil's was his to bestow, and he had been pleased with his choice. Mr. Paul Woodhull was young, earnest in his duties, and genuinely cared about his pastoral sheep. He had a little wife equally young, earnest, and caring. Too bad neither could carry a tune anywhere.

He rode toward his own fields, the sun warm on his back and welcome in October. Soon it would be cold and the snow would come. As Sepoy carried him up the gradual slope to his hayfield, he noticed the woman walking through the field. He smiled, wondering for the umpteenth time who she was. He had noticed her first in August's heat, when she walked with only a bonnet dangling down her back. All he could tell about her was that she was slender but not tall, and possessed dark hair. Since September she had been cloaked as well as bonneted. He had mentioned her to Mama once over dinner, but Louisa Chard—she who knew all shire news—only shrugged. "Perhaps she is a relation of the Wetherbys, and you know I do not visit them," was her pointed comment.

He rode toward her once out of curiosity, when she crossed his land, but she only edged away the closer he came, so he changed his mind. If I were a lone woman, I would not choose to be harassed by a stranger on horseback, he reasoned, and gave her a wide berth. He was always mindful of her, even if he never asked anyone else who she was. He even dreamed about her once, and woke up embarrassed and puzzled with his body. He vowed not to think about her again, and he seldom did, even if he saw her every day.

For no real reason, he turned to watch her this time as she skirted the boggy patch in the low spot on the path that had probably been there since Hadrian built his wall. She stepped over the creek that ran so cold, and continued her steady pace to the top of the rise. He noticed that she was walking more slowly than in

August, and then his attention was taken by his men in the hay field; he did not think of her again.

Chard worked all week on his farm at that same steady pace which had characterized his army service in India, and which had earned him the nickname, Lord Mark Time. It was a stupid name bestowed on him by a few fellow officers, and never used by his own men, who knew him best. He thought about it one night, and considered that those officers even now lay rotting in India, having discovered in the last minute of their lives and far too late to profit from, that steadiness usually overrules flash and dash. It had proved to be the quality most in demand at the Kaitna ford in Assaye, at any rate.

"Mama, am I stodgy?" he asked suddenly.

Lady Wythe looked up quickly from her solitaire hand. "Well, not precisely, Pete," she said finally, after rearranging some cards. "Careful, perhaps, and certainly reliable." She laid down the rest of the cards, sweeping them together to shuffle and cut again. She folded her hands in front of her. "I would call you firm of mind, but only a little set in your ways."

"Predictable?" He couldn't resist a smile at the look on her face. "Now be honest, Mama."

"You are predictable, indeed, but it doesn't follow that this is a defect," she protested.

He glanced at the mantelpiece clock. "It is nine o'clock, my dear, and my usual bedtime," he said. "Perhaps I will astound you and remain awake until midnight!"

She laughed as she rang the bell for tea. "You would astound me, indeed, for I know you have been in the saddle since after breakfast."

I *am* much too predictable, he thought, as he stared into the fire hours later, his eyes dry from reading. Mama had given up on him two hours ago and kissed him good night, and still he sat reading, and wondering what he was trying to prove, and to whom.

He paid in the morning by oversleeping, with the consequence that St. Phil's was full when he arrived. He knew that he could march down the aisle and take his patron's pew, where for centuries Marquises of Wythe had slumbered through services, but he was not so inclined. Mama sat there even now, with Emma and Will, but there was a shyness about him that made him ill wish to call attention to his tardiness. Lucy used to relish her late arrival, and the opportunity to peacock her way to the family box. He chose not to.

Will noticed him as he genuflected then sat in the back, and came down the aisle to join him. Will's clothes smelled faintly of camphor and it was a reminder, along with the hay, grain, and fruit of the vine tucked in his barns, that the season had turned. He noticed that Will's wrists were shooting out of his sleeves. His son would be nine early in the New Year. Mama would scoff at the expense, but Chard decided that it was time for Will to meet his own tailor. I will take him to Durham, and we will both be measured, he thought, pleased with himself.

They stood and bowed when the acolyte bore the cross down the aisle. The smell of incense rose in his nostrils, and then the little procession was past. As he sat down again, he noticed a woman well-bundled in her cloak standing in the aisle, hesitating. He motioned to Will to move closer to him and give her room, but she chose instead to seat herself directly in front of him.

He sat back, concentrating as always on the service because he cared what Mr. Woodhull said, and he felt a genuine need to express himself in prayer. I am so blessed, he thought simply; it follows that I should be grateful, even if gratitude is not stylish. They rose for a hymn. As usual, he prepared to flinch at the unfortunate lack of musical ability among his tenants and fellow parishioners. That he did not, he owed entirely to the woman standing in front of him.

He had never heard a more beautiful voice, full-throated and rich with a vibrato that was just enough without overpowering the simple hymn they sang.

"Oh, Papa."

He glanced down at Will, who appeared to be caught in the same musical web. He put his arm around his son and they enjoyed the pleasure of a beautiful voice together.

He was hard put to direct his attention to the rest of the service. When he and Will returned to the pew after taking the Sacrament, he tried to see who she was, but she had returned to the pew before him and knelt with her head down, as he should be doing. Instead, he knelt behind her again and watched her. Only a moment's concentration assured him that she was the woman who walked the hills. The cloak was shabby up close.

From what he could tell, she was small but sturdy. She was the happy possessor of a wealth of black hair long and managed into a tidy mass at the back of her neck. He could see nothing remarkable about her—no ribands, no jewelry—until a baby in the pew behind him burst into sudden wails and she turned around involuntarily. She was beautiful. Her eyes were wide and dark, her features perfectly proportioned, and her lips of tender shape. To Chard's honest delight, she smiled at either him or Will before she turned back around.

When the Mass ended, he wanted to speak to her, but he found himself hard put to think of a proper introduction. To his knowledge, she was not a tenant, so there was no connection. From the look of her cloak, clean but well worn, she was not of his social circle. While he puzzled on what to do, and nodded and smiled to various friends, she escaped and his ordeal was over.

He took his time leaving the church, waiting until the last parishioner had congratulated Mr. Woodhull on his sermon. He held out his hand before the vicar could give him the little bow that always embarrassed him. The vicar shook his hand instead.

"My lord, I trust you found the sermon to your liking. I remembered your fondness for that scripture which you commented upon at dinner last week."

Scripture? What scripture? Dinner? God bless me, I am an idiot, he thought wildly, before he had the good sense to nod with what he hoped looked like wisdom. "I appreciate your thoughtfulness, Mr. Woodhull," he said, praying that the vicar would not question him about the sermon. "Tell me, sir, if you can," he ventured, "do you know who was that lovely woman sitting in front of me? She has the most extraordinary voice."

"Ah yes, a rare thing in this parish," the vicar replied, with dry humor. "Has Lady Wythe commissioned you to help her find some voices for our Christmas competition?"

He was too honest to perjure himself further. "Not entirely, sir. I simply could not help but enjoy her voice. I will certainly inform my mother, of course," he added.

They were walking together toward the foyer. Chard looked up as they neared the entrance. The day had turned colder. He hoped that the beautiful woman had a ride home, wherever it was she lived. "Who is she?"

"You can only mean Junius Wetherby's little widow."

"Junius Wetherby?" he asked in surprise. "I had no

idea that rascal was married, much less dead." And what a relief that is, he thought without a qualm. He only remembered Junius as a care-for-nobody who gave the district a bad stink.

"And yet, it is no puzzle why they are keeping it so quiet." He looked around him again. "I gather that the Wetherbys, despairing of the church, bought the scamp a lieutenancy, which took him to Portugal." The vicar moved closer. "Apparently he met Rosie, promptly married her, and about a week later, fell out of a window while he was drunk."

Chard blinked in surprise. The vicar shook his head. "The Wetherbys sent for his body and his effects, and Rosie showed up, too, to everyone's amazement."

"Is she Portuguese?"

"No. From what I have learned of the whole business—which is precious little—she is the daughter of a Welsh color sergeant. Imagine how that sets with the Wetherbys, who probably think even captains are not sufficiently elevated!"

He had no love for the Wetherbys, but Chard winced anyway. "Trust Junius to disrupt, even from beyond the grave," he said. "Well, good day, Mr. Woodhull."

"Good day, my lord. Remind your mother of the necessity of recruiting a choir, if you will, sir. She promised, and I shall hold her to it."

They were waiting for him in the family carriage, but he indicated Sepoy tied nearby and motioned them on. The wind was picking up now, and he quickly regretted that he had not tied his horse behind the carriage and joined his mother and children inside. In his rush to not be late to church, he had forgotten his muffler, so he buttoned his overcoat as high as he could and resolved to move along quickly.

As Sepoy took him up the rocky path to home, the woman caught his eye again. Head down, she struggled across the field toward the Wetherby estate, which was still two miles distant. He stopped a moment and watched her, then continued on his way.

"She is Welsh, Mama," he said over Sunday dinner. "Perhaps that accounts for the beautiful voice. Oh, and she is a sergeant's daughter."

"She smiled at me," Will added.

"No, I think it was at me, son," Chard teased.

"No, Papa," Will said, sure of himself.

"Obviously she has had a profound effect on both of you!" Mama declared. With a glance at her grandson, she leaned across the table. "But, Pete, really! A sergeant's daughter *and* a Wetherby? That is more strain than any of us can stand." She laughed. "Can you *imagine* how things must be at the Wetherbys? No, I do not think we want to get embroiled in that."

"It was just a suggestion, Mama. Her voice is so pretty."

And her face, he thought later that night as he wrestled with accounts in the bookroom. It had been the most fleeting of glances, and by nightfall now, he remembered only the beauty of her eyes. He put down his pencil and rubbed his temples, where the headache was beginning. I must admit it, he thought. She stirs me. One glance and she stirs me. No wonder wretched Junius was a goner. He chuckled softly. And I do believe she did smile at Will.

By the end of the week the last of the hay was stacked in ricks and he faced the fact that he must have another barn. A visit to the Corn Exchange sent him home smiling with the news that corn was up and that the year would enjoy a prosperous conclusion. The day ended less satisfactorily with the sight of Rosie Wetherby walking in the cold. From the warmth of his carriage, he reached the glum conclusion that quite possibly she was not wanted at the Wetherbys and chose to walk away her days out of bleak necessity.

He was on the verge of mentioning something about his suspicions to Mama, but she gave him news of her own. "Son, I have succumbed to the fact that I must beg for a good soprano, even if she is a sergeant's daughter and a Wetherby," Mama said as soon as the footman served dinner and left the room. "I have written a note to the Wetherbys, stating that I will call on Monday."

"Take Will along," Emma teased.

Will, bless his calm demeanor, ignored his sister. "I would be happy to escort Grandmama," he declared, which left Emma with nothing to say.

"I will be depending on tenors and basses dropping from the sky before practice begins in two weeks," Lady Wythe said, then set down her fork in exasperation. "I so want a good Christmas choir for once, if only so my friends who reside within the parishes of Saints Anselm and Peter will not quiz me from Christmas to Lent!"

"Would you consider changing your circle of acquaintances?" Chard asked with a slight smile. "Or perhaps becoming a Muslim."

"Certainly not! I will find singers!"

As it turned out, by nine o'clock while she lamented in the sitting room and he read to Emma and Will in his own bed, events smiled upon Lady Wythe. Her daughter wrote a hasty, tear-splattered note to tell of chicken pox among her offspring and the dire necessity of her mother's presence immediately in Leeds. The welcome news was handed to her by postal express. The courier had scarcely left the house when she arrived at her son's bedroom, letter held triumphantly aloft.

"Pete, I am needed in Leeds!" She handed the letter to him and sat on his bed. "Now *how* can I possibly help Mr. Woodhull locate singers?"

He looked at her as warning bells went off in his head. "Mama, you don't imagine for one moment that this task of yours is to pass to me."

She gathered her grandchildren to her side. "Children, I cannot believe your father would fail me at this desperate moment when young lives are at stake in Leeds!"

"From chicken pox?" Will asked, always practical.

"It is scarcely fatal, Mama," Chard stated, but knew when he was defeated. "Bella needs you, I am sure. We'll manage here."

"And the choir?"

In his mind, ruin, disgrace, and another year's humiliation in the Christmas competition passed in review. "I will discharge your duty, my dear. Now get Truitt to help you pack. If I know Bella, she needs you this instant. I will escort you."

Leaving his children in the care of housekeeper, butler, and numerous doting servants, Lord Wythe took his mother south to Leeds and the open arms of his little sister Bella. He lingered long enough to observe the ravages of chicken pox among his nieces and nephews, notice that Bella was increasing again, and visit some former brothers in arms for needed information. Equipped with it, he wrote a few letters, walked the floor one night with a particularly feverish niece, and returned at noon on Monday at peace with himself and possessed of a plan.

Mercy, but I am tired, he thought as he changed clothes, ate standing up because he was tired of sitting, and kept one eye on the clock.

"I can go with you to the Wetherbys, Papa," Will offered.

"Perhaps not this first time," he replied, "but I do appreciate your interest, son." He took longer than usual with his neck cloth, and wished for the first time in years that he had a valet. "How is that?" he asked finally.

"A little crooked," Will said. "Bend down, Papa."

Chard did as he was advised and Will tugged on the neck cloth. The result was much the same, but he complimented his son, and let him carry his hat to the side door, where his butler handed him his overcoat again. He took the hat from Will. "I am off to hunt the wild soprano, my boy," he said and Will laughed. "Do wish me luck."

To be fair, there really wasn't anything the matter with the Wetherbys, he decided. He knew that if someone were to ask him point blank, that he would be hard-pressed to explain his dislike. But there you are: I do not like Sir Rufus Wetherby or his family, he thought as Sepoy stepped along with his usual sangfroid. He decided that Sir Rufus was very much like a cat that had insinuated himself into their household years ago. Someone—was it Bella?—named the beast Wooster for no discernible reason. Wooster had showed up one night at the servant's entrance, hollering and importuning, and then zipped in when someone opened the door, as if he had forgotten something inside.

Wooster never left, Chard remembered with a smile. He usurped the best spot before the fireplace, and always rushed to the scraps bowl before the other more polite household felines. In his rush to be first, he invariably ate too much and then threw it up, after much upheaval and noise. He would dash back to the bowl and repeat the process before the cook got disgusted and threw Wooster out. Wooster never learned. He was always there, first in line, when the door opened.

Bella loved the disgusting creature, but Papa threatened to anchor the cat in the driveway and run over it with the barouche.

That would be Sir Rufus, Chard thought. He has to be first at the food bowl. He is merely a baronet, yet he takes what he thinks are the best spots in the Corn Exchange, or the tavern, or even at church, when it suits him to go. Lord, it must chafe him that the Wythe box is so prominently situated, Chard thought. I believe he would have felt right at home with Cortez or Pizarro, rushing about and claiming things in the name of Spain. Sir Rufus is oblivious to the disdain of others, and thinks himself quite my equal.

Chard owned to some discomfort over that last thought. "I wish he would not fawn and slaver over me because I am a marquis and he is a baronet, Sepoy," he told his horse. "It smacks of the shop and embarrasses me. Perhaps that is why I never visit him."

The house, while large, never looked as though it belonged there. Chard gazed around him as he waited for someone to open the door. He decided that the general lack of permanence may have been partly to blame because of the painfully fake Greek temple that some misguided Wetherby had considered high art placed far too close to the front entrance. Mushrooms, he thought, then had the good grace to blush, and wonder perhaps if the first Lord Wythe centuries ago had been rendered insufferable by *his* title.

The butler ushered him in, asked his name, gulped almost audibly, then backed out of the hallway to leave him standing there like a delivery boy at the wrong door. Chard grinned when he heard Lady Wetherby shouting, "Sir Rufus! Sir Rufus!" into some nether part of the building. *Sir Rufus?* he thought in huge delight. I wonder if she calls him that while he rogers her?

So it was that he had a large smile on his face when

Rosie Wetherby entered the hall. He had only enjoyed the tiniest glimpse of her beauty a week ago during Mass, but surely no Wetherby by birth ever looked so good. It was Rosie. His smile deepened.

She carried her cloak over her arm, as though she were intent upon an expedition. "Oh, excuse me," she said, and to his pleasure, her voice had that pleasant lilt to it so typical of the Welsh.

"You really don't want to go outside," he said, without introducing himself.

"Oh, but I do," she returned as she raised her arms to swing the cloak around her shoulders.

He noticed then that she was pregnant, and farther along than Bella. Oh ho, Mrs. Wetherby, so this is why you are walking slower in October than you did in August, he thought, pleasantly stirred by the lovely sight of her, so graceful in her maternity.

"Well, keep your head down," he advised, as he came to her side to open the door. "Don't go too far from the house. If it starts to sleet, the stones will be slick."

She looked at him. "You're more solicitous than every Wetherby on the place," she whispered, her eyes merry. "They just tell me not to track in mud."

He laughed, wished he had some clever reply to dash off, and stopped short, the hairs on his neck rising, when Lady Wetherby shrieked behind him, "Lord Wythe! How honored we are! For heaven's sake, Rosie, close the door before he catches a cold!"

Rosie Wetherby did as she was told. For all her bulk, Lady Wetherby managed to leap in front of him to curtsy, her sausage curls at last century's style bobbing like demented watch springs. "We are so honored, my lord! And isn't that like your clever mother to let us think she was coming!"

"She was," he replied, stepping back a pace to ward

off such enthusiasm, and bumping into Rosie. "Pardon me, my dear." He turned around to look at Rosie Wetherby's loveliness. "You are . . . ?"

"Rosie Wetherby," she said, and held out her hand, which he shook.

"You should say, 'Mrs. Junius Wetherby, my lord,' and then curtsy!" Lady Wetherby admonished.

"Lord Wythe! We are honored!"

He looked around again, his head ringing with so much exclamation in a tight space, to see Sir Rufus advancing upon him, bowing as he came. Suddenly the hall was much too small, and all he wanted was out. He looked at the door handle with some longing, noticed Rosie's laughing eyes on him, and struggled to control the hilarity that warred with the chagrin inside him.

He held up his hands in self-defense as Sir Rufus minced closer. "My mother was called away by family business and I am merely discharging a duty for her, sir," he said, talking much too fast and feeling out of breath from the exertion of confronting more than one Wetherby at a time. As they looked at him, their expressions rapt, he grabbed Rosie by the hand and pulled her closer to him, closer than he intended, but his surprise move caught her off balance and she leaned against him. "I need a soprano for the Christmas choir," he said.

"Rosie, my lord? *That* is why you have come?" Lady Wetherby asked, making no attempt to hide her disappointment.

Well, hells bells, did you think I was going to ask you to dinner? he thought sourly, as he helped Rosie right her soft bulk, which—truth to tell—felt so good. "That's why," he finished lamely. He almost didn't trust himself to look at Rosie Wetherby because she was making small sounds in her throat that sounded suspiciously like laughter. He did look, because he knew he had to enjoy her up close as long as he could. "We really are a dreadful choir, my dear, and we need some help."

Sir Rufus and his wife crowded closer, and on a sudden whim, Chard whipped up the hood on Rosie's cloak and opened the door. "I think Mrs. Junius Wetherby and I will discuss this outside on a short walk," he told them firmly as he closed the door practically on their noses.

He took her hand because he feared that the front steps would be slick. They were not, but he did not relinquish her. They walked quickly down the steps, mainly because she was tugging at him to hurry. He understood a moment later when she stood behind a yew tree and laughed.

A few minutes later he gave her his handkerchief to wipe her eyes. "Oh, I do not know what you must think of me, but I don't know when I have seen anything so funny," she said when she could speak. She looked up at him, and he wondered how one human could be so lovely.

"They . . . they are a tad overwhelming," he agreed.

"I could tell, sir," she replied, and indicated a park close to the house. "I always find myself with an urge for a long walk."

He took her firmly by the arm again, appraising her and wondering how far along she was. "I know. I often see you walking my land," he said.

She stopped. "Perhaps I should apologize for trespassing," she said.

"No need. I'm sure the doctor has told you it is good exercise."

She blushed and looked away. "I've not seen a doctor. The Wetherbys think that is a needless expense. Bother it, Lord Wythe, *I* am a needless expense here.

There. I have said it." She continued walking. "I will be happy to sing in your choir. Promise me it will keep me from this house day and night!"

"I wish I could," he replied, not sure what to say. Mama would tell me I have stumbled onto a real bumblebroth, he thought. Good manners dictated that he say nothing, but for once in his life, he ignored it. Put me on the same acreage with the Wetherbys and I lose all propriety. "I . . . we . . . none of us had any idea that Junius Wetherby was married, much less deceased, Mrs. Wetherby."

He winced at his own words. I wonder anyone lets me off my own place, he thought, as he wondered if she would reply to something so ill-mannered.

"And what are they saying?" she asked quietly. She sat down on one of the more than ugly benches designed to look like a fallen log.

He stood beside her. "That you are Rosie Morgan, a Welsh sergeant's daughter with the army in Portugal."

"That's true," she said, then turned to look him straight in the eye. "But I have never earned my living on my back. My da was a good man."

"I am certain he was." It sounded stupid the minute he said it, as though he didn't believe her, and was just being polite.

Rosie Wetherby must have thought so, too. She gave him a patient smile. "That is not enough for you, is it? It certainly isn't for the Wetherbys."

He gritted his teeth, realized how much he disliked being lumped with the Wetherbys, and knew she was right. A veteran of marriage, he did the wisest thing when dealing with women who were right: he said nothing, and looked as contrite as possible.

"My mother was the daughter of a vicar in Bath, well educated, but perhaps not handsome enough to attract one of her own kind who never looked beyond a pretty face," Rosie explained, with the air of someone who had explained this too many times. "They met at church, and Mama lost her heart." She smiled. "And her mind, too, some would say. Da thought she was beautiful."

He picked up the narrative. "Oh, dear. Were there recriminations and threats, and tears and hasty words that no one could retract?"

She nodded. "Mama eloped with Sergeant Owen Morgan, and her father in all Christian charity told her never to return. She did not." Rosie Wetherby gave him a level look. "Yes, she married beneath her. No, it doesn't follow that she was unhappy. I do not know anyone who had a happier childhood than I did."

He was silent, thinking how kindly she had just set him down.

"The Wetherbys do not believe a word of this, naturally. Perhaps you don't, either, but it is the truth."

"So you have lived everywhere, and frankly led the kind of life that I know my children would envy."

She smiled again, but without that patient, wary look. "Do you know, I suppose I have. Of course, Mama insisted on teaching me manners, and niceties and airs, I suppose, but none seemed to mind that. Da taught me to sing."

"So I have noted."

"I was born in Jamaica, and lived in Canada and Ceylon." She sighed. "Mama died there, and Da and I soldiered on."

"You've never lived in England?"

"Never." She shivered and looked about her at the snow falling. "I cannot seem to get warm enough."

Not in that cloak, he thought. "And then it was Portugal? And Junius Wetherby?"

"Da died there," she said simply, quickly. "Junius Wetherby was a lieutenant in his regiment—Da was color sergeant—and he offered me 'protection.' " She made a face.

Chard nodded. He knew what that meant. "No choice, eh?" he asked quietly.

"Well, let us just say I made him improve his offer until it included marriage. I have followed the drum all my life, Lord Wythe." She smiled. "I suspect I knew more about soldiering than Junius, but we'll never know."

"I hear he met with a distressing accident," Chard said when her silence lengthened.

"Aye, he did," she agreed. "Only four days after our marriage, he was drinking with his comrades and sitting in a third-story window. He leaned back to laugh at someone's joke, forgot where he was, and lost his balance. Ah, me."

The sleet began that he had been predicting ever since he left his house. Rosie Wetherby shivered and moved closer to him, but made no move to rise and go inside. He looked at the house, wondering just how bad it was indoors for her to prefer sleet. "You . . . you chose England?"

"What could I do?" Her expression hardened for a moment. "I wouldn't know my grandfather the vicar if he came up and shook hands—which he would never do—and I couldn't stay with the army, of course. Junius had just enough money to get me almost here."

"Almost?" He was nearly afraid to ask.

She pulled her cloak tighter and hunched over, as though trying in some unconscious, involuntary way to keep her unborn child dry. "It got me as far as Durham."

"But that is twenty-five miles away," he exclaimed, caught up in her story. "What did you do?"

"I walked, sir!" she replied, making no effort to hide

the amusement in her eyes. "I told you I had followed the infantry from my birth."

"Yes, but—"

She laid her hand on his arm briefly, lightly. "Lord Wythe, it was summer and at least there are no snipers between Durham and here!"

He laughed along with her. "I'm an idiot," he apologized.

"No, you're not," she replied. "I hardly need tell you that I came as a complete surprise to the Wetherbys."

He closed his eyes, tried to imagine the scene, and discovered that he could not.

Rosie must have been watching his face. "Yes, it was every bit that bad!" she assured him, then made a face of her own. "And what do I discover but that Junius was a third son, and someone who did not figure very high even in Wetherby estimation."

"Yes, he has . . . had two older brothers," Chard said.

". . . where he told me he was only child and heir," she continued. She looked back at the house again. "Mrs. Wetherby grudges me every bite I eat, and counts the silverware every time I leave the dining room. I know she does not believe a word I have said. It's much more pleasant to walk outside, Lord Wythe, even in weather like this."

She was silent for a moment as the sleet pounded down. It cannot be good for you to sit out here, he thought, wanting to edge himself even closer and offer what puny protection she could derive from his body. Should I put my arm around her? he asked himself, and decided that he should not.

"You would like me in the choir?" she asked, reminding him of his purpose.

"Indeed I would! Will and I—Will is my son—sat behind you at Mass two weeks ago, and were quite captivated by your voice."

"Will." Without any self-consciousness, she scrutinized his face, and then he saw a smile of recognition in her eyes. "Yes, you were right behind me. His eyes are like yours."

"Yes, I suppose they are." He hesitated, then plunged ahead. "He's been telling his sister Emma for two weeks now that you smiled at him and not me. He was quite taken with you."

She laughed. "I like children." She touched his arm again. "Tell me about this choir, my lord."

"It is without question the worst choir in all the district," he said promptly. "Possibly in the entire British Isles. Every year our three neighboring parishes meet at one or the other's church before Midnight Mass. We were each supposed to sing a hymn or a carol, but the whole thing has gotten rather elaborate and become a competition." He stood up suddenly and pulled her to her feet. "Mrs. Wetherby, it is too cold to sit here! Shall we at least walk?"

He tucked his arm firmly through hers and she offered no objection. She let him lead her down a line of overgrown shrubs that had the virtue of masking the house. His arm, with hers tucked close, rested ever so slightly on her ample belly.

"We have little talent, but some of us—my mother among them—feel a real need to win just once."

"You don't care one way or the other?"

He surprised himself by shaking his head. "Not really. The fun for me is just to sing with Will, even if we are not very good."

"Then Will is lucky," she said. She looked at him, and through the freezing rain that made her cheeks so pale, he could see little spots of color. She rested her other hand lightly on her belly. "As you can tell, I will be big as a house by Christmas."

He smiled at her frankness, thinking of Lucy, who

hid away during her confinement with Will. I suppose she did not want the neighbors to think what we were doing to make a baby, he reflected with some amusement. "No matter. You are not tall, and we can hide you behind some altos." He cleared his throat. "I plan to continue my recruitment."

"In the neighborhood?" she asked. "My lord, you said this parish is short on good voices."

"Ah, well, I am recruiting rather farther afield than my mother intended," he admitted. "She was supposed to keep this appointment with you today, but her grandchildren in Leeds have chicken pox and she is there."

"So you have taken charge?"

"Why, yes, I have. You are my first project." He led her toward the house. "And if you should come down with a sore throat, I will be disturbed, as choir practice begins on Tuesday next. Let me take you indoors, Mrs. Wetherby."

She offered no objection, but he had to tug her along. Even then, she stood a moment at the front steps, her eyes bleak. "Do you know, I think they are trying to figure out how to turn me away, my lord," she murmured, as though it were merely an interesting complication. "It is a good thing that Christmas is only two months away. Perhaps the charity of the season will overtake them. Good day, Lord Wythe."

He nodded good-bye because he could do nothing more, mounted his cold horse, and took his leave. He looked back once to see Rosie still standing in the doorway, as though she intended to bolt back into the cold and snow once he was out of sight. Don't, Rosie, he pled silently. Stay inside where it is warm, even if the inmates are unfriendly.

"I have a soprano," he announced over dinner. The

news was received with reservation from Will and interest from Emma.

"Papa, she is only one soprano," his ever-practical son reminded him.

"True, Will. That is indisputable. You must look at this like a brigade major."

"Which you were, Papa," Will said with pride.

He winked at his son and took Emma upon his lap there at the dinner table. "It is like this, son"—he began, lining up three small bowls that even now the footman was attempting to fill with pudding—"if you put your best soldier between your two greenest recruits, what happens?"

Will looked at the three bowls. "Oh, I see," he said, then looked at Peter with a frown. "Mrs. Wetherby is going to teach the other sopranos to shoot, spit, and swear?"

Emma laughed. Peter hugged his daughter to his shoulder so Will could not see his huge grin. "My dear Will, she will teach them to sing, and give them her confidence. And whoever told you about shooting, spitting, and swearing?"

"Why, you, Papa," Will said with a grin of his own. "But is she going to be enough?"

"I am depending on more," he replied.

"From where, Papa?" Emmie asked as she ate her dessert.

"Oh, here and there," he said, knowing that his vague answer would never satisfy Emma. "From . . . from the Great North Road, my dear."

"Papa, that is far-fetched," she told him, then turned her attention to the pudding.

The house was quiet after he heard their prayers and tucked them in their beds. He stood a long while watching them as he always did, whether he was dog-tired from harvest, or weary from the irregularity of lambing in the raw Northumberland spring. Emma had been nearly a year old by the time he returned from India after the six-month-old news of Lucy's death in childbirth. And there was Will then, almost four, and big-eyed with the sight of him in his sunfaded, patched uniform, a stranger from another planet. He had spent many nights in the nursery, reacquainting himself with his son and meeting his daughter. Now that Lucy was gone, resigning his commission was the easiest thing he ever did. He knew he would find enough challenge in Northumberland's dales to keep him there, barring a French invasion.

As he stood there that night, grateful in his love for his children, he was teased with another thought, one that had not crossed his mind in more years than he could name. I want a wife, he thought.

The thought stayed with him as he checked all the doors, sent his old butler protesting off to bed, and sat himself down in the library, prepared to stare at the flames until they turned into coals. He spent more time at the window, watching the first snowfall of winter lay itself down in a thick blanket. When he finally lay down to sleep in the quiet house, he was at peace with himself. This was a good day, he thought. I wonder what tomorrow will bring?

Tomorrow brought a valet by the name of Owen Llewellyn with a note from Colonel James Rhys of the Welsh Fusiliers, who knew a good joke when he heard one. "You may return him if you wish," the note read, "but if he suits, keep him." After a rather querulous paragraph about the vicissitudes of waging peace in the wilds of Kent, Colonel Rhys wrote farewell, and wished to be remembered respectfully, etc. etc. to the Dowager Lady Wythe.

Chard examined his new valet, noting his dark

Welsh eyes and slight build. There remained only one question, and he asked it. "Tenor or bass?"

"Tenor, sir!" the valet responded with a snap-to and clicking of heels. He burst into "Men of Harlech," which even brought Chard's old butler wheezing up the stairs to stand transfixed by the bookroom door until the recital ended.

"Admirable, Llewellyn," Chard said when the man finished, still standing at attention. "You will be a remarkable valet. Just keep my clothes clean, make sure my shaving water is hot, and . . . Llewellyn, are you paying close attention?"

"Yes, sir!"

"Under no circumstances are you to go outside without a muffler around your neck."

"No, sir!"

As it turned out, he was too busy that day to worry much about Rosie Wetherby. He found himself welcoming a new under-bailiff, one Dafydd Williams from Cardiff, who by coincidence or divine intervention, sang bass. It gave him not a qualm to see young Williams safely bestowed into respectable quarters and to hear the glad tidings of great joy that Williams was recently married to his lovely Meg of Llanduff near Cardiff.

"And does she . . . ?"

"Alto, my lord."

"Send for her at once."

In fact, he would have gone to his mattress a happy man, except that Emmie was cross through dinner, refused her favorite baked apple with cream dessert, and was feverish by bedtime. He knew it was more than a crochet when Emma, most independent of his children, let him hold her on his lap until she fell into fitful slumber. He was not at all surprised when she came to his bed in the middle of the night, crying and clutching her throat. He kissed her, pulled her in close, and dozed and woke with her the rest of the night.

Dr. Barker called it catarrh and ordered bed rest and warm liquids. "I see this so often when the season turns to winter," he said with a hand on Chard's shoulder. "I expect Emma will be grumpy and melancholy in equal parts. Give her these fever powders every four hours. Do you have someone to watch her?"

He didn't, actually. He knew better than to bother Mama, busy with chicken pox in Leeds. The housekeeper had left only yesterday morning to visit her ailing sister in Durham, and she had burdened the maids with a long list of assignments. His old bailiff's wife was nursing lumbago, and the lovely Meg from Llanduff was not expected yet.

Will sat with his sister that morning while Chard worked in the bookroom with his bailiff, completing plans for the new barn and settling housing arrangements for the construction crew he expected any day. By noon, Will was worried and Emma in tears.

"Papa, she does not even argue with me," Will said over luncheon. "I mean, I told her that I could beat her to flinders at jackstraws and she just nodded!"

"This is serious, indeed."

He had a plan. In fact, as he stood at Emma's window, he realized that this was only one of many plans he had been scheming ever since Mama shouldered him with the choir. It had occurred to him last night, and nothing since then had convinced him that it was a silly idea. Quite the contrary: the more he thought about it, the better it sounded. He told his footman to summon the carriage.

The Wetherby estate was shrouded in fog as he drove up, and he liked it that way. The unspeakably stupid Greek temple was invisible, and the house itself, with its superabundance of trim and dormers, was mercifully indistinct.

Lady Wetherby insisted on plying him with eclairs and macaroons in her sitting room even though he really wanted hot coffee. She listened to his recitation—practiced in the carriage on the drive over—and shook her head.

"Rosie is really quite common," she said, leaning closer and licking the chocolate from the eclairs off her fingers. "I should wonder that you don't worry it will rub off."

"I will take that chance, madam," he replied, focusing his attention on a hideous vase of peacock feathers as Lady Wetherby dabbed at the crumbs on her bosom. "I need her help with Emma for a few days, if you think you can spare her."

"As to that, of course," Lady Wetherby said. "Truth to tell, I was wondering what to do with her this week." She edged even closer, to his dismay. "My darling Claude's fiancée is coming for a visit, and I do not want her to have to rub shoulders with someone from such a low class as Rosie!" She shuddered, and her greasy curls shook. "She tells a story about being well-born and her manners are pretty enough, but I cannot believe any of it. I wonder what Junius was thinking?"

Junius never thought much, that I can recall, Chard reflected to himself. Serves him right for getting drunk and falling out a window. If I had been but four days married to Rosie, I wouldn't have been sucking on sour mash with my comrades.

"Well, madam?" he asked finally, hoping to put enough curl in two words to remind her—somewhere below the level of her dim awareness—that he was a marquis.

It must have worked. She rose, curtsied until he feared for her corset stays, and left the room. In remarkably short order, Rosie Wetherby appeared in the doorway, satchel in hand, her cloak over her arm.

He rose quickly, pleased all over again at the sight of her. "So you will help me, Mrs. Wetherby?" he asked simply.

"You know I will," Rosie replied. She dabbed her hand across her eyes and he noticed as he came closer to help her with her cloak that there were tears in them.

"Are you all right?" he asked, speaking close to her ear as he put her cloak around her slender shoulders.

"Never better," she assured him. "I told Lady Wetherby I would return when you no longer needed me."

He knew that he would embarrass her if he uttered the first reply that rose to his active brain, but he was beginning to surprise himself with the fertility of his imagination. "It shouldn't be above a week. On behalf of my child, I do appreciate your help."

Lady Wetherby returned, all smiles, to see them out of the house. More particularly, she patted his arm, ignored her daughter-in-law, and made so much of him that he wanted to snatch Rosie in his arms and run screaming from the house. As it was, he closed the door on Lady Wetherby before she was entirely finished speaking, took a firm grasp on Rosie because the steps were icy, and escorted her quite carefully to his conveyance.

"I really don't have very good balance these days," she confessed as he helped her into the carriage. "Do you know, Lord Wythe, sometimes I look in the mirror and wonder where Rosie Morgan has got to."

"Would you change things?" he asked, berating himself silently that he had never managed to learn the art of small talk.

"Some things," she admitted. She rested her hand on

her belly. "Not all. But that's the way life is, isn't it? I learned that in the regiment, and it was a good school."

He nodded, made sure of the warming pan at her feet, and tucked a blanket around her. She smiled her thanks at him, then looked out the window. He noticed that she dabbed at her eyes once or twice in the short drive, but he knew he had not earned the liberty to ask her how he could help.

"Emma is six," he said finally, as the carriage turned into his estate. "She is independent, outspoken, and rather thinks she commands her brother and me."

"Does she?" Rosie asked.

"Oh, probably," he agreed, noting again that he was not embarrassed to show his complaisance to Rosie Wetherby. "I would do anything for her." He touched her arm. "If she knows that, at least she has the grace not to hold it over me like a sword."

"Lord Wythe, do you not have a wife?" she asked finally.

He was surprised that Lady Wetherby—she who could spread stories like farmers spread manure—had not unrolled his whole genealogy before her. *I wonder if they even talk, except when that harpy berates her daughter-in-law and tells her how common she is?*

"She died when Emma was born. I was serving in India. I returned home and resigned my commission." He stopped, dissatisfied with how brusque he sounded. He was silent as the carriage rolled to a stop. He contrasted the welcome of his home—large to be sure, and gray like the Wetherbys'—with the estate he had come from, and found it wanting in no way.

The footman was there in the drive to help Rosie from the carriage, but Chard assumed that responsibility, letting her lean for a moment against his shoulder as she got her balance. She gripped his hand, then relaxed when she saw that the walk was shoveled and there was no ice on the steps. He felt a twinge of pride as she looked about her, a smile on her face.

"I like the white trim," she said, then looked up at him, her eyes bright. "Tell me, sir, does the stone turn pink when the sun sets?"

"More of a lavender," he replied as he helped her up the steps. "You should see it in the spring when the flowers are up in the window boxes." And when the lawn is green and seems to roll right down to the stream, and the lambs are stiff-legged and bonking about, and the orchard is a dazzle of apple blossoms. "I love it here." What a clunchy thing to say he berated himself, but she smiled at him, and there was nothing but kindness in her brown eyes.

He took her right upstairs to Emma's room. Will sat there, his chin on his palm, watching his sister. Emma opened her eyes when she heard him enter the room.

Rosie did not know his children, but she did not hang back in the doorway. She came forward right beside him, first to stop at Will's chair. "You must be Will. How lucky Emma is to have a brother who will watch her."

Will leaped to his feet and Chard had to turn away to hide his smile. Oh, Rosie, think of the conquests you have made, he thought.

"Wou—would you like this seat?" Will asked.

She smiled at him, but shook her head and turned to Emma. "Not now, my dear, but thank you. I rather think I will sit with Emma."

"Emma, this is Mrs. Wetherby," he said softly as Rosie settled herself on the bed. "She's here as long as you need her."

To his amazement, independent Emma heaved a sigh and reached for Rosie, who gathered her close. "My throat hurts," she whispered, then burst into tears.

Chard blinked, then felt his face redden with embarrassment. "Mrs. Wetherby, you must think we are unfeeling brutes here," he said. "Truly, we have seen to her care."

She glanced at him over her shoulder as she smoothed Emmie's tangled hair. "Never mind that, sir. Sometimes a little lady just needs a mother." She wiped Emmie's face with the damp cloth that Will handed her. "And what a fine brother she has! My dear, could you go downstairs and talk your cook out of a half-cup of treacle, some mint, and a spoon? Emmie, with Will's help, your throat will be better in two shakes. My lord, please hand me the hairbrush over there. Nothing does a body better than a good hair brushing."

They both did as she said. When he closed the door quietly, Emmie's eyes were closed and Rosie was brushing her hair and humming to her.

"Papa, she's good," Will said as they went downstairs together. "Did Mama do things like that?"

Probably not, he thought. Lucy had told him on several occasions how much she disliked the sickroom, and mewling, puking babies. "Of course she did," he lied. "You're just too young to remember." He touched his son's shoulder. "You're going to discharge your duty with the cook? Good." He rested his hand on Will's head for a brief moment. "Just think, son: maybe you could come down with something, too."

Will grinned at him. "Or you, Papa."

How tempting that would be, he thought later that afternoon when he let himself into Emma's room. Dressed in a fresh nightgown, his daughter slept. The room smelled of lavender and clean sheets. Rosie sat in the chair with her feet resting on the bed, an open book on what remained of her lap, her eyes closed, too. She opened them, even though he was sure he had not made any noise.

"I'm sorry," he whispered. "I did not mean to wake you."

She sat up, her neat hair coming out of its pins, and to his mind, incredibly appealing. "I should be awake, my lord," she whispered back. "You will think me none too attentive."

He sat carefully on the bed so as not to disturb his daughter, but also not to miss a single opportunity to admire Rosie Wetherby. "I . . . Will and I are convinced that you really must be an angel."

She put her hand over her mouth so she would not laugh out loud, but her eyes were merry. "I doubt that in my present condition I could fly too well, sir!" she looked at her charge. "She is better, isn't she? You have a lovely daughter. Does she look like her mother?"

"Like Lucy? No," he replied, amused by his own thoughts. "She is her own person." He admired Emma's serenity, after a night of restless sleep. Hers and mine, he thought, suddenly tired.

He was aware that Rosie Wetherby was watching him with that same look she had earlier trained on Emma. "I am fine!" he protested, to her unspoken question. "Just a little tired."

"And you were likely up all night with Emma, weren't you?" she asked. "I hope you are not planning to sit up with her tonight, my lord."

"Well, yes, actually."

"No," she said. "I am going to be sharing Emma's room and whatever she needs I can give her. I have already spoken to the footman and he is arranging a cot for me."

"That is truly too much trouble for you," he said, but it sounded weak to his own ears.

"It is no trouble," she replied. "I cannot tell you what a relief it is to be useful to someone. Thank you for asking me, my lord."

The pleasure truly is mine, he thought, as he nodded to her, took another look at Emma, and left the room. There was something so restful about Rosie Wetherby, he decided as he went slowly down the stairs to the bookroom. It may have been her condition that made her so. He liked the deliberate way she did things, from brushing Emma's hair to touching Will's shoulder when he brought her what she needed from Cook. She seems to be studying our comfort, he thought, and what a pleasant thing that is. I wish she would touch me, he thought suddenly, then blushed and set his mind firmly on the ledgers on his desk.

God, please take me away from these, he thought later, as the afternoon waned. He made a face and closed the ledger, adding it to the stack on the desk. My barns are full, my stocks are high, I could probably buy Paris if I wanted it. Why the restlessness? "Lord, grant me a diversion from stodgy prosperity," he said, then looked out the window and smiled.

They were coming. It could only be his construction crew for the new barn, hired by his old one-armed colonel, retired now in Wales. One, two, three, four, he counted as he stood by the window, and they have brought all their tools. He glanced at his desk, with its drawing of the barn he needed, and then the copy of Franz Josef Haydn's "The Heavens Are Telling" lying next to it. "But more to the point," he said out loud as he took a tug at his neck cloth and looked for his coat, "can these builders sing?"

They could and did, he discovered, and with the same enthusiasm that his new valet had shown. It was starting to snow again, and the temperature was dropping even as he stood there in the driveway, hands in his pockets, as the men gathered around. To his unutterable joy they looked at each other, someone hummed a note, and they sang "While Shepherds

Watched Their Flocks by Night." The song rang with all the fervor that he remembered from the Welsh Fusiliers in India, singing in spite of, or perhaps because of, the worst conditions.

How was it that the Welsh can even make the closing notes hang in the air, as though they sing in a cathedral? He sighed with pleasure. One of the men stepped forward, didn't quite bow (which pleased him even more), and introduced himself as Daniel ap Jones, late sergeant of the Fusiliers and a graduate, like himself, of the hard school of Assaye. "I outrank them others, sir," he said, indicating the other singers. "Your old friend in Swansea indicated that you might like that song, considering that it's a local favorite."

"Aye, it is, Jones, think on," he replied, lapsing gracefully into the color of local speech. He looked down the lane again as another conveyance approached, then back at Jones, a question in his eyes.

"Our wives," Jones said. "T'old colonel thought you could use them, too."

"I am in heaven, Jones," he replied simply. "And do they sing as divinely as you?"

The men looked at each other. "All except Lloyd's wife, sir," Jones explained, the remorse deep in his voice. The other builders chuckled and nudged the one who must be Lloyd. "He married Gracie Biddle from Devon and she can't even carry a note to the corner and back."

"Ah, lad! Me auld lady can cook!"

Lord bless the military, he thought. The whole unloading of wives, children, household goods, and tools was accomplished with a certain precision that made him proud, even though he was six years removed from the army. "Just long enough, I suppose, for me to forget what a tedious, nasty business it really was," he said to Rosie that night, his feet propped on Emma's bed, as he relaxed in a chair he drew up close.

Rosie nodded. "Glorious once in a while on parade." She sat next to Emma on the bed, her fingers light on the child's hair. "Did you ever fight with the Fusiliers, my lord?"

He nodded. "I commanded an excellent brigade, my dear, but I was always glad when the Fusiliers were close by." He looked at his daughter, who rested, dreamy-eyed and at peace with herself, against Rosie's round belly. "And now, my dearest Emma, you have been tended, coddled, fed, read to, and entertained for the better part of the day by someone much kinder and softer than your father. Let me recommend sleep to you now."

Rosie smiled at him, and he could only smile back, because she was irresistible. "Emma assures me that you are kindness, itself, my lord," she teased.

He bent over to kiss his daughter, but stopped when he noticed how round her eyes had become. She was looking at Rosie, a question in her eyes.

"The little one always gets lively in the evenings, Emma," the woman explained, resting her hand on her belly. "Only think how busy I will be when she . . . or he . . . is born."

Emma let out a sigh, her eyes still filled with amazement as she pressed her ear against Rosie. Before he could stop her, she grabbed his hand and placed it against Rosie's side. "Papa! Can you imagine anything half so wonderful?"

He could not. As embarrassed as he was, Chard knew Emma would be upset if he snatched his hand away. Trusting that Rosie would not smite him for his most ragged of manners, he kept his hand where Emma held it, touched by the tumult within. He remembered better times with Lucy, when she had wrapped her arms around him as they lay in bed, and he had felt the steady kicking of their unborn son against his back. "It *is* wonderful, Emma," he agreed, sorry that his voice was not more steady. He took his hand slowly away, too shy to look at the Welsh woman.

"Did I do that, too?" Emma asked him in hushed tones.

"I'm certain you did, love," he assured her.

She sat up. "But you don't know?"

"I wasn't there. I was in India." Oh, that is hardly going to satisfy her, he thought, not this daughter who questions everything. He held his breath, exasperated with himself.

Emma frowned at him, and he knew he was trapped into more explanation than he wanted to begin, especially under the amused glance of Rosie Wetherby. "Then how . . ." she paused, her frown deepening. "Grandma told me—"

To his relief, Rosie came to his rescue. "My dear, do you think your questions can keep until your grandma returns?"

Emma nestled next to Rosie again. "Do you mean that my father does not know the answers?" she asked softly.

Peter laughed. "No, you scamp! It is merely that this is a subject not to be discussed lightly."

"I promise I won't tell Will," Emma whispered. "I only want to know how babies get in and how they get out. That is not so much to ask."

"No, it is not," he agreed, reminding himself that if he had wanted an easy path, he could still be in the army—with Wellington now in Spain—and far away from questions that made him sweat more than combat.

"Do you know, Emma, I can answer those very

questions," Rosie said finally, "that is, if you father will allow me."

Quite possibly I will kneel at your feet and worship the ground that you glide over, he thought. "Mrs. Wetherby, you're on," he said, without allowing her a millisecond to change her mind. He kissed his daughter. "Good night, my dear."

Emma kept her arms around his neck. "Papa, you could stay and listen, too. Perhaps you will learn something."

He laughed and kissed her again. I probably would, he thought as he stood in the doorway and watched the two of them with their heads together. How odd, Mrs. Wetherby, how odd. I do not know you well, but I trust you. Your mother-in-law claims that you are common, but I call you uncommon.

Uncommon fine, he considered, as he relaxed in the next bedchamber, listening to Will read his geography and paying no attention to his description of the land of Serendip. True, he had been no farther from his holdings than Leeds in the past six years, but he knew he had never seen finer brown eyes anywhere. Her lips were full, and seemed as generous as her nature. True, it would take a man with a greater imagination than he possessed to divine what a figure she really had, but he hoped, with a wistfulness that surprised him, that her bosom truly was that ample, under more normal circumstances.

"It that how it is, Papa?"

"I'm afraid so, son," he replied with a shake of his head. I am undone over a woman seven months gone with child who is the daughter of a Welsh color sergeant, and worse and worse, the widow of a scamp with cheese where his brains should have been. "There's no explaining it."

He looked up to see Will frowning at him over the

top of his geography. "Papa, all I wanted to know was
whether the water is truly that blue in Colombo's har-
bor."

Chard blinked. "Son, I had my mind elsewhere."

"Next door, Papa?" Will asked, and Chard started
again. Lord, am I so transparent?

"Well, yes, actually," he managed.

Will closed the book and came to him where he sat.
Chard made room for him. "Papa, I am worried about
Emma, too, but I think that Rosie—"

". . . Mrs. Wetherby," he said automatically.

"She wanted me to call her Rosie," Will said. "Rosie
can manage Emma, so you needn't worry and get all
blank in the face."

And blank in the head, he thought. "Son, it is time
for bed."

"Papa?"

"Hmm?"

"Do you think Rosie would wait for me to grow up
so I could marry her? That's what I would most like to
do."

Chard smiled down at his son. "I think you should
not place too large a wager on the matter. Come now,
and climb into bed."

Will did as he was told. "Maybe someone like Rosie
then?" he amended after Chard kissed him good night.
There is no one like Rosie, Chard thought as he closed
the door and went quietly downstairs.

She was waiting for him in the sitting room before
the fireplace, where the butler had directed her, ready
to pour tea. He seldom drank tea in the evening, because he hated to get up in the middle of the night to
deal with its consequences, but he took a cup from
Rosie and then made sure she had the most comfortable chair, with a pillow behind her back.

"I trust now that Emma is armed with enough infor-

mation to make her dangerous at family gatherings?"
he joked as Rosie relaxed into the chair. He pushed a
low stool under her feet when she raised them. "Do I
dare take her anywhere?"

The woman sipped the tea appreciatively and leaned
back. "Of course! I assured her that everything I told
her was privileged information and that she was not to
divulge it to any of her friends. Or Will, she assured
me." She laughed and leaned forward to touch his
wrist as he sat close to her. "She is so bright."

He cleared his throat. "It . . . it doesn't embarrass you
to talk about such things?"

She thought a moment then shook her head. "Children like to know what is going on, sir. It's only life."

"So it is," he said. He was silent then, looking into
the fire, and feeling no need to talk. It was enough to
sit with Rosie.

He was working up to some conversation when his
bailiff came into the room with idle nonsense about
grain storage that could not wait until morning, apparently. With real reluctance he offered his apologies to
Rosie, set Cook's good biscuits closer to her elbow, and
followed his bailiff to the bookroom, hating every step
of the way.

He knew she would be gone to bed when he returned, so he almost did not go into the sitting room
again, when his bailiff was through. I should at least
ring for my footman so he can remove the tea, he
thought, as he hesitated at the door.

The room was dark now, the fire settling into a glow
of coals that reminded him of Christmas. I wonder
where I will find my Yule log this year? he thought
idly. And I am certain that it will take me all of the next
month to figure out a way to invite Rosie Wetherby to
celebrate the season with us without all her deplorable
in-laws sniffing at her heels.

He went to throw himself down in his chair again, but there was Rosie where he had left her, only asleep this time, her head pillowed against the chair wing, her feet tucked under her now. Without a word, he sat himself on the stool where her feet had been, relishing the sight of her.

"Rosie? Rosie?" He called her name quietly, and she did not waken. Oh, too bad, he thought with real pleasure as he carefully picked her up and went to the stairs. She was hardly a weight at all as he climbed the stairs with his Christmas soprano. She settled against his arm as though she belonged there and he was hard put to let her down, even when he stood over her cot.

He put her down with great reluctance, pleased at the boneless way she slept. This was not a woman to thrash about, or walk the floor for no reason, growing more irritable by the moment, and berating him because this was Northumberland, and not London. With a sigh, Rosie Wetherby succumbed to the mattress, made it her own, and offered no objection when he removed her shoes.

Her stockings were clean, but darned many times. He picked up one of the shoes he had set down, and looked at the run-down heel and the sole thin from walking. He knew he was in no position to offer her anything, and he could think of no subterfuge that would trick her into accepting even a pair of cotton stockings from him. This is a season of giving, and as a widower, I cannot give her clothing. It would only appear forward or suggestive of mischief, he thought.

He blew out the candle on the nightstand and turned to go. Some impulse turned him around again, him, the least impulsive of men. He knelt beside the bed and rested his hand on her belly again. The baby inside was sleeping now, for all he knew. With a smile, he pressed steadily on Rosie's side until the little one moved away from his hand, then kicked back, to his delight. He lightened the pressure of his hand and tensed all over when Rosie murmured something, and covered his hand with her own. I do not dare move, he thought in panic. The baby continued to kick, and in another moment, Rosie's hand was heavy as she returned to deeper sleep.

He waited another moment beside the bed until her breathing was regular again, but even then he was not inclined to leave the room. He sat for a while in the chair, content to watch them both, until he realized with a guilty pang that his valet—the tenor—was probably waiting up for him. At least Owen Llewellyn is not the sort to wring his hands and grieve if I am late, he thought as he left the room quietly. And I did tell him never to wait up for me.

To his relief, Llewellyn was asleep in his little corner of the dressing room. He had laid out Chard's nightshirt and robe, and the fire was just high enough for comfort. In a moment Chard was in bed, if vaguely disappointed with his solitude. Emma will not want me tonight, he thought, his hands behind his head as he stared at the ceiling. Will seldom gets up in the night. At least his feet were not cold; Llewellyn had thoughtfully placed a warming pan in his bed.

Soon Christmas will be upon us, he thought, closing his eyes and enjoying the warmth. Mama will ask me what I would like for a present, and I will never be able to think of anything, as usual. We will probably go to Bella's, provided her little criminals are over the chicken pox. Brother-in-law Matthew will carve the goose, and Bella will look at me in that soft way of hers. She will assure me that it would be no trouble to find me an agreeable widow, or a maiden lady who would be relieved to splice herself to a farmer with a pedigree (however little he bothered about it), considerable wealth, and two children.

"There is no reason for a woman of fashion or sense to marry you!" she had raged at him during his recent visit to deposit Mama. "I have always thought you handsome, but you *will* insist upon wearing your clothes until they are fit for nothing but the rag bag, and it must have been months since someone with skill cut your hair."

He grinned in the dark, remembering how his mild comment that at least he did not stink and never scratched in public had only served to propel her irritation to undreamed-of heights. He knew they should both be embarrassed because Mama had had to intervene, as she had been doing for more than thirty years, but Lord forgive me, it is still fun to tease my little sister Belly.

His thoughts changed direction. He turned over on his side and looked out the window. He had forgotten to close the draperies, but then, he seldom closed them. The stars were as bright as the coming of winter could make them. He thought then of Haydn, and his choir, all bedded down for the night, and ready to begin building him a barn tomorrow. This will be a choir competition that no one forgets, he thought, and it was his last thought before the sky brightened with dawn.

Even though he and Will hurried through breakfast with Emma and Rosie, the Welsh carpenters were already hard at work when they arrived at the building site. Lord bless me, they are singing, he thought as they approached the farm yard. I am in heaven. He and Will just stood and listened, arm in arm, admiring the crispness of the notes in the cold morning.

"Why are they so good, Papa?" Will asked, his voice hushed and reverent as the carpenters, to the rhythm of hammers and saws, sang a hymn they were both familiar with.

"Some say it is merely because they are from Wales," Chard replied.

"Emma would call that a silly reason," Will said after a moment's thought.

"What would you say?"

His son smiled. "I would say it didn't matter, as long as they sing so well."

Chard nodded. No question that you are my son, he thought, pleased with himself. I suppose it irritates Emmie, but some things just can't be explained.

They helped where they could that morning, but it was soon obvious to Chard that his old friend in Wales had chosen this crew for both singing and building capacities. He was glad enough to retreat inside after sharing lunch with his crew in the shelter of the cow barn close by. Will shivered with cold, even though Chard knew he would never admit it.

"Will, perhaps we should rescue Mrs. Wetherby from Emma for an hour or two. You wouldn't mind entertaining your sister, would you?" he asked, careful to overlook Will's chattering teeth.

"If you think they won't miss us here, Papa," he said.

Chard shook his head. "They can spare us, lad."

They arrived upstairs to find the doctor with Emma, thumping her for soundness, while Rosie sat in the window seat, relaxed and yet watchful at the same time. I have seen cats guard their kittens like that, Chard thought with amusement. He joined her in the window seat.

"I suppose I must hope that he declares Emma sound of wind and limb," she whispered to him finally.

"You 'suppose'?" Chard asked, surprised.

She nodded, not taking her eyes from the doctor. "You will not need me anymore when he declares her fit."

He could say nothing to that because she was right. Now that is a dreadful turn of events, he thought, then thrashed himself mentally for not considering the eventuality. Lord, I am a butterfly, living for the moment, he told himself in disgust. While I would never wish Emma ill, too bad Rosie is such a proficient nurse.

"Excellent, excellent, Lord Wythe!" the doctor declared as he straightened up. "Another day and Emma will be sound as a roast. Right, my dear?" he beamed at her, as Emma glared back and tugged at her nightgown.

He walked the doctor downstairs, only half-listening to his story of neighborhood illnesses and all the while thinking, my Lord, tomorrow I will have to return Rosie to those deplorable Wetherbys. Lady Wetherby will never spend a penny to take Rosie to the silk warehouse for even a pair of stockings, much less a cloak that isn't full of holes. I wonder if Rosie even has a single nightgown or nappie for the baby? The thought upset him as nothing else could. He remembered all the care and attention he had lavished on Lucy when she was waiting Will's arrival: her clothes, the special food, a cradle specially made, and more nightgowns, sacques, and receiving blankets than Will could ever use.

"Doctor, when you return tomorrow, would you ask Mrs. Wetherby if she would like to talk to you about her approaching confinement?" he asked as they stood together by the front door. "I am also quite willing to take on the charge for that event, because she has been so helpful to me here. I will let that be my gift of thanks."

"I suppose this means that the Wetherbys are doing

nothing for her?" the doctor asked. He must not have expected an answer because he hurried on. "We've been hearing things in the village." He allowed the footman to help him into his coat. "Ah, me. Of course I will speak to her tomorrow." He sighed again. "Things must have been at a pretty pass for her in Portugal if she thought marrying Junius Wetherby would improve her situation."

"From what she has told me, her hand was forced. She is surely not the first to contract a disastrous alliance under a fog of optimism," Chard heard himself saying. Where did *that* come from? he asked himself.

After his return from India, Chard had resolved that he would not think about Lucy and what had gone before, but as he sat in the tub that afternoon, chin on his knees, he found that he could not help it. There was no point now in asking himself why he had ever agreed to the wedding. He had not needed her money; there was no land of any value that came with her; his parents (not hers) were under no obligation. He had met her at an assembly ball in Durham, but he had met other young ladies there before. True, she was a pleasure to look at, and the daughter of a well-connected family, but that was all.

I would never have pursued the affair on my own, he decided as he soaped himself and let Owen Llewellyn pour warm water over him. My family has always known me to be shy, and bless their hearts, they thought to help. The thing is, why did I ever let them talk me into it? And more to the point, am I still so pliable?

He thought he was not. No farmer was more resistant to panic than he, especially in the Corn Exchange, when the buyers were more irritating than fleas, calling bids. He had the instinct to know when the bid would go no higher, and wait until then.

He had stood firm at Assaye when he wanted to scream and run and dig a hole somewhere and drop himself in it. In a voice as calm as though he had asked someone to pass the bread at table, he had gone from man to man, encouraging, prompting, standing tall as shot and shell whizzed around him at the Kaitna ford. What was it about Lucy Monroe that he had been unable to cry off, when he knew he wanted to? Why was he so unable?

I should never have listened to all my friends and relations telling me what a prize I was getting in Lucy Monroe, he thought as he wrapped himself in his robe and sat looking out the window. What little conversation we had before marriage showed her to be a shallow, vain little thing. I should have withdrawn my offer, taken my lumps, and left the field.

He winced and felt his shoulders grow cold, even though the room was well-heated. Instead, I married her and discovered quickly that my wife was no fun. She was fueled by no love, like, or even lust, and saw no more to me than a title for herself and the promise of London, in the which I sadly disappointed her. She hated every minute of her confinement with Will and never wanted me near her again. Almost never.

His lips set in firm lines, Chard dressed quickly, shaved, and tidied up after himself before he remembered that he had a valet to do all that now. The sad thing is, he told himself as he went downstairs to dinner, I like women. If Lucy had shown any pleasure in it at all, we could have had some famous romps in bed. And now there is nothing. He paused on the bottom step. I am too much an honorable man to go near a doxy, even though none of the longings have left me. I work hard because I need to be tired every night. I am afraid to make another attempt. When left to my own devices, I am a coward. Shame on me.

He was grateful that he did not have to make conversation on the way to choir practice. He had filled his carriage with the Welsh women, and the men came after in the gig and on horseback. Rosie Wetherby sat next to him, her eyes bright with the pleasure of being with her father's countrywomen. He glanced at Rosie, who was crammed so tightly against him that he could feel her baby kick. It should have flattered him that she was so loath to leave his house tomorrow, but it only sank him deeper, knowing there was nothing he could do to stop it.

St. Philemon's was brightly lit, and he was gratified to see so many carriages, gigs, and blanketed horses there. He drew his singers around him for a moment of strategy before they went inside. "I know you will do your best," he said simply, then laughed and shook his head as some of the veterans of Wellington's army grinned at him. "Lads! I know what you are thinking! Although I must sound like every officer who has ever exhorted you on the field of battle, believe me, this is more important than Agincourt and Blenheim combined!"

He enjoyed their laughter, and continued, to their amusement, in his brigade major voice. "If we do not have a good choir, my mother will be sorely disappointed. I will have to sneak into a back pew at St. Phil's every Sunday morning, and the vicar will preach deadly sermons from Leviticus or Revelation to take his revenge upon me. Do your best. England may not care much, but I do."

The steps were icy, so he turned instinctively to look for Rosie, found her at his side, grasped her by the elbow, and helped her indoors without saying a word.

Once inside, he looked at her. "That was silly, wasn't it?" he said.

She shook her head. "Lord Wythe, do you know what your singers are already saying about you?"

"I can't imagine." And he couldn't. While he had admired the Fusiliers in India, he had never commanded them. "Well, maybe I can," he amended, as he walked with her to the choir seats at the front of the chapel. "I am Lord Mark Time, eh?"

He could tell he had surprised her with that nickname. "Oh, no!" she exclaimed. "Mostly they are excited to be working for you, because they remember you from India." She leaned closer. "Were you really a legend there?"

It was his turn to stare. "Not that I know of," he replied honestly. "They must have me confused with someone else."

"No, they don't," she replied. "Men like that don't confuse their heroes."

"I never imagined—" he began.

"You probably never did," she said.

He looked at her. "I'm not the quickest man on the planet."

"Yes, you are," she said. "What you also are is humble, and I think it must be so rare that no one recognizes it." She touched his arm. "For your children's sake, please never change."

He stared at her. No one had ever spoken to him like that before, and her words fell on him like warm rain. He had no idea what to say, and was relieved when the choirmaster asked them to take their seats. His face still blazing with embarrassment, Chard settled her between two of the weakest sopranos and took his place with the basses. His under-bailiff made room for him, leaning close to whisper, "Sir, thank you for sending for Meg."

He shrugged off any reply, his eyes on the choirmaster. "Really, my lord, you'll like Meg's voice," Dafydd Williams assured him. "I think she can be made useful around the estate, too, sir."

Startled, Chard glanced at his under-bailiff then looked down at the music the bass on the other side was handing him. I wonder, Williams, if you would believe me if I told you that I wasn't thinking about your wife's voice when I sent for her? he thought. I wanted you to have Meg close, and that was all.

"Doesn't matter about the estate, Williams," he whispered back, even as the choirmaster—no respector of marquises—glared at him. "You have a nice little cottage. Just let her keep it for you." He laughed, then put his hand over his mouth when the choirmaster started in his direction. "Consider it an early Christmas present."

The St. Philomen's Christmas choir waited a few minutes more to allow two latecomers to seat themselves, and Chard looked over his contribution of singers, noting with a brigade major's strategic eye how wisely they had spaced themselves among the uninitiated. I appear to have three sopranos, two altos, three tenors, and three basses, he observed.

With half an ear, he listened to the choirmaster's usual greeting, which contained, as it did every year, equal parts of resignation and exhortation, mingled with sufficient rue to dampen even the celestial enthusiasm of a multitude of the Heavenly Host. I must suggest to Mr. Woodhull after Christmas that it is time to replace our choirmaster, he thought, then smiled at the idea of approaching his vicar, who would not recognize a tune even if it bit his bottom. He will wonder why I am so inclined, but offer no resistance. Ah, well. This is one of the few occasions in life when being a marquis and the holder of Woodhull's living will carry the day, he told himself.

The choirmaster cleared his throat and everyone looked up expectantly. "My dears, let us not tackle the Haydn immediately, but warm up first on a hymn." He turned to the organist. "May I suggest 'The Mighty Power of God Unfolding'? A note please, sir, if you will."

It was a rousing, familiar hymn and everyone knew it. The sound of incredible, perfect harmony exploded in the church, booming from wall to wall with all the majesty the hymnist must have intended, but which had never before been even remotely achieved at St. Phil's. By the end of the first stanza, the choirmaster was gripping the lectern, his knuckles white. At the completion of the chorus, he waved the choir to a halt and staggered to a seat.

A soprano and a tenor from the front row reached him first, fanning him with Haydn, while an alto loosened his neck cloth. He sat for a long moment under their ministrations, then waved them back to their seats with a hand that shook. The doctor, who only dreamed that he was a bass, took his pulse, then helped him to his feet. He guided him back to the lectern and the choirmaster clamped his hands firmly again, a changed man.

It was still a moment before he could speak. "My dears, the strangest thing happened," he said finally, and he sounded like a different man. "I dreamed that you were singing, and in tune. How singular." He looked down at the music before him, but to Chard's view, he was not actually seeing anything. "I am certain it was a trick of hearing. Let us tempt fate again and try a mellower hymn. 'Lambs Sweetly Feeding,' if you will be so kind, my dears."

The soft beginning was no more difficult than the

magnificent spiritual call to arms that had preceded it.
As led by the Welsh singers, each note was sustained,
melodic, and softer than dew on the hillside. Chard did
not sing, preferring to listen to those around him and
enjoy their special national gift. He noticed that others
of the choir were doing the same thing. The Welsh
singers could not have been more oblivious. They sang
with the fervor peculiar to their race, fervor he had remembered all these years, and thousands of miles from
dry Indian washes and the scorch of a sun that burned
up everything but song.

The hymn ended, the choirmaster closing it with all
the feeling and artistry of a man half his age. "This is a
miracle," he declared. "My dears, do let us examine the
Haydn before us." He leaned forward to confide in
them. "I admit I was wondering if we would have the
capacity for this selection. Wasn't I the silly one?"

They sang for more than an hour, the choirmaster in
such a state of bliss that his wife had to tug at his arm
finally. When that effort proved fruitless, she dragged
his watch from his coat pocket, opened it, and waved it
under his nose like smelling salts. "Very well, if we
must," he grumbled.

We must, thought Chard. He glanced at Rosie, who
was starting to droop. In another moment they were
dismissed and he was at Rosie's side. Without a word
he helped her into her cloak and assisted her from the
church. She was quiet on the ride home, and he could
think of nothing to say. It was enough to sit next to her.
Before they turned into the lane before Wythe, she
leaned against him, asleep.

Sitting there in the dark carriage, with the other
women silent and sleepy around him, too, he realized
with a pang how much he missed the conversation of
women at night. True, Lucy had not been the warmest
of females, but early in their marriage he had enjoyed

her inconsequential chatter about the events of the day, told in all its minutia from her point of view. It was always different from his, and it charmed him somehow to know that women were different creatures entirely. I miss that, he thought as the carriage came to a stop and Rosie woke up. She apologized for crowding him, but he only smiled and helped her down.

Will was asleep when they checked on him. To Chard's eyes, his son was sleeping peacefully, but Rosie had to tug up the blanket higher, and smooth his hair before she would leave the room. This must be what mothers do, he thought as he watched her bend down awkwardly to kiss him. I am sure Lucy never did.

Gracie Biddle Jones, who could not carry a tune, had volunteered to sit with Emma. When they came in the room, she said good night quickly and left the room. Rosie felt Emma's forehead and nodded in satisfaction. She turned and held out her hand to him. "Good night, my lord." He had no excuse to stay, so he went to his own room, knowing somehow that he would be awake all night.

When the doctor arrived in the morning, he went first to Rosie as he had promised, spending some time with her, in another room separate from Emma. He came out to assure Chard that Mrs. Wetherby was strong as a little French pony and right as a trivet.

"Doctor, all similes aside, will she do?" Chard asked point blank as he walked with him to Emma's room.

The doctor laughed and clamped his hand on Chard's shoulder. "Someone would think it was your baby, laddie, and not poor Junius Wetherby's!" he exclaimed. "She's fine, and she knows to send for me when her time comes." He frowned then. "Can't trust the Wetherbys with so much sense."

The doctor passed sentence next in Emmie's room and doomed Rosie Wetherby to expulsion by his cheery news that Emma "simply couldn't be more fine, and aren't we all happy about that?"

No one was. Will dragged around with a long face as Rosie carried her small bundle downstairs. Emma was a thundercloud, refusing to be placated with his promise of a ride on horseback with him as soon as she was a little better. And Chard knew he had not felt so dreary since that long voyage from India when he had paced the deck and wondered what he would do.

The day was fine enough so he took the gig. As they rode along, Rosie turned her face up to the sun. "I do not suppose there will be many more fine days like this." She looked at him. "Does winter come early and stay long here?"

"Aye," he said simply, berating himself that he had no conversation. If he possessed any glibness, he could at least tell her how much he appreciated her help, and if had enough nerve—not the battlefield kind but the sitting-room sort—he could confess in an offhand, insouciant sort of way that she had certainly inspired him into thinking about looking for a wife. As it was, he was silent and miserable.

"My lord, is there a workhouse hereabout?" Rosie asked suddenly.

Her question dumbfounded him and he nearly dropped the reins. "A *what*?" he asked.

A workhouse," she repeated, softer this time, as though she hated to say it again. She looked at him, as if trying to decide if she could really speak. The words came from her mouth as if pulled with tongs. "Lady Wetherby says that will be my fate."

"She must be joking," he said finally when he could speak. "Come to think of it, she has always been overly dramatic." The Wetherby house was in sight now and he slowed the horse without thinking. "Surely you misunderstood her." He turned his attention to the horse, unsure of what to do in the face of such a question. "I am certain you did, Mrs. Wetherby. Pay it no mind," he added hastily.

She was a long time silent, and he knew somehow that he had failed her. "I probably misunderstood her," she said, her voice low, her eyes down. "And here we are now." Rosie held out her hand to him. "I can get out by myself, my lord. No need to trouble yourself."

He protested, but she was out of the gig before he had time to get down. She retrieved her bundle from the back and gave a small curtsy. "My lord, make sure Emmie stays indoors for a few days, and tell Will . . ." Her voice trailed off and she could not look at him. "Well, just tell him good-bye." Then she was gone inside.

He rode home knowing he had failed her somehow, and it bothered him through what remained of the day and into dinner. Weary with everything, he pushed away his favorite Yorkshire pudding, which only brought consternation to the footman's face and Cook upstairs in tears. His evening was spent in tense kitchen diplomacy that left him with a headache, an inclination to chew nails, and the thought that if he were married, his wife could handle the domestic turmoil that now fell to his lot.

Oh, Lord, I am making a muddle of my life, he thought as he went to bed. My daughter still pouts because Rosie is gone, my son mopes about, and I am a coward where women are concerned. What *was* it that Rosie meant by her remark about a workhouse?

He saw her in the morning as he rode toward the new barn. She walked slowly on a distant hill, leaning into a stiff wind. "Rosie, go inside," he muttered to Sepoy. "Surely it is not that bad at the Wetherbys."

Because he made a point from then on to ride a different way to the barn, he did not see her again until the next choir practice. He had arranged for Dafydd Williams and his lovely Meg—here now, and truly a beauty—to pick up Rosie for practice.

He wondered all day what he would say to her, but that night she came to him and spared him the trouble of a first move. She held out two folded pieces of paper. "My lord, if you don't mind, I wanted to write to Will and Emma, and want to spare the expense of the penny post."

He pocketed the letters. "I'll be happy to see that they get your letters. You can probably depend upon prompt replies." He hesitated. "They miss you, Mrs. Wetherby."

To his chagrin, tears welled in her eyes. She struggled to control them, and he flogged himself because he did not have the courage to take her hand, or say something—anything. She was about to speak to him when the choirmaster rapped on the lectern for their attention.

Halfway through the Haydn, Peter Chard admitted to himself that it was not beyond the realm of possibility that Rosie Wetherby loved his children nearly as much as he did. When the choirmaster finished by easing them through favorite passages from Handel's *Messiah*, it came to Chard that he loved Rosie Wetherby, daughter of a Welsh sergeant and a foolish, wellborn lass, widow to the most worthless Wetherby on the planet, and mother soon of that man's child. *I am a fool where women are concerned,* he concluded simply.

He thought about Rosie constantly through November and into December. Letters came and went regularly between Rosie and his children, delivered during choir practice. He hated himself for it, but he read

Will's letters from Rosie after his son went to bed. Emma had secreted hers someplace where he could not find them. He had occasion to thank God that Will possessed a less suspicious nature.

They were funny, well-written letters, telling about things she saw on her walks, mentioning last week's Northern Lights and describing events from Portugal, the West Indies, and Canada, where she had adventured with the army when she was young and in her father's care. Chard wrote her several letters of his own, which he never mailed.

He pinned his hopes on Christmas coming soon. The choir was fine beyond words, and there was no way they could ever lose the competition this year. Life will return to normal, he told himself, even though he knew that was the biggest lie he had ever perpetuated. Well, the second biggest. I must talk to her, he told himself over and over, the day of the last practice.

Snow was falling and Dafydd and Meg were late with Rosie. There was only time for them to slide into their seats before the choirmaster's downbeat. Chard sang with his eye on Rosie. Even in the dim church light he could tell that she was more pale than usual. When he caught her eye once, there was such a look of utter hopelessness on her face that he could only stare and wonder.

The choirmaster kept them long after the hour for the practice to end. "This is our final rehearsal, my dears," he reminded them. He leaned forward in conspiratorial fashion. "I have heard rumors that our efforts have not gone unnoticed at St. Peter's and St. Anselm's." He permitted himself the luxury of a chuckle. "I have even heard that they are worried."

I am worried, Chard thought, with another look at Rosie. When the choirmaster released them, Chard rose to go to her, only to be collared by Mrs. Barker, the doctor's wife, who chose that moment, of all the moments in the cosmos, to thank him for his clever idea of finding all those Welsh singers. She went on and on as he watched Dafydd help Meg and Rosie into their cloaks.

"Excuse me, Mrs. Barker," he said finally. He hurried down the aisle and outside, holding out the letters from his children as Williams handed Rosie into the gig. "Mrs. Wetherby, these are for you," he said, handing them to her.

Williams took his seat in the gig, made sure the blanket was snug around Meg, then looked at him expectantly. Rosie opened her mouth to speak, then closed it again. She tried to smile, then handed him letters for his children. "Good-bye, sir," she said as Williams spoke to the horse.

To the best of his memory, she had never said goodbye to him. Usually it was, "Next week then, sir?" The thought troubled him all the way home.

Next morning, he remembered the letters and went to the bookroom for them. There were three instead of two. With fingers that shook, he opened the one addressed to him, read it, then called for his carriage. He ignored the startled looks of his butler and downstairs maid as he ran down the hall, pulling on his overcoat as he went and not even bothering to stop for his hat. "Spring'um," was all he said to his coachman after giving the direction of the Wetherby estate.

Halfway there, he became aware that Rosie's letter was still crumpled in his fist. He smoothed it out and read the words again. Not that he had forgotten them from the first reading—he knew they were burned in his brain forever. "They are turning me out, sir, because they do not want me around when their precious Claude marries his high stickler from Durham. I am not sure precisely what their plan is, but Lady

Wetherby has made it quite plain that I am not part of the family circle. She swears she has proof that my baby is not Junius's, but she does not produce it. I am sorry that I could not accommodate you and sing in the Christmas choir, but they have assured me that I will be gone by then. Please accept my kindest regards for your good health and fortune. Remember me to your children."

He didn't bother to raise the stupid gargoyle knocker on the Wetherby's front door but barged into the house, shouting for Rosie. Lady Wetherby, teacup in hand, came from the breakfast room followed by Claude, looking more oafish than usual.

"Where is Rosie?" he demanded, grabbing Claude by his shirt front and backing him up against the wall, where he began to cry and plead for his mother. Chard shook Claude like a terrier shakes a rat and repeated his question six inches from the sobbing man's face.

Lady Wetherby's shrieks of "Murder! Murder!" brought Sir Rufus from his bookroom. As Chard slammed Claude against the wall again and Lady Wetherby screamed, Sir Rufus leaped back inside the bookroom and locked the door. Well, I like that, Chard thought as he gave Claude a final shake and let go of him.

A door opened upstairs. Chard looked up to the first-floor landing, then took the stairs two at a time to stand by Rosie Wetherby. "I need some help," she said simply. "If you could—"

"Get your cloak," he interrupted.

Without another word she did as he said. He followed her into her room, one quick glance telling him about the paucity of Rosie's life with the Wetherbys. There was no fire in the grate, no carpet on the floor, nothing of any color besides the pictures Emma had been drawing and sending each week. He was almost surprised to see that they had allowed her a bed.

"Is there anything you want to take with you?" he asked, furious with himself for his lack of courage in love.

"N—no," she stammered, "just my bonnet."

"No baby clothes, nothing of your own?" He wished his voice was not rising, but it was.

She shook her head and took a step away from him. "I have nothing."

"Come then." He took her by the hand and helped her down the stairs, taking them slowly because she could not move fast, trying to calm himself because he knew he was frightening her.

The door Sir Rufus had retreated behind was still closed, but he gave it a good kick as they passed it. He stopped in front of Lady Wetherby and narrowed his eyes. "You people are deplorable," he said, all his fury focused now in those few words.

Lady Wetherby glared back. "Dear Lucy must be spinning in her tomb. I am amazed what lengths you will go to for a soprano." She sneered.

"You don't know me," he replied.

Rosie burst into tears in the carriage, and he had the good sense to hold her close. When she wiped her eyes finally with his handkerchief and blew her nose, he held her away from him a little and took a deep breath.

"Mrs. Wetherby—Rosie, if you please—would you mind terribly if we took a bolt over the border and spliced ourselves?"

He could not overlook the surprise in her eyes. "You can't be serious, my lord," she said.

"Never more so, Rosie. I can't have my best soprano vanishing a week before we sing," he teased. This won't do, he thought as he saw the confusion in her beautiful eyes, red now with weeping. "I love you, Rose. Won't you marry me?"

She nodded, then blew her nose again.

As man and wife they returned from Scotland quite late that night, both considerably shocked by what they had done. Well, I am shocked, Chard reasoned as they rode in silence. I had no idea I was so impulsive. He glanced at Rosie's profile, calm now after a storm of tears before and after the brief ceremony. And you, my love?

The house was dark, which suited him. He helped Rosie upstairs to his own room, found one of his night-shirts for her, turned down the coverlet on the side of the bed that would be hers, and went downstairs to write to his mother. When he came to bed, Rosie was asleep. She made no protest when he gathered as much of her close as he could and went to sleep. He couldn't remember a better night's rest.

In the morning, Will and Emma were pop-eyed, as-tounded, and then silent for the space of a few seconds when they heard the news. Then Emma burst into tears and threw herself into Rosie's arms, which only set off his wife again. Will leaned against him. "Papa, why do they do that? I'm happy, but it doesn't follow that I want to cry."

"Oh, Will," was all Chard could manage. Let him find out someday on his own time how skittish preg-nant women were.

In answer to his letter, Mama was home in jig time to gasp and scold and storm and rage about the sitting room while he listened, his hands behind his head, his long legs stretched out in front of him, content. The sight of him so relaxed seemed to set her off further, but he could not help himself. He had never felt better. Rosie was upstairs in his—their—bed because Dr.

Barker said she needed rest. Already her complexion was pinking up again and her eyes had that familiar sparkle.

"Son, you have not heard a word I have said!" Louisa Chard concluded. She had not even removed her traveling coat, and was only now stripping off her gloves.

"I have," he replied. "Let me see: the entire village thinks I have run mad in my attempt to retain my best soprano. And my favorite: Lord Wythe is cuckoo, probably the result of inbreeding among England's better houses." He gave his mother a sunny smile. "Was that the gist?"

Mama gave him a look that would melt glass. "You have made us a laughingstock. You are giving the protection of your name, position, and honors to a common soldier's daughter who is bearing a child of this shire's most notorious scoundrel!"

He smiled. "That's it, Mama." He straightened up then. "Mama, I am a farmer. Times passes pretty regularly here. I'll continue farming, Will and Emma will thrive, the new little one will fit right in, and we'll be happy. I hope you can adjust, Mama. If not, there is the dower house, or Bella."

Mama left that afternoon, after another row when he asked her to remain to at least hear the choir he had got together, "At your command, I might add." She chose instead to return to Bella's for a good sulk, and it bothered him less than he would have thought.

Rosie came downstairs a day later, her serenity restored. She didn't say much to any of them, and he did not press her. Every now and then he would catch her just watching him. You are wondering what kind of a queer fish you have caught, aren't you, my dear? he thought. There was a question in her eyes, but until she found the courage to ask it, he would not intrude on what remained of her pride and dignity.

Christmas Eve brought a skiff of snow in the morning. The house smelled of candied fruit, rum sauce, and cinnamon. He and Will spent the afternoon finding baby clothes in the storeroom. They took their findings to Rosie, who was resting again. He knew she would cry at the sight of all those clothes, and she did, sobbing into another of his handkerchiefs as she folded and unfolded the mound of nightgowns and blankets.

He helped her dress that night for the competition, buttoning up the back of her dress, pausing to kiss her neck before the last few buttons. She looked around in surprise and then smiled at him. "I know I am a trial." She took his hand where it rested on her shoulder. "I do need to ask you something, Peter. It's a favor. No, no, it is not that—" She stopped. "It's something I need to know."

"Do I really love you, or have I done this to secure a soprano?" he asked softly.

She gasped, then turned around and took his face in both hands. "No! I do not doubt that you love me," she said with sudden ferocity that made him go weak inside. "I've always known that. It is something else." She raised herself to kiss his lips, standing sideways to accomplish this because of her bulk.

His arms were around her, his face in her hair. He wanted to kiss her again, but Emma bounded into their room and tugged at his shirt. "Papa, Will says we have to hurry." She grinned up at Rosie. "Do you like to kiss my father?"

"Very much, my dear," Rosie replied promptly. She released him and sat on the bed. "Emmie, if you will help me with my shoes, that will give your father time to tuck in his shirttail and slap a little color back into his face."

They rode to St. Anselm's, the most distant of the three churches, but the largest. He was pleased to see the nice fit of the kid gloves he had bought her that morning. She rested her hand in his, gripping it tight at intervals.

"Nervous?" he asked.

She nodded. "Can we talk tonight?" she asked as the carriage stopped and the children clambered out. "I still have a question. Please."

Suddenly he knew what it was she needed to know, and he also knew that he had a great secret for her, too. We will certainly have to trust each other, he thought. He felt a rush of love for her that left him almost reeling. "Of course," he whispered back as he rose to help her from the carriage.

At the entrance to the church, she stopped suddenly and leaned against him for a long moment. "Afraid?" he asked.

She nodded, but said nothing. People stared at them as they came into the church, but he did not care. His life and happiness were no one's business but his own. He knew his neighbors; in time they would come to know and appreciate his wife.

He was about to sit down with the rest of St. Phil's choir when his old bailiff who never came to church shouldered his way through the crowd. "My lord! My lord!" he was shouting, as the church fell silent. "Your barn! It's on fire!"

Without a word, the Welshmen in the choir rose at once and followed him out of the church. In minutes they were on their way across fields to Wythe and the distant barn. Let it be a little thing, he pleaded as they rode toward the high, thin plume that grew more black and dense as they approached.

To his intense relief, the new barn was intact. "Look

there, sir, just beyond," one of the men shouted. "It is the old cow barn!"

So it was. The old structure that had probably been a tool shed since the Bishop of Durham's days was blazing away, the roof gone, the stones so hot they popped. He motioned them all to stand back, then looked around to discover that everything he had stored there—old tools, extra pails, spare rope, harness needing repair—was lined up neatly on the grass.

He smiled. It didn't take a genius . . . "I think that St. Phil's marvelous, majestic choir has been diddled by an Anglican arsonist," he said. "Someone from St. Anselm's or St. Pete's has thoughtfully selected my most expendable, distant outbuilding to burn, after removing anything of value inside."

Dafydd Williams shook his head. "I don't know, sir, but what you Northumberlanders aren't more trouble than all those Mahrattas at Assaye," he murmured.

Someone started to laugh. "How did the *Welsh* get a name for being troublemakers, sir?" someone else asked.

Chard looked around him, in perfect charity with his wonderful choir. "Ah, well, maybe next year. Come, lads. Since they so thoughtfully left us the pails, let us extinguish this little diversion. Let us sing, too, while we're at it."

Smoky and soot-covered, they returned to St. Anselm's long after both the competition and services were over. Another Christmas had come. It only remained to collect his wife and children and go home. "Mr. Woodhull," he said to his vicar, who waited inside the church, "it was only a small blaze, and not my new barn. Merry Christmas!"

"Don't you want to know what happened?" the vicar asked as Chard looked around for his wife.

"Eh?"

Mr. Woodhull gripped his arm, completely forgetting his place. "My lord, we won!"

"That's not possible," Chard said. "Almost the whole men's section was with me. And may I suggest that you advise the vicars of our neighboring parishes to preach an occasional sermon on repentance!"

"We won," the vicar repeated. "When it looked like you would not return in time, the choirmaster suggested that we turn to the *Messiah*. You know, that selection you had been using as a warming exercise?"

He nodded. The vicar smiled. "And when Mrs. Weth—Lady Wythe sang that part, 'And gently lead those who are with young,' there was not a dry eye in the building."

As the words sank in, he stared at the vicar. "But— but who sang the other parts? The Welsh men were gone!"

"We had the Welshwomen, of course, and let us say that either our Lord chose to smile on us for one night, or perhaps, just perhaps, our choir has been learning from masters. Congratulations, my lord."

"I'm delighted," Chard said, suddenly tired and in need of his own bed and Rosie to keep him warm. "Where's my wife?"

It was the vicar's turn to stare. "I thought you came from Wythe."

"No. We came right here from the upper pasture. What's wrong?"

Mr. Woodhull took his arm and started him for the door. "When Lady Wythe finished singing, she asked to be taken right home. Lord Wythe, I do believe you had better hurry there. It may be that our Lord is sharing His birthday with someone else."

*   *   *

He set records getting to Wythe, his mind a perfect turmoil. She had been so quiet all day, and then she kept gripping his hand at intervals on the ride to St. Anselm's. I remain an idiot, he told himself in exasperation. She was in labor and I didn't even know it. What a clunch Rosie has yoked herself to! Obviously she hasn't a clue in the world how to choose a husband. I had better be her last one, or no telling what trouble she will get into.

Emma and Will were both asleep on the sofa in the upstairs hall, and he passed them quietly. The doctor stood on the landing, as well as two of the Welsh women.

"Didn't you say January?" he asked the doctor. "I distinctly remember January."

The women laughed. "They come when they're ready. She has a daughter," one of them said as he opened the door.

He went inside on tiptoe, taking off his smoky overcoat and then washing his hands and face before coming to the bed where Rosie lay with her little one. He sat beside them, staring at the pretty morsel cradled so carefully in her arms. She was as beautiful as her mother, with the same dark hair.

"Rosie, she's a wonder," he whispered.

Her eyes were closed, but he knew she was awake. Too tired to open her eyes, he thought. And I was putting out a stupid fire. "I wish I could have been here, Rosie," he said simply. "It won't happen again like this. You had to know the baby was coming. Why didn't you tell me?"

She opened her eyes and his heart melted with the expression in them. You're going to love me, even if I am stupid and stodgy, and unimaginative, aren't you? he thought.

With an effort, she moved her hand from the baby to cover his hand. "I don't think you really cared if we won or not, did you?"

He shook his head and kissed her. "You know it never really mattered. Did it matter to you?"

She nodded. "Singing matters. I had to be there."

He got up, took off his shoes, and lay down on her other side. "I think you cut it a little close, love."

She nodded again. She turned her head to look at her baby. "I have something I should have asked you sooner."

He put a finger to her lips and then raised up on his elbow so he could watch her expression. "Let me spill my budget first. If I am not mistaken, it will answer your question." He cleared his throat, wondering just how far back to go. Begin at the beginning, he told himself. "After Will was born, Lucy didn't want anything more to do with me."

"She was an idiot," Rosie murmured, her eyes closed again.

"Well, yes, but that's neither here nor there. I was in Ireland with the regiment, and we were headed to India. I was summoned home."

"Summoned?"

"Yes, and it did surprise me, because I was pretty sure from things I had heard, that Lucy was grazing in other pastures."

Rosie opened her eyes wide and stared at him. "Did you know the man?"

"Yes, indeed. Someone rather high-placed in the government. You'd know the name, but I can be a gentleman. Lucy obviously wanted me to share her bed, but I chose not to, and left the next morning for India, as I had planned."

He paused and waited, knowing that Rosie was quick. "Emma?" she gasped.

". . . is another man's child. I had been summoned home to Lucy's bed to do my conjugal duty and avoid a scandal. I knew it from the moment I heard of Lucy's death in childbirth. Letters are so slow to India, my love."

Rosie was silent, taking in what he was saying. She pulled her own daughter closer, and as he watched, the tears slid from her eyes to puddle in her hair still damp from the sweat of childbirth. He let her cry, knowing that he had answered her question.

"During that terrible voyage home, I thought about what I would do. Everyone thought Emma was mine, but I knew different. I could have created a dreadful scene. It might even have toppled a government I am not too fond of."

"But you could not," Rosie said, burrowing closer to him. "That would have destroyed Emma."

He felt his own tears rising this time. "Rosie, I looked down at that innocent baby, and I could not do it. Emma may not be bone of my bone like Will, but she is my daughter." He patted her hip. "And that, wife, is my great secret. I trust you to keep it. I'll never fail your . . . our daughter, either. She is already mine, because she is yours."

Instead of answering him, she handed him her baby, and it was all the response he needed. He sat up, holding his new daughter as Rosie rested her head against his leg.

"Depend on me," he whispered as he kissed the little one. "Depend on me."

Melody

❄

Anne Barbour

I

Some might have called the ancient country church picturesque. It stood beneath lowering skies, huddled amid bare trees and a tumble of mossy gravestones, its roots seeming to have spread through the centuries. The man who moved uncertainly among the graves shivered inside the warmth of his sheepskin coat.

Tacitus was right, he thought sourly. England was a cold, misty, unpleasant place. The damp seemed to penetrate his very bones. Lord, he must have been out of his mind to come here. He was an American, for God's sake. He did not belong in this land of chilblains and propriety.

He gazed about him and sighed. On the other hand, he supposed the setting was perfect, considering his purpose. As he moved past several rain-slicked tombstones, his eyes narrowed. He approached an area separate from the other graves, protected by a decorative fence. Opening the gate, he stepped inside.

"Weston," he murmured, running his fingers over the letters carved into a mossy headstone. How strange to behold the surname, repeated so many times, in this alien environment.

Crossing to another corner of the enclosed area, he

examined two stones, set apart from the others by their obvious newness and the fact that they stood straight as sentinels guarding the mounded plots at their feet.

"George Weston," read the first one, "Sixth Earl of Sandborne." "William Weston," read the second, "Seventh Earl of Sandborne."

Both had met their Maker in the Year of Our Lord, 1814.

"Almost two years ago," whispered the man. While he had been busy with his own interests in Pennsylvania, disaster had struck persons far away and unknown to him, but whose deaths would have a profound impact on him.

He shivered again and moved out of the iron enclosure toward the horse standing at the edge of the graveyard. He glanced cursorily at the church as he passed, noting the pine boughs that were affixed to the door. The red ribbon binding them provided the only color in the scene.

A little early for decoration, was it not? Christmas was, after all, well over a month away. The idea snaked through him with a forlorn twist. Not that this Christmas would be any lonelier than those of the last few years, spent huddled over the meager comfort of a campfire.

Another image sprang unbidden to his mind, of a large, comfortable dwelling in Philadelphia, redolent of pine and warmed by family and candlelight and laughter and love. He grimaced, remembering the small interloper who stood alone, seemingly forever on the outside looking in.

He straightened. No. He would not think of all that now. He had come a very long way, and he had business to attend to. He'd best get on with it and stop maundering in sodden churchyards.

Moving to mount his horse, he halted abruptly as a sound reached him from inside the church. It drifted over the tombstones, faint yet beckoning, seeming as alien to this bleak environment as an orchid might be, blooming suddenly at his feet. It was a woman, singing a Christmas carol. Her voice was profoundly pure and of such an aching sweetness that her song seemed to fill him with a breathless sense of impending magic.

" . . . and the running of the deer," she sang, and to his surprise, the American felt tears spring to his eyes. A moment later, he heard, "And Mary bore sweet Jesus Christ on Christmas Day in the morn," as the singer drew the carol to a close.

The man waited motionless for several minutes, then, on an impulse, moved toward the church. He had mounted the crumbling stone steps to grasp the door handle, when suddenly it swung out toward him. He stumbled and fell back as a slight figure propelled itself into his arms.

"Oh!" the figure, revealed as a young woman, exclaimed. "I'm so sorry! I did not know anyone was here."

The man steadied himself as she clung to him to avoid falling. He laughed awkwardly.

"It is I who should apologize. Tell me, was it your voice I just heard?"

The woman blushed, but said nothing, merely nodding her head.

"If I may say so, ma'am, you are prodigiously talented. I very much enjoyed listening to you."

"Thank you," she replied, a little breathlessly. She seemed somewhat flustered—at his compliment? Or at being addressed by a stranger? He took her arm to assist her down the stairs, and when they reached the bottom of the short flight, she stepped back to look at him. The man was struck by the fact that, although the woman seemed very plain in almost every other aspect, she was possessed of a very fine pair of eyes. They were a clear, light gray, fringed with a long, dark sweep of lash. Her brows were a delicate, winged tracery.

Moving his gaze to the rest of her face, Josh drew in a startled breath. She was disfigured by a scar that ran from her temple down her jawline, until it reached the side of her neck. The wound that caused it had been deep, but it was pale now, and no longer as conspicuous as it must once have been.

Schooling his features to an expression of blank courtesy, Josh returned her regard. Only a crescent of her dark hair could be seen beneath a voluminous, gray bonnet, and she was almost obliterated by the heavy cloak that covered her from head to toe.

"You are a stranger here, sir?" she asked at last.

"Very much so," the man replied with a smile. He took her hand, and bowed, continuing. "I am from America. I—"

At his words, she jerked spasmodically and pulled her hand away. "I'm sorry," she said again. "I must go."

She hurried away toward a small gig that stood on the other side of the church. He stared after her for a few moments, then shrugged and moved to his horse. Swinging into the saddle, he slapped the reins, and the animal clattered off down the lane.

II

"My goodness!" In the small, black gig that sped down the lane in the opposite direction, Melody Fairfax exclaimed once again. "My goodness!"

Could it really be he? At the Court they had given

up on the prospect of his ever arriving—but, who else could it be? Striding through the old graveyard in an outlandish coat, he'd seemed as alien as—well—as alien as the American he claimed to be.

Such a coat had probably never been seen in the Kentish village of Westonbury, she thought with a grin, but somehow it suited the man. He was tall and rangy, yet he moved with an almost feral grace. He did not wear a hat, and his hair, black as storm-drenched slate, fell in damp tendrils over a broad forehead. His eyes, in startling contrast, were a clear, deep green, lucid and polished as carved jade. His features were regular, if somewhat harsh and weathered. He appeared to be somewhat older than her own nine and twenty years.

Somehow, she hadn't pictured him as being so large. Perhaps because the others, though they were tall men, did not give the impression of taking up more physical space than their dimensions warranted—as did the lanky specimen she'd just met. Nor did they possess a manifest and unsettling maleness that was as natural to him as the easy informality of his speech.

She supposed she should have made for home immediately to tell the others. If only she had not promised the vicar's wife to stop by with a receipt needed that afternoon.

Melody continued on her way, a small smile curving her lips as she envisioned the stranger's reception at Sandborne Park.

III

A very short time later, after passing a lengthy section of high, stone wall, the American turned in at a wide gate flanked by two stone lions. He followed a long, winding drive lined with willows whose branches, laden with the weight of freezing moisture, hung almost to the ground.

As his horse trotted around the final curve of the drive, he stopped in astonishment. George Willis, the London attorney who served as the Weston family agent, had described the manor house as impressive, but now the man realized that Willis's words had been inadequate. The place was magnificent. It was of Tudor design, its symmetry accented by several ranks of long windows.

Drawing up with a flourish before the house, the man ascended a broad flight of stairs that culminated in a massive entrance door. Firmly, he wielded the heavy brass knocker, and the resulting clang could be heard echoing inside the house.

At length, the door was opened by a personage of such impressive mien that the man stepped back involuntarily.

"Um," he said tentatively, "I'm looking for—"

The apparition cast a cursory glance over the visitor.

"If," he intoned frigidly, "you seek the Earl of Sandborne, his lordship is not home at present."

He began to close the door, adding as he did so in a tone of austere admonishment, "The tradesmen's entrance is around to the rear."

The American glanced down over his clothing. All right, he would admit his garb was less than fashionable. Certainly not what one would wear if one expected to be admitted to this grand establishment. However . . .

He pushed against the door, and at the man's expression of astonished affront, said mildly, "Oh, but the earl is here, for I am he. My name is Joshua Weston. You are the butler, I take it. Surely, you must be expecting me?"

The butler's mouth dropped open, working emptily for several moments. At last, he drew himself up, apparently prepared to dispute such an obviously fallacious statement. He must have thought better of that notion, however, for after eyeing Josh briefly, he opened the door grudgingly.

"We knew of the possibility—that is . . . I do apologize if I have been in error, sir, but . . ." Once again he allowed his pained gaze to travel over the sheepskin coat and the serviceable breeches that accompanied it. "I am Forbes."

Without waiting for the butler's acquiescence Josh moved past him into an imposing entrance hall. Forbes opened his mouth, closed it once again, and glanced out at the horse standing at the foot of the steps.

"Is there—? That is, I do not see a coach, sir—my lord."

"No," said Josh Weston with an apologetic grin. "I came on horseback."

"From London—on horseback!" echoed Forbes faintly. "I see. Well, ah—very good, my lord. I shall have someone see to the, er, animal."

He transferred his gaze to the horse and his expression lightened somewhat. The man before him might or might not be the Earl of Sandborne, but his knowledge of horse flesh could not be in doubt.

"Thank you, Forbes," replied Josh imperturbably. "Do you see the portmanteau strapped to the saddle? Would you have it taken up to wherever I'm to stay? My trunk should be along in a day or two."

"Of course—my lord." Forbes bowed and, in some bemusement, assisted Josh in removing the sheepskin coat. "If you will follow me, I shall inform her ladyship of your arrival."

"Her ladyship?"

"The countess, my lord. Lady Sandborne. The dowager countess, I should say."

"Oh. Yes. Of course."

Forbes turned. He was a large man, with an empurpled countenance that spoke of years of good wine and rich food. His stately progress across the hall's marbled expanse put Josh very much in mind of a galleon plowing the waves.

The butler led Josh to one of several small salons that lay along the hall's perimeter.

"If you will wait here, my lord, I shall return momentarily."

So he was not to be allowed at large in the establishment, thought Josh with some amusement, until he had been vetted. Well, that was to be expected. This is what he got for arriving at Sandborne Park on his own, sans a complement of retainers and attorneys—and looking as though he'd come fresh from the colonial backwoods. Which, of course, in a manner of speaking, he had.

Unwilling to trust his angular frame to any of the Louis Quatorze chairs that dotted the salon, he wandered about the room, idly examining Dresden shepherdesses and Wedgwood nymphs. He had just begun on the paintings lining the walls when Forbes, true to his word, reappeared.

This time he guided Josh up the great staircase that ascended from the hall and forked into two sweeping branches before reaching the next floor. From there it was a short journey to another salon, this one more spacious and even more elegantly furnished than the one downstairs.

"The Earl of Sandborne, my lady."

The words echoed strangely in Josh's ears.

Seated in a wing chair near the window, her slippered feet resting on an embroidered stool, a woman awaited him. She was slight of build, with short, gray hair that clustered about her small head in a tumble of curls, but her bearing was regal. She nodded at the newcomer, her demeanor stiff and vaguely unwelcoming. Smiling faintly, she held out her hand.

"Mr. Weston?" she asked tentatively.

"Yes, ma'am," he replied, choosing for the moment to ignore the "mister." He took the proffered hand and brushed his lips across cool, slender fingers.

"I am Lady Sandborne." She gestured him to another chair. "George Willis wrote to tell us that a man calling himself Joshua Weston had arrived in England," she said at last. "However, we were not sure when to expect you."

"I call myself Joshua Weston because that is my name," retorted Josh. "Mr. Willis intended to accompany me," he continued after a moment. "However, he came down with an ague a couple of days ago. He made arrangements to send one of his clerks in his stead, but I told him I was quite capable of making my way down here on my own. I do have credentials," he added stiffly.

Lady Sandborne raised her head, and for the first time, studied Josh's face. She relaxed suddenly.

"Yes, of course you do," she said softly, "but they are unnecessary. I should have known the instant I saw you. You are very like your grandfather in appearance—the late fifth earl, that is."

Josh, too, relaxed.

"It's just that it is so very odd," continued Lady Sandborne. "When Sandborne—my husband—passed away two years ago, without male issue, and when his brother followed him only a few months later, we were absolutely stunned. We knew that your father, as the third son, would have been next in line, but word reached us years ago of his death. And, of course, we thought that you—"

"Yes, Mister Willis explained all that," interrupted Josh harshly. "I've seen the letters written by my mother, when my life was despaired of."

"Yes, and when we heard nothing after that, we were sure that you had not survived infancy. The message we received from the attorneys a few months ago was the first indication any of us had of your existence. At any rate"—she continued after a brief pause—"you are here now, dear boy. Welcome to your new home."

At her words, Josh started. His home? He almost smiled. He had never really had a home. The man who had raised him, his father's business partner, Eli Betterman, had provided him with food and shelter and a measure of kindness, but Uncle Eli's house had never, by any stretch of a boy's most determined imagination, been home.

And now, here he was in a great, empty palace of a house, where his voice echoed off the walls. He was once again among strangers, and this woman bade him welcome and told him he was home.

"Actually," he said rather stiffly, "I shan't be staying long."

"What?"

"I plan to return to America as soon as I have apprised myself of my situation here."

Lady Sandborne's jaw dropped, and she gaped at him in astonishment.

"But—this is your home, now. You can't—"

"My lady, this is *not* my home. You must see that I do not belong here, and I do not wish to stay any longer than it will take to assure myself that the estate is being cared for competently. I shall return for visits from time to time, but I shall reside in Philadelphia."

The dowager's lined features crumpled in distress. "But, you are the earl, the head of the family."

"I am sorry to overset you, my lady, but I will not be staying."

Josh uttered the words with such finality that the countess, who had brought a handkerchief to her eyes, straightened. She gazed at him for a long moment, and then said simply. "Then I suppose there is nothing more to be said, except that I—we—shall do everything in our power to change your mind."

Josh smiled thinly, but said nothing more.

"It is unfortunate," continued Lady Sandborne, as though the previous conversation had not taken place, "that Arthur and Mary are not here to greet you, but they will be home shortly."

"Arthur and—oh, yes, Mister Willis explained about them, too. Arthur is the son of my father's younger brother." Josh spoke the words hesitantly. "I understand he thought himself to be the new holder of the title."

Aunt Helen raised her hand dismissively. "Yes, but that's of no account. However, they live here, you know. Mary is expecting their first child."

"I see," replied Josh, feeling suddenly rather overwhelmed.

Lady Sandborne rose smoothly. "You have many other cousins and aunts and uncles, of course. You will meet Mary and Arthur at dinner and you will make the acquaintance of the rest at the Christmas ball. It is held here every year. My goodness, it's almost dinnertime now. I'm sure you will want to freshen up." She stopped, her voice uncertain. "You do have something—?"

"Yes," Josh said again, rather stiffly this time. "I do have an ensemble that I hope very much you will consider acceptable for dinner, my lady."

"Oh!" She flushed. "I did not mean—that is—do call me Aunt Helen," she finished in a rush.

"Thank you, my—Aunt Helen, I shall be pleased to do so, if you will call me Josh."

"Oh. No, I don't think— I may address you as Sandborne, of course, but—"

"I would much prefer Josh. I don't think I am ready for Sandborne yet. Where I come from, it is customary to call family members—and friends—by their first names, and I am used to Josh."

Lady Sandborne smiled suddenly, and Josh realized she was not as old as he had first thought. She rose and moved to tug on the bellpull. "Very well, Josh. I shall deliver you into the hands of Mrs. Gresham, our housekeeper, who will show you to your chambers. The master's suite has been prepared for you."

"The—oh. Yes, of course. Thank you. It will take me a day or two just to acquaint myself with all this." He waved a hand about him. "That is," he amended hastily, "my house."

"To be sure, dear boy. Although—"

At this moment, a scratching at the door heralded the entrance of a stout, matronly woman. Even to Josh's untutored eye, her conservative garb, starched apron, and the ring of keys that hung from her waist proclaimed her to be the housekeeper of this premier establishment.

"My lord," said Lady Sandborne, and the words rang strangely in his ears, "allow me to present Mrs. Gresham, our housekeeper. She will show you to the master's suite."

Mrs. Gresham's prominent blue eyes were wide with curiosity, but she said only, "Good afternoon, my lord. Welcome to Sandborne Court. It will be my pleasure to serve you." She bobbed a respectful curtsy, and stood expectantly at the door.

With a nod to Lady Sandborne and a promise to present himself in a chamber known as the Blue Saloon at dinnertime, he moved to join Mrs. Gresham. After a slight contretemps during which Josh stood aside to allow the housekeeper to precede him through the door, while Mrs. Gresham determinedly held her ground, waiting for Josh to precede her, the two departed sedately from the room and back through the seemingly endless miles of corridor to the great stairway.

As they walked in silence, Josh stared about him. Despite his confident words earlier about "his house," he felt thoroughly intimidated by its grandeur. It was impossible to believe that all this magnificence indeed belonged to him. He could chop up the Louis Quatorze furnishings for firewood, if he so chose. He could, should the mood strike him, order that all the walls be painted bright green. He could replace the silk and velvet hangings with burlap, if he wished. What he could not do, he realized with a pang, was think of this great overstuffed barn as home.

He walked on with Mrs. Gresham, oppressed by the genteel silence that surrounded them. The housekeeper guided Josh up one more flight of stairs and they traversed several more corridors. At last, she paused and, opening one of the doors that lined the corridor, ushered Josh into a spacious chamber.

"I think you will find everything in order, my lord," she said, scouring the room with her gaze. She gestured toward the adjoining chamber where his portmanteau had been set on a small bench at the foot of an enormous canopy bed. "I understand," she said expressionlessly, "that your man did not accompany you."

Josh cleared his throat. "Actually, I do not have a, er, man. I—I have not had time to acquire one."

"Very well, sir," the housekeeper replied austerely. "I shall send one of the footmen up to see to your things and to assist you in dressing for dinner."

Feeling a ridiculous need to assert himself at this point, Josh raised his hand.

"That won't be necessary, Mrs. Gresham. I have lived without a personal servant all my life and I am used to doing for myself. I would prefer to stow my own gear. That is, I shall put my own things away, and prepare for dinner myself. Tomorrow morning you may send someone to me, but for this evening, I believe I shall muddle through on my own."

Mrs. Gresham stiffened alarmingly and opened her mouth as though to remonstrate with this barbarian who had somehow breeched the sanctity of Sandborne Court, but as Josh continued to gaze at her amiably but with unmistakable authority, she instead produced a respectful smile. She curtsied again.

"Of course, my lord. The dressing gong will sound in about an hour. If you will ring when you are ready to go downstairs, one of the housemaids will show you to the Blue Saloon, where the family customarily gathers before dinner."

"Thank you, Mrs. Gresham."

As the door closed behind the housekeeper, Josh sank into one of the comfortable chairs placed near the window. He glanced about his sitting room. It was handsomely furnished with pieces that might have been in place since the house was built. A secretary desk stood in one corner and an ornate dresser in another. In the bedchamber, a massive wardrobe spread across one wall, and a commode and washstand were set against another. The bed was hung with forest-green velvet, lavishly embroidered and matched by the window draperies. Amid such casual grandeur,

Josh's shabby portmanteau took on a very humble aspect, indeed.

Josh turned to the window, where he found himself facing an expansive prospect. The clouds had dissipated, and a wintry sun slanted across a sweep of lawn. Incredible that it could still be so green at this time of year. In the distance, a small herd of deer browsed on the shores of an ornamental lake, and farther away yet, the rolling hills of the Kentish weald were a purple shadow against the horizon.

He wondered how far toward those hills his estate stretched. He would have to make it one of his first priorities to ride over his acreage with the estate agent and—what was the name Willis had given him? Brickley. His land steward.

He repeated the words, rolling them over his tongue. His land steward. Steward of his land. The phrase still seemed meaningless to him. How could he possibly hope to consider this—this fiefdom—his home?

He remained for some minutes lost in contemplation of his startling change in status. At last, he shrugged and rose to unpack his portmanteau, a task that took a distressingly short time. Placing hairbrush and comb on the handsome washstand that stood near his bed, he glanced around again, somehow hopeful that the appearance of these commonplace items might create a certain homeyness in this alien environment.

They did not. He sighed and paced the floor for a few moments before straightening his shoulders. Turning, he moved to the imposing wardrobe.

IV

In another part of the house, Melody, returned home a few minutes earlier, entered her bedchamber, located not far from that of Lady Sandborne. She moved to her dressing table, her thoughts still filled with the man she had met at the church. Forbes had told her of his arrival at the Court. What was he doing now? she wondered.

Melody gazed unseeing into the mirror. Almost every day for three years she had stood thus, preparing herself for another evening in attendance on the countess. She should consider herself fortunate, for her ladyship was a considerate employer, and a certain distant friendship had grown between them.

Lord knew, reflected Melody, that she was fit for little else beyond acting as a lady's companion. Aside from her musical talent, she had no skills. And, with her physical flaws, she was not likely to attract a husband—as her mother had often reminded her.

Not that she had any such aspirations. Not many eligible young men had come her way over the course of her nine and twenty years, and those she had met inevitably drifted toward more likely prospects. Fortunately, if her hand had never been solicited, neither had her heart ever been touched. She had her music and her books, and a few friends. Surely, that was enough to make one content with one's lot.

Why, then, did her thoughts keep returning to the stranger in the churchyard? The answer, she supposed, was simple enough. If he really was the Earl of Sandborne, which she had no reason to doubt, his presence at the Court might well have a profound effect on those who lived here.

Sighing, she brought her attention to her reflection in the mirror and began to brush her thick, dark hair.

V

Taking advantage of the pitcher of water that had been placed on the washstand, Josh made himself as presentable as possible and donned his evening attire. Again, he was conscious that his raiment left much to be desired, for, although the dark coat and light breeches, with accompanying silk waistcoat, might certainly suffice for an evening in even the most aristocratic homes in Philadelphia, it lacked the fashionable styling he had observed sported by the young bucks in London.

Affixing an emerald stickpin, a bequest from his father, to his cravat, he pronounced himself ready to face the world—or at least, that small portion of it who awaited him in the Blue Saloon. He moved to the door and stepped out into the corridor. Making his way back to the main staircase, he wondered if he should not be carving arrows into the furniture as he passed. It wouldn't do to lose one's way in this warren. It might take weeks for his starved, lifeless body to be found, cast up against a forgotten credenza.

He hailed a passing footman, who provided directions to the Blue Saloon. Making his way through more corridors, he stopped occasionally to peep into the various chambers that lay in his path. One of these was, apparently, a music room, for it contained a harp, an enormous grand piano, and one or two cabinets overflowing with sheet music. Hesitantly, he crossed toward the piano. He did not seat himself, but his fingers, as though of their own volition, stretched over the keys.

The next moment, his hands formed into fists and, turning, he all but hurtled from the chamber.

In the corridor, he leaned against the wall, breathing as heavily as though he had just run the length of the house. Which was perfectly absurd, of course. Following the footman's instructions, he continued on his way until at last he reached his destination. The Blue Saloon contained only one occupant.

The young woman from the church sat at a tambour frame set near a long window to catch the last rays of the sun. She looked up when Josh entered, and a slight flush spread over her pale cheeks. He advanced into the room with hand outstretched, and as he approached, she blinked nervously. It could now be seen that her dark hair, free of the bonnet, was pulled back into an uncompromising knot, upon which rested a modest lace cap. Her gown, even less fashionable than his own ensemble, was made of some dark-bluish stuff, with a high neckline, and it was unadorned by so much as a cameo pin. The figure beneath this creation appeared trim enough, but the gown was so ill-fitting, it was difficult to ascertain its parameters.

"Good evening, ma'am," he said in some surprise. "We meet again. Perhaps now we may make our names known to each other. I am Josh Weston."

She seemed disturbed out of all proportion at this informal greeting, and gasped slightly as she rose to put out a hesitant hand, rather as though she had been asked to place it in a bear trap.

"Ah! Sandborne, you are down betimes."

Josh whirled about, to behold Lady Sandborne. She entered the room with a swish of silken skirts, her gray curls fluttering as she moved.

"I see you have met Melody."

The young woman blushed even more furiously as she shook her head spasmodically.

"No, my lady. I—that is—he—we—"

She subsided into a strangled gurgle.

"I was just introducing myself, Aunt Helen." Josh's smile included the younger woman.

"Ah," said Lady Sandborne again. "Allow me to do the honors, then. Lord Sandborne, may I present Miss Melody Fairfax, my companion? Melody is the daughter of a dear friend of mine, and she has been with me for four years, now."

Once more, Josh put out his hand. "How do you do, Miss Fairfax? I am indeed pleased to make your acquaintance—again."

Lady Sandborne's brows rose questioningly and Josh, with a smile at Miss Fairfax, told of their brief meeting earlier in the day.

"My lord," said the young woman. "I did not know— That is, it is an honor to . . ."

Miss Fairfax trailed off into an incoherent murmur and Josh knew a stab of pity. So very plain—and in addition, disfigured. No wonder she found herself forced to spend her days as companion to an old lady. An unfortunate situation, no matter how amiable the old lady might be.

On the other hand, he mused, bowing over her hand, perhaps she considered herself fortunate in securing a position that might provide her with a haven for some years to come.

Miss Fairfax, after assisting Lady Sandborne into a comfortable chair, took one nearby, abandoning the tambour frame.

Having acknowledged her presence, Lady Sandborne apparently forgot her companion's existence except to request, a few minutes later, that her spectacles be fetched from her bedchamber. Miss Fairfax departed silently to perform this task.

The countess turned to Josh, but before she could speak again, the door opened to admit a man and a woman. The man appeared to be about five-and-twenty and was very thin, with wispy brown hair that drifted untidily over forehead and cheeks. He smiled absently as his gaze encountered Josh. The woman who entered on the man's arm, was a few years younger. She was slender, except for a slight swelling at her waist, and not unattractive but for her expression of discontent. She smiled not at all.

"Mary!" exclaimed Lady Sandborne. "And Arthur. You are just in time to meet your cousin." The dowager performed the introductions gracefully, and bade the newcomers to chairs nearby. Arthur Weston, clasping Josh's hand in a cordial if somewhat limp grip, proclaimed himself to be pleased to make the acquaintance of his newly discovered relative. His wife, on the other hand, contained her pleasure admirably.

"Good evening, Mister Weston," she sniffed. "What a surprise to learn that you truly exist."

"You must address him as Sandborne, Mary," the countess said reprovingly, with an apologetic glance toward Josh.

"Yes, I suppose I must," replied Mary, with a barely perceptible nod. "Forgive me. I'm afraid I still haven't recovered from the shock of learning that a backwoodsman from the American frontier is now the head of our family."

Josh stared at her.

"Philadelphia is hardly on the frontier, madame. It is a cultured city, and—

Arthur Weston cleared his throat noisily. "Steady on, m'dear," he said mildly. "Can't hold that against him. It's not his fault he was born in the back of beyond."

Josh, stiff with affronted astonishment, bowed. "Why, thank you, Arthur." To Mary, he responded smoothly, "Mrs. Weston, I do apologize for my being an American. I fear that life among the savages has ill prepared me for the gracious courtesy displayed by more civilized members of society, such as yourself."

Mary did not reply, but flushed and sat down with a flounce. Lady Sandborne's hands fluttered. "Josh arrived just a few hours ago. He is trying to become acquainted with the Court, and I was just about to offer my services as guide tomorrow morning." She turned to Josh. "That is, if you are free. I know Mister Brickley is anxious to meet with you. Ah, thank you, Melody," she said to her companion, who had just reentered the room with the spectacles.

Arthur and Mary nodded briefly in greeting. Arthur made no move to rise, and Miss Fairfax removed herself to a chair a little apart from the grouping containing her ladyship and the two gentlemen. Josh stood.

"Do sit here, Miss Fairfax. I'll just move that chair closer."

Before she could protest, Josh lifted the chair to a position closer to Lady Sandborne.

For the first time, Miss Fairfax looked directly at Josh, and he was surprised to note an expression of gratitude in her gaze. Once again, he was struck by the beauty of her eyes. In fact, a closer observation proved that Miss Fairfax was not so very plain, after all. If it were not for the scar she might be considered attractive. She was possessed of a small, straight nose and her generously curved mouth was sweet and well-formed. She had little pretense to beauty, but in a more becoming gown and with a hairstyle that might serve to conceal rather than emphasize the scar, there was no doubt she would show to advantage.

Josh smiled at her reassuringly and turned his attention to Mary, who was speaking querulously. "Of course—my *lord*. I suppose your first order of business is to survey your new domain."

Arthur twisted to gaze at his wife in mild surprise, and Lady Sandborne gasped.

"Mary!"

The younger woman shifted uncomfortably. "I am sorry to be so abrupt, but—Cousin Joshua—you may as well be aware that I think this is all so unfair! It is Arthur who should hold the title." She glared at Josh. "He had moved into the master's suite, you know."

"But, Mary," expostulated Arthur, his spectacles sliding down his nose, "you know I never had any wish to assume the title. Dashed nuisance, I always thought it. I'm much too busy with my work to take on any additional responsibilities."

"It would not have been necessary for you to have concerned yourself with the responsibilities," snapped Mary, and Josh knew somehow that this conversation had taken place many times. "You have plenty of people to take care of all that for you. Anyway," she continued, tears springing to her pale blue eyes, "we would have spent most of our time in London. Where the museums and libraries are," she said hastily. "We would have taken our place in society, and our children"—she patted her abdomen—"would have made splendid marriages! It is all ruined now," she concluded pettishly. "Everything has been taken from us by this—this usurper." She waved an angry hand at Josh, who uttered a choked sound of indignation.

"You are being foolish beyond permission, Mary." Lady Sandborne interposed at last, her eyes sparking with anger. "The title was never Arthur's to begin with, so your rantings about usurpation are perfectly ridiculous. You might as well blame Josh for being born, which even you must admit, is patently absurd."

Mary said nothing more, but settled back with a grunt into her chair. What a perfectly dreadful young woman, thought Josh, appalled. Arthur apparently was undisturbed by being ousted from the position he had thought was his. It was his wife who was greedy for the status and privilege the title would confer.

It was brought to Josh with some dismay that, despite his reluctance to travel to England to spend a few weeks in this—this monument to the feudal system, he had hoped, deep within him, that his unknown relatives would attempt to make him welcome.

He shrugged and turned once more to Lady Sandborne.

"Tell me, Aunt Helen—" he began, but at this point, Forbes entered the room to announce that dinner was served. Lady Sandborne rose to lead the way from the Blue Saloon to the dining parlor.

This chamber proved to be as large and imposing as Josh had expected. It boasted a heavily carved mantelpiece, and landscapes by fashionable artists lined the walls. The mahogany table fairly bristled with shining cutlery, bowls, fine china, and glassware. The centerpiece consisted of an enormous epergne depicting the not-altogether-appetizing subject of Hercules beheading the Hydra monster. It was flanked by several massive candelabra.

Forbes rather ostentatiously pulled out the chair at the table's head for Josh, and Lady Sandborne took her place at his right. Mary seated herself at Josh's left and Arthur settled in next to her. Miss Fairfax took a chair next to the countess.

A stiff silence fell on the group, broken only by the clink of cutlery and glassware as the meal was served by liveried footmen.

Melody glanced surreptitiously at Lord Sandborne from beneath her lashes. Despite the awkwardness of his situation and his modest attire, he seemed entirely in command of the situation. She wondered what was going on behind those remarkable green eyes. How strange all this must seem to him. Yet from the casual manner in which he accepted the presence of the footman ladling his soup, he might have dined in this chamber all his life.

Arthur, who had apparently not noticed the lack of conversation, spoke up at last. "Did I tell you, m'dear," he said to Mary, "I found the most interesting reference in Gregorson today? He avers, you know that the Twentieth Legion, stationed in Chester, was responsible for most of the building of the Antonine Wall. This is arrant nonsense, of course, for there has never been any sign of their involvement there. In addition, it is widely recognized that it was the Second Augusta who were responsible for the construction of the wall. However, Gregorson points out—"

"Josh," interrupted Lady Sandborne, a note of desperation in her tone, "you must tell us something about yourself. After all, we know almost nothing of your life in the Colonies."

"There is not a great deal to tell, Aunt Helen," replied Josh. "My father had remained on reasonably amicable terms with the family after he emigrated to the Colonies. In fact, he and my grandfather corresponded from time to time after his arrival there."

"Yes," said Lady Sandborne with a laugh. "I remember your father. A handsome devil, he was, and a simmering bundle of raw energy."

Josh smiled. "So I've heard. The partnership he formed with Eli Betterman thrived, and the firm of Weston and Betterman became one of the premier mercantile establishments of the New World. At about this time, Father met Elizabeth Thorne, the daughter of a local tradesman. They were married less than a year after that. I'm told they were very happy in the short time they had together, but Father died in a carriage accident while Mother was expecting her first and only child—me."

"How very sad," interposed Lady Sandborne, dabbing at her eyes with a wisp of handkerchief. "Your poor mama—she almost lost you in infancy and then she, herself, died when you were less than two years old. How fortunate for you that Mr. Betterman took you in."

Josh smiled faintly. "Yes, Uncle Eli planned that I would take over the business when he retired. He was more than somewhat dismayed at the news that I had suddenly become the Eighth Earl of Sandborne, but it was he who encouraged me to sail to this country to take up the reins, so to speak."

The others nodded in polite incomprehension. Glancing at Melody Fairfax, Josh found himself the recipient of a wide-eyed, fascinated stare.

"But, what were you doing living in the forest— miles away from the city?" exclaimed Lady Sandborne. "If you had a home in Philadelphia, and a secure position there . . ."

Josh felt a sudden tension spread through him, but forced himself to relax. "For the past few years I have spent quite a bit of time traveling along the Susquehanna and Delaware rivers, trading with the Indians. We—that is Uncle Eli and I—have a fairly large interest in the fur trade." He paused to draw a deep breath. "You see, I was betrothed for a while, but my fiancée—passed away. I—I found myself at loose ends and eventually decided to head for the woods."

He spoke with a calm he was far from feeling. He found that he was gripping his fork with an intensity that nearly bent the utensil in half. He felt the old darkness looming over him once again—the emptiness and sense of bitterness and the crushing guilt that had pursued him for so long.

Melody, observing him, felt her own stomach clench. Dear Lord, the man was still overcome with grief for his lost love. And—yes, there was something else to be seen in the harsh planes of his face. It was not only grief that afflicted him, she realized with a start. There was something that went much deeper, she was sure of it.

He regaled the company for the rest of the meal with anecdotes from his travels. Arthur roused himself from his meditations, and even Mary seemed interested, despite herself. Miss Fairfax, seeming to forget both her shyness and her humble position in the household, pelted him with questions. Josh found himself warming to this unusual young woman as he told of life in the far reaches of the New World. At length, as the last spoonful of an excellent trifle had been disposed of, Lady Sandborne rose to lead the ladies from the dining parlor. Melody, following the dowager from the room, cast a glance back toward Lord Sandborne, only to find him gazing at her speculatively. She felt her cheeks go hot and cursed her wretched tendency to blush whenever anyone so much as took notice of her.

Not to her great surprise, the ladies had barely settled themselves in the Blue Saloon when Lord Sandborne and his cousin appeared in the doorway. Evidently the two had made short work of their brandy and port. Melody grinned inwardly. She would like to have been a fly on the wall during that time-honored social ritual between such mismatched participants.

Lady Sandborne welcomed her nephews and gestured toward Melody.

"And now, my dear, it's time for the treat I promised Josh. Will you favor us with a song or two?"

Without demur, Melody rose to seat herself at the harp. Here, at least, she felt completely at home, for when she sang she knew herself to be competent and in control.

Mary took a chair next to Lady Sandborne, and, glancing at Josh, commenced what appeared to be an injured diatribe against the usurper in their midst. Arthur sat near her in bemused silence, apparently devoting himself to further contemplation of the Twentieth Roman Legion. Mary did not stop talking, nor did Lady Sandborne stop interposing ineffectual rebuttals as Melody began to stroke the harp strings.

She had chosen a simple Mozart aria for her offering, and Josh fell immediately under the spell of her glorious voice, despite the sibilant wrangling taking place behind him. At length, however, he was forced to a peremptory, "Hush, please!" before the two combatants fell silent.

"Very nice, Melody," was Lady Sandborne's absent comment as the last notes of the song died away. "Why don't you give us one of those Irish ballads you do so well?"

Melody lifted her hands once more to the harp, but Josh interposed. "I wonder if, instead, you would mind singing the carol you were practicing in the church—'The Holly and The Ivy.'"

"Oh. Yes. I will be performing that for the Christmas service. I'm afraid I do not know the harp accompaniment for that—and, I do not play the pianoforte."

A twinge of apprehension rose inside Josh. He drew a deep breath.

"Perhaps I can help," he said, much to his own astonishment. "I have—I have played the piano in the past. Would you accept my assistance?"

Melody hesitated. "Of course," she said at last.

Lady Sandborne's brows lifted slightly, and a muted snort issued from Mary, but Josh rose to settle himself at the piano. His hands lifted, he turned to Melody.

"What key do you prefer?" he asked.

"Oh!" she replied, for some reason flustered. "'D will be fine."

As Josh ran through a few experimental chords, his hands felt stiff and unresponsive. He settled into the simplest accompaniment he could produce for the carol. As the song progressed, however, his fingers relaxed and seemed to move of their own volition in an embroidery of the melody that poured so effortlessly from Miss Fairfax's throat.

Entranced, Josh absorbed the liquid cascade of music, and as he listened, it seemed to him that his soul was awakening from the dark winter that had possessed it for so long. Which was patently ridiculous, of course. How could one song, no matter the talent of the singer, accomplish what three years of solitude and hardship could not? Still, he was swept, as he had been on hearing her voice in the churchyard, by that breathless sense of something extraordinary about to happen.

He became aware that Miss Fairfax had fallen silent and was staring at him in perplexity. Catching his gaze, she faltered.

"Oh, do pardon me, my lord. It's just that you play remarkably well, and—and—"

Josh grinned. "You did not expect such a display from a barbarian newly arrived from the edge of civilization?"

The young woman flushed a deep rose, and he was again struck by the purity of her features, a purity that was in no way diminished by the scar that lay along her cheek like a leafy tendril. As she returned to her chair, he glanced at Lady Sandborne and Mary, who had at last fallen silent and sat in bored attention. Arthur had apparently fallen asleep. Good Lord, had they no appreciation for the lark who lived in their midst? True, she gave more the appearance of a very plain wren, but surely her remarkable talent should produce more than their attitude of patient forbearance. With an effort, he returned his attention to Lady Sandborne, who was speaking enthusiastically.

"It will be the premier event of the season, of course, and everyone from miles around will attend."

"I beg your pardon?" Josh asked absently.

"Why, the Christmas ball, of course. I think I spoke of it to you earlier. It's been a tradition here at the Court for years. It always takes place during the last week before Christmas, so it's only a few weeks away. Forbes and Mrs. Gresham have been deep in plans for some time.

"As I said before, it will be a chance for you to meet the rest of your newfound family. Hopefully, you will have encountered most of your neighbors by then," she continued, "but the ball will give you an opportunity to greet those more far flung. Now, Josh dear, I hope you will not take offense, but we really must do something about your wardrobe. What you are wearing no doubt serves for a respectable visiting American, but more is expected of a peer of the realm, you know."

Josh opened his mouth, but after a moment's thought, stilled the protest that had formed on his lips. His aunt was right, he supposed. If he was going to fill the position of an earl, even temporarily, he might as well look the part.

Arthur yawned ostentatiously.

"Umm." He rose. "It's been rather a long day, and I believe I'm for bed." He assisted his wife to her feet. "I should think you would be fagged as well, Aunt Helen. It's well past your usual bedtime."

Lady Sandborne looked up, startled. "Why, yes, dear, you're right. My, I don't know when the evening has flown so. Good night, Josh. I look forward to showing you all the glories of Sandborne Court in the morning. Melody?"

Miss Fairfax rose to take the dowager's arm and the group left the room.

Josh moved slowly back to the piano, and for some moments, stood staring at it with clenched fists. He had not touched a piano since Dorothea's death, and tonight, with scarcely a moment's hesitation, he had played an accompaniment for Miss Fairfax. It would have been churlish not to oblige, of course, but did his willingness indicate that Dorothea's memory had begun to fade?

No! He must not allow that to happen. A love such as he and Dorothea had shared must not be allowed to drift into oblivion like last season's roses. To turn away from her memory seemed like a negation of all he had felt for her—and a confirmation of his responsibility for her death.

He became aware that someone had entered the room behind him and turned to observe Miss Fairfax standing at the door.

"Oh!" she exclaimed, startled. "I thought you would be—that is, Lady Sandborne forgot her spectacles."

She entered the room, moving gracefully toward the chair recently vacated by the countess. "She will want them at hand when she awakes in the morning."

Picking up the spectacles from a nearby table, she turned again toward the door, but stopped uncertainly in the center of the room. "I see you have returned to the piano," she said, smiling, "but I did not hear any music."

Josh rose hastily. "No. I was not playing—merely thinking about it."

Her winged brows rose questioningly and her mouth quirked in mischief. "I have heard of many piano theories, but I do not believe I have ever heard of the 'think' method."

Josh felt his breath catch in his throat. Why, the little gray companion could be absolutely enchanting when her eyes took on that impish sparkle. He returned her smile.

"The fact is," he said awkwardly, "I have not played for a very long time. I used to be rather good at it," he continued, "but—something happened."

"I'm so sorry. I did not mean to pry."

"Not at all. It's just that—" He expelled a long breath and sank down on a settee, drawing Miss Fairfax with him. "I think I have always loved music, particularly the piano. I found I had a talent for it, and despite Uncle Eli's objections, I spent the better part of my youth studying and practicing. I even tried my hand at composing, and eventually became an accomplished musician." He gestured diffidently. "I say this not to boast, but so you will understand my dedication to the instrument."

He grinned. "Although I imagine I do not need to tell you anything on the subject. Anyone who sings as gloriously as you must have spent a great deal of time on her art."

She did not seem discommoded by his compliment, but nodded seriously. "Indeed, my lord. It is not so much that I wished to pursue an interest in music, but that—well, I can't *not* sing. It just seems to well up inside me until it—it explodes!"

Josh laughed. "Precisely."

He sobered abruptly. "And then I met Dorothea. Actually, she was the daughter of one of Uncle Eli's business associates and we had known each other for most of our lives. It was not, however, until she returned from a year abroad with her mother that we— that is—we had both grown up during her absence.

She had changed from a rather gawky, snub-nosed girl into a dazzling beauty, and I, though my transformation was not nearly so spectacular, had at least grown taller. I promptly joined the army of her admirers, and I could not believe my good fortune, when she seemed to return my regard." He laughed again. "I made the most complete ass of myself. I wrote odes to her blue eyes and even dashed off a sonata in her honor."

Miss Fairfax smiled. "I'll wager she was a lover of music and was swept off her feet by your musical ardor."

Josh frowned. "I thought so, at any rate." He glanced down at his fingers. "However"—he sighed, his eyes clouding in memory—"I had reached the point where I was being asked to perform, and such was the reception granted my efforts that I thought seriously of taking up the piano as a career rather than going into business. I was fortunate in the fact that, through Uncle Eli and the share in his company that was mine through my father, I could live comfortably, if not lavishly. But, Dorothea thought—as did Uncle Eli and his family—that it was beneath me to actually earn money from something as plebeian as performing on a stage."

Josh halted abruptly. Good Lord, what was he thinking of, gabbling on like this? He had never spoken so to a living soul—and he had known this young woman for only a few hours!

"I'm sorry—" he said somewhat painfully.

"Oh, no!" protested Miss Fairfax. "I think a life as a professional pianist would be wonderful. In fact, I had similar aspirations myself—as a singer, that is."

"Did you?" Josh asked interestedly. "Why did you not pursue this possibility? I should imagine you would have taken London by storm."

She blushed. "Well, such was my fantasy, though I should imagine the reality would have been a great deal less enthusiastic. The reason I did not make a stab at it, of course, was my family."

"They objected?"

She sighed, much as Josh had done a few minutes earlier. "You see, my lord, my—"

"Miss Fairfax," said Josh with mock severity, "as I told my aunt some hours ago, I fear I shall never become used to 'my lord.' I wish you will call me Josh. It is what I have answered to all my life, and I'm much too long in the tooth to change my ways now."

"Oh, but I don't think— That is—perhaps you did not understand Lady Sandborne fully. I am a paid companion."

"Yes," replied Josh gently. "I do understand that, but where I come from it is commonplace for persons in your position to call family members by their first names. In America, we set little store by formality."

"So I've heard," responded Miss Fairfax dryly. "Very well, my lo—Josh, but if her ladyship has any objection—"

"I'm sure she will not." Josh inserted an authoritative note into his voice. "And, I shall call you Melody, if I may. My American upbringing again," he added hastily as she drew a deep breath. "And Melody is such a lovely name, it is a shame not to make more use of it. Now"—he continued before she could dispute this dictum—"you were telling me of your plans to become a professional singer. Why did your family object?"

Melody's gaze flew to his, and an unaccountable stirring made itself felt deep in his interior.

"My father is a baronet," she replied hesitantly. "Not an exalted title, but one he is proud of. He and my mother were horrified at the idea of their daughter going on the stage, like a common—"

"Piano player?" asked Josh in some amusement. "Tell me," he continued, "if I am not being forward, how did it happen that you were contemplating the need to earn your own way in the world?"

Melody shrugged. "Oh, it was the usual. My father inherited an estate and a more than modest competence, but he was addicted to gambling in its most virulent form. By the time I was sixteen, we were in serious financial difficulties. I have two younger sisters, and they took after my mother. That is, they are very beautiful and vivacious. It was hoped they would make advantageous marriages, but with no dowry, their situations were bleak. It seemed to me the only way we could come about was for me to earn enough money to provide at least one of the girls with a season. My music master had some connections in London, and he felt sure he could help me. He said he had little doubt I would enjoy a measure of success."

"An understatement if I ever heard one," said Josh, smiling.

"My mother always felt somewhat uncomfortable about my singing. She said that it was unseemly. 'Plain is as plain does,' she would tell me. 'A young woman who has so few prospects as you, dearest, should not put herself forward.'"

Josh was appalled. "She said that? To you? Her daughter?"

Melody smiled ruefully. "She was only being kind, Josh. She was an absolute diamond, and she always felt badly for me, I think, that I was not. And then, when I acquired this"—her fingers reached up to brush the scar—"she knew that I could never make a match. She knew I must face the fact squarely and make the best of my life."

Josh could only gape at Melody. Good Lord! Because she was not a raving beauty, and had been further marred by an injury, the girl actually thought of herself as worthless! And what was worse, she had conveyed that concept to everyone around her. He had seen ample evidence in the demeanor of Lady Sandborne and Mary and Arthur toward her. When they noticed her at all, it was with the condescending kindness they might bestow on a feeble-minded scullery maid. It was as though her self-effacing style completely smothered the beauty and sparkle that lay beneath. My God, what had her mother been thinking of to so twist her daughter's concept of herself?

"How did it happen?" he asked at last.

"A childhood accident. I was playing in the barn and fell from the loft into an armful of pitchforks that had been stacked against the wall. The doctor said I was lucky I had not lost an eye." Josh shivered involuntarily, and Melody uttered a short, bitter laugh. "Sometimes, I used to think it would have been better if the pitchforks had pierced my heart."

Immediately, she pressed her fingers against her mouth. "No, I do not mean that, of course. It was only my self-pity speaking. For, I must tell you, for a while, I fancied my life was over." She essayed a weak laugh. "As you can see, I was a rather gothic-romance sort of young woman. I have since taken my mother's words to heart and have, indeed, tried to make something of my life. I am content now."

For a long moment, Josh said nothing. Then, leaning forward, he took Melody's hand. "You very much mistake the situation." Josh spoke softly, but he was surprised at the intensity he heard in his voice. "You must know that you are lovely, despite the care that you have taken to represent yourself as plain and uninteresting. You are obviously intelligent and possessed of wit. In addition, you are gifted with a magnificent talent. Any man would be honored to take you as wife."

For several long moments, Melody was silent. Never had a man spoken to her thus! Her heart was pounding as though she were being pursued by demons and her stomach churned unpleasantly.

Why was he saying these things to her? Things she knew to be patently false, except for the part about her purposeful self-effacement. How had he discerned that, when no one else ever had? Otherwise the things he said were so absurd she would have laughed had she not been so astonished. Was he perpetrating some sort of cruel joke? She had been the butt of many such in the past, but somehow the Earl of Sandborne had not struck her as the type to amuse himself at another's expense.

She forced herself to meet his gaze, and once more she knew a quivering sensation in the pit of her stomach. There was no mockery in his jeweled gaze, only a perceptive sensitivity that drew an unthinking and wholly unguarded response from deep within her.

Instantly, she stiffened, marshaling her defenses. He was being kind to a spinster with an unfortunate burden, one who was hopelessly flawed and without prospect. Yes, that was it. She felt a surge of resentment that he should see her as such an obvious object of pity, but the next moment, she chided herself. Compassion was a virtue, and the earl could only be commended for his consideration. She must not mind his clumsiness in choosing words that could only make her more painfully aware of her defects.

She gulped. "Thank you—Josh. It was—nice of you to say that." She removed her hand from his, experiencing a strange sense of loss as she did so. She rose awkwardly. "I must say good night to you now."

She turned to leave the room, but was stayed as Josh lifted his hands to her shoulders. He smiled into her eyes. "You think I am offering you Spanish coin. I am not, little lark. You are a jewel, albeit glowing unnoticed, and you must never think otherwise." Bending his head, he brushed the scar with his lips, then bent to her mouth. So light and so impersonal was his touch that it could hardly be called a kiss, but Melody jerked as though he had bitten her.

Uttering a strangled sound, she whirled and ran from the room, leaving Josh to stare bemusedly after her.

What the devil had possessed him to behave so? he wondered. My God, he had actually kissed a woman he had met but a few hours earlier. A gently bred maiden to boot. Had he taken leave of his senses?

Yes, he had. He had acted in a moment of complete mindlessness, guided only by an instinct that had been as insistent as it was unpremeditated. To be sure, he had felt a connection with Lady Sandborne's unprepossessing companion from the moment he had been caught up in the beauty of her song in the churchyard. He was angry, as anyone would be, at the way she had been virtually ignored by her family and now her employers. He was even angrier that Melody apparently felt compelled to shroud her gifts in a submissive demeanor and an unflattering style of dress.

That was no reason, however, for him to maul her as though she had been a flirtatious chambermaid.

But no, surely he was making too much of this. He had not really mauled Melody Fairfax. His kiss had been—well—almost paternal. Yes, that was it, a mere salute of friendship. Surely, despite her startlement, Melody had received it as such and would think no more about it. Nor would he.

Casting one more glance at the piano, he left the music room and repaired to his bedchamber.

In her own room, Melody stood motionless, her fingers pressed to her lips. How could he have behaved so? How could he have followed what appeared to be a genuine attempt at kindness with such an assault? Did he see her as that humorous stereotype, an ugly old maid, desperate for the attentions of a man? A convenient outlet for his base passions?

Even as these reflections whirled chaotically in her brain she realized their foolishness. His kiss had been totally lacking in passion. It was almost brotherly, in fact, although she had rarely received such a sign of affection from anyone in her family. The earl had not assaulted her. The kiss had been merely a gesture of kindness, but . . . His lips had been warm against hers. And firm.

And she was making entirely too much of the incident. He had acted in a spirit of distant kindness and that was all there was to it. She would place no further significance on what had been, after all, merely a careless gesture on the earl's part.

Her resolutions firmly in place, she began her preparations for bed. Once she had retired, however, it was many minutes before she was able to compose herself for sleep.

VI

The following morning Lady Sandborne strode briskly into the breakfast room as Josh was finishing a hearty repast of eggs, a largish beefsteak, and scones. Melody entered behind her, blushing when her gaze encountered that of the earl.

Pinning an impersonal smile to his lips, Josh greeted both ladies and urged them to seats at the table.

"No, my dear," caroled the countess, "we have already breakfasted. I merely wished to see if you are ready for your tour. I thought we'd better get to it before Mr. Brickley arrives."

"I shall attend to that correspondence, my lady," interposed Melody, backing out of the room. "If you will just ring when you—"

"Nonsense," retorted Lady Sandborne. "You know as much or more about the house than I. You can repair any of my omissions and add anything that comes into your head. Come along, both of you."

The countess led the way from the breakfast room to the main hall, and from there up the sweeping staircase to the floors above. With sporadic interpolations by Melody, she chattered all the way of Restoration staircases, Jacobean galleries, and Grecian anterooms. Josh was swept into drawing rooms and other assorted chambers, as well as guest bedchambers and, of course, the State chamber in which, he was assured, had slept three kings, a queen, and the odd princess or two. At the end of an hour, they arrived in the Long Gallery, which stretched the length of the house.

The walls of this vast chamber were lined with family portraits, and as the countess led him along, Josh's interest increased, for several of the gentlemen pictured might have been hosed and bewigged versions of himself.

Reaching the far end of the gallery, they stopped before a group portrait. In its center, a boy stood within the protective curve of his mother's arm. He was about seven years old, and he stared gravely out at the world through a pair of expressive gray eyes.

"Is this my father?" asked Josh softly.

"Yes. All four of the brothers were included in this portrait. The oldest, of course"—she indicated the tallest boy, standing straight and proud next to his father—"is George, my late husband. Next to him is William, and then your father, John. Seated in your grandmother's lap is their youngest, Foster. They were a handsome group, do you not agree?"

"Yes." Josh whispered the word as a hot, pricking sensation rose behind his eyelids. These people meant nothing to him, really. Not even the boy who had grown up to become his father, for he had never known the man. Yet, it was impossible not to feel the bond of kinship that seemed to reach out to him from beyond the canvas and paint. These were *his* people! They were not important to him, of course, but still he felt drawn to the portrait.

He turned, aware that Lady Sandborne was speaking once more.

"I remember the boys very well, you know, for, as I told you, our parents were good friends. They rarely let me in on their games when we visited, but I can still remember them—in this very gallery. They used to run races, screaming with laughter. George always won, of course, but occasionally he would let the others catch up to him. John always tried harder than the others. I can see him now—his face red with effort and determination.

Josh turned to look down the length of the chamber. He could almost see them, too. George shouting encouragement, little Foster struggling to keep up on his short, stubby legs, and William and John trying valiantly to outdo each other.

He caught Melody's glance on him, her gray eyes warm with empathy. Was she reading his thoughts? He shifted uncomfortably. Dammit, he didn't want her inside his mind. He had spent a lifetime guarding his feelings, and he preferred to keep his own counsel.

He nodded curtly. "Again, I thank you for your time and trouble, ladies, but if you will point me to the earl's—or, rather, my study, I must be on my way. That is where I promised to meet Mr. Brickley in— good Lord, fifteen minutes ago!" he exclaimed, pulling out his watch.

The countess directed Josh to a handsomely appointed chamber on the ground floor of the house, and he arrived somewhat breathless to find his steward awaiting him.

Their conversation was amicable and informative. Josh was pleased to discover that, according to the accounts spread before him, Sandborne Court and the other estates now in his possession, were in good stead.

Following their discussion, Mr. Brickley drove him about the estate. Their travels, encompassing the park, the Home Farm and various smaller farms and tenancies, took the remainder of the day, and at the end, Josh was pleased at the confirmation of his initial assessment of Mr. Brickley's husbandry. Good, he thought, he could leave the Court in short order, secure in the knowledge that his lands were in good hands. By the first of the year, his work in England might be done and he could return home in good conscience.

Return home? Well, no, not precisely. He would simply be going back to the place where he had lived all his life. A different thing, altogether.

He would have, he considered some days later, little compunction in leaving his new family, for he seemed to make little impact in their lives. As he familiarized himself with his new domain, he saw Arthur only infrequently, for his scholarly cousin spent most of his time in a crowded little study in his own family quarters. Upon visiting him there one day, Josh was astonished at the depth of the man's interest in Roman Britain. The room was laced with bookshelves that

overflowed with moth-eaten tomes bearing Latin ti-
tles. Almost every surface was covered with crumpled
notes, old maps, and such impedimenta as models of
ancient forts, coins, and even pieces of rusted armor.

Mary, while profoundly uninterested in her husband's avocation, spent most of her time as well in the
family quarters. What she did there, Josh was unable
to fathom, since she seemed to have no hobbies of her
own. She maintained her chill disapproval of Josh's
presence at the Court, and on the rare occasions when
she and Arthur graced the huge dining chamber with
their presence, she turned a resolutely cold shoulder to
her new cousin.

Aunt Helen, while more visible, was usually immersed in village activities. She took her duties as lady
of the manor seriously, and made frequent social calls.
She also busied herself in visiting tenants or planning
charity events with the vicar's wife, usually with
Melody at her side.

Josh found this situation, somewhat to his surprise,
highly unsatisfactory. On the occasions when he was
permitted conversation with the little companion, he
found her company pleasant in the extreme. With her,
he felt he could be himself. He relished the sparkle of
interest that would appear in her gray eyes when he
spoke of his homeland across the sea.

He spent a great deal of time with Mr. Brickley, a
tall man with perceptive brown eyes, who had served
the Weston family for most of his three and fifty years.
Josh also became acquainted with various and sundry
neighbors, all of whom apparently found it necessary
to visit the Court on some pretext or other during the
first week of his arrival.

With the rest of the family, he attended church in
the village on Sunday. At his first Sunday service, he
was obviously the focus of attention from the county

gentry down to the lowliest laborers. Josh was made more than somewhat uncomfortable by this, yet another indication of his sudden rise in status. On the other hand, he discovered to his surprise that he enjoyed the service. The vicar, a plain, no-nonsense sort of man, delivered a plain, no-nonsense sort of sermon, and the occasion was further enhanced by the offertory delivery of Bach's "Jesu, Joy of Man's Desiring," by Melody. Unfortunately, her accompanist, the village's oldest inhabitant, he was told, played very badly, her arthritic fingers stumbling over the keys of an ancient organ, rendering the morning hideous with discord.

Afterward, Josh stood on the steps of the church, exchanging pleasantries with his new neighbors, the county landowners. These worthies, he soon discovered, were not so different from their American counterparts. Bluff and hearty, their minds seldom rising above the current crop conditions and the prices thereof, they were nonetheless good people, and ones with whom he soon established a surprising rapport. Their wives, to a woman, determined immediately that what was supremely lacking in his life was a wife. They seemed to come to a unanimous decision that their first priority in life was to assist him in remedying this sad want. Josh found himself the recipient of invitations to countless dinner parties, balls, routs, and soirees, all made the more frenetic by the imminent approach of Christmas.

Indeed, Josh noted that the season was beginning to creep into his house in hesitant increments, heralded first by bits of greenery swagged in the entry hall and pine boughs over the mantelpieces.

One morning, he entered the breakfast room to find Melody dining in solitary state. He lifted his brows in surprise.

"You are not with Aunt Helen this morning?"

Melody's eyes twinkled. "I have been banished. Lady Sandborne has declared that she's full of crotchets today and plans to spend the day catching up on her correspondence. I usually help her with that, but she says she would rather write to her particular friends herself."

"Ah," replied Josh, unaccountably pleased. "Then perhaps you would care to join me after breakfast for a ride. Brickley is a hard taskmaster, but I find that if I creep out early enough I can usually elude him for a good gallop before taking up my daily chores."

The idea seemed to take Melody by surprise.

"Oh!" she exclaimed, her eyes wide. "But—but, I am not dressed for riding. I don't think—"

"How long would it take you to change?" asked Josh mildly, not to be put off.

Seeming to come to a decision, Melody rose abruptly. A smile like the dawning sun spread across her features. "Not very long at all," she replied in a lilting tone. "If you will wait, I shall join you in just a few minutes."

As Melody hastened up the stairs, her heart beat wildly. She was being foolish beyond bounds, she chided herself. The prospect of a couple of hours spent with a man was not enough to cause this sense of exhilaration, this singing in her blood. The earl, of course, was not just any man. She had come to enjoy his presence at the Court far more than a spinster of limited expectations should. She relished the intelligence that shone from his extraordinary emerald eyes, and his kindness, and—oh, the solid, reassuring strength of him.

Hurriedly, she donned her habit, wishing uncharacteristically that she possessed one of more fashionable styling. At least it fit her better than most of her

gowns. She reached for her hat, noting with a twinge
of satisfaction that it, at least possessed a modicum of
style. One of Lady Sandborne's castoffs, it was fash-
ioned as a military shako, with a dashing feather
swooping down from the brim. Ruthlessly, Melody
crushed it atop her hair and, pausing only to push a
few stray tendrils under the brim, she turned toward
the door.

Sometime later, my lord the Earl of Sandborne and
Miss Melody Fairfax cantered sedately out of the sta-
bleyard, moving in the direction of the Home Farm.
They chattered amiably of inconsequential matters, although Josh found himself hard pressed to keep his
mind on the conversation. He had been summarily
taken aback at Melody's appearance upon returning to
the breakfast parlor.

Her tailored habit revealed the figure that he had
only guessed at previously. The soft swell of bosom
and hip were perfectly delineated beneath the serviceable fabric. Her hat, with just a touch of dash, comple-
mented her ensemble, and the jaunty feather that
curved along her cheek served to mask her scar.

Her countenance fairly shone with anticipation, and
the effect, combined with the impact of her sparkling
eyes and her lovely smile, was altogether dazzling. My
God, Melody Fairfax might not be a certified beauty,
but without her protective shroud, her aspect was
more than sufficient to set a man's blood pounding.

They maintained their slow pace until they reached
the hedge that formed the boundary between the farm
and the open fields and woodland that lay beyond.
Josh turned to Melody.

"Are you for a gallop?" he asked, smiling.

"Oh yes," she answered gleefully. "It is one of the
things I love most, peltering over the hills with the
wind in my face."

Suiting her words to action, she spurred the little mare provided her by Lady Sandborne. She waved gaily as she sped away over the frozen grassland, and, grinning, Josh clapped his heels against his mount. He experienced no difficulty in overtaking her, and neck and neck they flew toward the woodland that lay a few miles ahead. Upon reaching their destination, they halted, exhilarated and well-pleased with themselves.

"My, that was glorious!" exclaimed Melody.

They had by now entered the woods and lightly frosted leaves crackled beneath the horses' hooves as they slowed to a leisurely walk. For a while they rode in a companionable silence.

"I have not heard you at the piano," Melody said at last, "except as an accompanist."

Josh drew in a swift breath.

"No."

"You do not wish to take up your avocation?" She smiled. "Or are you still immersed in the 'think' method?"

"What? Oh. No. That is—I have been busy." He added in a rush, "I'm not sure I wish to pursue my former hobby." Josh found that he was perspiring profusely.

"Forgive me—Josh, but it seems like a slap in the face of God to turn your back on such a gift."

Josh flushed. "I suppose it is, but . . . Oh, the devil take it!" he exclaimed, slapping his thigh with the reins he held loosely in one hand. "I have a good reason for not wishing to approach the keyboard," he concluded stiffly.

He glanced at Melody, but her face revealed only a waiting courtesy. Impulsively, he jumped from his horse and held out his hand to help her dismount. She lifted her brows questioningly, but slid from her saddle into his waiting arms.

Noting abstractedly that his hands nearly spanned her slender waist, he began speaking.

"I started to tell you the other night about Dorothea, my fiancée. Our disagreement over my playing intensified over the course of our betrothal. Then, one night"—his green eyes grew distant—"I had been invited to perform at a concert given by some music students of my acquaintance. The money taken in was to benefit a proposed school of music.

"Dorothea did not want me to be a part of it. It smelled, she said, too much like playing for hire. We argued at length, but in the end, I decided to participate. We were still brangling when I left her house. Shortly afterwards, she changed her mind and, remorseful, set out after me. It was in the autumn of the year and a hard, chill rain was falling. Her carriage broke down and she was forced to wait on the road for over an hour. She was soaked to the skin." He drew a long, shuddering breath. "She caught an inflammation of the lungs and died within a week."

"Oh!" gasped Melody. "How awful for you. But—"

Josh began walking, and Melody stumbled after him.

"Don't you see?" he continued. "It was all my fault. It was my obsession with my music that had caused her death. Thus, music ceased to be my joy. I could not face the piano, for there was no song in my soul. I did not make a formal vow never to play again, but I have been unable to do so—at least until I accompanied you on the first night of my arrival. I became rather a recluse, I'm afraid and that's when I started making treks into the wilderness."

For a long moment, Melody gazed at him consideringly.

"And did your decision bring you happiness?" She spoke quietly, but with a slight edge to her tone.

"What?" he asked in some surprise. "I—well, I suppose I developed a certain sense of peace."

"As well you might"—Melody continued, the sharpness in her voice now pronounced—"having abandoned all your responsibilities."

"Responsiblities?" asked Josh blankly. "But, I had none."

Melody whirled to face him. "Forgive me for saying so,"she said breathlessly, "but you left the family who had raised you, and it sounds very much as though you left your Uncle Eli in the lurch. In addition, you took it upon yourself to deny a talent that is given to very few. Such a gift comes with a responsibility, you know, to share it with others."

Her voice shook, whether with temerity at her outspokenness or simply her anger, Josh could not tell. She paused for a moment to draw a long breath before plunging into her conclusion. "It seems to me, my lord earl, that you have been wallowing in self-pity and what one can only consider your ridiculous feelings of guilt. How could you possibly feel responsible for a rainstorm? Or the breakdown of Dorothea's carriage? If she had loved you enough to accompany you in the first place—"

"What?" said Josh again in outraged astonishment. He stepped forward to grasp her shoulders. "What the devil gives you the right to scold me like an errant schoolboy? I might say you have little room to talk, Miss Fairfax."

"M-me?" squeaked Melody.

"Yes, you. You are an attractive woman, yourself possessed of a remarkable gift. Yet, you have let yourself be bullied by your family and you have chosen to hide yourself in clothes a scullery maid would scorn and to bury yourself here in a household that hasn't the sense to appreciate the treasure in their midst!"

Melody wrenched herself from his grip and fell back a step. Dear Lord, what was she about? She had felt compelled by a force beyond her understanding to reach out to him, but how could she have spoken so to a man she barely knew, let alone one who was, for all intents and purposes, her employer?

For several moments, the two stared at one another in mutual mortification. At last, Josh spoke stiffly.

"Perhaps we should return to the house."

Wordlessly, Melody swung about to her horse. Josh assisted her into her saddle, and they rode swiftly and silently back to the house. She did not see him again until that evening, when the family gathered for dinner in the Blue Saloon.

As it happened, Melody was the first to arrive there. What, she wondered in some trepidation, would be the earl's reaction on beholding her this evening? When Josh entered only a few moments later, Melody stiffened, and after a mechanical exchange of pleasantries with him, fell silent. She turned and ran her hand self-consciously along the mantelpiece. Bringing her fingertip up for a thorough examination, she said at last in a colorless voice.

"I owe you an apology, my—Josh. I had no right to speak so."

"I said a few unfortunate things, myself," said Josh, a smile tugging at his lips. "Phew! Who would have suspected that such a spitfire lurked beneath the very proper exterior of Miss Melody Fairfax?"

Melody flushed. "I assure you, my lord, I do not ordinarily indulge myself in such unbecoming displays of spirit."

"Then perhaps you should do so more often." He lifted a hand to tuck away a tendril of hair that had escaped the confines of her cap. "Temper becomes you."

To her discomfiture, his gaze intensified. "And I

want to tell you—" He halted and dropped his hand abruptly as voices sounded in the corridor. A moment later, Mary and Arthur entered the room and Melody turned away hastily. Her heart pounded. What had he started to say?

During dinner, conversation was general, although as usual, Mary remained frigidly oblivious to the earl's presence. By an unspoken agreement, the others ignored her display of bad manners. At length the countess spoke up.

"Now then, Josh, I want to talk to you all about the Christmas ball."

"But," he said, bewildered, "I thought all the arrangements had been made. Mrs. Gresham told me we've been receiving notes for weeks accepting invitations that were sent out some time ago."

"Yes," intoned the dowager austerely. "But that does not mean everything is in place. I was not at all pleased with the foodstuffs sent by Gunter's last year. The lobster was definitely off, in my opinion. I rather think we might try Fortnum and Mason this year. They have a much wider selection and their prices, so Cook informs me, are more reasonable. Also, they deliver in a more timely fashion, or so I am told."

"Are not our own people capable of preparing the food?" asked Josh, startled. He had not realized the apparent scope of this family Christmas celebration.

"Yes, of course. That is, they do well enough for the ordinary things—pastries, sandwiches, and so on— but, for the more exotic items, such as lobster puffs and the *croquembouche*, a caterer is a necessity."

"I see," said Josh gravely. "I suppose the musicians must be hired in London, as well."

"Well, naturally. In past years, we used a group from Canterbury, but the violinist and the cellist were, unfortunately, addicted to strong drink."

"A common affliction among creatively endowed persons, I understand." Josh's tone was still serious, but Melody was not deceived. She perceived without difficulty the amusement that twinkled in his eyes.

An exhaustive discussion followed, mostly between Mary and Lady Sandborne, involving the merits of the various orchestras to be obtained in the city, as well as the quantity and quality of the food required for the ball, the quality of the candles, the placement of the greenery, and the advisability of allowing the guests' children to participate in the festivities.

Melody followed the conversation distractedly. Her opinion on the critical decisions regarding the ball was not, of course, sought. Which, she reflected, was a good thing, since she was having difficulty fixing her attention on any of them. Her thoughts dwelled on what it was that the earl had wished to speak to her about.

She remained silent through the rest of the meal, and when the ladies rose, she cast her own gaze to the floor as she followed Lady Sandborne from the room. Her tactics were for naught, however, for upon the gentlemen's arrival in the music room, Josh strode unerringly to where she sat and settled himself in the chair next to her.

"Will you sing for us tonight, little lark?" he asked in a low voice.

Since he had made the same request every night since his arrival, she was not surprised, but her pulse quickened—as it always did in response.

"Yes," she replied, as she had every night, "but only if you will accompany me."

"Of course, I will. In fact"—he hesitated—"I wanted to talk to you about that. What you said this morning—out in the woods— It made me very angry at the time. No," he added hastily as Melody put up her hand in a defensive gesture, "I have thought about it—thoroughly." He drew a deep breath. "And I have come to the conclusion that you were right. I have been indulging in what was really nothing more than a prolonged fit of the sulks for the last three years over an incident that, while it was undoubtedly a tragedy, was not my fault."

Melody could only stare at him in astonishment.

"I shall always retain the memory of Dorothea in a corner of my heart, but I must finally admit to myself that she and I were not truly suited and would have made one another miserable." He drew in a long breath. "I have, therefore, vowed to renew my acquaintance with the piano. I'm sadly rusty, and I shall probably drive the household mad, but I intend to practice diligently in order to regain whatever skill I possessed before flouncing off upriver."

Josh did not reveal to Melody the extent of his further reflections during the course of his rather long afternoon. He had spent considerable time wondering why a few succinct, if more than somewhat infuriated, words from a woman he scarcely knew had effected such a profound response from him. Certainly, other people had told him he was being foolish to abandon his comfortable life in Philadelphia for the rigors of life in the forest. Uncle Eli had expounded at length on the subject, as had his friends, all to no avail.

Yet, one small, perceptive female had made him realize within a few short weeks of their acquaintance the futility and the self-indulgence of his behavior. Not only that, but she had engendered a certain joy in him—simply through the pleasure of her company.

He felt as though he had known her all his life. Such a trite phrase, but so very meaningful. During his time at the Court, he had learned more about her—her tastes, her opinions on everything from the Corn Laws to the Regent's marriage to the poetry of Byron—and the more he discovered, the more he wished to know. Being with her was like embarking on an exploration of a new and fascinating country.

It was a fine thing, he told himself, to have found a friend among the alien corn.

He took her hand and led her to the piano. Seating himself, he drifted into the first chords of Purcell's "Fairest Isle." Hesitant at first, and then gaining strength, her glorious voice blended with the notes and for the next hour, oblivious to their audience, they made music together.

Melody scarcely noticed the passage of time. She was aware only of Josh's long, sensitive fingers on the keys and her own response to the sound he created. The music seemed to flow from her effortlessly, almost without thought.

How very odd, she thought. She and the earl had quarreled. The words she had hurled at him had been born of a genuine concern, but it was not surprising that she had angered him. Yet, he had valued her sentiment and had taken her intemperate speech to heart. How long had it been since anyone actually valued her opinion?

Why, it was almost as though he considered her a friend. The thought warmed her. She had few friends—the vicar and his wife, the daughter of a nearby squire, a couple of former school friends in London. With none of these, however, did she feel the odd and wholly unexpected sense of connection she experienced with the earl. She uttered a small sigh of contentment, contemplating the void in her life that now seemed filled.

Melody sang on, her heart so full she could hardly bring out the words. As the song drew to a close, she turned to Josh.

"I think that about finishes me for the evening," she

said with a laugh. "Perhaps—that is—you have said you are out of practice, but could you favor us with a solo selection?"

She returned to her chair, leaving Josh seated at the piano, a thoughtful frown on his face. A moment later, he lifted his hands and brought them down in a simple but achingly beautiful melody. Melody listened, enraptured. It was obvious that Josh had not exaggerated when he spoke of his artistic skill, for he possessed the rare gift of drawing not just notes from the great instrument, but seemingly the very soul of the music itself. Even Lady Sandborne and Mary ceased their conversation to listen.

"Oh!" breathed Melody when he had finished. "That was magnificent. But—I think I have heard that piece before." She lifted her brows questioningly.

"It was written by Herr Ludwig van Beethoven. It is his Sonata Number Two in C Sharp Minor, the first movement. Some call it 'The Moonlight Sonata.' It is not technically difficult, but is exquisitely crafted—as you say, a magnificent piece of music."

Lady Sandborne crowed her delight. "I had no idea you were so talented, Josh. You must play the organ at the church. It would be a refreshing treat from poor Miss Verney's efforts. Perhaps a special presentation at the offertory on Christmas Day."

Thus, Josh entered another phase of his tenure at the Court. He continued his sessions with Mr. Brickley, absorbing with gratitude the older man's intelligence and expertise and his dedication to the Weston family. He found himself growing more interested every day in the management of the estate, and learned, almost without conscious effort, the price of wool, the best markets for the other fruits of the estate, and the needs and desires of his tenants. He learned who among these could be relied upon to produce an honest day's work for a fair wage, and who must be prodded into effort. He discovered a great enjoyment in visiting the cottages to assure himself that all was in good order.

He plunged into county activities. The hunt was nearly over for the year, but he took part in one or two outings among good-natured raillery on his ignorance of proper protocol. The snickers turned to cries of admiration, however, when, on shooting expeditions, he unfailingly hit his mark.

Most of all, however, he relished the hours spent in the music room. His former proficiency returned to him with surprising speed, and he engaged frequently in duets with Melody on the harp. He even began lessons with her on the piano and was delighted by the aptitude she displayed almost immediately.

Meanwhile, preparations continued apace for Christmas. From the beginning of December onward, guests arrived almost on a daily basis at the Court's great front doors. Relatives, close and distant, poured in from all points of the compass. Surrounded by an ever-widening galaxy of cousins, aunts, nephews, and nieces, Josh gave vent to his bewilderment one afternoon as he sat at the piano with Melody.

"I have twice confused cousin George with cousin Harold," he complained, his fingers wandering aimlessly over the keys. "And, I have recently paired each of them with females other than their wives. I cannot remember if Aunt Letitia Weston is a member of the Wiltshire or the Sussex branch of the family, nor can I ever remember Uncle Septimus's last name, except that it is not Weston, since he is, apparently not a blood relation."

Melody laughed. "I suppose it must be difficult for you, acquiring an instantaneous—to say nothing of multitudinous—family."

"Oh, but—" Josh began, ready to dispute her. He realized suddenly that he could not. How could he explain to her that, though the people streaming into the manor house were related to him, he could not possibly consider them family?

Family, to him, meant what the members of his Uncle Eli's flock had shared—at least all of them but him. Bonds of affection and tradition forged over generations—a fierce loyalty to one another and an abiding interest in each other's welfare. Though he was now the head of his own household, he was coldly aware that he and his newfound relatives felt nothing for each other beyond a mild interest. And that was how he preferred it. He certainly did not wish for any encumbrance in his life.

He considered that he had done his duty as the Earl of Sandborne. He had surveyed his little realm and found it good. His lands were in good stead, and those who worked it were well cared for. When the members of his extended family made their departure from the old homestead after Christmas, the earl would be at the head of the pack. After a brief tour of his other estates in various parts of England, he would be off on the first available ship from Bristol.

He would return for the occasional visit, of course, but his home was in America, and his life as well. He must remember that, he concluded, wondering why this plan, so eminently reasonable in its conception, seemed to be losing some of its luster of late.

"No, no," he said to Melody, shaking off his reflections. "You must lift your fingers higher during this passage. Every note must sound clear and crisp."

He gazed fondly on her as she bent earnestly to her task. She was flushed with her endeavors and her lovely hair had almost completely escaped the confines of her cap, with curls drifting in an enticing manner about her cheeks. Her magnificent eyes were narrowed in concentration. He knew an unwelcome urge to place his lips just there, at her temple, where a faint pulse beat beneath a satiny feather of hair.

Good Lord! he thought, startled. Where had that thought come from? Melody was his aunt's companion, a confirmed spinster—and his friend. Of course, he realized with a painful twinge. That was what had been bothering him. He would miss Melody when he returned to America. He would miss her laughter and her wit and her songs. Most of all, he would miss their long, late-night chats after Lady Sandborne had retired.

He jumped as Melody's fingers splayed over the keys in a discordant jangle.

"Drat!" she exclaimed. "I shall never get through this passage without blundering. I fail to understand," she continued indignantly, "why composers can't simply write everything in the key of C. Why must they make us struggle with all these sharps and flats? In addition, why can't they realize that not all pianists are men? Look at this chord! I cannot possibly make my hand stretch to cover it." She turned to face her mentor, blowing a wisp of hair from her eyes.

Smothering a chuckle, Josh lifted one of her hands in his.

"To be sure, composers are an inconsiderate lot. However, I think if you strive for more flexibility in your wrists, you will experience less difficulty with those unruly sharps and flats, and perhaps we will allow you to turn this particularly menacing chord into an arpeggio."

Turning, Melody repeated the passage, this time without error, dispatching the last chord in a ripple of notes. She lifted her hands with a flourish.

"Brava!" cried Josh, planting a noisy kiss on her

cheek just as Lady Sandborne put her head in the door.

The countess said nothing, but halted abruptly, watching unseen as the two erupted in laughter. Josh removed the piece of music from the piano, replaced it with another, and began a prosaic series of instructions to his pupil. Slowly, Lady Sandborne backed from the room. Closing the door behind her, she pursed her lips thoughtfully, her eyes narrowing in speculation. She remained in this pose for several moments before she at last opened the door once more, this time rattling the handle briskly.

"Melody, dear," she said in a clear voice. "There you are. I do apologize for interrupting your lesson, but I need your help."

Melody jumped from the piano stool at once. "Of course, my lady. Goodness, it is almost eleven o'clock! I am so sorry. I did not realize I had been away from you for so long. Do you wish to continue with the correspondence we started yesterday?"

"Yes. I owe letters to half the persons of my acquaintance, and I really must take care of it now before I all but sink out of sight beneath the Christmas muddle. How are the lessons coming?" she asked, as Melody moved toward her.

"Famously," replied Josh with a laugh. "She has begun—" But Aunt Helen had already turned away, her interest dissipated. His eyes narrowed. It occurred to him that he must have a long talk with his aunt before he left, on the subject of Miss Melody Fairfax. To be sure, Melody was not mistreated, but her ladyship must be apprised of Melody's importance to him as a valued friend and the necessity of according her more respect in the household. Aunt Helen, as well as Mary and Arthur, must be made aware of the importance of treating her as one of the family. They must cherish her and make her realize her worth.

He returned to the piano and launched into a rather melancholy Bach fugue.

VII

For Melody, it seemed as though the Christmas season had never before contained so much sparkle and anticipation. As the house filled with the chatter of the gathering Westons, her duties increased. She found herself heavily occupied with countless demands on her time, from assuring that Great-aunt Horatia's breakfast tea was served at just the right temperature to finding suitable occupations for the numerous Weston progeny now inhabiting the nursery floor. Still, she found time to assist in decorating the house. Luxuriant boughs of pine, holly, and mistletoe were hung in every room, bound with garlands of gaily colored ribbon. The scent of holiday potpourri issued from strategically placed bowls all over the house.

In her room, she crafted gifts for the family, a pair of slippers for Lady Sandborne, a set of pen wipers for Arthur, and an embroidered reticule for Mary. After some thought, she had sent to a friend in London for a set of piano variations of Josh's favorite, Herr van Beethoven, published just last year. They now reposed in the bottom drawer of her dressing table and she spent an inordinate amount of time picturing the pleasure on his face when she presented him with her gift.

She realized she was becoming entirely too fond of the earl. At first, she had simply enjoyed the fact that she had found a friend, but of late she was forced to admit that her feelings for him were growing far beyond friendship. She relished his companionship, but it was not, she realized guiltily, only his wit and intel-

ligence and kindness that she cherished. She reveled in
the warmth of his laughter and loved to watch the fire-
light reflected on the planes of his face as they lingered
in conversation late at night. She was fascinated by the
strength of his fingers on the keyboard and in the performance of such mundane tasks as slicing a piece of
fruit or mending a pen nub.

She was being unpardonably foolish, yet she could
not deny herself his company. It seemed that her
whole day centered around the moments spent with
him at mealtimes or in the music room.

The full extent of her folly was brought to her with
unpleasant abruptness one evening at dinner. The
Christmas ball was now less than a week away and
the house had become as full as it could hold. The
state dining chamber had been opened and every
place around the massive table was filled with guests.
Melody, seated as usual near the foot of the table
where Lady Sandborne reigned, had been addressing
herself to the gentleman on her right, cousin Harold
Weston. If the truth were told, she was not properly
attending to the conversation, which consisted of a
rather ponderous monologue on soil conditions in
Northumberland. Lady Sandborne's voice caught her
attention.

"Yes, of course, Charlotte Ponsonby is a very good
sort of girl, but I hardly think her a suitable match for
Josh. Maribelle Grant, however, would be perfect."

Netta Weston Graham, Countess of Mayfield, seated
at Lady Sandborne's right, nodded sagely. Melody
gasped. It was as though a chill wind had blown
through the dining room, dimming the candlelight
and settling just below her rib cage. She listened as the
conversation swirled around her. She was unac-
quainted with anyone named Charlotte Ponsonby, but
Maribelle Grant was the daughter of a viscount living

within two days' ride of the Court. She and her family were fairly frequent visitors, and they had accepted with alacrity Lady Sandborne's invitation to the Christmas ball.

Had the countess been pursuing her own agenda in inviting the viscount's family? Melody knew a moment of self-chastisement, realizing with appalling clarity that she should have expected something like this. Good Lord, she knew full well that one of Josh's first priorities as the new Earl of Sandborne must be to seek out a worthy bride. The succession must be secured, after all.

Now that this critical circumstance had been brought home to her, Melody's brain whirled in a dismal fog of speculation. Josh had said nothing to her of being on the hunt for a wife, but perhaps he felt that his marital plans were none of her business. Which, of course, they were not.

But, what would his marriage mean to her? To the precious rapport that had grown between them? In all likelihood he would forget her very existence once he married. It would be his new wife with whom he would share his music. Would he give her piano lessons as well?

The thought of Josh's head bent close to Maribelle Grant's golden curls caused an unexpected wave of pure pain to course through her. Dear Lord, what was the matter with her? How could she have allowed her silly, spinsterish fancies to have carried her so far?

She became dimly aware that Harold Weston was again contributing to her scant knowledge of farming technology in the north country. She was also aware that she was developing a thundering headache, and she experienced an urgent desire to flee the dining chamber for the haven of her bedchamber.

Such behavior would be unthinkable, of course, so

Melody smiled and nodded and interjected the occasional question, turning from Harold Weston after a suitable interval to address herself to the equally boring Sir Philip Weston on her left.

After dinner she was offered a respite, as those conversing in the music room paid her little attention, as usual. When the gentlemen entered the chamber, Melody remained determinedly on the other side of the room from Josh. Seeing him now in a new and painful perspective, she could not bring herself to participate in even the most inconsequential conversation with him. Though he approached her several times, she took care to avoid him. Actually, she was called upon to make little conversation with anyone, and once again she was grateful as the others present looked through and around her as though she were transparent. She was not even asked to sing on this night, as courtesy demanded that the time allotted for the evening's entertainment be given wholly to the visitors, some of whom were possessed of a modicum of musical talent and others who, regrettably, were not.

To Melody's relief, the company broke up betimes, and with some alacrity, she accompanied Lady Sandborne upstairs to bed at an early hour. She sent a wistful glance back at Josh to find that he was staring after her in some perplexity.

What the devil was the matter with Melody? wondered Josh, watching with a frown as she whisked herself from the room after his aunt. She'd been looking blue as a megrim ever since dinner. And she'd hardly spoken to him all evening. He stood aside as Mary pushed past him on her way to the door. He bade her a pleasant good night and was rewarded as usual with a cold sniff. Blast the woman, anyway, he thought distractedly. Could she not unbend even at

Christmas? He shrugged. It mattered not to him if his newfound cousin wished him to perdition. She and the woolly-witted Arthur would soon be nothing but a memory.

Josh did not retire with the rest of party, but lingered in the music room, seating himself at the keyboard. Restlessly, he skimmed through a Mozart divertimento, dropping his hands at the end to gaze sightlessly before him. He was surprised to discover the extent of his dismay at Melody's withdrawal from him. He realized that he had grown not just accustomed, but almost dependent on her unobtrusive companionship. He felt deprived when he must do without her conversation, or glances shared with her across the room.

He sighed. Yes, he would miss her when he left England. Perhaps he might persuade Aunt Helen to visit him in America, bringing her companion with her. He would enjoy showing Melody the wonders of his native land. He could just picture her, wide-eyed in Philadelphia, or even, perhaps, paddling with him in a canoe on the Susquehanna. She would—

He brought his reflections to an abrupt conclusion. He was beginning to sound as though he wanted Melody as a permanent fixture in his life. Which was patently absurd. Melody's life lay here in England, as his lay across the Atlantic. If she chose to leave his aunt, she could look forward to a stellar career in the concert halls of London. He, in turn, wished for nothing more than to return to his former life. His business interests would surely occupy him fully, as they always had.

He rose abruptly to pinch out the candles and he left the darkened room swiftly. As he mounted the stairway ascending from the hall, he almost collided with a small figure just descending.

"Oh!" Melody cried faintly. "Josh! I did not see you there in the shadows!"

She had removed her cap, and Josh noted with a tightening of his throat that her hair had been released from its unrelenting knot, flowing over her shoulders in enticing abandon.

"But, I thought you abed long ago," he said in some bemusement.

"I just settled Lady Sandborne for the night and wished to read for a while before seeking my own rest. I had nothing in my chambers, so I thought to find something in the library."

"Ah." Josh stepped aside to let her pass, but laid a hand on her arm as she passed. "Is—is anything troubling you, Melody?"

She gasped slightly. "Me? No, of course not. Why do you ask?"

"You seemed rather, um, distracted this evening."

"Oh. I was—well, I was thinking about—about my family."

"I suppose you must miss them at this time of year."

"Oh." She said again. "Yes, of course." She breathed a small sigh of relief. Apparently, he had accepted her blatant lie. "Although, " she continued hastily, "I am enjoying the presence of so many of your family."

Josh smiled. He had turned to escort her to her destination and they were now crossing the center of the hall. He gestured toward the greenery that hung above their heads.

"You have done much to bring the spirit of the season into my home," he said quietly. Looking up again, he halted and, following his gaze, Melody stiffened. There, suspended from a swag of pine hung a huge bunch of mistletoe, bound with a scarlet ribbon. Smiling, he grasped her shoulders lightly.

She knew he was going to kiss her, yet, as his head

bent over hers, she did nothing to stay him. Instead, she swayed into the hard curve of his body as though her own had been created expressly for this purpose. His lips came down on hers, gently at first, but as an immediate response shuddered through her, the kiss deepened and grew urgent. His arms encircled her to clasp her to him tightly until she felt she might never breathe again, but her hands went up to pull him even closer. Her fingers twined into the silky darkness of his hair where it lay against his collar.

The feel of his mouth on hers, the strength of the muscular frame pressed so needfully against her shattered whatever rational thought remained to her and she was appalled at the whimper she heard emerging from her throat. She felt as though she were being consumed by the flame that shot through her at his touch and she was conscious only of the wanting that seemed to permeate her being. She was not sure what it was she yearned for so insistently. She knew only that she needed him to go on kissing her, to continue this delicious chaos within her and to increase the swirls of fireworks where his hands moved along her spine.

Under his persistent teasing, her lips opened beneath his, but at this point, Josh slowly drew back from her. Almost sagging in his arms, she looked up at him, seeing her own dazed wonderment mirrored in his jeweled eyes.

"I think," he said huskily, "I'd better stop while I still can."

She could only nod in unwilling agreement.

"I suppose I should apologize"—he continued, his voice soft as fur—"but I find that I cannot. So, I will just say good night, little lark, and I hope your dreams will be as sweet as mine."

His mouth slanted across hers one last time, gently

and with infinite sweetness. Then, he turned and moved swiftly up the stairs.

VIII

"I am not sure about the color of this floss," said Lady Sandborne dubiously. "Do you think the red too gaudy?"

The countess sat in her sitting room, her slippered feet resting on a stool. Her needle gleamed as it pierced the snowy lawn of the handkerchief on which she was embroidering a monogram for Arthur. Near her, Melody sat engaged on a similar task, inserting the last stitches in the reticule she crafted for Mary.

"Mmm," replied Melody thoughtfully. "I suppose it is a departure from the traditional white, but I think Arthur could stand a touch of gaudy in his life."

Lady Sandborne laughed. "I agree." She glanced sharply at her companion and after a moment's hesitation, she spoke again. "You are looking uncommonly well of late, Melody."

Melody glanced up, startled. "Why, thank you, my lady."

"Yes, there seems to be a certain sparkle about you."

Melody gasped a little. "It must be Christmas, ma'am. The anticipation and all."

Melody dropped her gaze again to her embroidery, her heart pounding uncomfortably. What a time for her ladyship to acquire a sudden perception where her companion was concerned. Was her newfound happiness really so noticeable? she wondered guiltily.

It had been two days since the meeting between her and Josh in the shadowed recesses of the hall stairway. He had been out with Mr. Brickley and Mr. Wiggs, the Sandborne Court bailiff, on an inspection tour of some intended repairs on the tenants' cottages, so she had seen little of him during that time. But the memory of the strength of his arms about her and the feel of his lips against hers was still with her.

Her intent to visit the library forgotten, she had ascended the stairs in a haze of joy. Josh Weston loved her! He had not said so, but the depth of the emotion he had displayed just now told its own tale. No man could kiss a woman like that unless he had given his heart to her.

Not that she was an expert on such intimacies, of course. She had been the recipient of only three kisses from men in her life other than family. One was of the experimental variety from the butcher's boy when she was thirteen and two later on from males who apparently felt that a female as flawed as she would be grateful for the opportunity to indulge in a bit of tickle and squeeze.

Never had she experienced the shattering passion she had found in Josh's embrace. Never had she dreamed that a single kiss could be so satisfying yet plunge one into such a whirlwind of desire.

How odd, that she had not known until that moment that she loved him. She had welcomed his friendship as a desert flower might drink in the season's first rain, but the knowledge of her love for him had laid hidden in the recesses of her heart. Had it been that way for him?

She did not allow herself to think ahead. Josh was a peer of the realm, and peers did not ally themselves with impoverished maidens, no matter how gently bred. His family obviously wished him to marry well. How could she possibly fit into his future?

No. She would not think of that now. She would—

She came to with a start, realizing that Lady Sandborne was speaking again.

"Goodness, the ball will be upon us in two days and

I still have not decided what to give Josh for Christmas. It seems odd to think that a fortnight ago, we hardly knew of his existence. Have you planned a gift for him?"

Melody could feel herself blushing. "Why, yes, as a matter of fact, I have." She described the music she had purchased through her friend.

"What a splendid idea. Perhaps I could find something similar. For, it will not do to give him something too large." She paused and said deliberately, "The item must be small enough to carry with him easily on shipboard."

"What?" Melody stared blankly at the countess.

"When he returns to America. Why, has he not told you? He will be leaving the Court shortly after Christmas—or, at least so he says. My dear, what is it?" she asked at an involuntary sound from Melody.

"N-nothing, my lady. I have pricked my finger, merely." Melody's stunned gaze fell to her fingers and she watched as the small circle of blood beneath her needle spread on the silk of the reticule.

She could not have heard aright.

"No," she breathed. "He cannot be thinking of leaving."

"Well, but he is. In fact, he seems determined, as he informed me on his arrival. And, he mentioned it again just yesterday." Lady Helen uttered a short laugh. "I was unwise enough to broach the subject of marriage to him. I did not mention Maribelle Grant, even though she and her family arrived on Saturday last. Charlotte Ponsonby and her mother are here, too, of course. Where was I? Oh, yes. I merely remarked on how full the house has become and that there might be among the guests a young lady of good birth who would make him a good wife. He simply smiled and told me that he does not plan to marry. As you can imagine I was taken completely aback. 'Not plan to marry?' I asked in what I can only think of as justifiable indignation. 'What about the succession?' Would you believe, he just smiled again and said the Weston family would have to rely on Arthur and his progeny to continue the line. Meanwhile, he said, he still plans to sail off to America at the earliest opportunity, as that is where his interests lie. Although, he added as an afterthought, he does plan a visit now and then. A visit now and then! Where his interests lie! Did you ever hear the like?"

Melody felt as though she were slowly turning to stone. *Yesterday?* After she had surrendered a piece of her soul to him in that shattering kiss, he had spoken to his aunt of leaving? Their embrace had meant nothing to him?

"What is it my dear?" asked the countess, her sharp eyes scrutinizing her companion. "You are quite pale."

With what seemed a supreme effort, Melody raised her gaze. "Actually, my lady, I am feeling rather unwell. I think it must have been the breakfast kippers. If you do not mind, I believe I shall retire from you for a while."

"Of course, dear," replied Lady Sandborne solicitously. As Melody rose slowly to her feet, however, she laid a hand on the younger woman's arm.

"Melody," she began hesitantly, "I am sorry to have been the bearer of bad news. No," she continued as Melody raised a limp hand in protest, "I know how— how fond you have become of Josh. I am still trying to persuade him to stay in England, but you must realize, that if he does, he must marry." Her eyes grew thoughtful and speculative as she continued. "He must ally himself with a suitable *parti*, but it appears he is one of those men who will not marry where they cannot love. It will be a task for me to find someone who embodies both of those criteria."

From somewhere, Melody dredged up a smile and pinned it to her lips. "Of course, my lady. I wish his lordship well, no matter what his plans."

With what she hoped was a regal nod, she moved to the door, feeling as though at any moment she might break into a thousand painful shards of ice.

In the sanctuary of her bedchamber, she lowered herself carefully into a chair by the fire. How could she have been so stupid as to read a declaration of love into what was obviously no more than a moment's dalliance for the Earl of Sandborne? Even a woman so unschooled as herself should have realized that a single kiss does not a commitment make. The scene at the bottom of the staircase had been merely a pleasant interlude for Josh.

For that matter, how could she have been so stupid as to fall in love with a peer? Or with any man with eyes in his head? Many years ago, she had taken her mother's precepts to heart. How could she have forgotten them in the presence of a pair of heart-stopping jade eyes and a smile that could melt glaciers?

Well, she had been brought to the enormity of her mistake, and she would not repeat it. If it killed her—and it very likely might—she would henceforth treat the earl with such cool courtesy that he would apprehend without difficulty that she, too, looked on that midnight kiss with nothing but a slight distaste that she had so far forgotten herself.

If, as the earl had stated, he planned to leave the Court in a short time, so much the better. She would be glad to get him out of her life so that she could begin the painful business of getting him out of her heart. Please God, he would not heed Lady Sandborne's pleas to stay in England. She did not think she could remain at the Court while the earl courted and wed his suitable *parti* and produced children with her.

After many more minutes of fruitless reflection, which served only to plunge her farther into a seemingly bottomless pit of misery, she rose slowly from her chair by the fire and left the room to resume her duties as Lady Sandborne's paid companion.

IX

The day of Lord Sandborne's Christmas ball dawned bright and clear, and the house hummed with activity. Footmen scurried to accomplish last-minute tasks, kitchen maids basted roasts and prepared sauces, and flustered abigails prepared their mistresses for the evening's festivities. The gentlemen merely tried to stay out of the way.

A few minutes before she was due to accompany Lady Sandborne downstairs, Melody stood once more before her mirror, staring in some bemusement at her image. With the assistance of her employer's seamstress, she had crafted her own ball gown and she was amazed at the results. She had started it some weeks ago at a time when she still wished to present herself before the earl in an ensemble that, in the words of the seamstress, would "knock any man into flinders." The gown was simple in design, made of a dark green silk over which lay a tunic of cream-colored gauze embroidered with a border of flowers that matched the silk. Her décolletage, while modest by prevailing standards, exposed a generous mound of soft, white bosom and her hair, *sans* cap, had been brushed into a shining coil, piled atop her head. Polished curls fell on either side of her cheeks, almost obliterating the tracery of her scar, and amid them, she had tucked a small sprig of holly.

Melody could not believe her eyes. While not a diamond of the first water, the woman before her could certainly be classed as a semiprecious stone of good quality.

And none of it mattered two straws, she thought dismally. All her dreams of smiting the earl with a *coup de foudre* were now so much dust. She had already discovered she possessed the power to lure him into a few moments of stolen passion. Unfortunately, a fleeting pleasure was not what she wanted—even if it did look as though that was all she was going to get.

In all probability, Josh would request her hand in a dance tonight, for he would consider it part of his familial duty to propel his aunt's companion in a turn about the floor. She would certainly accede, for it would be unpardonably rude to refuse this participation in a minor social ritual. In addition, a refusal would indicate to him her heartbreak. She would rather die than have him know of the anguish that lay concealed in her breast.

With a ragged sigh, she draped a shawl of gossamer over her shoulders and left her chamber.

In the master's suite, Josh also stood before his mirror. In accordance with his aunt's wishes, he had expanded his wardrobe to include a new ensemble for the ball. He was forced to admit that he felt complete to a shade, as they said over here. In fact, he should be supremely satisfied, he thought with some asperity. Tonight's ball was the signal of the completion of his present duties as the Earl of Sandborne. He would take his position at the head of the stairs and greet visiting Westons and Weston friends. He would dance with the ladies and converse jovially with the gentlemen, and when it was all over, he would be free to shake the dust of Sandborne Court from his well-shod feet.

Yes, indeed, all had gone according to plan.

Then why was he permeated by this emptiness—this sense of destiny unfulfilled?

He plucked irritably at an invisible scrap of lint on his sleeve. He well knew the reason for his dissatisfaction, and it lay in the diminutive form of Miss Melody Fairfax. He had not left the Court and he had already begun to miss her, for he had not seen her above once or twice since their encounter at the foot of the stairs. She'd been busy with ball preparations, he supposed, as well as to attending to the needs of his guests. In addition, she'd taken to dining in her chamber. They had not even met in the music room.

He had begun to wonder of late if there was perhaps another reason for her disappearance from his life. Was it possible that she had taken snuff at his—his display of affection? She certainly hadn't seemed to mind at the time. He shivered involuntarily at the memory of her response to his kiss.

Surely, he mused uneasily, she had not read more into the episode than he had intended. He was very fond of Melody, and he had merely been expressing that fondness. She was an attractive young woman, he told himself, at least when she allowed herself to emerge from her drab cocoon. A man could not be faulted for wanting to take her in his arms for a moment of mutual pleasure.

He snorted. Who was he trying to hornswoggle? When Melody had hurried toward him down the stairs in the candlelight, with her mahogany hair falling about her shoulders, he had been entranced. He'd intended only a brief salute, but when she returned his kiss with such sweetness and fire, he had nearly lost control. She had been all womanly curves and giving innocence and her passion had ignited his.

He wanted to believe that it was simply because he

had been without a woman for so long that he had gone up like an incendiary bomb at her touch. But, deep within him, he knew better. She was different from anyone he had ever known. In a few short weeks, she had stolen into his heart and become almost as important to him as his breath. He realized with a sudden, stunning burst of clarity that the magic he had sensed on the day of his arrival had indeed come to pass—in the form of a small, unobtrusive angel. The fact was inescapable. He was in love with Melody Fairfax.

And in a few short days, he would leave her.

Was he mad? Was he turning his back on the only chance for happiness he was likely to be offered in this lifetime, simply because of a disastrous experience back when he'd been too young to know better? And because he knew it was his destiny to be forever an outsider looking in at the happiness of others?

On the other hand, he had grown so accustomed to this role that he now felt comfortable in it. He was his own man and that was how he preferred it. He relished the freedom to live his life as he saw fit, whether in the comfort of Philadelphia or in the wilds of the land along the Susquehanna.

He was still talking to himself in this vein as he left his chambers and made his way downstairs, but on an impulse, he made a detour on his way downstairs. Most of the guests had long since repaired to the ballroom, which was situated in another wing of the house; thus there was no one in the long gallery as he entered quietly. He walked slowly past the portraits, his footsteps echoing on the polished floor.

He had not been here since the morning of Aunt Helen's tour, and now he found himself studying the faces before him with renewed interest. Hmm. He could see a definite resemblance between the Honor-

able Horace Weston (1732–1759) and cousin Arthur.
Lady Amelia Weston, who had arrived last week from
Northumberland, was the spitting image of her great-
great-great-grandfather. He noted with some surprise
that the second Earl of Weston (1655–1704) had been
painted as he sat in a carved oaken chair that, if Josh
was not mistaken, currently reposed in his study.

At last, he came to the portrait of his father and his
uncles. Good God, he hadn't had so much as a sip of
Christmas punch yet, but he could swear a twinkle of
kinship and understanding shone in the eyes of
sixteen-year-old George.

Josh glanced back along the corridor, at the line of
portraits stretching back along its length. He could almost fancy himself a leaf on the tallermost branch of a
giant oak, gazing down at his roots, spread far below
him. He had thought himself completely alone, he reflected in some wonderment, but he was not. Like
anyone else, he was descended from a line of human
beings that stretched into the mists of antiquity. Unlike many others, however, he had been granted the
opportunity to know the names and appearances of
his progenitors from several generations back.

He made his way from the chamber, still mulling
over this concept, which had not previously occurred
to him. On reaching the portal leading to the East
Wing, he stopped to gaze over a swirling sea of party-
goers, all of whom had donned their gayest apparel.
As he moved among them, they turned to greet him
and to wish him a happy Christmas.

His eyes searched the throng, but he did not perceive the one he sought. He made his way slowly upstairs into the ballroom proper, stopping at frequent
intervals to exchange conversation with cousins,
nieces, and friends of the family. At one point, he
halted abruptly to avoid being thrown almost into the

arms of Mary Weston. He turned away, feeling little inclined to endure yet another freezing set-down from Arthur's wife. Altering course, he drifted behind a nearby potted palm just in time to catch the tail end of a conversation between her and a woman whom he recognized as a visitor from London.

"Really, Mary, my dear," this person was cooing, "I certainly commiserate with you. It must have been dreadful for you when Arthur was virtually pushed out of the succession, all to make way for a barbarian from—where is it?—Pennsylvania or some other impossible place in the American wilderness. Only fancy," she tittered, "an untutored savage as the Earl of Sandborne!"

Josh stiffened unconsciously into a defensive posture, awaiting Mary's response. The next moment his jaw dropped and his eyes widened in disbelief as his cousin snapped, "Pennsylvania is not some impossible place in the American wilderness, Sarah. I'll have you know that Philadelphia is—is a cultured city. In addition, Josh is as much of a gentleman—and more—than anyone of my acquaintance."

Her companion's eyes widened in shock and she sniffed audibly. With a swish of her skirts she turned away from Mary, who swung about in another direction. She thus bumped into Josh, who had moved out from behind his palm tree in order to fully absorb the genteel confrontation.

"Oh!" she gasped, startled. Then, observing Josh's bemused countenance, she grinned sheepishly. "Sarah Bliss has always been insufferable, and you're—well, you're family. Besides, I have decided I may·have been rather—extreme—in my previous judgment of you."

Bobbing her head, she pushed past him, leaving Josh to stare after her, openmouthed.

"Josh! There you are." It was Lady Sandborne,

gowned in a robe of burgundy velvet. On her gray curls perched a matching turban embellished with a spray of diamonds. "Heavens, I thought you must have taken a wrong turn at the conservatory. Come with me now to receive our guests, for we must begin the dancing soon."

Still pondering Mary's abrupt volte-face, Josh followed his aunt to the head of the staircase, where they took up their positions. The next minutes passed in a blur of hands pressed against his and lips put against his cheek. The guests, obviously in a festive mood, expressed their pleasure at being among those present, and many of them made it a point to tell him of their happiness that he had at last come home to take his place as the head of the Weston family. To his surprise, they seemed eminently sincere in these sentiments.

It was not until almost all the ball attendees had trooped past the line composed of himself, Aunt Helen, Arthur, and Mary, that Josh saw Melody. He halted mid-sentence at his first glimpse of her, standing some distance apart. It would be too much to say that she was the center of attention, but she had gathered a small court of attentive gentlemen about her. The reason, thought Josh, stunned, was easy to perceive.

Melody was a dream of Christmas in a gown that clung lovingly to her curves. All the sparkle of the brilliants scattered over her tunic seemed to gather in her luminous gray eyes as she spoke shyly first with one and then another of her admirers.

She lifted her head under his scrutiny, and across the distance that separated them, their gazes met and held. Some of the brilliance seemed to fade from her eyes, but at last she nodded courteously before returning to the gentlemen.

My God, he thought, a curious sensation stirring within him. It was the self-effacing companion garbed in ill-fitting gowns with whom he had fallen in love, but tonight . . . His heart swelled with a pleasure that was almost painful.

"Melody is in looks, is she not?" whispered Aunt Helen. Speechless, Josh nodded.

"I'm so glad she chose to dress for the occasion," continued his aunt. "I have been urging her for some time to come out of the—the tent of obscurity with which she has chosen to cover herself for so long." She paused before speaking again. "And I am glad you and she seemed to have established such a, er, rapport."

At a certain note in her voice, Josh swung to look at her. The countess promptly dropped her gaze. "She is a fine young woman, Josh. I would not see her hurt."

"I would be the last person in the world to hurt Melody," declared Josh.

"Sometimes one can inflict pain without the slightest intention. Are you still planning to leave after Christmas?" she asked in an apparent non sequitur. Josh glanced at her sharply.

"Yes. Or—no." He listened to himself in some surprise. "I don't know. It is time I went home," he concluded a little desperately.

Lady Sandborne sighed. "I had hoped you'd come to realize that you *are* home, Josh. This is where you belong, my dear boy. Here, among your family and friends, all of whom are growing to love you," she added gently before turning to greet the next guest.

Blindly, Josh swung away from her and stumbled toward the sound of an orchestra playing. For some moments, he stood staring at those in the ballroom. The musicians had swung into a country dance, and the chamber was filled with warmth and music and

laughter. Again, he felt a stirring within him, as
though something large and heavy, a burden carried
for too long, had cracked and shifted. He realized with
wonder that, though he was outside, looking in, he
was not an interloper. All he had to do was to enter
and be welcomed, for he was home—among his family, the family for which he had unknowingly been
searching all his life.

He looked about for Melody, but he could not—no,
there she was, dancing with cousin Farlow Bryce, from
Lancashire. Josh leaned against a decorative column,
his arms folded across his chest, watching her. As
though aware of his observation, she stumbled slightly
in the intricate steps of the dance, and once again, her
eyes met his. She colored a little and transferred her
gaze to her partner.

When the country dance had ended, he approached
her, but her hand was solicited immediately by a
young sprig whom he recognized as Miles Weston,
oldest son of the Surrey Westons.

Recalled to his duty by a minatory stare from Aunt
Helen, he requested his aunt Lucretia's hand for the
next dance, a quadrille. The one after that was a waltz,
and his partner was Maribelle Grant, she of the yellow
curls and hopeful gleam in her eye.

To the young lady's obvious disappointment, he did
not ask for a second dance. At the first intermission, as
the musicians laid down their instruments and thirstily
eyed the refreshments set out for them, Josh girded his
loins and hurried to the spot where Melody stood in
conversation with several young ladies.

Grasping her hand, he laid it on his arm, and murmuring polite excuses to the other ladies, he led her
away from the group.

"Josh!" Melody exclaimed. "What in the world—?"

"I have been trying to get you to myself all evening,

with absolutely no luck. I blame you for looking like a fairy tale come to life, but that is neither here nor there. I would have a word with you, young Melody."

He knew he was babbling, but a strange excitement filled him, causing his blood to fizz like champagne.

"Really, Josh, you can't just walk out of the ballroom with me and leave everyone wondering—"

"I can and I will. It's a bit nippy outside for a stroll on the terrace, but how about a turn in the conservatory?"

"But—" protested Melody, to no avail. Josh merely tightened his grip and led her through corridors and passageways until they reached the ground-floor conservatory, now empty of all other company.

Good heavens, what was wrong with the man? thought Melody. Her heart had leapt in her breast like a stricken bird when she had sighted him for the first time that evening. Looking impossibly handsome in his ball attire, he was every inch a peer of the realm. What a very good thing she had her emotions firmly in check, so that his appearance had absolutely no effect on her other than to cause a constriction in her breathing for a few minutes. How fortunate that she had planned out the course of her behavior toward him during his remaining tenure at Sandborne Court and thus could confront him with her usual composure.

She turned to him as he ushered her into the conservatory and breathing in the cool, earth-scented dampness of the chamber, she said icily, "Now, then, what was it you wished to discuss with me?"

"I guess I should start with the other night," Josh began, observing her unpromising demeanor with some dismay.

"The other night?" She lifted her brows in apparent bewilderment. "Oh, yes—when you kissed me. Yes, I suppose you do owe me an apology for that, but never mind. I have all but forgotten the incident."

"You have?" This was not going at all as Josh had envisioned. "I—I'm sorry to hear that."

Melody's curved brows lifted again, but she said nothing.

"Because," continued Josh, "kissing you was the highlight of my visit to England so far and"—he moved closer and lifted one of her curls in his fingers—"I was hoping to repeat the occasion."

Melody's velvet gray eyes were transformed instantly into boiling little infernos of fury.

"How dare you, sir! Do you think me Haymarket ware? A piece of muslin with whom you can while away the tedium of the hours before you leave Sandborne Court?" Behind the anger, Josh caught the glitter of tears unshed.

"Leave Sandborne—? Oh, God, Melody—I—I'm sorry. I never meant—" He drew in a deep breath. "Lord, I'm making an unutterable mull of this. Look— I mean, listen, please. Hear me out."

He drew her onto a bench beneath a spreading Empress tree.

"Yes, I thought to leave the Court and England. I never intended to stay any longer than it would take to put my affairs in order here. It never occurred to me that I could fit in here—that I could consider it my home.

"But then, something unexpected happened. I found acceptance—and love. I thought that being the Earl of Sandborne would be a burden, but instead it has become my salvation. I find I *like* being the earl, with what seems like a million relatives, and responsibilities and duties and—and everything that goes with it. I plan to stay," he concluded shakily. "I shall want to journey to America now and then, but here is where my roots lie—and so shall I, someday, in the good earth of England."

Trembling, Melody found that her throat had tightened so she could hardly speak. "I am happy for you, Josh," she whispered. "Truly, I am."

She realized that she spoke the truth. She had sensed an underlying sadness in the Earl of Sandborne, from the moment she had met him in that dismal churchyard. She had guessed at the reasons, but had not known until now how deep his unhappiness had run. Her mind whirled with the implications of what he had just told her. She loved this man, and she was glad he had found peace in the bonds of the family he had sought for so long.

But, what of her situation? He would marry. Lady Sandborne would see to that. She simply could not remain at the Court to watch while his new bride took her position as chatelaine of his home and mother of his children. Trying to draw her emotions back into the tight little ball in which they were customarily confined, she became aware that Josh was speaking once more.

"Thank you, my dear. However, there is one thing I need to cement my position as head of the Weston clan—a countess."

Oh, God. Was he about to tell her he planned to offer for Maribelle Grant? She lifted her head only to encounter his polished jade gaze fixed intently on her. Her heart began to thud wildly. His expression certainly was not that of a man on the verge of declaring his intent to wed another woman.

She swallowed convulsively. "Yes," she said, a little wildly. "The Earl of Sandborne must make it one of his first priority to choose a proper wife. Aunt Helen thought perhaps—"

"Aunt Helen's feelings in the matter do not interest

me," interrupted Josh gently, and it seemed to Melody that his jeweled eyes fairly glowed with the fire that lay banked behind them. "What concerns me are your feelings."

"M-mine?" Melody's heart was now beating so frantically it seemed to flood her entire being.

"Melody, I found something else here at Sandborne, a woman who fills my life with song and my heart with joy. My dearest lark, we have not known each other for long, but we have become friends. I value that more than I can say, but—oh, dear God, I want so much more from you. I want you to be my wife—to share my new life—to make music with me—and babies. Lots of babies."

It seemed to Melody that a great well had opened up within her, spreading happiness into every pore and a dizzy delight that surged through her veins.

"Josh—" she began.

"I know it is probably too soon to be speaking to you like this, and if you wish, I'll wait until you think you might love me. But, oh, my darling lark, could you at least tell me I have a chance?"

His eyes were green fire and Melody thought she might be consumed in them. She drew a shuddering breath.

"Yes, it is soon, Josh, but I've discovered that it is possible to fall in love in a very short time."

Josh's eyes widened incredulously, and with a gasp of joy, he pulled her into his arms. His mouth came down on hers in a kiss that shook her to her soul. Once more, a shattering response swept through her, and she pressed against him. It was many moments before she was able to return herself to coherent thought.

"Oh, my love," she said with a little gasp. "Whatever will Lady Sandborne think? I'm quite sure she had Miss Grant in mind for your bride—or Charlotte

Ponsonby. She will certainly not think I am an acceptable substitute."

"I think we need not worry about Aunt Helen," he replied with a chuckle. "Unless I'm much mistaken, the bride she has in mind is neither of those staggeringly eligible damsels, but a certain soon-to-be-former lady's companion."

He bent his head once more to his beloved, and after several moments, Melody spoke in a ragged whisper.

"I never dreamed of such happiness, Josh. You have brought me the joy of Christmas."

Josh gathered her close once more. "And you are my Christmas wish come true, little lark," he whispered into the fragrance of her hair, "for all my Christmases to come."

Melody swayed in his arms, her heart too full for speech. Her heart was so full of joy, she thought she might burst. She reached to brush her lips against Josh's cheek.

"Yes, my dearest love. For all our Christmases to come."

♪   ♪   ♪   ♪   ♪   ♪

For many years afterward, it became a Christmas tradition in the little church at Westonbury for the Earl of Sandborne to play the splendid organ that was his gift to the village. Afterward, he would play an accompaniment for his countess as she raised her voice in a glorious medley that always included "The Holly and the Ivy." In later years, they were joined by their children, and later still, by grandchildren and great-grandchildren. To the last man, woman, and child, the villagers agreed that it was the music of Lord and Lady Sandborne that made Christmas in Westonbury.